THE BODY ON THE ROCKS

THOMAS HAUCK

Editor: Kim Smith
Cover art: Thomas A. Hauck
Back cover portrait photo: Kim Smith
Proofreaders: Alex Hauck, J.M. Hallock

"A Good Day to Bury Charlie" was first published by *Over My Dead Body! The Mystery Magazine Online* (overmydeadbody.com).

ISBN-13: 978-0615949529 (Avanti Literary)
ISBN-10: 0615949525

AVANTI LITERARY
Chrismarkdetective.com

Contents

Preface

It was by chance that I first met the man known within these pages as Chris Mark.

One of the benefits of living near Gloucester Harbor is that you can walk just about anywhere and experience something interesting—you can smell the salt air, hear the cries of seagulls, see the time-honored labor of the fishermen. On a crisp fall day I had left my office to stretch my legs, and sure enough there was plenty of activity on the wharves and in the working harbor. I soon found myself strolling along the Jodrey State Fish Pier. Along the west side of the pier by the fish freezing plant the big hundred-foot steel-hulled vessels were unloading their catches. On the east side the smaller fishing boats were coming and going from their berths, and at the southern end a few seals basked on the exposed rocks of what in the old days had been called Five Pound Island. The indolent seals ignored the men casting for stripers off the edge of the pier high above the ebb tide.

Out of idle curiosity I strolled over to a vessel that had recently been in the news—a sleek fifty-foot pleasure cruiser once owned by a local contracting tycoon named Roger Smolley. The boat was a beauty, with teak decks, a spacious main salon and galley, and a master stateroom that reportedly boasted a fifty-inch plasma screen.

On sultry summer weekends the boat had been Smolley's floating love shack where he entertained a succession of girlfriends. The good times rolled until the long-suffering Mrs. Smolley marched down to the pier with a loaded thirty-eight and put an end to her husband's cheatin' ways. Since Mrs. Smolley only possessed enough skill with a gun to hit her target with one shot out of six, the female guest who was on board that evening escaped the hail of bullets and ran off into the night, dressed only in her faux-pearl earrings.

After Mrs. Smolley had been arrested, tried, and packed off to prison, the cruiser—aptly named *Sweet Revenge*—remained tied up at the pier in a state of legal limbo.

Yes, my curiosity was ghoulish; I wanted to see what everyone was calling the "Death Boat." I supposed this was a deliciously ironical inversion of *The Love Boat*.

I stood on the edge of the pier surveying the *Sweet Revenge*. After the murder it had been the subject of sensational headlines in the *Gloucester Tribune*, but in subsequent months both the crime and the boat had faded from public consciousness. Now the forlorn floating pleasure palace waited for its fate to be decided by the courts.

The only clues to the macabre history of the craft were the bright orange "NO TRESPASSING" sign stuck in the helm windshield and the piece of plywood that had been fitted into a forward porthole, the glass of which had been blown out by one of Mrs. Smolley's errant bullets.

Having satiated my morbid curiosity, I was turning to leave when I noticed a man standing a few feet away. He was about thirty, tall, and very fit, but the way he stood suggested that in order to balance himself he had to align his bones at odd angles, almost as if he had once been knocked apart and the pieces hastily reassembled.

He glanced up and gave me a nod. I remember that one of his eyes drilled into me like a laser beam, while the other eye didn't have quite the same focus.

"Quite a story, isn't it?" I said.

He replied that it was, and we started talking. It turned out that he was a veteran of the Iraq War—hence the problem with the eye—and a private detective. Of the *Sweet Revenge* he had personal knowledge. Weeks before the shooting, the wife, Regina Smolley, had contacted him. She said that she suspected her husband of infidelity. To my new friend she had seemed unstable and potentially violent, but he had taken the case because that's what investigators do. It didn't take him long to produce photographic evidence of Roger Smolley's philandering. The detective had implored his client to keep her cool, get a lawyer, and clean his clock in court. She agreed to take the legal road. Then she went home, got drunk, took her husband's revolver, and went to the *Sweet Revenge* to get a quickie divorce.

In the detective business you see people at their worst, said the man. What they do to each other is just a more intimate form of warfare than what he had experienced on the streets of Baghdad. He felt badly that one his clients had shot another human being, even if the victim was a no-good bum. In his work his goal was not to create more disorder in an already bad situation, but to bring order out of chaos. Sometimes he succeeded, sometimes not.

Then he shrugged and asked me what I did for a living. I told him I was a writer. That seemed to arouse his curiosity. What kind of writer? he asked. Practically anything, I replied. I write my own books—thrillers mostly—as well as ghostwrite and edit books for clients.

The man said that he had a head full of stories. He thought they would make for a good book. He professed not to be a writer, only a guy who had been around and had something to say about people and the things they did to each other, both good and bad.

Over drinks in a booth at the Tiller Restaurant we hammered out the basics of a deal. He'd tell me the stories and I'd write them up. He wanted them to be told in the third person, and he wanted me to change all the names and the key details so that client confidentiality wouldn't be compromised.

"You'll need to change my name, too," he said.

I asked him what name he wanted.

"I dunno," he said. "How about Chris Mark? It sounds like an ordinary name. I want people to know that I'm just a regular guy who has one marketable skill: I can help people solve their toughest problems."

Having proposed a new name for himself, he then insisted that the name of his adopted hometown—the port city of Gloucester—remain unchanged. Chris told me that after his discharge from the Marine Corps he had taken his savings and bought a small house in Gloucester, a town he had often visited with his late parents. He said that he liked Gloucester for its rugged coastline and broad beaches that offered good surfing, and because the town was a microcosm of a much larger region, with a vibrant mix of industry, art, and history that made life interesting. He really hadn't thought about a career and had done a succession of odd jobs until one night at the Red Lantern bar he had successfully defused a brewing fistfight between two guys who wanted the same girl. Gradually he got the reputation as a guy who could see through the bullshit that people created to deceive both themselves and others. This led to him getting hired as a private investigator. It was not a job that he had made any effort to choose or even to prepare himself for, but he was good at it and he made enough money at it to suppress any desire to seek alternate employment.

In months following our first meeting, when we each had spare time we'd get together over a bottle of Jack Daniels and he would narrate his stories while I wrote them down. Eventually he gave me enough material to fill several books. We decided to present an initial batch of twelve, to be followed by subsequent collections. I smoothed out the rough edges of his narratives and did some fact checking, and the result is this book. Some of the stories are whodunits and others read more like thrillers. It's a world that most people enjoy visiting but wouldn't want to live in.

Chris Mark and I thank you for reading.

Thomas Hauck
March 2014

Captain Sal's Final Voyage

The body was that of a white male. Age about fifty. Grey hair, long on the sides. The face, hands and forearms were deeply lined from decades of working on the open ocean.

"When did he die?" asked Chris Mark.

"Today's Saturday," replied the medical examiner. "He was lying on the deck of the boat, exposed to the elements. I'd say Tuesday night or early Wednesday."

"Cause of death?" asked Mark.

"Massive skull fractures. Someone or something hit him hard. Twice—once at the base of the skull, and again on the right side. Either blow would have been fatal."

"Maybe a boom on the boat?"

"Nah," said police chief Ray Frontiero. "The *Little Princess* was set up for lobstering. No boom. Someone whacked him."

"Robbery?" asked Mark.

"Nope," said the chief. "Cash and credit cards still in his wallet."

"Hmm," said Mark noncommittally.

An hour earlier Chris Mark had been at home, getting ready to go surfing. Sure, Gloucester is not exactly Maui or Malibu. You have to wear a wetsuit six months out of the year when the water temperature at Good Harbor Beach dips into the chilly fifties and even the frigid forties, but that's one reason why local surfers stubbornly wait for the waves. It's not for everybody. The warm-weather riders get quickly weeded out. When Mark surfed, the cold water cleared his mind, especially when he was hung over. He was trying mightily to make such occasions less frequent— the hangovers, not the surfing—and for the most part he had been succeeding. But last night had offered the perfect trifecta of temptation: a good band at the Anchor Club, an attractive blonde, and a bartender who didn't skimp on the Wild Turkey. A good time was had by all. In the morning Mark had thanked his overnight guest before trying to clear the hammers from his head with a cold shower. He had been looking forward to the bracing salt air and the slap of waves against the board when his phone rang. The caller ID indicated Chief Frontiero. Mark felt obliged to answer.

The chief knew very well that Mark was not looking for hard action. On the streets of Baghdad Mark had too often escaped death by inches. In war a bullet goes wide or a bomb is defused with only seconds to spare, and you live to patrol another day. After slipping from death's greedy grasp more times than he deserved, he had been nailed by a roadside IED and shipped home, his nerves shot and his body ravaged.

Mark had first met Ray Frontiero when he was working for a client. In the course of the investigation —a routine spousal cheating affair—Mark had uncovered the fact that the husband was not only very bad at hiding his multiple affairs with various waitresses around town but that he was at the center of a major gun running operation. Mark felt that it was only sporting to share this knowledge with the police, and in return for setting up what became a major bust Frontiero took the damaged Iraq War vet under his protective wing.

Mark respected the chief. He was a good guy who for too many years had been working diligently to make Gloucester a safe place. Sometimes he needed a fresh pair of eyes on a case. When he called it meant that Mark was going to do a job without making any money, which was inconvenient. It was sort of like performing a community service. In return, the chief gave him access to police resources. In the long run it was a fair deal.

"Okay, I'll check it out," Mark had replied after hearing the chief relate the story of the discovery of the drifting boat and the body lying on its deck. Half an hour later he found himself at the office of the medical examiner, gazing down at the corpse of Sal Cromisi, the late captain of the *Little Princess*.

"When you're a fisherman you figure your worst enemies are the weather and the waves," said Frontiero. "You don't expect to go like this. It's got the waterfront rattled and the mayor has already told me that it's not good for tourism, as if I didn't already know that. I'd like you to see what you can find."

"Where's the widow now?"

"At their home, over on Prospect Street."

People die in the waters around Gloucester on a regular basis. Mostly they get swept off the rocks and into the pounding surf. Fishermen get lost at sea, too. Once in a while a crewmember will expire onboard a boat. Drugs, an undiagnosed heart condition, drowning after a fall—there are many ways to go. This case was unusual, thought Mark as he wheeled his Camaro through streets congested with out-of-town tourists. You don't often see outright murder on a fishing boat. The fishermen—and the few fisherwomen —were a tough lot, but unfailingly loyal to each other.

After parking his Camaro across the street from the trim clapboard house, Mark went to the front door and found that it was open. In the tiny vestibule stood a man and a woman. Two mourners, friends of the family. She was holding a covered casserole dish. With a nod Mark squeezed by them and entered the living room. While it was crowded with people, the atmosphere was hushed. A few of the occupants turned and looked at Mark with the puzzled expression that signified "Who are you and why are you here?" Keeping a deferential demeanor, Mark surveyed the room. Frontiero had told him that he would recognize Judy Cromisi by her flamboyant red hair. His gaze drifted beyond the living room into the dining room.

There, standing at the table and fussing with a plate of cold cuts, was the widow.

Picking his way through the crowd, Mark approached the table. Judy was speaking to an older woman. In her hand she held a white handkerchief with which she occasionally dabbed her eyes.

While Mark paused for the opportunity to introduce himself, he looked around the room. While clean and tidy, it looked as if it not been redecorated in decades. The floral wallpaper was faded and the low plaster ceiling was crisscrossed with hairline cracks. There was not much money here. Fishing in Gloucester had become a tough business, and the only people getting wealthy were the owners of the big factory ships that worked the fishing grounds far offshore.

As was typical in many coastal houses, the artwork on the walls reflected the culture of the sea. There were small black-and-white photos of fishing vessels— probably ones owned by Sal Cromisi over the years— as well as a handful of pleasant seascapes painted in oils and framed in antique gold.

Atop the tall glass-doored cabinet, which displayed a quaint collection of teacups, saucers, and silver, rested an old wooden model of a trawler.

In the most commanding spot in the room, on the wall above the buffet table, hung a big painting of a two-masted ship riding gracefully at anchor in a harbor. Even through the layer of dull varnish Mark could appreciate the sublime evening air that enveloped a scene of perfect tranquility. The elegant ship was safely in port and everything was right with the world.

At that moment the woman who had been speaking to Judy Cromisi turned away. Mark took a step forward and extended his hand.

"Mrs. Cromisi?" he said.

She turned her sharp green eyes to his. "Yes?" Her voice was steady and clear.

"My name is Chris Mark."

She extended her hand, which Mark took briefly before releasing. Her touch was cool.

"Please accept my condolences on the passing of your husband," said Mark.

"Thank you," she said. "Did you know Sal?"

"No, I must confess that I never had the pleasure of meeting him. I'm an acquaintance of Chief Frontiero. I hope to provide some assistance to the chief and to the department."

"Oh, I see," she replied. "I hope that he finds out who did this. It's a terrible thing to be murdered on your own boat. It's just—" Her voice drifted off as she raised the handkerchief to dab her eyes. "If I can help in any way, please let me know."

"I know this a difficult time for you," said Mark. "But I see you have support." He gestured to the crowded rooms. "I know that Sal didn't have any brothers or sisters. Perhaps you have family here?"

"Only my brother," she replied. "Charles LaPierre. He drove up from New York. My two kids both live on the West Coast. They didn't know Sal that well; we've been married for only five years. I told them to stay where they are. They have their own families to worry about, and you know, with the expense of traveling across country—" Again she dabbed her eyes.

A man approached them and extended his hand. "Please accept my condolences on the loss of your husband," he said. "Sal was a good guy. I often saw him on the water because we worked the same area."

"You're a lobsterman?" asked Mark.

"Yeah. Name's Bill Travis. And you're—?"

"Chris Mark. I do some work for the city."

Travis gave Mark a cool glance and then made a little shrug. He turned to the widow. "Like I said, I'm sorry for your loss." He then moved away.

"This is a lovely old house," said Mark.

"From the late nineteenth century," replied Judy. "It was built by a shipwright."

Another man approached them. He was well dressed in a white tailored shirt and gray sports jacket. "Can I get you anything, Judy?" he said.

"No thanks; I'm fine," she replied. "Charles, this is—I'm sorry, was it Chris?"

"Yes," said Mark as he extended his hand. "Chris Mark. Nice to meet you. Judy just mentioned that you had driven up from New York."

Judy turned to Charles. "Mr. Mark is working with the police department."

"They're going to need all the help they can get," said Charles.

"Do you think this will be a tough case?" said Mark.

"Well, yeah," replied Charles. "The poor guy was found on his boat in the middle of the ocean. No one around for miles."

"Yes," said Mark. "Very strange. Mrs. Cromisi, when did you last see your husband?"

"Like I told the police," she said, "it was Tuesday, at dawn. He said he was going out to check his traps and that he'd be back by sunset. I wasn't feeling well, so that night I took a sleeping pill and went to bed early. When Sal wasn't back on Wednesday morning, I called the Coast Guard."

"How far off the coast does he go?"

"He's got traps all over Cape Ann. But they're not in deep water—you have to be able to haul them up."

"Well, thanks for your time," said Mark. "Charles, it was nice to meet you. Mrs. Cromisi is fortunate that you were able to be here during this difficult time. What do you do in New York?"

"I run a little art consulting company," replied Charles.

"Must be a fascinating business," said Mark.

"I do okay."

"Yes—well, thanks again," said Mark.

Outside, the weather had turned cool and cloudy. Mark drove the few blocks to the edge of the inner harbor with its fish and lobster dealers, boat yards, restaurants, and fuel and ice sellers. The streets and docks were alive with a vibrant mixture of fishermen, pleasure boaters, tourists off the coastal passenger ship anchored in the harbor, and the odd artist with an easel set up on the sidewalk.

Mark steered past the gate of the Coast Guard station with its big RESTRICTED AREA sign and parked by the front entrance next to a Gloucester police cruiser. A few minutes later, having passed through security, he walked out of the back of the building onto the big square pier. Tied up behind the angular Coast Guard cutter was a trim fishing boat. Painted on its stern was the name LITTLE PRINCESS.

On the pier, Chief Frontiero was standing with a man in a Coast Guard uniform. As Mark approached the chief saw him and nodded in the direction of the boat.

"There she is," said Frontiero. "Twenty-eight feet. Built in nineteen seventy-one by Jarvis as a pleasure craft. In the nineteen-nineties she was converted for lobstering. Single diesel engine. She's seen better days."

Mark went on board. While seaworthy, the *Little Princess* bore the scrapes and scars of a working vessel. Aside from a dozen empty lobster traps and some plastic bins neatly stacked at the stern, there was no loose gear. When Sal died, the boat had not been working the traps.

Frontiero joined him on the deck.

"Where was he found?" asked Mark.

"Lying here," replied Frontiero with a wave of his hand. "Near the hatch leading to the forward cabin area."

Mark examined the wheel and the controls. "I see that the keys are in the ignition. The throttle is about a quarter of the way up. He was cruising slow. When did the Coast Guard find the vessel—Thursday afternoon?"

"Yep."

"Thursday afternoon, twenty miles offshore. Was the engine running?"

"Nope. Out of gas."

"What's the range of this boat with a full tank?"

"With two hundred gallons?" said Frontiero. "Depending on the boat's speed and the weather, a long way. Maybe three hundred miles. But Sal knew how far he could go. His traps are within sight of land. Lobstering is strictly an inshore business."

"With a full tank you could expect to get well out into the open ocean," said Mark. "If Sal were expecting to spend the day tending to his traps, he would have taken more fuel. This boat left the dock with perhaps one gallon in the tank." He leaned in to peer at the instruments. "There's a gas gauge, but it says that it's three-quarters full."

"Yeah," said Frontiero. "Sal told me he was going to get it fixed. There's a short in the sensor in the fuel tank."

"The switch for the running light is turned to the 'on' position," said Mark.

"Maybe he was still operating the boat after sunset," offered Frontiero.

Mark scanned the cockpit. "There's nothing here that could hit him on the back of the head, unless he fell backward against the gunwale. No likely murder weapon. And the medical examiner said that he was hit with a lot of force—twice. Any blood on the deck?"

"Yes," replied Frontiero, "but it rained on Wednesday. Rough seas may have caused the body to shift. So we can't do much about reconstructing a crime scene—if there was one on this boat."

"You think he was killed somewhere else and brought to the boat?" said Mark.

"Gotta keep my options open," shrugged Frontiero.

Mark circled the small rear deck. He picked up a length of nylon rope. One end was neatly tied to a cleat on the stern, starboard side.

"This looks like a docking line," said Mark. "But it's too short. It's been cut. Where's the dock where the *Little Princess* was usually tied up?"

"Over at Kelsey's Wharf."

"Let's go."

Twenty minutes later the chief and Mark stood together on the rambling wooden wharf that jutted out into the harbor.

"We're off the beaten path, aren't we?" said Mark.

"Yeah," said Frontiero. "This is one of the oldest docks in the harbor and the one that's closest to the breakwater. Beyond the breakwater is the open ocean. Not many boats tie up here anymore because there's too much danger from heavy weather. When storms blow up this dock gets pounded. But space here is cheap and Sal didn't seem to mind that he wasn't in the heart of the harbor."

"Where would he tie up?"

Frontiero walked almost to the end of the pier. "Here. He had the last spot."

Mark sighted along the pier. "It's a straight shot to the open ocean," he said. "The *Little Princess* is twenty-eight feet long." Mark placed his hand on the side of one of the big round wooden pilings. "Sal would tie up the bow line here." Mark walked back towards shore and then stopped. "He'd tie the stern line to this piling." He got down on his hands and knees next to the piling and peered at the planks of the dock. "Chief—have a look," he said.

The chief bent down. "Looks like fresh cut marks in the planking."

"Yes. They look like they were made by a knife blade. And it's at the exact spot where it would be if you were hacking through the stern line of the boat."

"But why would Sal cut the line?" asked Frontiero. "Why not just untie it?"

"Good question," replied Mark. "My next stop is the fuel dealer."

Manny's Marine lay shouldered between a boat yard and the Seaport Landing, an upscale new restaurant and function facility built to cater to tourists and to the increasing traffic in small coastal cruise line ships. The ships could tie up at its spacious wharf and disgorge their mostly senior citizen passengers, who were then provided with plenty of opportunities to spend their cash in the boutiques and galleries perched invitingly within walking distance of the harbor.

Mark entered the cramped office. It smelled of fuel and canvas and paint. The shelves on the dark paneled walls were laden with cans of lubricant and degreaser, boxes of parts, tattered repair manuals from an era long before the Internet, fishing gear, and rolled-up charts. Behind the desk a man sat hunched over an old computer.

"You Chris Mark?" said the man without looking up.

"Yes. Mr. Reilly?"

"That's me. Chief Frontiero said you would be coming by to ask about Sal."

"Yep. You got a minute?"

After a few clicks Reilly took his hand off the mouse and leaned back in his chair. "Okay, let's talk. It's a shame about Sal. He was a good guy."

"You knew him well?"

Reilly rubbed his stubbled chin. "Sal and I graduated together from Gloucester High. That summer he went to work on the boats—or should I say, he went back to work on the boats, because he'd been fishing since he was a kid. I went to work for my dad, and here I am today, at the same damned desk I've been sitting at since I was eighteen. But times have changed. Back then we sold diesel fuel to a hundred boats. Now there are maybe thirty. We're barely hanging on. But you didn't come here to hear my problems. It's about Sal, right?"

"Yeah. The medical examiner says he was murdered. Do you know anyone who had it in for him?"

"No," Reilly shrugged. "Like I said, Sal was a respected guy. No problems with anyone."

"Did he have a business partner with his boat?'

"Nope. He owned the *Little Princess* outright. He was a one-man operation. It was the only way he could make any money."

"He bought fuel from you," said Mark. "When was the last time?"

Reilly peered at the computer and made a few clicks with the mouse. "A week ago last Tuesday. Filled the tank with one hundred and ninety gallons."

"During the lobstering season, how often would he fill up?'

"Once a week."

"So you would have expected him to be here a week later—on Tuesday or Wednesday?"

"Yeah."

"You know that his boat was found twenty miles offshore with an empty tank?"

Reilly shook his head. "It doesn't make any sense. He would never head out with only a gallon of fuel in his tank. It would be insane."

"The *Little Princess*—what do you suppose would be the insurance value if she were lost at sea?"

"Not much," said Reilly. "Given her age and condition, no more than thirty grand. She's only got a few more years left in her."

"Thanks," said Mark. "You've been a big help. By the way, did you ever meet Sal's wife?"

"Judy LaPierre? Sure. I was at their wedding. It was at the VFW hall. A nice affair. They even had a guy who sang Frank Sinatra songs. All the old ladies were swooning."

"Have you ever been to their house?"

"On Prospect Street? Yeah, on a few occasions. The last time was at Christmas. They had an open house and so I went there and hung out for a few hours. Sal had the Red Sox game on."

"Where was Judy?"

"In the kitchen with her girlfriends. I don't think that she likes Sal's fishing buddies. We're too rough around the edges for her taste."

"How'd they meet?"

"At the Elks Club. They hit it off and got married a few months later. It wasn't a big fancy ceremony—they were both adults and she had two grown kids. Then she moved into the house on Prospect Street."

"That was his house?"

"Oh, sure. He grew up in that house. It hasn't changed in years."

"Lots of paintings and photos of boats on the walls."

"From the glorious days of sail, y'know?" said Reilly. "When the number of fishermen lost at sea every year was counted in the hundreds."

"What's the old saying?" said Mark. "'That's not fish ye're buying—it's men's lives.'"

"You got that right," said Reilly.

Mark leaned nearer. "So tell me, Mr. Reilly, how did Sal and the missus get along? Any problems?"

"Sal never said nothing to me," Reilly shrugged. "But he was a quiet type. Stoic is the word. Did his job and paid his bills on time. Never late."

"No gambling, no women?"

"Not Sal," Reilly shook his head. "Some of the guys go to the casino at Mohegan Sun, drink bottom-shelf booze, and piss away their kids' college savings at the slots. Sal was never interested. He kept his mind on business."

Mark took his double bourbon and swished the glass to jumble the ice. His table at the Tiller Restaurant overlooked the Marine Railway, where they hauled up ships out of the water to scrape the hulls or fix the engines. On this particular evening the railway—so named because of the steel rails that descended into the water, providing a sturdy guide for the massive wheeled cradle that supported the boat being winched ashore—was host to an ungainly tugboat, a couple of sleek power yachts, and an old wooden schooner that had been dismasted. In the glow of the late setting sun the massive bulk of the elevated tugboat seemed oddly poignant, like a huge creature held aloft, carefully balanced by spindly legs.

The waitress delivered his swordfish special on its bed of barley, kiwi, and tomatoes, and as Mark ate he pondered the unfolding case. Certain facts were emerging. Sal was a decent guy who seemed to have had no enemies. He was a highly experienced seaman who would never have left port with only a gallon of fuel in his tank. Something strange had happened where the *Little Princess* was tied up at Kelsey's Wharf.

The police didn't find a cell phone on the body or on the boat. The killer may have gotten rid of it in the naïve belief that without Sal's phone there would be no phone records. The Gloucester Police had gotten a court order for the call records, and the report was due within twenty-four hours.

"Excuse me—" A female voice roused Mark from his thoughts. He looked up to see a woman wearing a floral blouse and white jeans.

"Yes, how may I help you?" said Mark.

The woman edged closer. "I saw you today at Sal and Judy's house, didn't I? I overheard you say that you were some sort of investigator."

"Yes—I'm helping Chief Frontiero. My name's Chris Mark. And you are—?"

"Patsy." The woman put her hand on the empty chair opposite Mark's. "Patsy Brumo. I hope you don't mind if I sit for a minute."

Before Mark could say, "Not at all," Patsy Brumo had eased her ample bottom into the seat.

"How about buying a lady a drink?" she said.

"Sure," said Mark. Something told him that it would be a worthwhile investment.

"A dry Martini," she said to the waitress. "Vermouth. With an olive." Then she leaned into Mark. "It's a shame about Sal."

"That's what people keep saying to me. Did you know him well?"

"I knew Sal since he was a kid. His ma Angie and I worked together at the ice company. She did the books and I ran the office. Nice family. Hard workers. No nonsense. We tried to fix up Sal with some of the girls we knew, but he didn't take to any of them. Angie wanted grandchildren. She was beside herself that Sal never married, and we had given up hope when he met Judy LaPierre. At last! we thought. But no kids. Angie resigned herself to her fate. At least Sal had found himself a good wife." Patsy's face turned sour.

"Things were not so good?" asked Mark.

Patsy took an unladylike gulp of her drink. "These Martini glasses are pathetic," she said. "Two little sips and it's gone."

"I'll get you another one," said Mark.

"That would be very nice. You're a good man to take care of Patsy. Anyway, it didn't take long before Judy started complaining. Nothing was good enough. Sal was always on his boat. They didn't have a new car. They never went anywhere on vacation."

"Didn't Judy understand what she was signing up for? Sal was a lobsterman."

"You know how it is. People come to Gloucester and see the harbor and the fishing boats, and they think it's all very romantic. After a while they realize it's just endless hard work."

"Okay—but there are lots of spouses who dream of a better life." Mark drained the last of his whiskey and signaled for another.

"True," said Patsy. "You can put me in that club. But there's more. Some of us girls think that Judy was seeing someone."

"A man?"

"Yes."

"This man have a name?"

"Let's just say that Judy spent a lot of time at Fred's Clam Shack."

"Fred Kane's place?"

"Yes. He makes a pile of money. In spring, summer, and fall he takes money from the tourists. Then in the winter he goes to Florida. He's got a condo in Tampa. He does all right."

"Did Sal know Fred?"

"Sure. Sal sold him lobsters. If you're a lobsterman around here, you know all the restaurant owners."

The waitress came over. "Will there be anything else?"

"No thanks," said Mark. "I'll take the check."

Patsy stood up, Martini glass in hand. "I'd better get back to my girlfriends at the bar. Don't want anybody getting the wrong idea."

"No, we don't," smiled Mark. "Thanks, Patsy. It was a pleasure to meet you."

Fred's Clam Shack was across town near the broad expanse of Good Harbor Beach, where families from the hot inland suburbs came to cool off on summer afternoons. They came in their minivans and SUVs packed with coolers, umbrellas, and toys for the kids. After paying twenty bucks to park in the paved lot they filed across the winding boardwalks to the hot sand and cold surf. At the end of the day, sunburned and tired, they'd trudge back to the parking lot and load up the car, and before hitting the highway back to Malden or Stoughton they'd grab an authentic beach dinner of fried clams or pizza washed down with a few cold beers at Fred's.

When Chris Mark pulled open the front door at Fred's, it was near closing time. The counter girl was wiping down the tables as a few stragglers finished up their soggy fries and melting ice cream, or assembled their grumpy kids for the long ride home.

Mark approached the girl wielding the rag.

"Hi there—is Fred around?"

"In the back," she said after a quick glance at the late visitor. "You want to order something? I think the kitchen may still be open."

"No thanks."

"Fred!" she called. "Someone here to see you!"

A moment later a middle-aged man, very fit, came out through the kitchen door. He didn't look as though he had been cooking. With a wary expression he approached Mark.

"Yes—how can I help you?" he said. His voice had the sound of hard stone.

"My name's Chris Mark. I'm looking into the death of Sal Cromisi. Perhaps we can sit down for a minute."

Fred showed Mark to a clean booth near the back. "How about a beer? Crissie! Two Bud Lights!"

Mark had no time to object to the choice of beverage. The two men sat down, facing each other across the narrow table of polyurethaned wood.

"You a cop?" said Fred. "Haven't seen you around before."

"I keep a low profile," replied Mark with palms up. "Just helping out Chief Frontiero. Crossin' the T's and dottin' the I's."

The waitress delivered two beers in tall plastic cups.

"Well, here's to Sal," said Fred as he raised his beer. "He was a good guy."

"Sure," said Mark, and he took a sip of the watery concoction. "You knew him well?"

"I knew him. Everyone did. In the old days I bought haddock from him, and then during the last ten years or so it was lobster. I'd see him at the Elks Club. He was a big Red Sox fan and he'd always watch the games there."

"How about his wife—Judy? Do you know her?"

Fred shrugged. "I see her now and then. Socially. With Sal. They only got married five years ago."

"Know of anybody who would want to kill Sal?"

Fred leaned so close so that Mark instinctively leaned back to give himself space. "Tell you what," said Fred. "Some of these lobstermen are pretty aggressive. Their traps are like their children. If they think you're messin' with them, they're likely to come after you."

"You mean like if you steal lobsters from their traps?"

"Yeah. It's a code of honor. No one touches another man's traps."

"Are you suggesting—?"

"No, no," Fred pulled back. "Sal was as clean as they come. But some of these guys get paranoid. All's I'm sayin' is that's the first place I'd look. In that community."

"You got any names?"

Fred swigged the last of his beer before setting down the plastic cup. He looked Mark in the eye. "I'll get back to you on that. Now if you'll excuse me, I gotta lock up."

Mark went out the front door to the parking lot, where there were only his Camaro and three other cars. Two of the cars were old clunkers that the kitchen help would drive. The third car was a Cadillac—a bit past its prime, but definitely the best of the bunch. After firing up the Camaro, Mark drove a few hundred yards down the road towards town. He pulled into a side road and waited.

Five minutes later the Cadillac passed him. Mark pulled out behind it. The Cadillac made its way along Eastern Avenue to the glittering lights of the harbor before turning up Prospect Street. It stopped a few houses from the Cromisi residence. Mark pulled over and watched Fred go inside the house. Five minutes later the front door opened and Fred stepped out. He was talking to someone who was still inside the house. Then the person stepped onto the front porch. It was Judy's brother, Charles LaPierre. They shook hands and Charles went back inside the house. Fred returned to his car and pulled away from the curb.

Maybe Fred was just paying his respects to the widow. Maybe it was something more.

Mark followed the twin vertical taillights out of downtown and south along the edge of the harbor. When the Cadillac arrived at Kelsey's Wharf, it turned not in the direction of the water but onto a road that went up a long, gently sloping hill. From the bottom of the hill Mark watched the taillights turn into a driveway.

He took out his phone. In a moment he had pulled up the home address of Fred Kane of Gloucester, Massachusetts: 34 Spring Lane. After stopping to see Judy Cromisi, Fred Kane had gone home.

On Sunday morning after a late breakfast of a Western omelet, grapefruit juice, and black coffee served up at the counter of the Three Cousins Diner, Mark returned to the Cromisi home. Judy's tired-looking Buick sat in the narrow driveway. Mark knocked on the front door and the widow answered. She was dressed in black slacks and a dark green blouse that made her hair appear even more brilliantly red.

"Mr. Mark," she said. "You're not in church?"

"It's too nice a morning," he replied. "Have you got a minute?"

"Yes, of course. More neighbors are coming by. When your beloved husband passes on, people bring you more food than you could eat in a year."

"They mean well," said Mark. He followed Judy into the living room. The house smelled like flowers and pasta. On the sofa sat two elderly women, who smiled at Mark. He nodded and smiled, which seemed to please them. On the coffee table was a plate heaped with pastries and Danish.

"Coffee?" said Judy. She had eased into the dining room, where on the table a carton of Dunkin' Donuts coffee rested on a tray along with china cups and saucers that Mark recognized as having come from the cabinet with the glass doors.

"No thanks," said Mark. "I'm good. I just wanted to go over a few things with you."

"You gettin' close to finding out who killed my husband?" Judy poured herself half a cup of coffee and filled the rest with cream. With a teaspoon she slowly stirred it to a uniform tan color.

"We have some ideas," said Mark. "But nothing definite, I'm sorry to say." It was at that moment that

Mark's gaze left the table and took in the rest of the room. On the wall above the buffet, where the day before he had seen the lovely painting of the two-masted boat riding at anchor, there was only a rectangular patch of unfaded wallpaper. "The painting that was there—it's been removed," he said reflexively.

Judy swiveled to look at the bare wall. "Oh yeah. That old thing. Charles took it."

"To New York?"

Judy shrugged. "He said he might be able to find a buyer for it. I have to be honest with you, Mr. Mark, without my husband's income I'm going to have to sell a lot more than one old painting. The bill collectors don't care if you're a widow. I'm having an appraiser come look at the house. I have no choice."

"Yes, I understand. It's not easy." Mark looked around the room. Nothing else had been removed.

"You have some questions for me?" said Judy. "I'm expecting some of the ladies here in a few minutes. They're so kind to keep me company."

"What time did you say your husband left on Tuesday?"

"It was at dawn. All the lobstermen leave at dawn."

"Did he go straight to his boat?"

"I suppose so. That's where he said he was going, and I've no reason to doubt him."

There was activity in the living room. A line of women entered and began to make their way past the Danish and towards the dining room. Each was carrying a covered dish.

"More food," said Judy.

"They're very thoughtful," said Mark. "I won't keep you. One more quick question—do you know Fred Kane? He lives over on Spring Lane. Directly across from Kelsey's Wharf."

"I've met him a few times," shrugged Judy. "He buys lobsters from Sal. Why?"

"No particular reason. His name came up. Thank you, Mrs. Cromisi. I'll stay in touch."

The Gloucester Museum of Art was housed in a former captain's house in the center of town. Over the years the building had been remodeled and expanded to accommodate the museum's growing collections of regional art as well as artifacts that included an actual fishing dory from the nineteenth century. The air inside was cool and dry, and once Mark had paid the five-dollar admission fee he spent a few minutes wandering the galleries looking at beach scenes, boat pictures, and depictions of men working the docks. While nearly everything that he saw had merit, the gallery that he found the most captivating was the one devoted to the works of Fitz Henry Lane, who in the decades before the Civil War specialized in scenes of Gloucester Harbor and the many ships that could be found there—at anchor, pulled up on shore for repair, or setting sail on the morning's high tide. In these pictures, whether small or the size of masterpieces, Mark saw a nation at peace, undisturbed by conflict, blessed by commerce, and in harmony with the natural world. The ships were often depicted in the rosy glow of sunset, riding at ease on calm waters, with sails slack, while men on the shore in the foreground engaged in some unhurried activity.

"Mr. Mark, you wished to see me?" A voice broke his reverie. He turned to see a man who had come noiselessly into the gallery.

"Yes—Mr. Hubert?"

"Please call me James." He stood beside Mark in front of the large painting that Mark had been studying. "This one is called 'Gloucester Harbor from Rocky Neck,'" said James. "Lane painted it in eighteen forty-four. It's got all of the qualities to make it one of his very best: the panoramic view, the beautifully rendered boats, and the feeling of perfect well-being. It was painted twenty years before the horrors of the Civil War. It was a fleeting time in this nation that has never since been repeated."

"As the director of the museum, you must know a lot about local collections," said Mark.

"I try to keep tabs on who's got what," he smiled. "You'd be surprised what people have in their houses."

"Just yesterday," said Mark, "I was in the home of Sal Cromisi, the lobsterman who was murdered. I was admiring a really lovely painting that was hanging in his dining room. It was about as big as this one, and showed a two-masted ship at anchor in a harbor. I suppose it was Gloucester Harbor. Anyway, the feeling was sublime—the same feeling that I get from these pictures. The same beautiful sense of peacefulness."

"Sal Cromisi?" said James. "Yes. I know of him. Terrible tragedy. About a month ago he approached the museum. He showed me a photograph of a painting that was hanging in his dining room. He said that since he had no children, he was considering rewriting his will so that after his death the painting would be given to the museum. He didn't know much about the painting other than it had been in his family for nearly a hundred years. When I saw the photo I was stunned. I recognized the work immediately. It was 'Schooner at Sunset' by Fitz Henry Lane. The last known record of the painting was that it had been sold by a dealer here in Gloucester in the late nineteenth century."

"What's the painting worth today?"

"Fitz Henry Lane paintings are highly coveted and rarely come on the market, and there would be intense interest not only from American buyers but from newly minted Chinese, Russian, and Middle Eastern billionaires. They're driving up prices for the very best works. The last record-breaking auction price for a major Fitz Henry Lane was set about ten years ago. The painting was 'Manchester Harbor' and the winning bid was five and a half million dollars. Because 'Schooner at Sunset' has everything you want in a major work by Lane, I would expect it to go for at least ten million dollars."

"Did you tell Sal this?"

"No. We're not allowed to offer valuation of works donated to the museum. I told him that it was a very significant work that we would be proud to display in this gallery. To get a valuation for tax purposes, I encouraged him to consult an independent appraiser."

"Did Sal come back?"

"No. He told me that he was very grateful for my positive response, and that he'd get the painting appraised."

"So you never saw him again?"

"Not to discuss the painting. But I did run into him on late Tuesday afternoon. At the bank."

"Did you talk to him?"

"Only for a moment. He was going out as I was going in. He held the door open for me. He mentioned that he had come back early from working on his boat because his wife wanted him to do a bunch of errands for her. Then he went on his way."

On the street outside the museum Mark called Chief Frontiero.

"Do you have some good news for me?" the chief asked.

"Maybe. I'd like you to send a diver over to Kelsey's Wharf. Check the harbor bottom for a murder weapon. And do you have Sal's cell phone records? Great. I'll be down to the station to look at them. And one more thing—contact the New York police. Tell them to pay a visit to an art dealer named Charles LaPierre."

Monday morning came grey and unseasonably raw. After breakfast Mark drove over to police headquarters to meet Chief Frontiero.

"Fred Kane is in the interview room," said the chief. "Judy Cromisi will be here in half an hour, as you requested."

Mark entered the interview room. Fred did not look happy.

"Listen—I got a business to run!" he scowled at Mark. "What the hell is this all about?"

Mark put a cardboard box on the table. He removed the lid and reached inside. "This is what this is all about," he said as he took from the box a plastic bag containing a heavy wrench. "It was recovered from the water next to where Sal tied up his boat."

"So what?" spat Fred.

"It's got your fingerprints on it."

"I—"

"There's more. Your phone records indicate that you called Sal at eight o'clock on Tuesday evening. The call lasted two minutes."

"He was on his boat."

"No he wasn't. From your house, you can see Kelsey's Wharf. You called Sal and told him that there was something wrong with his boat. Maybe you said that there was an intruder on the boat. You gallantly offered to meet him on the dock. He rushed over and you both boarded the *Little Princess*. When his back was turned you smashed him in the head with the wrench. When he was down you hit him again to make sure that he was dead. After tossing the wrench overboard, you untied the bowline, started the engine, turned on the running lights, and stepped off the boat and onto the dock. The boat was pulling against the stern line so you couldn't untie it. You had to cut it. Once the line was cut, the *Little Princess* cruised a straight course out of the harbor and into the open ocean. You thought the tank had plenty of fuel and that she'd get halfway to Europe before the engine quit. Your mistake. Less than an hour later the tank was dry. On those busy fishing grounds, the drifting boat was quickly spotted."

"I got no motive," protested Fred.

"Sure you do—the loving arms of the lonely widow and your share of ten million dollars. Your buddy Charles LaPierre took 'Schooner at Sunset' to New York, where he figures he can quickly line up a private buyer. The painting could be out of the country before ol' Sal is resting in his grave."

There was a moment of thick silence. Mark opened the door to the interview room and looked out into the hallway. Then he closed the door.

"Judy Cromisi is here," he said. "We fully expect her to deny any involvement and to pin the murder on you. She and her brother are looking forward to your taking the rap for first-degree murder. Massachusetts doesn't have the death penalty, so you'll be spending the rest of your life as a guest of the commonwealth at Cedar Junction. It's not a nice place."

"That bitch!" spat Fred. "It was her idea! Without telling Sal, she had Charles appraise the painting. When he told her it was worth ten million bucks she told me we'd be crazy not to get rid of Sal and cash in. She made sure he was at home on Tuesday night when I called."

Mark slid a pad of paper and a pen across the table. "Okay, Fred. Start writing. And don't leave out a single detail."

Confessions

"Where's the head?" asked Chris Mark.

Chief Ray Frontiero gave a shrug. His weary eyes scanned the gloomy woods. "Haven't found it yet. We've got every available man looking for it. I've ordered a search of today's trash pickup in the city."

"Any identification?"

"In the pocket of her slacks we found her driver's license," replied Frontiero. "Penny Dickert. Age thirty-five. Lives over in Riverdale. We're looking for next of kin."

Mark slapped a mosquito that had alighted on the back of his neck. The midday temperature had topped ninety, which for Gloucester, surrounded on three sides by the cool waters of the Atlantic Ocean, was a rare event in September. Mark looked at his hand. His palm showed a smear of red blood and bits of mangled insect parts. With the fingertips of his other hand he swept the debris. The fragments tumbled into the weeds.

"The cuts on the neck look ragged," he said.

"The medical examiner says the head was removed with a narrow saw blade," said Frontiero. "There was evidence of clumsiness. False starts. Particularly on the vertebrae. Not a medical doctor. An amateur." Frontiero paused before leaning close to Mark. "This was before your time, but years ago we had two other murders with the same characteristics. Dead women, heads cut off, bodies wrapped in plastic sheets, found here in the woods. We never caught the guy. The press called him the Demon of Dogtown. As time passed I thought that he either got killed or moved away. Looks like I was wrong."

"I remember reading stories about those old cases," said Mark. "The heads were never found."

Mark surveyed the jumble of trees and rocks that framed the scene. Here in the hidden heart of Cape Ann there were no houses, no roads—only rough trails that skirted the huge granite boulders and towering trees. Here and there the weekend hiker could discern the outlines of old foundations, the ghosts of the scattered nineteenth-century homesteads and shacks that once dotted this rugged landscape.

In these tangled woods, to find an object the size of a human head you'd have to practically step on it.

He slapped another mosquito. The sun burned bright and hot. The red cotton blouse worn by the headless corpse contrasted sharply with the vivid greens and earthy browns of ground upon which it lay.

"The murderer cuts off her head but doesn't bother to take her identification," Mark mused aloud. "He's not trying to hide her identity."

The medical examiner gave the signal for the body to be bagged. There was nothing more to be seen here. Chris Mark turned and made his way along the winding path to his car.

In his Camaro, safe from both the relentless mosquitoes and the television news reporters, Mark tapped his phone. A search for "Penny Dickert, Gloucester" yielded few results—just the usual misleading pages that promised deep secrets and delivered only useless pay-per-click advertising. Not even a Facebook page.

One search result appeared promising. Mark clicked through. The page was part of the website of the Independent Trinity Church. Mark had heard of the congregation. By New England standards they were rigidly fundamentalist. The search match was a photo caption. Under the image of three men and two women the text read, "Church standing committee at the first meeting of the year. Left to right: Bob Haskins, Garrett Didston, Penny Dickert, Melvin Thorp, Suzanne Greenleaf." The woman in the center was about thirty years old and the same physical type as the headless corpse—average height, slender. She was looking straight into the camera and smiling. Her shoulder-length brown hair was pulled away from her face, revealing the high forehead and arched eyebrows that gave her face an eager, inquisitive look. Like the other four, she was smiling while squinting into the bright sunlight that cast hard shadows under their chins.

The photo and its caption appeared on a page of the church newsletter. The issue of the newsletter carried a date in August of the previous year. Probably the photo was taken on a hot summer day just like this one.

It was the only online evidence that Mark found of Penny Dickert. In a world of silence, a single whisper can mean everything. Into his GPS he punched the address of the church. It was on the mainland in the western part of town, across the big bridge that spanned the Annisquam River.

Under the hot blue sky the plain box of the church building gleamed white. Topped by a stark steeple, the sharply peaked roof was clad in black shingles. All that was needed to complete the scene of American Gothic was a man and woman dressed in overalls and holding a pitchfork. After parking in the gravel lot next to a drab Oldsmobile, Mark walked past the low wooden sign upon which was carved and painted the words "INDEPENDENT TRINITY CHURCH - 1985." A smaller sign advertised "Bible Study Classes Every Tuesday" and "Thursday Evening— Everyone Welcome." Attached to the rectangular box of the church was a low clapboard-sided addition with its own door. Probably the office.

The bright sunlight made Mark squint. The only sounds were the buzz of locusts and the dull hum of a far-off lawn mower. The office door was aluminum. Should he knock or just enter? He chose the latter and pulled open the door. He entered a small office, dimly lit, and cooled by a window air conditioner. As his eyes adjusted to the light he saw a woman seated at a desk.

She clicked the computer mouse and swiveled to look at him.

"How may I help you?" she said with a lifetime of cheerfulness.

"My name's Chris Mark. I'm looking into the death of Penny Dickert."

"Oh—the dear child," said the woman. Her smile faded like a rapidly setting sun. "A terrible thing. I just saw it on the news. What happened? She was murdered?"

"Her body was found in Dogtown. That's all we can say. You knew her?"

"Yes. We all did. We're a very close-knit community. I'm sorry—I should introduce myself. I'm Wilma Dixon. The church secretary."

"Pleased to meet you. Is there somewhere we can talk?"

Wilma rose from her swivel chair. "Let's go into the kitchen. There's some lemonade in the refrigerator." Wilma led Mark through a doorway and into a small kitchen furnished with a table and four chairs. As Mark took a seat she busied herself with two plastic tumblers and a pitcher of pink lemonade.

Mark accepted the tumbler that Wilma handed to him. The lemonade was cold and tasted like corn syrup dissolved in tap water.

"I saw Penny's photo in the church bulletin," offered Mark. "It's posted online. On the church website."

"Yes—the standing committee," said Wilma. Now that she was seated across from him, Mark was able to get a better sense of her. No makeup, save for clear nail polish. Smooth skin like freshly risen bread dough. Soft brown hair, no coloring. Plain gold studs in her ears. Her manner was direct and unaffected. Clearly she felt no compulsion to improve upon the physical attributes given to her by God.

"How long has Penny been a member of the church?" asked Mark.

"She came to us about two years ago. From Boston. She had an epiphany and dedicated herself to her salvation."

"What was her life like before she joined the church?"

"From what I could gather, it was not healthy. In the city she did what so many young people do—went out drinking, had boyfriends. She did not honor herself. That changed when she came here. She put it all behind her."

"She got herself elected to the standing committee very quickly."

Wilma nodded. "She was dedicated to the church. She placed herself under the guidance of our pastor and became very involved here. In fact, she was supposed to present her confessional this Sunday. Poor thing—she never had the opportunity to cleanse her soul."

"Cleanse her soul of what?"

"Past sins. Things that are offensive to God. You cannot enter the kingdom of heaven without confessing your sins. Everyone knows that. We've all made our confessions."

In an effort to be polite, Mark took a swallow of the lemonade. But he did not want to drain the glass for fear that Wilma would offer him a refill. He set the plastic tumbler on the table.

"This confession is public?" asked Mark.

"Of course," replied Wilma. "What else would it be? You unburden your soul in front of the congregation."

"Does anyone know in advance what you're going to say?"

"Yes. You write it out. You inform anyone to whom you've done wrong. You tell the pastor. By the time you get up in front of the congregation, half of them already know what you're going to say."

"And what do people confess? Big stuff or just little things?"

"All sins are 'big stuff,' as you say," said Wilma. "Being angry, stealing, going against God, infidelity, intoxication—all of those things. Whatever leads you away from God."

"Public confession must be difficult to do, especially if you've done something to hurt another person."

Wilma nodded. "It can be painful, but it's a small price to pay when you consider the alternative."

"Your immortal soul," said Mark.

"Yes."

"Do you know what Penny planned to confess?"

"No. I presume that nothing she was going to say involved me. The pastor knows her confession, and some others know also. But we do not judge. It does not matter whether I know or I don't know. It's not about me. It's between the confessor and God."

"I understand," said Mark. "Wilma, you've been very helpful. Thank you for your time. I'm sorry for the loss of one who was close to you. Do you happen to know if the pastor is in?"

"I think John's in his office." She stood up and went to the door through which she and Mark had entered the kitchen, and then from the church office into the church itself. It was a plain space with rows of polished pews and a simple cross above the altar. There were no images of saints or even of Jesus. Twin overhead ceiling fans lazily stirred the stifling air. Wilma led Mark to the opposite side of the room to a door that opened onto a short hallway that ran parallel to the building. They came to a door that was ajar. Wilma knocked and a man said, "Come in."

"John, there's a man here wishing to speak to you about Penny Dickert," said Wilma as they entered a square room with one window and one desk. Behind the desk sat a lanky man with a shock of white hair. He turned his piercing eyes in Mark's direction.

"My name's Chris Mark. I'm investigating the death of Ms. Dickert. May I have a word with you?"

"Certainly." The pastor's voice was soft but self assured. "Please have a seat. We're absolutely shocked. She was a good woman."

As Wilma closed the door behind her Mark drew up one of the two plain wooden chairs that were parked against the wall. In contrast to the oven-like church, the office was as cold as a refrigerator.

"Do the police know what happened?" asked the pastor.

"All that we can say is that her body was found in Dogtown. You knew her well?"

"As well as anyone. She was active in the church. Everyone liked her."

"Wilma told me that Penny was preparing to present a confession before the congregation. Is that true?"

John looked directly at Mark, into his eyes, and said nothing. Mark's expression remained as blank as a sphinx. After a moment John leaned back in his chair, widening the distance between them. Mark leaned forward slightly to compensate. There was no sound except the drone of the room air conditioner.

John blinked. "Yes, she was. This coming Sunday. It's something that every member of our family does."

"And it's public? Anyone can hear it?"

"Yes—anyone in the congregation."

"I understand that Penny wrote it out. May I see a copy?"

John hesitated.

In his head, thought Mark, he's running through the presumed sequence of events. Deny this intruder Mark. The police then go to a judge. The judge rules that it's not privileged communication because the whole point of the confession is that it's public. The cops come back with a search warrant and tear the place apart.

John reached into a drawer of his desk and withdrew two sheets of paper. Without a word he went to the small portable copy machine and made a copy of each of the sheets. He handed the copies to Mark before replacing the originals in his desk drawer.

"Penny told me that she wasn't one hundred percent certain that she wanted to go through with it," said the pastor. "She was going to give me her decision this week. I asked her why she was hesitating. She said it was a private matter between her and God. I urged her to keep her promise to the church and to herself, and to seek forgiveness for her sins."

Mark glanced at the neatly typewritten paragraphs with Penny's signature at the end. He folded the sheets and slipped them into the inside pocket of his jacket before standing up.

"Thank you, Pastor John," he said. "I'll get back to you."

At his desk in his home office Mark unfolded the sheets and, after smoothing out the creases, began to read.

CONFESSION OF PENNY DICKERT

This is my confession given freely before God.

I have committed the sin of adultery.

When I lived in Boston I worked as a media consultant for a public relations company. Our offices were on High Street, in the Financial District. At the time, it was a job and a career that I had dreamed of. My role was to assist and advise the firm's female clients who, by the nature of their work, either appeared in the public eye or at high-profile events in their industry. These appearances required our clients to be impeccably groomed and accessorized. Many of them didn't have the time to worry about these things, so they hired us to do the worrying for them. I would meet privately with my client, determine the best look for her, go shopping, find makeup artists and hair people, and assemble the team that would make sure that the client looked perfect. My job involved meetings at four-star restaurants, shopping at the finest stores, and visiting our clients in their offices at some of Boston's best addresses.

I say this not to excuse or justify my sins, but to explain the circumstances.

One of our clients was the chief executive officer of a prominent real estate investment company. She was constantly on the go and my boss suggested to her that she use my services. She readily agreed, and our first appointment was set for her office on a Tuesday morning.

This was a big account and I felt the pressure to perform and to please her. Our meeting went well. We reviewed her calendar of personal appearances and the image that she wanted to project. I suggested a few wardrobe adjustments—simple things like making sure her skirts covered her knees and wearing suits that were not too tight. She proved to be a good client who was willing to set aside her own preconceptions in favor of a look that was more appropriate to what she wanted to accomplish.

Our first breakthrough came when she had to address a gathering of a thousand industry leaders at a convention in New York. She was apprehensive. Her first choice was a drab beige skirt and blazer. This was not going to help her. I found a stunning red power suit that had visual impact. She loved it, and after she had made her presentation she sent me an email saying that she had never felt so confident.

I knew that my client was married. She wore an engagement ring and a wedding ring, and on her desk was a framed photo of her with her husband and their teenaged son. The photo looked as if it had been taken on a tropical island. It never occurred to me that she was interested in anything other than a professional relationship. But a few weeks after the New York convention, she invited me to lunch at the restaurant of the Adams Hotel in Boston's Financial District. It was a place frequented by high-powered executives. Of course I accepted. We met at one o'clock. During our lunch she asked me questions about where I lived (in the South End) and if I had a boyfriend (no, I did not). In retrospect I should have been suspicious, but I was flattered that one of our biggest clients was taking a personal interest in me.

When the check came, which she insisted upon paying, she asked me if I had a few minutes of free time. I said sure, no problem. My client said that her company maintained a suite at the hotel for out-of-town visitors. She didn't care for the décor, and would I mind having a look? I replied that of course I'd be delighted.

We went up to the twentieth floor. In the elevator she stood very close to me, and when the door opened she took my arm and guided me down the hall. She seemed a bit tipsy—we had shared a bottle of sparkling wine at lunch—and I was having fun and excited to be with her.

The suite was indeed drab, and we spent a few minutes discussing paint colors and carpets. Then she took me to the window to show me the view. Suddenly she turned to me and told me that I had magic eyes. Those were her exact words— "magic eyes." At first I assumed she was complimenting me on my taste as a consultant. I thanked her and told her that the pleasure was all mine. She came close to me—close enough that I could smell her makeup. After putting her hand on my arm she leaned closer and kissed me on the lips.

If someone had told me that this was going to happen to me, I would have replied that I was sure I would find it utterly repellent. And at first I was startled. But I did not pull away. The first thought that entered my mind was that we ought to move away from the window because someone might see us. I may have said something to that effect because she took my hand and led me to the bed. She sat me down and kissed me again—harder this time, and with more passion.

I won't go into the details. Suffice to say that we engaged in intimate relations of the kind that are condemned by the Bible, and they are condemned not only because she was married but because they are unclean. I know that now.

We left the room about an hour later. I was giddy. I felt as though I had stepped into another world. In many ways it was scary. I felt unbalanced.

The next time we spoke was the following Friday. She was scheduled to appear on a local television talk show. I prepped her and she behaved as she always had, as if nothing had happened. I became worried. Had I displeased her? Had I not satisfied her?

When she called me on Monday and asked me if I were free for lunch the next day, I admit that I felt a thrill. I had won her approval. The feeling was seductive. We had lunch in the same hotel restaurant and when the meal was over she gave me a smile and asked if I wanted to see the room again.

I confess that I was hoping she would ask me. I had worn expensive lingerie and had meticulously groomed myself. I was determined to please her.

Our relationship continued for about six months. As time went on I became uneasy. At her demand, our intimate relations, which at the outset seemed like a harmless and loving diversion, became increasingly disturbing. My client asked me to do things that I thought were unnatural and frightening. I worried that I was in danger, and I began to have sleepless nights. I started taking sleeping pills and it became more difficult to concentrate at work. On more than one occasion my boss asked me if I were feeling all right. I told her that everything was fine, but I knew that everything was not fine.

It was on a weekend drive to Gloucester that I happened to pass by the Independent Trinity Church. For some reason I stopped. It was a beautiful autumn day and the trees were golden. The church building seemed so simple and so pure. I got out of my car and on an impulse tried the door. It was open. I went inside and sat in one of the pews. As the light faded towards evening a man came up to me and told me that he needed to lock up. The man turned out to be Pastor John.

You all know the rest. I visited the church on weekends, and eventually decided that I needed to take care of myself. I quit my job. I was relieved, I guess, that it was over. I sold my condo in Boston and bought a small house here in Gloucester. That was two years ago. Pastor John let me join the church without making a public confession, but now I'm ready. I'm sorry for my sins and seek forgiveness from you, my neighbors, as well as from God.

Signed, Penny Dickert.

Chris Mark got up from his desk, went to the kitchen, and poured himself a double Jack Daniels on the rocks. As he stood in the kitchen he downed a hefty slug. The burning in his throat felt good. With drink in hand he went back to his desk and clicked on his computer. A quick search confirmed what he suspected was true.

There was only one woman who, during the past decade, had been the CEO of a leading real estate investment firm in Boston. Rachel Garrison had recently left the firm with the intention of entering politics. She was currently embroiled in a heated election to become the next governor of Massachusetts.

Garrison's campaign website, which touted her belief in strong family values, said that she and her husband lived in Weston, a wealthy bedroom community about an hour from Gloucester. Their son Lawrence had taken a leave of absence from college to work on his mother's campaign.

Another search revealed that they owned a summer home on the coast just north of Lanesville. It was about two miles from where the body had been found.

"My detectives are pissed off that you're involved in this investigation," said Chief Frontiero. He took a vigorous stab at his pork chop. Normally a quiet restaurant on a weekday afternoon, today the Seaport Landing was crowded with a load of Midwestern tourists who had been ferried in from the big boxy cruise ship that had anchored that afternoon in the deep outer harbor.

Looking across the table, Chris Mark wondered why it had taken so long for the chief's men to express resentment. He swirled the beer in his glass. "Tell me to go away and I will. No skin off my back. If your guys can crack this case, fine. They didn't fifteen years ago."

"Why don't you let me put you on my payroll, for chrissakes," said the chief. "You clear cases faster than anyone else in New England. I'll give you a badge and a gun, and my guys will shut up."

"No thanks," replied Mark. "I like my freedom. My tour of duty in Iraq gave me enough of the regimented life. Right now I'm enjoying my lunch. This swordfish isn't bad. The manager said it came off the boat this morning. While we're here, let's talk business. Come on, Ray, give me something about Penny Dickert. After all, I've practically solved this thing for you."

As Frontiero carefully picked the last of the meat off the bone, he leaned across the table and lowered his voice. "Just before we got here I received a call. We found the head in a load of trash from Lanesville. It had been put into one of those purple plastic trash bags that all the homeowners in Gloucester have to use. Wads of newspapers had been stuffed into the bag too—I suppose to make it look bigger so the trash pickup guy wouldn't notice. In the head there was a bullet. It entered the eye socket and bounced off the back of the cranium."

"A low-power round," said Mark.

"Yeah. A twenty-two. Probably fired from a short-barreled weapon, like a ladies' handgun. The bullet is intact. We could get a match if we had a weapon."

"So now we know why the head was cut off."

"Yeah—to hide the evidence," said Frontiero as he took a hunk of bread from the basket. Then he put it back into the basket. "I gotta stop eating this stuff. My doctor says I have to lose ten pounds. No more bread, no more pasta. This diet is killing me."

"Pasta is killing you. What are the dates on the newspapers?"

"Three dates: September tenth, eleventh, and twelfth. Monday, Tuesday, Wednesday."

"It looks like our murderer is a subscriber to the *Tribune*. The medical examiner says that Penny was killed on Wednesday night—last night—between eight and midnight. The hiker found her body today at eleven. The head was put out with today's trash. In Lanesville they pick up the trash between ten in the morning and noon."

"I'm still hungry," said Frontiero.

"You'll get used to it," replied Mark. "Your stomach shrinks. After a while it takes less food to fill you up. The time line is clear. Penny Dickert was murdered Wednesday night and her body was dumped in Dogtown. The head was put out with the trash on Thursday morning. You'd assume the murderer wouldn't leave the bag on the street overnight. Too risky. They'd wait until the morning, just before the trash truck came around."

"The Demon of Dogtown?" said Frontiero.

"Maybe. Or someone who read about him in the newspaper."

At that moment Frontiero's phone buzzed. He glanced at the screen. "Ah—this could be interesting." He put the phone to his ear. "Tell me some good news. Okay. That is good news. Yeah. Thanks." He put away the phone. "We have a witness who saw a car in Dogtown at eleven o'clock last night."

Mark called for the check. "If you don't mind, chief, I'm going to take a drive."

Chris Mark turned his Camaro off the main road that leads from Gloucester to its northern neighbor, Rockport. The setting sun over Ipswich Bay to the west streamed its rays through the tunnel of arching trees and forced Mark to lower his visor. The driveway curved to the north, providing relief from the late afternoon glare.

After passing a rambling stone wall, the Garrison house came into view. An imposing but ramshackle shingled beach house, it gave the appearance of unforced wealth and ease. Like many summer estates along the North Shore it had been built over many decades as a series of additions, with each one attempting to match the architectural style of its predecessor. To the right, a garage nestled against a wall of shrubs. In front of the closed doors of the garage was parked a blue Mercedes station wagon. On the sloping lawn two kayaks lay casually abandoned, as if their owners had just returned from a trip picking blueberries on one of the beachfront meadows that dot the western side of Cape Ann.

After parking his car on the side of the gravel driveway, Mark walked the stone-paved path to the front porch. He paused to listen. In the dense heat there was no sound except the distant shush of the waves against the rocks. Mark knocked. There were footsteps before the door was pulled open by a middle-aged man.

"Henry Garrison? My name's Chris Mark. I'd like to have a few words with you."

"About what?" said the man. With a burly forearm he leaned against the doorframe.

"Penny Dickert, and your station wagon."

Henry Garrison gave an offhand shrug. "Come in, Mr. Mark. I can't imagine how I can help." Stepping aside, he allowed Mark to enter a dark vestibule that opened onto a big living room on one side and a hallway on another. Henry Garrison led Mark to the spacious living room. There were wicker chairs and a chintz sofa, and on the mantle rested a model of a square-rigged ship. At the far end next to a big window was a French door that opened onto a covered porch. Through the open door Mark could see the bright gleam of the ocean. A sultry breeze swished against the sheer curtains framing the window.

"Are your wife and son at home?" asked Mark.

"Mrs. Garrison is at a meeting. Lawrence went to the store. They're both due back any minute. Have a seat, Mr. Mark."

"I'll stand, thanks. Mr. Garrison, do you know Penny Dickert?"

"Can't say that I do." Henry Garrison went to the wet bar and picked up a bottle of single malt Scotch. He turned to Mark. "Drink? Might cool you off. This heat's a killer."

"No thanks. Mr. Garrison, we have a serious problem."

"What would that be?" replied Henry Garrison as he dropped two ice cubes into the highball glass.

"We have a witness."

"A witness to what?" Henry Garrison brought the glass to his lips after recorking the bottle. "I only drink single malts, Mr. Mark. Don't care for blends."

"We have a witness who saw your Mercedes station wagon in Dogtown on Wednesday night. It was parked at the spot where the body of Penny Dickert was found."

"So what?" replied Henry Garrison.

"There's something else," said Mark. "Information that the police haven't released yet. We recovered the head, Mr. Garrison. I know why the head was cut from the body."

"It was the Demon of Dogtown, of course. You should be making an effort to catch him rather than making wild insinuations against innocent people." Drink in hand, Henry Garrison slouched into a wicker chair.

"Her head was cut off for a very practical reason," replied Mark. "To get rid of the evidence."

"What evidence? That the poor woman had a head?"

"The evidence of the twenty-two caliber slug that was lodged in her cranial cavity. Interesting thing about twenty-twos: they haven't got much momentum. When you shoot someone in the eye socket—as Ms. Dickert was—the bullet hasn't got enough force to break out through the back of the skull. So it just bounces around inside the cranial cavity and turns the brain into cottage cheese. That's why many professional hit men use twenty-twos. When you shoot the victim in the head at close range, the impact doesn't make a mess but the wound is lethal."

"So what?" said Henry Garrison in a tone that had become more wary.

"We have the bullet. And we're confident that it'll match the twenty-two-caliber Ruger pistol that's registered to your son Lawrence. He stated on the license application that the purpose was for shooting varmints. The evidence against him is piling up. What I'm hoping is that he'll provide a full confession and take a plea deal. It will go much better for him."

At that moment Mark heard the front door open and shut, and the sound of footsteps in the vestibule.

"In here," called Henry Garrison.

"Henry, I really need you to call the exterminator," said the unseen woman. "There's a wasps' nest on the front porch and—" When she entered the room she stopped. "I'm sorry—who is this?"

"He's an investigator," said Henry Garrison, who had gotten to his feet.

"My name's Chris Mark, Mrs. Garrison. I'm afraid that I've brought some bad news. Your son Lawrence is under suspicion for the murder of Penny Dickert."

Rachel Garrison stood ramrod straight in her flawless navy blue suit. Under her perfect helmet of highlighted hair her brown eyes flashed in anger. She set her purse on the table by the door.

"I need to call my public relations people," she said.

Henry Garrison approached his wife. "Don't you think we should talk about this?"

"Talk about what?" she snapped.

"Our son."

"We'll get him the very best lawyer. I know who to call—Bernard Copley. No one's better. We can prove that it was a terrible accident. Make a deal. Whatever we do, we need to get this off the front pages as quickly as possible. The election is in six weeks. That's not much time. We cannot afford to let this derail my campaign."

"Mrs. Garrison, do you believe your son to be guilty?" asked Chris Mark.

"I admit to nothing," she retorted. "What I'm saying is that we are going to spare no expense to get him the very best lawyers who can cut a deal and get this resolved as soon as possible. Nothing will be gained by dragging our names through the mud."

"Rachel, what are you saying?" asked Henry Garrison. "Are you throwing Lawrence under the bus?"

"It is what it is," said Rachel Garrison. "Lawrence never amounted to anything. He's a disappointment. I'm sorry, Henry, but the truth can be painful. There's no reason to sugarcoat it. Our son just doesn't measure up. It cannot be helped. What cannot be allowed to fail is this campaign. Too much is at stake."

Mark looked at Henry Garrison. "The evidence is overwhelming, Mr. Garrison. Your son's gun was the murder weapon. He cut off the head and then used the Mercedes to dump the body. The next morning he put out the head with the trash. It was an elaborate plot based on what he had read in the papers about the Demon of Dogtown. If this goes to trial, your son is going to jail for a very long time. It would be better if he confessed."

"Confessed?" sputtered Henry Garrison. He slumped into the chair and put his head in his hands. "No—I cannot let my son be railroaded. He has his entire life ahead of him. I'm retired. I've had my run." He raised his head and looked Mark in the eye. "I'm ready to confess my part in this crime."

"Henry, shut up!" hissed Rachel Garrison. "You have no idea what you're doing!"

"Yes I do. Mr. Mark, I will tell you what I know. Last night I arrived home at ten o'clock in the evening. The lights were on but the place was quiet. I called to my wife. I thought perhaps that she was out attending a campaign event that I had forgotten about. I was about to go into the library to make myself a drink when I heard her answer. She was in the kitchen with Lawrence. They both came into the vestibule. I knew instantly that something was wrong—not so much from Rachel, who is always very self-composed, but by Lawrence's behavior. He seemed to be very nervous. I think that his hands were shaking. I asked them what was going on. Rachel said that something terrible had happened. There had been an accident. A bad accident with Lawrence's gun. A woman was dead in the library.

"I rushed into the library. The woman was lying on her back on the floor. At first I didn't see any wounds or even any blood. Then when I bent over her face I saw a small hole in her right eye. It was consistent with a small caliber bullet. The woman—whom I had never seen before—had no pulse and was clearly dead. I lifted her head and felt the back of it for an exit wound. There was no hole and no blood.

"I was horrified and said of course we needed to call the police. Rachel insisted that we not call the police. It would destroy her campaign and ruin her career for no reason. What was done was done. What we had to do was get rid of the body.

"I demanded to know who the woman was and how she came to be shot to death in our home. After sending Lawrence outside to check on the woman's car, Rachel told me that her name was Penny and that she was a deranged stalker who had come to the house and had demanded money.

"Money for what? I asked. Rachel replied that the woman claimed to have evidence that the two of them had been involved in some sort of sexual affair. The woman wanted a million dollars to keep it quiet; otherwise she was going to make a public statement.

"I asked my wife why she didn't go to the police. Rachel's response was that it was too close to the election. The press would have a field day, and even though the stories were baseless it would give her opponent a huge boost. She had decided to reason with the woman and perhaps give her a small payment to get rid of her. It was to this end that my wife had invited the woman to our home. To talk to her and to offer her some reasonable amount to go away.

"Foolishly, Lawrence had burst into the room and, in a misguided attempt to assist his mother, had brandished his varmint pistol. Rachel told me that the woman had lunged at Lawrence. They struggled and the gun went off. The woman fell to the floor. My wife and son panicked. Lawrence suggested dumping the body in Dogtown. Rachel brought up the problem of the bullet, which was still in the woman's head. Leaving the body on the floor, they went into the kitchen to get rubber gloves and some sort of tool to try to dig out the bullet.

"That's when I came home. After convincing them to abandon the idea of recovering the bullet, I decided to go along with my wife and refrain from dialing nine-one-one. The woman was dead and nothing was going to bring her back. But we had the problem of her body and what to do with it. Rachel suggested we bury her in the far corner of the back yard. No way was that going to happen—I did not want anyone's dead body buried on our property. I remembered the stories about the Demon of Dogtown. I had read about the murders in the newspaper. Two women had been found dead. Decapitated. It seemed like a plausible scenario. I wrapped the body in plastic and carried it out to the garage, where I keep my power tools. I laid the body with the head and shoulders over a shallow plastic tub, unwrapped the head and neck areas, and used an electric reciprocating saw to cut off the head. Then I tightly re-wrapped the body and loaded it into the station wagon. I took the body to Dogtown, where I dumped it. When I returned home, after putting the head into a trash bag with newspapers to give it bulk, I cleaned up the garage. I threw the saw into the ocean. The next morning when I heard the garbage truck coming, I hurried out to the curb and added the bag with the head to the other trash bags. A minute later it was picked up and thrown into the truck."

Chris Mark let Henry Garrison's words linger in the sultry air. Rachel Garrison said nothing.

"Mr. Garrison," said Mark, "you've just confessed to several crimes, but the seriousness of your situation depends upon the investigation into the facts surrounding the death of Penny Dickert. You say that she came here seeking money. Did you know that she was prepared to make a public confession at her church? Although she was not going to state your wife's name, after reading her confession it took me about five minutes to figure out the person's identity."

At that moment the front door opened and Mark heard footsteps. Into the room came a lanky young man who looked like a taller and skinnier version of his father.

"Lawrence," said Rachel Garrison, "Mr. Mark is here to talk to us about the death of that young woman."

"Oh—yeah," said Lawrence. He set his bag of groceries on a chair. His eyes went from his mother to his father.

"We were just telling Mr. Mark," continued Rachel Garrison, "that we're going to spare no expense to provide you with the finest legal defense possible. What happened was a tragic accident. No one meant to shoot that woman. She came here to blackmail this family. Your father and I will stand behind you every step of the way."

"Stand behind me?" said Lawrence. "I didn't do anything."

"Lawrence," insisted his mother, "you know how important this campaign is. Nothing can be allowed to stop it. We all need to stick together. When I'm governor I'll immediately commute your sentence. We'll take care of you. Please—tell Mr. Mark how you shot Penny Dickert."

"How I shot Penny Dickert?" said Lawrence. His face went white. "Mother, what are you saying? I wasn't even in the room! I heard the gunshot when I was upstairs!"

"Mrs. Garrison, why don't you tell us what really happened," said Mark.

"What happened" —Rachel Garrison was now shouting— "was that my son pointed his gun at that woman to frighten her! She lunged at him and they wrestled and the gun went off. It was a horrible accident. If that woman had never come here and had kept her hands to herself, none of this would have ever happened."

"Wait a minute," said Lawrence. "Mother, I'm not going to jail for you! I'm sorry—I just can't do that. I don't care if you're going to be governor. It's just not right!"

"Lawrence," said Mark, "why don't you tell me exactly what happened."

The room was silent.

"Son, tell us what happened," said Henry Garrison.

"Henry, you stay the hell out of this!" shouted Rachel Garrison.

"Mother," said Lawrence calmly, "I'm not going to sacrifice myself. I'm just not going to do it. Mr. Mark, here's what happened. I was at home yesterday evening. I was in my room upstairs listening to music. My mother came to my door. She asked to borrow my varmint pistol. I asked her why. She said that a woman was coming over and that she wanted to show it to her. To teach her about self defense. Okay, I said. I got the gun and handed it to her. She asked if it were loaded. I said of course not—I would never in a million years keep a loaded gun in my room. She asked me to put in a couple of rounds. Just to show the woman. I said okay, but you'd better be careful. So I put three rounds in the clip and showed her how to load and unload the clip. I showed her how the safety worked, and to make sure the safety was always on. She said okay, and took the gun.

"I went back to listening to music. About a half-hour later I heard a gunshot. I thought, oh shit, the gun's gone off. I hope no one got hurt. I hurried downstairs. I found mom in the library. The gun was in her hand. A woman was lying on the floor. I asked mom what happened. She said the woman had attacked her and the gun went off. We needed to get the bullet out of her head. Mom hustled me into the kitchen. I thought the whole thing was crazy! But I went along with what mom said. Then dad came home. Mother talked to him, and he took the body away. Mom told me to get the woman's car keys. She told me to drive the woman's car to a street in downtown Gloucester. I needed to wear gloves when I touched the car. Mom followed me, and I parked the car and walked away. It's probably still there.

"That's all. Mom drove me home as if nothing had happened. Today I saw the television news stories about the murdered woman found in the woods, and the fact that the police thought it might be the return of the Demon of Dogtown. It seemed unreal. I knew that the woman had been in our house. She had been killed in our house."

Henry Garrison faced his wife. "Rachel, we've been married for twenty-five years. I've always stood by your side. I was ready to commit to your run for the governor's office. But we cannot go on. It's over. A woman is dead. I encourage you to give up. Confess everything. If the woman attacked you, so be it. If you shot her in cold blood, I hope that you'll have the strength to say so."

Rachel Garrison collapsed into a chair as a single tear welled in the corner of her eye. Her eyes seemed to focus on a place far in the distance.

"Idiots," she muttered. "I'm surrounded by idiots."

From outside came the sounds of vehicles pulling up to the house, heavy footsteps on the porch floorboards, and an insistent knock on the door.

"That would be the police," said Chris Mark. "They've brought three sets of handcuffs."

Melody of Death

Even by the old money standards of Eastern Point, the imposing residence was grand. From the broad front porch you could see beyond the private road and the sheltering trees to the white curl of the waves of the Atlantic Ocean crashing against the rocks of Brace Cove, while at the rear of the house the majestic brick terrace was only a few steps from the dock jutting proudly into Gloucester Harbor. There you could watch the fishing boats as they chugged past the great granite breakwater and headed out to the open sea for a day or a week of trawling or gillnetting.

"Water front and back," the realtor had told newly minted millionaire musician Ty Massy when she had shown him the property earlier that year. "It's extraordinary, isn't it? The ocean and the harbor. There are few other places on the East Coast where you'll find such a combination."

Massy had shrugged, neither agreeing nor disagreeing. He had been brought up in Boston's tough neighborhood of Dorchester and he knew not to appear enthusiastic. He wanted the house but he could also walk away. There were many other estates on which he could drop five million dollars in cash.

That's what a string of hit records can do for you. Almost overnight they can take you from your girlfriend's sofa to a mansion on the ocean. If your head is screwed on straight, you can leverage your success. If you're young or foolish, you'll squander it on dope and your fawning posse, and find yourself back on welfare before you know it. Ty Massy had been working in the music business for ten years and knew what it was like to live hand to mouth. He was clear-eyed about his success.

After some haggling, Massy had bought the mansion on Eastern Point for four and a half million. Paying cash had helped bring the price down.

Because he was a public figure, there was a lot of information in the media about his life and career. Not all of it was flattering. Some of it was the usual stuff of rock stardom—drugs and wild parties. Not so much in the past few years; as he got older Massy had curbed his most flagrant excesses. There were also stories about money problems, sinister lawyers, the Svengali-like manager, the greedy posse. How much was real and how much was sensationalism was hard to figure. For a rock star any press is good press, and the slightest ripple or rumor was inevitably exaggerated for the benefit of both tabloid and CD sales. As long as no one got hurt, everyone came out a winner.

And now the kid from Dorchester who made it big lay in that house with a bullet through his chest.

Chris Mark closed the file that the Gloucester police had assembled on Ty Massy. He pondered what he had read in the file and what he had seen at the mansion on Eastern Point a few hours earlier.

He had just returned to his own house after a morning of surfing at Long Beach, the big swath of sand that straddles Gloucester and its northern neighbor Rockport. There had been three-foot waves and he had caught a few good ones. From nine to five in the summertime you're not allowed to surf at Long Beach—it's too dangerous because of all of the tourists in the water—but from September through May you can surf anytime. On this particular early spring day the beach had been host to only a few hardy dog walkers. The water temperature was a bracing forty-five degrees, so a wetsuit had been in order.

As Mark toweled off after his shower the phone rang. Chief Frontiero. A murder. The victim was a wealthy musician on Eastern Point. Could Mark have a look? Mark had hurriedly dressed in jeans and a Red Sox sweatshirt before driving his Camaro down the road to the address he had been given. It was a long two miles from the working-class neighborhood on the harbor where Mark lived to the tony enclave of Eastern Point. Despite the fact it was a public area, the homeowners paid to have a guard patrol the entrance to Eastern Point Boulevard. The guard had no legal authority to keep anyone out, but his presence made the residents feel better.

At the Massy house, Mark had eased past the cluster of local news trucks with their rooftop dish antennas and parked his car behind the white medical examiner's van. After nodding to the city cops who were keeping watch at the front door he entered the big gloomy vestibule. Straight ahead through the French doors of the dining room he could see the glitter of the harbor.

The decor was a mashup of two centuries. Heavy oak furniture counterpointed by pieces of bright modern art. Traditional paintings on the paneled walls interspersed with promotional posters of Ty Massy. Clearly the rising star had bought the place lock, stock, and barrel; and while his wife had tried in vain to make their newly acquired home look respectable, Massey had put his own stuff wherever it would fit. The effect was discordant.

"The studio's down here," Chief Frontiero had said with a nod to a door set in the wall underneath the grand stairway. Mark followed him downstairs and found himself in a short hallway whose walls were covered with framed presentation pieces from Massy's record company that contained facsimile gold and platinum CDs. The hallway led to a spacious sound-proof recording room with two separate isolation booths. Around the room were guitar cases, road cases, mic stands, and all the gear you'd find in a place designed to make hit records.

Through another door was the control room, with its big old-fashioned analog mixing board along with newer digital equipment. In one corner of the control room was what looked like a big walk-in closet with shelves lining the walls.

The body of Ty Massy lay slumped over an electronic Yamaha keyboard. He was dressed in a white t-shirt and jeans. The shirt was stained crimson from the blood that had gushed from the single gunshot wound to his chest.

His right hand rested on the black and white keys. The left arm was flopped over the keyboard's control board. Mark stepped closer. Here and there on the Yamaha's sleek surface were smudged bloodstains, as if Massy's bloody fingers had been groping.

"Time of death?" asked Mark.

"Sometime around midnight last night," replied the medical examiner.

"How long did he live after being shot?" asked Mark.

"I won't know until after the autopsy, but my guess is that the bullet tore through his lower trachea. His lungs filled with blood and in a few seconds he was unconscious. Dead in two or three minutes."

"Looks like he was capable of motion," said Mark.

"Motion of his extremities, yes. Talking, no."

"He was facing his attacker when he was shot?" said Mark.

"Yes," replied the medical examiner. "He was probably conscious for thirty seconds. Enough time to turn around and then collapse on the keyboard."

"Bullet?"

"Drilled through him and smashed into the steel frame of an electrical junction box," said the chief. "Flattened. Nine millimeter, but that's all we can tell. No murder weapon found."

"Any sign of forced entry?" asked Mark. "Robbery?"

"No to both."

"Who else lives in the house?"

"His wife," said Frontiero. "But lots of people come and go—a studio assistant, various musicians, management people, and assorted hangers-on. We're developing a list."

"A regular traveling circus," said Mark.

"The neighbors regularly complained about the traffic. One night Massy and his crew set up a bunch of amps and a drum kit on the back terrace and had a jam session. If you were a Ty Massy fan, it would have been a once in a lifetime experience. The neighbors didn't see it that way and the station was bombarded with calls. We had to send a unit down there to put a damper on the Lollapalooza of Eastern Point. But Massy was cool and agreed to move the impromptu concert inside the house."

"Who's the nearest neighbor?"

"Mrs. Ruth Copley. Her blood is so blue you could use it as antifreeze in your car."

"Where's the wife now?" asked Mark.

"Liz Madison is upstairs in the house—in their private quarters."

After ascending the broad curving staircase, Mark found the widow sitting in a small sunroom that faced the harbor.

"Liz Madison?" asked Mark.

"Yes," she said. Her voice was ragged from lack of sleep. "Are you from the police? I've already told them what I know."

"My name's Chris Mark. I'm an investigator. I'm sorry for your loss. May I have a few moments? I know you've been through a terrible experience."

"Of course. Please." She motioned to one of the three other chairs placed around the elegant little table. Mark sat down.

"How long have you known Ty Massy?"

"For two years. We met at a party in Boston. We dated for a while and then I moved in with him when he bought this house."

"When was that?"

"Six months ago. We got married a month later. We flew to Barbados. He wanted a very small private ceremony. My mom's deceased and my dad's a drunk, so I didn't care about having a big wedding."

"With a big star like Ty Massy, it must be tough to stay under the paparazzi radar."

"Avoiding them is a lot easier than you think. The publicity whores who complain the loudest about having no privacy are the first ones to make sure everyone knows where they're going."

"Some of your Eastern Point neighbors have not been too pleased about having a rock star in the neighborhood," said Mark. "Any trouble with them?"

Liz looked at Mark with hard blue eyes. "I told Ty he was crazy to buy this house. It's too close to the other houses, even if they're all mansions. He needed a place with more space around it. But he insisted. He liked the location. So yeah, whenever we had a party the stuffy old neighbors would call the cops."

"So I suppose you'll be selling the house."

She shrugged. "Maybe. But the fact that it was the scene of a murder may make it tough to sell. I'm in no hurry."

"Any problems with the people who ran Ty's business—his manager or music publisher?"

"When you're making money the way Ty was, everyone falls all over themselves to suck up to you. They all kissed his ass. But what they wanted was their share of the pie. Ty was a human ATM machine. They stood in line with their wallets open. Anyway, I tried to stay out of his financial affairs. I'm not one of those clutching show business wives."

"Who runs his business?"

"His manager is a guy named Gabson Cage. He's the chief beancounter. Ty's also got a lawyer in Boston, a woman named Dora Walker."

"They come around the house?"

"Sure. The house is always full of people. Ty liked to do everything here. He was relentlessly creative. He always had a song in his head and he needed a place to put down his ideas right away, before they 'escaped into the ether,' as he would say. It was something that I got used to. At any moment he'd stop what he was doing—even eating dinner—and run over to the nearest piano or keyboard. 'You never know,' he would say. 'This could be a good song. You gotta let it out.'

With an electronic keyboard he'd use the internal memory to record his idea. Then he'd go back to it later."

"So it made sense that he put a recording studio in his house, and made his house open to his retinue," said Mark. "It was the center of his creativity."

"Yes," said Liz. "He could record finished tracks and simply upload them to the record company. In fact, he was talking about getting rid of his record company. Cut out the middleman, the way the band Radiohead did. Sell directly through iTunes or online. What did he need a record company for? No one buys records anymore. It's all downloads. Anyway, this house became a very busy place. We wanted to have children—" she paused to gather her emotions. Presently she continued. "Forgive me. If we were going to stay here and have a family, we needed to exert some control. I got tired of finding random roadies and musicians upstairs in what I thought were our private quarters. I told Ty that no one except he, the housekeeper, and I were allowed above the first floor. I wanted the upper floors to be just for us. If the music people needed to come and go, they could stay in the studio and on the first floor."

"Where were you at midnight yesterday evening?"

"Upstairs in our bedroom watching a rerun of *Law & Order*. I dozed off. Then Jack Lamprey— Ty's road manager—came running upstairs and woke me up. I was angry at him until I realized how upset he was. He was the one who found Ty. I went down to the studio with him. Then we called the police. It was a terrible, exhausting night."

"You didn't hear the gunshot?"

"No. The studio is totally soundproof. You could set a bomb off in there and no one would know."

"Thanks, Ms. Madison. You've been very helpful."

Mark went downstairs, where he saw that the medical examiner was removing the body.

"Anything useful turn up?" asked Mark.

"No shell casing found," said Frontiero. "There are no security cameras inside the house. At this point, all we have is the statement by the road manager that he came down to the studio just after midnight and found the body. He said there was an odor of gunpowder. Then he called the missus."

"Is the business manager here?" asked Mark.

"Gabson Cage? Yeah. He's on the back terrace. We're finishing up with him now."

Outside on the terrace the air smelled of salt and seaweed. In the harbor a whale watch boat slowly cruised towards its wharf, laden with tourists who had gotten an up-close-and-personal look at some of the great denizens of the deep as they frolicked in Massachusetts Bay. Standing by the low stone wall of the terrace was a man wearing a sports jacket, jeans, and snakeskin boots.

"Beautiful view," said Mark.

"I suppose," said Cage. "I'm more of a mountain guy myself. But Ty liked it."

"You discovered him when he was an unknown, right?"

"If you can call it that. I started working with him when he was still playing clubs in Boston. I got him a record deal and then put him on the road. We spent month after month in a beat-up minivan, criss-crossing the country playing clubs, colleges, and festivals. It was a long hard slog to the top. We didn't make any money until his last two or three CDs. Then the floodgates opened."

"Was he working on a new CD?" asked Mark.

"Ty was *always* working. He was never far from his keyboard. He was constantly writing songs. Sometimes just fragments of songs, melodies, chord changes—whatever came into his head. He's got enough material in the can for ten more records. Hell, he's even got his next Christmas album ready to ship."

"I heard that he was thinking about not renewing his contract with his record company. He wanted to sell directly to his fans."

"A bad idea," replied Cage. "Ty didn't understand that even in today's digital marketplace, record companies do more than sell your tracks. They provide a whole host of services including promotion and accounting. They can help you reach new audiences. I wanted Ty to focus on being creative and let other people do the everyday stuff of selling."

"Were you here last night?" asked Mark.

"Yep. I was hanging out in the living room watching the game on TV. Some of the guys in the touring band were there too. We were supposed to be having a meeting about the upcoming fall tour. Ty wanted to play some dates in China, which would have been a logistical nightmare. I tried to tell him that in China we would get robbed blind. He said he'd think about it. I had planned on going back to Boston today."

"What do you recall happened at the time of the shooting?"

"Around midnight Ty suddenly got up and said he had to go down to the studio. He had an idea for a song. It was late and this was not what anyone wanted, but what can you do? The muse had struck. So off he went. I sat there for a while watching the game, and then I hit the bathroom and took a leak. I came out of the bathroom and went into the kitchen. That's when I heard shouting—you know, commotion. Liz was very upset and Jack was trying to calm her down. Jack told me that Ty bad been shot."

Mark thumbed through some papers that he had in folder. He paused to look at one of them. "I see that Ty was in New York last week. He stayed at the Four Seasons for one night. It's on East Fifty-Seventh Street. Do you know why he was there?"

"Nope," shrugged Cage. "I didn't track his every move. Maybe he was meeting up with someone he wanted to use on a record. Ty got around. He was very sociable. Knew a lot of the top players."

"You carry a gun, don't you?" asked Mark.

"You bet," replied Cage tersely. "So does Jack. And Ty had a nine-millimeter. Maybe other people around

here carry too. I got a license. I started packing back in
the early days when we were playing crummy clubs in
bad neighborhoods. We'd get paid in cash. I wanted
some security."

"Lots of guns in the house," mused Mark. "Well, the
good news is that the cops found the bullet. Dug it out
of the wall."

"Can they match it?" asked Cage.

"Not sure," shrugged Mark. "You'll be the first to
know." At that moment Mark saw the road manager
step onto the terrace. "Thanks for the information. If
you'll excuse me—"

"No problem," said Cage.

Chris Mark introduced himself to Jack Lamprey
and steered him to a quiet corner of the terrace.

"You've had a rough night," said Mark. "You
discovered the body?"

"Yeah," nodded Jack. He took out a cigarette and lit
it. "Been tryin' to quit. But this is just too much. Ty
and I go back a long way. I started with him when his
first record came out. We were playing gigs where
there were ten people in the audience. Then the next
week there were fifty people. Then five hundred. It
kept getting better. During the last tour he drew an
average of twenty thousand a night."

"Can you tell me what happened last night?"

"We were having a sort of half-meeting, half-watch-
the-playoff-game session in the living room. Talking
about the next tour."

"Going to China," said Mark. "I heard it was going
to be a challenge."

"Dora Walker—Ty's lawyer—and Gab were
opposed. Said the timing wasn't right. It didn't matter
to me. Just give me a stage and somewhere to plug in
the amps and I can give you a show. The challenge is
more from the managerial side. The money, the
contracts. Anyway, we were sitting around when Ty
suddenly got up and went down to the studio. That
took the wind out of the discussion—you can't talk
anything important without the main guy being

there—so everyone sort of wandered away. After half an hour I decided to go downstairs and see if Ty wanted to continue the meeting. I tiptoed my way down and didn't hear anything."

"Tiptoed?"

"Not literally. But Ty had always made it very clear that when he was hashing out an idea he didn't want to be disturbed. He'd get pissed if you barged in. So I proceeded very carefully. I figured I could tell if he were in the middle of something creative, and then I'd just go back upstairs and tell everyone to call it a night. But all I heard was the sound of a sequencer."

"A sequencer?"

"Yeah. It's like a tape loop. You can play a bunch of notes on the keyboard, put them into its memory, and have it played back endlessly. You know the classic Who album *Who's Next*? Lots of sequencers. On top of the sequence of notes you can layer on other sounds—chords, melodies, whatever. So I stopped for a moment and I heard the sequencer. I called out "Hey, Ty." No answer. I went into the control room. The first thing I noticed was the smell of gunpowder. Then I saw Ty. He was slumped over the keyboard. I went to him but there was blood everywhere and he seemed to be dead. I shut off the damned sequencer because the sound was incredibly irritating. I ran upstairs to get Liz. I had to wake her up—she had fallen asleep watching TV. She came down and then we called the police."

"How long was it before you came back downstairs with Liz?"

"From the time I left Ty in the control room? Maybe three minutes."

"And when you got back downstairs, everything was the same?"

"Yeah. Ty was still lying there. Liz screamed and went to him. I pulled her off of him because, you know, someone had shot him and I've seen enough cop shows to know that you don't want to mess up evidence."

"You immediately assumed that it was murder and not suicide?"

"Are you kidding?" scoffed Lamprey. "Ty had big plans. He wanted to go global. Play all around the world. He had tons of tracks in the can. He was on a roll. No reason for him to kill himself."

"Any idea who would want him dead? Maybe a dope dealer?"

"Ty Massy was clean. He had only two vices: weed and women."

"Groupies on the road?"

"On the road, at home, anywhere. If they were available, so was he."

"But he was married," said Mark.

Lamprey gave a wry smile. "Part of the road manager's job is to keep the wife in the dark, my friend."

Mrs. Copley's house was even older and more grand than Massy's. A ten-foot brick wall discouraged sightseers. To gain entrance to the property Mark was required to ease his Camaro alongside the squawk box and, when prompted by the scratchy voice, identify himself, after which the big iron gate swung wide. His tires crunched on the short gravel drive as Mark steered his car to the stately portico that hooded the tall front door and its hanging lantern. A moment after Mark had pressed the doorbell and heard the distant echo of the chimes, the door opened. Standing before him was a trim woman who looked like sixty going on forty.

"Mr. Mark?" she said in a clear voice. "Ruth Copley. Please come in."

Mark entered the foyer and followed the lady of the house into the library. She offered him a seat in one of the big leather chairs, and when he had settled himself she sat down on the overstuffed sofa.

"This is a stunning house," said Mark.

"It was built in the nineteen-twenties by a wealthy railroad man. He lived in New York. It was a summer place. They say that F. Scott Fitzgerald came here once. But who knows? People love to tell stories. My husband bought the place in the nineteen seventies. It was a wreck. It took us five years to restore it to its former condition. We see ourselves as stewards, not owners. Since my husband retired we live here year 'round. Now, Mr. Mark, what can I tell you about Mr. Massy?"

"Did you know him?"

"Not personally. He only moved in last year. We lead very busy lives. I understand he was in the music business."

"Yes, and there were complaints about the traffic and the noise," said Mark.

Ruth Copley nodded. "Many of the neighbors were concerned that he was running his music business out of his house. People were coming and going at all hours of the day and night. Not like drug buyers, I suppose, whom you imagine pulling up and then driving away, but visitors who'd stay for awhile. Now I know that when you're a musician your life is perhaps more unstructured than other peoples' lives, but this area is not zoned for business. It's strictly residential. We value our peace and quiet. We just weren't sure this was the appropriate neighborhood for Mr. Massy's lifestyle."

"Loud music?"

"Not every day. I've heard that the basement recording studio is soundproof. But yes, when they had parties, there was noise and traffic. I called the police myself on a few occasions."

"According to police records, you've called fourteen times."

Mrs. Copley gave a shrug. "It was noisy."

"Aside from those issues, any significant problems?"

"Do you mean personally between us? Not really," said Ruth Copley.

"Anything ever get out of control on the Massy property?" asked Mark.

"Aside from the usual antics you expect at late-night parties, there was only one time. A week ago. Tuesday. In the middle of the afternoon, which was usually a very quiet time at the Massy house. I was gardening near the property line. We have rose bushes there. I heard an argument. It sounded like two men were shouting at each other by the front door. I confess that I moved closer to the property line to try to hear them better. I caught a bit of what was being said. A voice yelled, "Don't screw me over! I made you and I can break you!" Then I heard a car door slam and the car left the driveway."

"Was it Massy's voice, or someone else's?"

"I have no idea who it was," shrugged Mrs. Copley. "It sounded like a woman."

"Did you see the car?"

"No, I'm sorry. It was obscured by the wall and the row of lilacs."

"Whaddaya got for me?" asked Chief Frontiero as Mark sidled into his downtown office. The chief shoved a pile of file folders to a corner of his big grey desk, as if clearing a space would somehow make room for bigger and more potent nuggets of information.

Mark sat in the chair facing the desk. "Before we begin, do you have that list of the people who were at the house last night?"

"Yep." He slid a paper across the desk. Mark picked it up.

"There are—let's see—twelve names here. A bunch of musicians, two roadies, the wife who claims to have been asleep upstairs, the road manager, the business manager, the lawyer, and the studio assistant. The question is, who would want to shoot Ty Massy, and—assuming it was one person who acted alone—how could they have been in the studio alone with Massy?"

"Maybe they all did it—like in that Agatha Christie novel."

"*Murder on the Orient Express*," said Mark. "The only problem with that theory is that Massy was shot with one bullet. Not twelve stab wounds. Let's get down to business. It's highly unlikely that unless Massy was fooling around with one of their girlfriends, any of the musicians or roadies would have a motive to kill Massy. They would have absolutely nothing to gain. That narrows our field to the heavyweights—the road manager, the business manager, the lawyer, and the studio assistant."

"Don't forget the wife."

"Yes," agreed Mark. "And the wife. Five people. The motive could be money or control."

"Control?"

"Over Massy's assets. Celebrities often become worth more after they die. Look at Elvis Presley and Michael Jackson. Their estates are money machines. Jimi Hendrix has released more albums after his death than he did when he was alive. The top dead celebrities—from Elizabeth Taylor to Bob Marley and even Albert Einstein—make tens of millions every year. It all goes into the pockets of whoever controls their estate. Ty Massy has just joined this élite group."

"So all we need to do is follow the money," said Frontiero.

"Easier said than done. It may take years for all of the legal claims to get sorted out. Meanwhile we have a murderer to catch. And we can't rule out other possibilities. A crazed stalker could have gained access to the house. People were coming and going all the time."

"And there's the wife," added Frontiero. "She gets wind of him cheating on her, goes down to the studio, plugs him, and runs back upstairs before anyone knows what's happened. When Jack Lamprey told her about her husband's death, she was supposedly asleep. But no one else was in the room."

"Lamprey and the wife could be in it together," said Mark. "Okay. I've got another person to interview—the studio sound engineer. He's a local guy. Lives down-town."

The grand old Victorian had seen better days. On the mailbox unit attached to the wall outside the front door Chris Mark confirmed the name: Roger Griffin, 2A. After climbing the creaking staircase to the second floor landing, Mark paused to listen. From behind the door of unit 2A came the sound of music. Heavy metal—Black Sabbath, in fact. In response to his knock the music stopped and the door opened a crack. A bearded face peered out. "Yeah?"

"Roger Griffin? My name's Chris Mark. I want to talk to you about the death of Ty Massy."

"Okay," said the bearded face grudgingly. The door opened. Before Mark stood a young man about twenty-five, flannel shirt, old jeans, Timberland boots. "You wanna come in?"

"That's the usual procedure," said Mark. He stepped across the threshold and entered a studio apartment that was bigger than he expected. There was a leather sofa, flat screen TV, boxes of vinyl records, and racks of audio gear. In front of the window overlooking the harbor, the dining room table was clean and there was a vase of fresh tulips in the center. A woman's touch, surmised Mark.

As Mark sat down at the table he noticed a surfboard leaning against the wall by the door. It seemed huge, even in the big room. "Been out lately?" asked Mark with a nod to the board.

"I try and go as often as I can," answered Griffin. "Went up to New Hampshire last week for a competition. Didn't win anything but had a good time."

"I'll have to go up there sometime. Having a steady gig in the area is a good deal if you're a surfer. How did you meet Ty Massy?"

"A friend of mine in Boston knows him. Sorry, *knew* him. He found out that Ty had bought a place up here and was building a studio. I had done some work on one of Ty's records, and Ty remembered who I was. So he invited me over to the studio and I helped him with some tracks. I just sort of started working for him regular. Finally he said that he'd put me on a weekly salary. I thought sure, why not? Could be a cool thing and good for my resume."

"What was Massy working on when he died?"

"Just a bunch of tracks. He always had songs in the works. They ranged from rough demos to finished cuts. When it was time to put out a new CD—the next one was going to be in the fall, with the tour—he'd assemble the best ten or twelve songs, and that would be the CD."

"He wanted to cut ties with his label?"

"I heard him talk about it. He figured that he didn't need them. But his contract with them called for three more CDs, so it wasn't going to happen anytime soon. Ty could have just given them three crappy records to get out of his contract, but that's not the way he operated. He wanted every release to be good."

"The tour was going to be big?" asked Mark.

"Ty wanted it to be big. He wanted to go up to the next level. He wanted to play stadiums. It takes a big organization. Professionals. There is no margin for error."

"What did Gabson Cage have to say about this?"

"He's lucky he's gotten this far. Half of what he earns goes up his nose. Whenever I see him at the house, he seems out of it. Not connected. He's always on his cell phone but I have no idea who he's talking to. Ty tried to keep him out of the studio. He told Gab that he needed his creative space. What he really wanted was for Gab to stay out of his hair."

"Ty went to New York last week. Know the reason why?"

"No. He told me that he might have some news for me soon. I got the impression that he was working on some sort of deal."

Mark heard footsteps outside in the hallway. The door to the apartment suddenly opened and a young woman entered. She gave Mark a wide-eyed stare before stammering, "Oh—sorry, baby, I didn't know you had company."

"No problem," said Roger. "Polly, this is Chris Mark. He's asking about Ty's murder."

Polly tossed her blonde mane. "Such a terrible thing! He was a sweet man." She glanced at Roger. "Well, you know what I mean. I know that Roger enjoyed working with him."

"Were you at the house last night too?" asked Mark.

"Umm—" said Polly.

"It's okay," said Roger. "She was there. Only for a while. Liz didn't like seeing girlfriends in the house. She said that it was bad enough that all the guys were over there, but she understood it was Ty's business. She drew the line at the girlfriends. Said she didn't want the place to become party central. Once when Polly and I stopped by, Liz came down to the studio to talk to Ty about something. Polly hid in the storage closet until Liz had gone back upstairs. It seems very silly but we wanted to keep the peace, y'know? The last thing I wanted was to get the wife upset. You never want to get Liz upset."

"She has a temper?" asked Mark.

"She'll rip your face off," said Polly.

"Thanks." Mark rose to leave. "Oh—one last thing. How often did Massy use a sequencer?"

Roger shrugged. "Once in a while. It was just another tool. The Yamaha portable grand piano keyboard that he always used has a recording function. You just hit the record button and play whatever you want. It's stored in the memory. It's simple."

"That's the one he was playing when he was shot?"

"Yeah," nodded Roger.

"Have you received Ty Massy's phone records?" asked Chris Mark as he shuffled through his notes.

"Yes," replied Chief Frontiero. "Just got 'em."

The orange rays from the setting sun slanted through the Venetian blinds of the chief's office. "Been a long day," sighed the chief as Mark studied the report. "What say when we're done we repair to the Harbor Oyster House for a cold beer and some fried clams?"

"Sounds good," said Mark. "But first—check out the phone log for last Tuesday. When Massy was in New York. He called his wife at two o'clock, just after checking into the Four Seasons. Probably to let her know he got there in one piece. The next call was to a guy named Stan Hotchkiss at Live Nation. They're on West Forty-Second Street."

"What's Live Nation?"

"A huge entertainment conglomerate. They happen to manage some very big artists like Madonna, U2, and Jay-Z. They do it all: tours, management, merchandising, media. Hotchkiss is a biggie at Live Nation. He would not waste his time on any artist who was not poised to be a global brand."

"You think that Ty Massy was talking to him?"

"Yep. Do you have that bill from the Four Seasons?"

After hunting through a pile of printouts, Frontiero handed Mark a piece of paper.

"Yeah—here it is," said Mark. "A charge for a car service. The destination was Two-Twenty West Forty-Second Street. That's Live Nation. The car stayed there for three hours before taking Massy to a restaurant. Then to a night club."

"A three-hour meeting with a big management company," said Frontiero. "Interesting."

"Let's put a call to Stan Hotchkiss," said Mark. He punched a number on his phone. After a series of negotiations with a string of receptionists and assistants, Mark gave an "okay" sign to Frontiero.

"Stan Hotchkiss? Thanks for taking my call. My name's Chris Mark. I'm investigating the death of Ty Massy. Yes sir, it's a terrible tragedy. No sir, we have no new information. What I need from you is a list of the names of the people who were at the meeting with Mr. Massy last Tuesday in your office. Okay. Thanks very much. Yes, I'll call back with any further questions." Mark ended the call. "He's emailing me the list. Ah—here it is. I'll send you a copy. There. Let's see... six people. Massy, Hotchkiss, and three more from Live Nation, including one of their lawyers. Name number six is Irving Kerman. Let's see—he's a high-powered New York attorney who represents entertainment people. Musicians, singers, actors. He'd be there to represent his new client Ty Massy."

"Didn't Massy have a Boston attorney?" asked Frontiero.

"Yeah. Dora Walker. On the basis of this meeting in New York, I'd say that Massy was looking to make a big change in his career and his business." Mark sat back and rubbed his eyes. "It's late. I like the idea of hitting the Oyster House. Give us a chance to step back and take the long view of this case."

It was a five-minute walk from Frontiero's office to the restaurant on Rogers Street by the harbor. The place was half full, mostly with locals; the mobs of tourists would not arrive in full force until after Memorial Day. Mark and Frontiero found a booth and the waitress soon brought their orders of fried clams, fishcakes, and cold beers.

"There's no shortage of people who have a motive to kill Ty Massy," said Mark. "There's big money at stake. Record sales and music publishing could provide millions for years. Whoever is on the gravy train now would be on it for the rest of their lives. Consider the grieving widow. She could have accomplished two goals at once: get rid of her cheating spouse and position herself as the director of a vast financial empire, just like Priscilla Presley. She could even turn the house into a shrine, just like Graceland."

"Oh my God," said Frontiero. "That would give the neighbors on Eastern Point heart attacks. Can you see tour buses full of gawkers from the suburbs pulling up in front of the Massy mansion?"

"The key is to determine who actually has contractual control of Ty Massy's creative product," said Mark. "It may not be his wife. It may be the manager or the lawyer."

"Let's not forget the angle that it could be purely a crime of passion," added Frontiero. "Ty Massy was a womanizer. He could have been fooling around with the girlfriend of any one of those guys. He gets pissed, goes down there to confront Massy, and shoots him."

Mark took a last long swig of his beer before setting the bottle on the table. He signaled the waitress for the check. "There's one more thing I need to check out. We need to go back to the house. Bring along a couple of uniformed officers. Have them wait in the wings. We may need them."

An hour later Chris Mark stood in the center of the spacious living room, with its grand piano and stone fireplace. Seated around the room were the people who had been in the house for the past twenty-four hours.

"What's this all about?" demanded Liz Madison. "Why is everyone still here, in my house?"

"*Your* house?" said Gabson Cage sharply.

"It's going be hers soon enough," said Dora Walker.

"Well, Mr. Mark, what do you have for us?" asked Jack Lamprey. "I'm sure that all of us are anxious to get out of here and go home."

"I do have something for you," said Mark. "As you can see, here on the table is Ty Massy's Yamaha keyboard. It's the same one that he was sitting at when he was shot. Chief Frontiero can testify as to the chain of custody. It has not been tampered with or cleaned since the shooting. It is exactly as it was found, just after Ty Massy was murdered."

"Okay, so what about it?" said Walker.

"We've been talking about Ty Massy quite a bit since his death, and I've learned a lot about him. He had his faults, but there is no doubt that he was a great musical talent and phenomenally successful. One of the most salient character traits that each and every one of you mentioned about him was that he was relentlessly creative. He was always thinking of new songs. They'd pop into his head and he'd rush off to record them. It didn't matter what he was doing—at dinner, on the beach, on the tour bus—if he had an idea, he'd make sure that he put it down somehow. On tape, on his mobile phone, on a napkin. Or—" Mark turned to the keyboard— "on this."

"It was turned on when I found him," volunteered Lamprey. "The sequencer."

"Yes, the sequencer," said Mark. "You turned it off." Mark leaned over the instrument. "I believe you pushed this button, correct?"

"Yes," said Roger Griffin.

"So if I pushed the same button again, the sequencer would start, and would play the same prerecorded pattern?"

"Yep," said Griffin.

"Okay," said Mark. "Let's give it a try." A hush came over the room as Mark pressed the bloodstained button. A series of notes filled the air. They cycled quickly and then repeated.

"It doesn't sound like much," said Liz Madison. "Just a bunch of notes."

"I don't get it," said Walker. "Was this a song that Ty was working on when he died?"

"Actually," said Mark, "based on the bloody fingerprints on the keyboard, I believe that Ty Massy wrote this series of notes *after* he was shot. He lived just long enough to press the record button and play the keys."

"But why?" demanded Cage.

Mark looked the manager in the eye. "Because Ty Massy wanted to name his killer."

"How?" said the widow.

"Roger, you've got a good ear," said Mark. "You tell me if I'm playing the correct sequence." He went to the grand piano and tapped out seven notes.

"Yeah," said Griffin. "That's it. You've got it. Those are the seven notes that Ty played."

"What are the notes?" said Lamprey. "What's the big deal?"

Mark turned to the group. He nodded to the uniformed officers who were waiting by the doors. "The notes that Ty Massy played and recorded are these: G, A, B; and then C, A, G, and E. The scale does not provide for an S, O, or N, so he didn't play them."

"Officers, place Mr. Cage under arrest," said Chief Frontiero.

"You're crazy!" shouted the manager.

"You almost got away with it," said Mark as Cage was being handcuffed. "You went down to the studio, found Massy alone, and shot him. You were going to finish him off with a second shot when you heard Jack Lamprey coming. So you hid in the utility closet until Lamprey had gone upstairs to awaken Liz Madison. By that time Massy was dead. You went to the kitchen and feigned surprise when word spread that Massy had been gunned down."

"But why did he do it?" asked Liz Madison.

"Your husband had recently returned from a meeting in New York with a new management company and a new lawyer," said Mark. "Massy was going to dump Gabson Cage and go global. Cage has a bad drug habit and Massy knew there was no way he could handle the next stage of his career. So Cage figured that if Massy were dead, as the last manager under contract he would have a continuing interest in Massy's estate. He'd be a part of all of the posthumous CD releases and the publishing empire. He could ride the Ty Massy gravy train until the day he died."

"Ty Massy owed me!" shouted Cage. "I brought him up from nothing. I mortgaged my house to launch his career. Week after week we spent on the road, playing every two-bit club from here to Florida. Sometimes we'd steal food from the kitchens of the clubs. We'd get one room at a crummy motel and five of us would sleep there. I paid for his first demos out of my own pocket. Then when he started to sell records and get bigger paychecks at gigs, the lawyers and accountants started showing up. Suddenly I wasn't good enough for him. He wanted a manager with a big office in New York. He was going to cut me loose and spread the word around that I had a drug problem. I said to him, 'Okay, just give me a cut. I get fifteen percent now, so give me two percent and I'll go away happy.' He refused! Said it was too much. The only problems I had were the vultures who were giving him bad advice. They were going to sell Ty Massy like toothpaste. They don't care about him. I cared about him!"

"And so you shot him," said Mark. "Officers, take him downtown."

Incident at Teal Pond

As he pondered the excruciating dullness of the party, Chris Mark took another sip of his Jim Beam. It was not that the people gathered here in the kitchen of the beachfront house of his surfing buddy Charlie were by nature boring; as individuals they were interesting enough. There was Ralph the banker—hiya, Ralph, good to see you too!—who had brought Janet the real estate agent. By the refrigerator stood Tom, the aspiring novelist, looking insecure. Kathy, the high school nurse, could be heard above the crowd talking about her recent trip to Puerto Rico. There were many others, all chatting and drinking on this New Year's Eve, waiting for the ball to drop in another two hours.

Chris Mark disliked crowded parties not because of the individual people present but because you had to shout to be heard, people were always jostling you, and he was uncomfortable talking while he was eating. But Charlie had invited him, and it would have been rude not to accept.

Two hours to go! With an inward sigh Mark eased past Ricardo—who courtesy of a trust fund lived quite nicely on a horse farm in Essex— before going through the door into the living room. It was quieter here, probably because the bar and the food were in the dining room. Sitting next to the fireplace was a woman. What was her name? Oh yes, Emilie. Mark had met her in passing. He liked her direct and down-to-earth quality. On the small sofa where she sat, the place next to her was empty.

"Mind if I join you?" said Mark.

She looked up. Even in the dim light her eyes were sky blue. "No—please do," she said with a warm smile.

After a few minutes of agreeable small talk, during which Mark's attention became more keenly focused on his new companion, she said to him, "In your work as a private detective, what's the toughest case of murder that you've had?"

Mark smiled. "There've been too many—I'd need a long time to tell you."

Emilie gave him a look that suggested she would be willing to give him the time—but not here at the party.

"Okay," she said. "How about the easiest case?"

"The easiest? I'll tell you one. It took me five minutes to solve."

"Really? A murder?"

"Really."

"I'd love to hear it."

"All right. I was in my office one afternoon. I was bored because I didn't have a case and the surf was flat. I was thinking about going to get a haircut when a woman came through the door. She was about forty years old, well dressed, and visibly distraught. I invited her to sit down. I asked her why she had come to see me.

"'It's my husband,' she told me. 'Tony Lamasin.'

"I had read about Lamasin in the papers. He had passed away under mysterious circumstances. I asked her if she were his wife, Joanne. She said yes, she was Joanne Lamasin.

"'Your husband died in some sort of accident in a canoe?' I said.

"'Yes,' she replied. 'The police are working on the case, but—'

"'Yes, I know,' I replied. 'They're very capable, but overwhelmed.'"

Mark took a sip of his whiskey. The melting ice had made it watery, but because he wanted to stick close to Emilie he didn't get up and go to the bar. In the fireplace the embers glowed orange. "The deceased was a successful businessman," he continued. Emilie nodded attentively. "Real estate developer. Wanted to build a high-rise apartment building over in West Gloucester, on a hill overlooking the harbor. Spectacular view. The zoning board had approved it. Some of the abutters opposed the plan, and others didn't care. You know how it is. Anyway, Lamasin was a workaholic who, much to his wife's annoyance, spent six days a week in his office. He had one recreational pastime: he loved to fish. He and his wife owned a cabin on Teal Pond. It's a small lake about a half-hour from here. He'd go out in a canoe and fish for smallmouth bass. Stay out for hours. Didn't really care if he caught anything. He loved all the accoutrements of the sport. He stored all of his lures in his favorite fishing vest, he wore the round-brimmed canvas hat—the works. I guess it gave him solace to be out on the pond. No telephone, no email, no one pestering him."

"I can understand," said Emilie.

"It was a Sunday morning," continued Mark. "Lamasin and his wife had driven from Gloucester to the cabin by the pond. While she busied herself with a book that she was writing, he went out in the canoe. It was an old wood-and-canvas job, an antique. No motor, just a paddle. After a half-hour Joanne got up from her desk and went to the porch to get some fresh air. From her vantage point she could see the pond. By some chance her husband was casting just offshore. She stood there idly on the porch watching her husband in his canoe when suddenly he leaned over. He clutched his chest and fell face-first into the canoe. She freaked out because she assumed he was having a heart attack. She called the police before running to the neighbor's house to borrow a boat. She and the neighbor ran to down to the neighbor's dock and got the boat. By this time, Joanne saw that the canoe was sinking."

"Sinking?" asked Emilie. "Why would it be sinking?"

"You'll see," replied Mark. "By the time the police came running down to the dock, Joanne and the neighbor had rowed out to her husband. Tony Lamasin was lying in the bottom of the canoe. The canoe had filled with water, and the water was bloody red. Lamasin appeared to be dead. Joanne and the neighbor weren't strong enough to lift him out of the canoe without tipping over their boat, so Joanne sat in the stern of the boat and held onto the prow of the waterlogged canoe while the neighbor rowed to shore."

"How awful," said Emilie. She shifted her weight on the sofa so that she was snuggled closer to Mark—an adjustment that he did not fail to notice and appreciate.

"They got the canoe to shore," said Mark. "The police took over the investigation."

"What did they find?" asked Emilie.

"Joanne Lamasin told me that her husband had been struck by a projectile of some sort. A steel dart or rod about four and a half inches long was sticking out of his chest. The rod had punctured the heart.

"I asked the widow if she had heard any gunshots. She replied that she had not."

"Maybe it was some sort of spear gun," offered Emilie.

"Nope," replied Mark. "Spear gun tips are always barbed. They have to be; otherwise the fish that you speared could swim free. This rod had a sharp point, but it was not barbed. I asked Joanne if the canoe had been examined. Yes, it had been. And what was found? Four small holes in the bottom. The police had theorized that the holes were caused by the steel dart as he thrashed around in the canoe after being impaled."

"Maybe it was some sort of crazy accident," said Emilie. Mark felt her thigh pressing closer against his. Her breath was warm as she leaned close to speak with him.

With a noncommittal shrug, Mark continued. "I asked Joanne to excuse me for a moment while I went to my computer. She waited while I performed some research. It took me less than five minutes before I turned to her and said, 'The person who killed your husband is Geoff Rezner.'"

"The widow was astonished. Geoff Rezner was her husband's business partner. She demanded that I explain. I told Joanne that the murder weapon was a vintage Soviet SPP-1 underwater pistol, which had been introduced in 1971. The SPP-1 fires steel darts that are four and a half inches long. For various complex reasons, a relatively long steel dart will travel through water with greater momentum and accuracy than a smaller conventional bullet. Because of the technical problems of chambering cartridges under water, the SPP-1 has four barrels in a two-over-two configuration. Each barrel contains one cartridge. Its ammunition is held in a square clip that is attached to the pistol's breech. When you've fired the four cartridges, you need to attach a fresh clip."

"So someone who was underwater shot him with this special gun?" asked Emilie breathlessly. "A scuba diver?"

"Yes," said Mark. He was beginning to deeply enjoy the closeness of Emilie's body. "The assassin knew where to find Lamasin's canoe. The water in Teal Pond is about fifteen feet deep, which for this operation was ideal. The murderer swam to the location and fired all four rounds up through the bottom of the canoe. Three missed, flying by Lamasin and falling harmlessly into the water some distance away. But they got Lamasin's attention and he leaned over to see what was happening in his canoe. The fourth shot hit him square in the chest. Four holes in the bottom of the canoe, one hole in the victim."

"But how did you determine the killer's identity?" asked Emilie.

"Simple process of elimination," replied Mark. "I went online to see who owned this type of rare and collectible firearm. I got a pool of several hundred names. Then I searched for those who were certified scuba divers. Four names were members of both groups. Because the murder took planning and was not a spontaneous thrill kill, I was looking for someone with a motive. The last man standing was Geoff Rezner. I notified the police, and when they questioned him he quickly confessed."

"Well, that certainly was exciting," said Emilie. Her eyes were shining and her lips moist.

At that moment a pudgy middle-aged man came and stood next to the sofa. He lingered closer than Mark would have liked.

Emilie turned to the man. "Hello, dear. My new friend Chris was just telling me about his work. He's a private detective."

"Pleased to meet you, Chris," said the man as he extended his pasty hand. "Robert Hawkson. Thank you for looking after my wife. I had some business to discuss in the kitchen. But now I'm free to enjoy the party."

"Sure," said Mark. "No problem." He was appalled. Why on earth did the hottest women so often marry dorky men? Robert Hawkson must have had a pile of money. Yes, of course—from the depths of Mark's memory the name slowly rose. Hawkson had sold his software company for over a hundred million dollars. Anyway, so much for Chris Mark's prospects with Emilie. He felt not a little bit snookered. With her husband not twenty feet away, why had she so shamelessly flirted?

At that moment it was not a figment of Chris Mark's imagination that Robert and Emilie exchanged knowing glances. Robert Hawkson gave a little nod to his wife.

Emilie turned to Mark and laid her hand lightly on his arm. "Robert and I would love to have you over tonight for a very special New Year's Eve celebration."

Mark's brain went into overdrive. He looked at Robert Hawkson, who gave him a sly smile before taking a sip of his Bud Light. Did he lick his lips as the can left his mouth?

"Thanks very much," said Mark to Emilie. "You ought to know that I didn't come here with anyone. It's only me."

"That's how we like it, if you know what I mean," smiled Robert Hawkson.

Emilie pressed close to Mark. "My husband likes to watch," she whispered in his ear. "And I like to show him."

An image flashed into Chris Mark's mind: the naked Emilie, a bouncing bed, and the leering, greedy eyes of her devoted husband.

As Chris Mark got to his feet he extended his hand to Emilie Hawkson. "It was a pleasure to meet you and your husband. Thank you for your very kind invitation. I'm sorry but I have another party that I must attend. A friend across town. I wish you both a very happy and prosperous New Year."

With those words Mark left the Hawksons, found his friend Charlie, and bade him good night before making his way through the crowd to the front door and into the cold and sobering night.

Inmate 67430-317

Everyone says that orange is the new black.

I wear orange all day, every day. At MCI-Framingham—the Bay State joint for female offenders—it's the color they give you.

Personally, when I wear orange I don't feel the slightest bit fashionable.

I'm here for what offense, you ask? You should understand that it's considered extremely rude to ask an inmate why they're incarcerated. The question exudes the stink of judgment. But since I'm putting pen to paper and writing this memoir, I'll tell you.

My first conviction was for a violation of Massachusetts Laws, Part Four, Title One, Chapter 265 (Crimes Against Persons), Section 16: Attempt to Murder. You can look it up for yourself online. To save you the trouble, the statute says this:

"Whoever attempts to commit murder by poisoning, drowning or strangling another person, or by any means not constituting an assault with intent to commit murder, shall be punished by imprisonment in the state prison for not more than twenty years."

Drowning and strangling are not my style. Poisoning—that was it. And you'll notice that the charge was *attempted* murder. Yeah, I screwed up. My intended victim still lives and breathes. He's probably at home right now, watching a hockey game on television. My little project cost me five years of my life while giving him the rest of his. But more about that later.

What pisses me off is that I was put here by that bigshot private detective Chris Mark. In my book, he's just a bastard who stuck his nose into my business.

Like a dog with a bone, he kept gnawing on my case until he got what he wanted.

Let me tell you how my life changed thanks to Chris Mark. The trial was a sham. Thanks to my idiotic lawyer I had no chance. As soon as the judge pronounced sentence, the goons in blue hustled me to an overheated van and took me back to jail. Two days later I was put on a bus with ten other women and driven to MCI-Framingham. I've been around the block a few times, but let me tell you this: When I walked through those gates it was major culture shock. The reality was worse than I had imagined. Not necessarily the physical appearance—I was prepared for cinderblock walls—but the gut-wrenching realization that I had left my freedom outside the gates.

From the bus we walked single file into the intake room. In my civilian clothes I stood in line with the other women. On the bus ride I had learned that four of them were new to the system, like me. The other five were recidivists who were making their second visit to prison. Drug charges, mostly. I was sentenced to the joint for the attempted murder of a human being, and these women were heading to the same joint for possession of some pot or a few grams of coke that, in most cases, they were carrying for their asshole boyfriends. Go figure. It's no wonder that the good ol' US of A has the highest incarceration rate of any civilized country on earth, and higher than many uncivilized countries too.

As they were processed, one by one the women left the room through an unmarked door.

After verifying my identity—yes, I was Angela Gentry—and checking my name off the list, the intake officer ordered me to go into the next room to change.

Okay, whatever. I went through the unmarked door and into a small room. A female corrections officer was sitting in a chair.

"Take everything off," she said.

"Everything?" I replied. What was this all about? I'm a normal woman, not a freak.

"You heard what I said," she said. "Now do it."

Okay—I could tell by the hardness in her eyes that she was as serious as a piece of glass in your carton of fried clams. As I stripped off my clothing she watched me like a hawk. When I was done, I stood there in my birthday suit. As she gawked and probed my body, she made check marks on her clipboard.

To break the ice I asked her if she ever found anything really weird on a new inmate, like a pet weasel between their legs.

The guard did not crack a smile.

"Okay," she finally said. "Bend over and cough."

Wow—this was getting ugly. You couldn't pay me enough to have her job. Well, maybe you could.

Finally, after feeling like a freshly caught flounder on display in the cooler at Stop & Shop, the inspection was complete. No contraband had been found.

The officer handed me three pairs of orange and black striped pants, five orange shirts, canvas shoes, a pair of pajamas, seven pairs of granny panties, five sports bras, socks, a winter hat, a winter coat, and a pair of steel-toed boots.

Steel-toed boots? All inmates receive steel-toed boots. They're for the women who work outside or have jobs where they need foot protection, such as the prison carpenter's assistant. Most of the inmates did not wear the boots. They just stashed them underneath their beds.

My civvies were bagged and taken to storage.

Wearing my new prison garb and looking like a Halloween bumblebee, I was sent to another room for a round of fingerprinting and photographs. A guard then handed me a red identification card that looked like a driver's license, but the mug shot labeled me as inmate number 66793-459.

"Take good care of that card," she said. "You'll need it. If you lose it, it'll cost you five bucks for a new one."

She gave me a set of dingy sheets, a pillow in a vinyl casing, a bottle of liquid soap, an unpackaged bar of hard soap about the size of a matchbox, a teensy black plastic comb, a toothbrush, a small tube of toothpaste, and a single-blade disposable razor.

Then she sent me on my way, through three remotely operated sets of sliding gates.

That was the first hour of the first day of my one thousand eight hundred and twenty-five days at MCI-Framingham. In case you're interested, that's forty-three thousand eight hundred hours, give or take a few. Trust me, I counted every one.

In prison, you soon get over the fact that you cannot go where you please and that you're never alone except in the toilet or the shower. The biggest problem is that you're mostly just bored. True, we all have our menial jobs; I work in the laundry. When we're not working or sleeping, we try to keep busy by inventing microwaved food items. You go to the commissary where they sell candy, cookies, pretzels, ice cream, popcorn, peanut butter, soup, oatmeal, bagels, and cheese. You can also buy a microwave bowl, eating utensils, and plastic cups. On every floor there's a microwave, and favorite microwave recipes are passed down from one inmate to another. We make all kinds of crap like microwaveable pickle wraps, taffy, cheesecake, potato logs, and chocolate cake. Because there's only one microwave on every floor, there's always a long line to use it.

Aside from microwaving random combinations of processed food items, my hobby is writing. When I get out of here I'm going to get my book published. Yes, I know that it's against the law to profit from your crime. I'll have to give all the profits to charity. My book will be called *I'll Never Wear Orange Again*. It will be a memoir. I'll reveal everything. Here's an excerpt that will give you a snapshot of how I ended up doing my first term in prison. I'm using the present tense to give the story immediacy. I learned that in my writer's group.

I hope you like it.

I'll Never Wear Orange Again
By Angela Gentry

I ask my husband which top I should wear to the writer's group meeting.

From the sofa he gives me a tired glance. "Either one would look fine," he replies.

This is not the answer that I'm hoping to hear. I cannot imagine that he sees no difference between them. Why can't he give me an honest opinion? He could have taken a moment to think about his response.

Standing before the mirror I carefully consider my choices. To anyone with eyes it would be obvious that the green shirt makes my waist look wide while the yellow knit is too low-cut and makes my boobs look like two lemons stuck to my chest.

I notice that Bill hasn't taken a drink of his Gatorade. What's he waiting for? I don't want to pressure him or make him suspicious. He says that he needs to stay home because of his illness, which is a good sign. I wish it didn't take so damned long. But I need to be very careful. Very methodical.

My hair is really a mess. I think it must be the weather. When I was a kid my hair had a nice natural curl. Now I look like I have a mop stuck on top of my head. Shapeless and lifeless. After Bill's funeral I'll get a trendy cut from the salon downtown. Rasida charges an arm and a leg and you have to sit there and listen to that horrible eighties music, and the chemical smell nearly chokes you. But to improve myself I will patiently endure a few hours of torture. I'm not ready to throw in the towel yet.

Perhaps I'll wear the green shirt. I can wear it with a belt to bring in my waist. But then I'll feel tight and I won't be able to breathe. I never was able to wear any of those support undergarments like Spanx. I hate feeling as though I'm a sausage stuffed into a casing. Screw the belt.

I want to look attractive, but not just for Bill. There are other men out there, and what's the harm in testing the waters? If Bill isn't interested at least I can keep some tiny spark alive. And anyway, I'll be on the market soon.

Come to think of it, at the last writer's group meeting Timothy seemed unusually attentive. He sat next to me, which he never did before, and he was very friendly. After the meeting we were chatting and having a glass of wine, and someone wanted to get by us so Timothy put his hand under my elbow to gently pull me aside. He didn't have to do that. I know that he touched my arm on purpose to gauge my reaction. I didn't pull away. I let him leave his hand under my elbow for as long as he wanted. It was only after we were standing together for a minute that he let go.

Timothy will be at the meeting tonight. I suppose I'm deluded. He'll show up with some blonde hottie and I'll feel like a fool for thinking that he found me attractive.

Of course Bill knows nothing about any of this because he takes me for granted. I could ride naked on a horse down the street and he wouldn't notice until he saw it on the evening news.

The green shirt is not going to work because I don't have the right shoes. My black pumps are much too formal with jeans, and the sneakers make me look like a farmer. I knew that I should have bought those cream-colored stacked heels I saw at the mall.

When Bill wants something he doesn't hesitate to spend money. Last month he charged three hundred dollars for Bon Jovi tickets. The concert is in two weeks. I almost told him not to bother getting tickets because he would be in no condition to go, but then I realized that it was better if we maintained appearances. The first time I saw Bon Jovi was when I was in college. I drove with some friends to New York and we stayed up all night and drove home at dawn. That was before I met Bill.

Bill tells me that he loves me and that we'll always be together and that I have nothing to worry about, but I'm no fool. The bottom line is that my dear husband's got a seven-figure trust fund and I cannot afford to leave my inheritance to chance. He has no other living relatives. I'm all he's got. When he goes, the cash will be mine.

Come to mama, my sweet gold nest egg!

I need to get a manicure. My nails look like a raccoon has been chewing on them. Maybe I'll make an appointment at the Vietnamese shop next to the bank. They do a nice job and they don't try to yack your ear off. They just quietly go about their business. You give them a five-dollar tip and they seem sincerely grateful. God only knows what they say about you after you leave. I don't trust any of them.

I discovered online that antifreeze is the key. I noticed that when Bill went jogging he would drink blue Gatorade. It seemed so simple. You put a couple of ounces of ethylene glycol in the Gatorade bottle and the person never knows. I read that ingestion of ethylene glycol leads to systemic toxicity beginning with central nervous system effects, followed by cardiopulmonary disturbance, and finally renal failure. Big words for something that will make you feel like crap. After a few weeks you die, and the medical examiner cannot determine the manner of death.

I had considered other methods, including electrocuting him in the bathtub. I decided that it had been done too many times in the movies. (Wasn't it *The Postman Always Rings Twice* with John Garfield and Lana Turner? I loved that movie. It was in black and white. Such beautiful cinematography.) The cops who investigated would quickly suspect that it wasn't an accident. Same with brake failure on the car. I know nothing about cars and wouldn't know where to begin to mess around with the brakes. I thought about an accidental gunshot, but we don't own any guns. I didn't want to hire a hit man because the person might squeal or blackmail me. It's better if it's done by me. Very quietly.

It took me a while to decide the final scene. One choice was that Bill could simply disappear. If I disposed of the corpse there would be no autopsy and no police investigation. The drawback is that I would have to wait seven years to have him declared legally dead. I can't wait that long to get his trust fund. It would also mean cutting him up or burying him in the back yard. Mrs. Rosenkrantz from next door is extremely nosey and I cannot imagine how I could manage to dig a hole and bury Bill without her finding out. Even more than that, the idea of handling a dead body makes my skin crawl. I suppose I could manage cutting off the arms and legs in the bathtub, but the head would be too much. All those gross sinews of the neck and the vertebrae that I'd have to saw through. The blood would not be a problem because I could get rid of it with bleach, but what if his eyes opened? It would be as if he were looking at me and watching me cut him apart. I'd have to make sure to use a powerful drain cleaner on the bathroom pipes because I've heard that the police will rip up the plumbing to search for traces of blood or guts.

I've been encouraging Bill to drink his Gatorade regularly. I tell him it will build up his strength. His bottle is on the table next to the sofa, just where I put it for him. But it looks full. I don't think that he has drunk any of it tonight. I must remember to buy some more. The bottle I gave him two days ago disappeared. He says that when it was empty he tossed it into a trashcan near the park. I would rather he give the empties to me so that I can thoroughly wash them before putting them into the recycling.

I want to get this over with. I'm a very patient and methodical person, but enough already. He's got to go.

I hear the doorbell ring. Who could be calling at this time of night? I hate it when people drop in unannounced. If it's a salesman or one of those creepy religious people, I'll tell them that unless they vacate the apartment building I will call the police. I cannot imagine how people like that get through the front door. It's supposed to be locked at all times. I've seen some of the college kids open the door for strangers. I've reprimanded them but they just shrug and flip their hair and turn up their iPods.

Bill is at the front door. Good. He can handle them. He's talking to a man in a leather jacket. Standing behind the guy in the jacket is a woman in a blue uniform. She's a cop. I didn't know they had female cops in this town.

I wish Bill would hurry up and get rid of those people at the door. There are three cops now. Two men and the female. They're entering the apartment. I wish Bill had not let them in because I haven't tidied up. The apartment is in no condition for guests. I regularly remind Bill to ask me about having visitors; it's only common courtesy. I was so relieved when Bill quit that awful poker club that used to meet here once a month. Let them take their silly games somewhere else.

All I need now is to find my earrings. I want to wear the single pearls that Bill gave me last year on our anniversary. I was amazed that he remembered, although the note I left stuck to his calendar may have helped. I like these earrings because it was on that day—our anniversary—that I decided that Bill needed to go away.

Bill is still here, but not for long. He'll be gone soon. And then I'll have the freedom to go wherever I want, whenever I want.

The female cop is standing behind me. Yes, of course my name is Angela Gentry. Who else would I be? No, I do not want to go with you. Take your hands off me. This is insulting. Bill, how could you do this to me, your loving wife? Traitor! I've promised myself to you 'til death do us part. The handcuffs are chafing my wrists. I've never touched a bottle of Gatorade. Around here Bill is the only one who drinks that stuff. Yes, you're damned right I'm going to be represented by a lawyer. I'm going to show all of you what a terrible mistake you're making.

The man in the leather jacket is talking to Bill. The man looks about thirty. Short hair, sharp eyes. Tough guy. The two of them look at me as I stand there handcuffed in my own living room. Gloating, I'm sure. And then it dawns on me. I've seen the guy around town. Here and there. At the grocery store and Starbucks. Has he been following me? The bastard!

"Who are you?" I say to him.

The man says nothing.

Bill shakes his head. "Sorry, dear, but two can play at your game. This is Chris Mark. I hired him to confirm that you're trying to poison me with ethylene glycol. It sucked having to pretend to be sick for so many weeks, but those days are over. I feel great and you're going to prison. I'm divorcing you and you will not get a penny of my trust fund. Sorry, Angela, you got greedy and it backfired."

"Chris Mark is your name?" I say to the guy in the leather jacket as the cop hustles me out the door. "I'll remember that name."

As soon as I finish my memoir and get out of the joint, I'll look for a publisher.

Okay—back to my story. While I was doing my first term, Bill divorced me. I don't blame him. After all, I tried to become his widow. He was too slick for me, the bastard. I heard that he moved to Washington State. Probably to put as much distance between us as possible.

I did not forget about Chris Mark.

I thought about him each and every day I was incarcerated. If it weren't for his meddling I'd have become a wealthy woman, wearing orange only because I bought it at Nordstrom's and not because it was prison issue.

Day after day, I patiently waited until I was free to exact my revenge. After five long years I said goodbye to my cellmates and took the last long walk down the cinderblock corridor to the room where they process you for release. I got my old clothes back, and they still fit me, no doubt because during my prison term I had tried hard to stay in shape. Many of the ladies here get fat because they do nothing but sleep and eat junk food from the commissary. Not me. For five years I exercised and stayed at my same weight.

The discharge officer gave me money for bus fare to Boston before they closed the gates behind me.

Unlike many people who walk out of prison after serving a long sentence, I was not adrift. I was not in search of meaning in my life. While the newly regained pleasure of walking under the open sky was seductive, I quickly focused on my plan. I knew exactly what I wanted to do, and every one of my choices and every one of my actions were bent towards my goal.

I was determined to eliminate Chris Mark. This was to be my purpose and my vocation. It would give my life as a free woman shape and meaning. Bill had slipped through my grasp; Chris Mark would not. When I walked out of that prison, I resolved never to be blown around like a leaf in the wind. I would not latch on to the first loser guy who promised to put a roof over my head. I had seen too many girls in prison use men as crutches and surrogate daddies. Not me. I was going to stand on my own two feet and make my tormentor pay the price for his meddling.

The *Gloucester Tribune* was my first source of information. A few days after my release, while I was getting settled at the YWCA in Boston, I read in the online edition of the *Tribune* that Chris Mark, the renowned private detective, had captured a guy who had murdered a lobsterman. The perp did it because he and the lobsterman's wife were having an affair. To enhance the motive for murder, it just so happened that the lobsterman owned an old painting that was worth ten million dollars. He had the thing hanging in his living room! Seems the wife figured out how valuable it was, so she conspired with her boyfriend to kill her husband and then auction off the painting.

The article confirmed that Chris Mark was still living in Gloucester. In that case, I was going to live there too.

I planned my relocation to Gloucester with exquisite care. My move was not to be merely physical. Not just a change of address and a new job. It was to be transformational. It was not to be Angela Gentry who would become a new resident of that coastal town. Angela Gentry was a convicted felon who needed to disappear. I chose a new name: Darlene Keller. No particular reason for those two names; I just thought they sounded good together. Hi, I'm Darlene Keller. Pleased to meet you.

Next came new hair: cut short and dyed black. I was pleased that when I walked through the door of the Y after my hair appointment the receptionist did not recognize me.

I went shopping online. It took me a few days to get up to speed on the vast world of underground internet commerce. After downloading the special Tor browser (it was free!), I logged onto the anonymous trading site called Gold Path, where you can buy anything that's on the black market—drugs, mostly, but also identification cards, guns, and anything else that's either illegal or controlled. You make payment using untraceable bitcoins. What I wanted was a new identity. A few days after emailing my newly taken selfie to a seller named Pirate Pete and paying him fifty bucks in bitcoins, I received in the mail a Massachusetts driver's license and a Social Security card. On the driver's license under my photo my new name was printed: Darlene Keller.

With my new identification I opened a checking account. Now I could pay my rent by writing checks from the account of Darlene Keller. I could even get a credit card!

But I was getting ahead of myself. My mission came first. It was time to make my move.

Having borrowed money from my brother—he sent me a check, I think, so I wouldn't visit him and his

perfect little family—I packed my few belongings and
took the train to Gloucester. After a forty-minute ride
north along the coast I arrived at the Gloucester train
station. The weather was unseasonably cool with a
light drizzle. My first stop was an apartment building
located within walking distance of the station. I had
seen a listing online for a single-bedroom unit for rent.
The building manager who rented the apartment to me
was at first concerned that I was unemployed. His
quick acceptance of my application may have been the
result of the quick blowjob that I bestowed upon him
as he sat behind his desk.

Within an hour of my arrival, I had the keys to unit
6B.

The next day I landed a job as a waitress in a local
seafood restaurant. It was the height of the summer
season and the place was packed from noon until ten
at night. The hours were long but the work was
bearable. I spent the next few weeks learning how to
extract tips from the tourists. I made enough money to
pay my rent, buy food, and put a down payment on a
used Ford.

With the basics of life taken care of, I could focus
all of my attention on the reason why I was living in
this dreary fishing town: to track and eliminate the
man who had taken away not only five years of my life
but a trust fund that would have been mine had my
dear husband followed the script and quietly passed
away after a lingering and mysterious illness. "He was
so young," the mourners would have said to each
other. "How especially sad for his wife—they had only
been married six years!" Yeah—six years that felt like a
lifetime. Add to those six years the five spent in prison,
and you've got eleven years down the drain.

A quick online search of property deed records had
revealed the home address of Chris Mark: 56
Blackburn Road, on the narrow peninsula of East
Gloucester, near the harbor. Google maps showed a
compact Cape. From the small back yard stretched an

expanse of dense trees. The nearest neighbor looked to be some distance away.

A check of the city directory revealed no one else living at that address.

During my weeks of preparation I had carefully considered a wide range of methods to accomplish my goal. The primary consideration was that on the heels of a suspicious death there comes—as everyone knows—a police investigation. I quickly decided that to lead the investigators down the wrong path I needed to avoid any methods that were traditionally associated with female killers. These included poison and any form of seduction. I eliminated schemes that were far beyond my expertise, such as bomb making. I also put aside any notion of hiring a hit man. I trusted no one. I knew that I had to do the job myself.

After much careful consideration and more than one discreet drive-by of Chris Mark's house, I decided that the best method would be to acquire a good hunting rifle, establish myself at a spot in the woods behind his house, and shoot him through a rear window, or maybe as he walked in his yard. The range was about an eighth of a mile. Two hundred and twenty yards. A challenge, but with a good scope it would be doable.

I looked forward to seeing Chris Mark's head explode into a pink mist as the bullet slammed into his skull.

My first task was to procure a rifle before joining a rifle range to hone my sharpshooting skills. I logged onto Gold Path, and after carefully reading customer reviews and gun owners' blogs I chose a Mossberg three-oh-eight. Lightweight, accurate, and cheap. The operative word was "cheap" because I bought two of them. Why two? You'll find out. After laying out a thousand dollars in bitcoins for the two rifles, two high-powered scopes, one sound suppressor, and five hundred rounds of solid copper ammo, I had the guns shipped to a mailbox I had rented at a local pack-and-ship store.

A week later as I unpacked my purchases I felt the thrill of a sinister Christmas: I was opening gifts I had given myself that would help me accomplish my deepest personal goal. As I hefted each of them in turn, my twin guns felt good in my hands. Heavy, long, and lethal. After attaching a scope to one of them I sighted through the open window. On the railroad station platform a few blocks away a man was standing, waiting for the train. As I kept his head pinned in the crosshairs I breathed ever so slowly. I squeezed the trigger. Click. It seemed so easy. This was the instrument of my revenge. I would not be a powerless victim, either of my ex-husband Bill or of Chris Mark.

Since Bill had divorced me and moved away, he was off my radar screen. Chris Mark would pay for both.

The next day I drove to the Essex Sportsman's Club, which is located deep in the woods in Gloucester and which admits women. An affable older gentleman named Gus showed me around. He asked me if I had shot a gun before. I told him yes—when I was kid my dad owned a twenty-two plinker and we used to shoot empty beer cans (with great success) and varmints, like squirrels (with no success).

The clubhouse had a kitchen, eight-foot pool table, and an antique soda machine stocked with locally brewed flavors. No booze—so much the better, I suppose, because I needed to keep a clear head. Gus took me out back to see the five-acre trout pond with little rowboats for fishing. Didn't seem to be much of a challenge to cast for captive fish in a trout pond, but hey, whatever turned them on.

What I wanted to see was the hundred-yard outdoor shooting range. It was really nothing more than an open wooden platform covered by a roof and facing a long, scrubby field. On the platform were tables with body-sized cutouts so that you could rest your elbows in a comfortable position as you held your gun. I noted that you could also either sit or lie prone on the floorboards, which is what I had in mind. In the woods above Chris Mark's house there were no tables or chairs, and I had to train under realistic conditions.

At the far end of the field a line of posts held the targets, and beyond that was a berm to catch the bullets.

I told Gus that I wanted to store my firearm at the club. He said that was perfectly fine as long as I didn't mind not having access to it after hours or when the club was closed. I said no problem; safety was my priority.

The next Monday, after taking the mandatory gun safety course at the club and earning my Firearms Safety Certificate, I filled out the firearms license application and submitted it to the Gloucester Police Department. This was the most harrowing step in establishing my new identity, because when you submit your application they take your fingerprints and run a background check. For the next two days I couldn't sleep and I barely ate, and every time a cop car cruised past me on the street I held my breath: I was convinced they had caught onto me and I was going to be sent back to prison.

On Wednesday afternoon a police sergeant called. He told me that my license was ready and that I could stop by headquarters and pick it up.

This had to be a trap. They were going to bust me the minute I walked in the station. Bravely I went there and showed the desk officer my identification. With a smile he handed me my license.

I practically ran out the door.

With one of my Mossbergs—I could now legally use it—I hurried to the range. There were three other shooters there—all men—and I set myself up at the far end, away from them. I wanted to concentrate and not socialize. The Mossberg felt good in my hands, and as I chambered the first round I imagined the gleaming copper projectile ripping into Chris Mark's head at two thousand feet per second. At that speed, he would never hear the shot that killed him.

The targets were ordinary eight-and-a-half-by-eleven sheets of paper printed with a bull's eye design. The solid red ball in the very center was three-quarters of an inch in diameter. This was surrounded by a solid black ball two inches in diameter. Then came two concentric circles: the inner one was four inches in diameter and the outer ring six inches, or about the width of a human head.

My first impression of my target, pinned to the frame on the post one hundred yards away, was that it was impossibly distant. Lying prone, I sighted through the scope and managed to slow my breathing and steady my hands enough to keep the bull's eye in the vicinity of the crosshairs. Slowly I squeezed the trigger.

Bang! The unexpected sound and sharp recoil made me flinch. Then I smelled the gunpowder, and I was transported back to my childhood with my dad's steady hand on my shoulder as he announced in his deep voice that I was the next Annie Oakley. It was a brief moment in time, like a butterfly in the garden—here and then gone in the blink of an eye. How rudely I had been awakened to the harsh reality of human treachery when on a winter night my father had abandoned us! It was so easy for the bastard to cut us loose without a care. As if we were fish that you could just throw back in the lake and we'd happily swim off. But that's the way of the world. Anyone who counts on loyalty or fidelity is a fool.

I peered through the scope. Near the edge of the paper was a small hole. I had hit the target! I fired another shot, and another. My hits were scattered. Not even a cluster, just random holes. But they all hit the paper.

At the end of the hour I put my rifle into the secure locker and signed the slip. The guys in the clubhouse were friendly, testing me to see if I were available. I was not. I was a rock, an island. No one was going to touch me.

After work that night I went for another reconnaissance of Chris Mark's house. I cruised slowly up

Blackburn road. To my relief his Camaro was not in the driveway and the house was dark. At the end of his road I came to an intersection. I turned left onto a narrow lane that was riddled with potholes. Swallow Lane, it was called. The lane went up the hill before curving to the right. I was in the woods now, and my headlights illuminated slender maple trees standing amongst towering hunks of ancient granite. I followed the lane over the spine of East Gloucester—the peninsula is only about a mile wide here—and came down the other side, where the lane met Atlantic Road and the shoreline.

Perfect. If I parked my car on Swallow Lane, I could make my getaway in the direction away from Mark's house, towards Atlantic Road.

Turning my car around, I drove back up the hill towards Mark's house. At the top of the hill the lane widened on the left side, giving just enough room to pull over and park under the canopy of trees. After I got out of the car I stood quietly and listened. From the woods came not a sound. Other than Mark's, the nearest house was at least a quarter-mile away through dense woods.

Under the pale light of the half moon I picked my way through the gloomy underbrush and over fallen tree trunks in the direction of Blackburn Road. Suddenly I heard a frantic rustle amongst the bushes. A rabbit perhaps, or a skunk. Then just as quickly all was quiet again.

My heart was pounding. My response to this trivial surprise was not acceptable. I needed to be cool, less jumpy. With great caution I continued forward. Of course I carried no flashlight, and I had to tread carefully. In my extended hand I held a slender branch to clear the dark space in front of me of spider webs.

With the moon over my left shoulder I crept slowly forward. Every few seconds I stopped to look and listen. Through the trees on the road far below I saw the headlights of a car as it drove towards Gloucester, and seeing the lights gave me a sense of distance. After the taillights of the car had disappeared I stepped forward again. My senses were on high alert for the slightest touch, the tiniest sound, the faintest glimmer of light. My foot landed on a brittle branch and it snapped with a crack that seemed impossibly loud. Who could not have heard that? I stopped again, barely allowing myself to breathe. In the treetops the wind sighed and from the harbor came the soft chug of a fishing boat's diesel at low throttle. Far in the distance—downtown Gloucester perhaps— a police siren faintly wailed.

Placing my hand on the rough bark of a broad tree trunk, I peered forward. Two hundred yards down the gentle slope I could discern the dark square bulk of the house of my target.

This spot would be perfect. It would be my hunting blind and my perch from which I would cut down the man who had ruined my life. I stood quietly for a moment, savoring the stillness of the shadowed woods and playing in my mind the scene as I squeezed off the lethal shot before slipping away to my waiting car. Long before the police arrived I would be on the road. After getting rid of the gun I'd go to a bar and establish an alibi.

I saw headlights come up Blackburn Road. First there was the dancing glow through the trees, and then as the vehicle came closer the pair of sharp lights came into view. With disinterest I watched them. Probably just someone driving by.

But the headlights slowed and then turned into Chris Mark's driveway. With my heart racing I saw the headlight beams sweep a brilliant arc across the small lawn before the car pulled up by the side of the house where there was a gravel turnaround. The lights were extinguished. It was then that I could see in the weak moonlight that the car was black and low. A Camaro. When the driver's door opened the interior light came on.

It was him. The man who had put me away.

In the passenger's seat was a woman. In the instant before she alighted from the car and the interior lights shut off I saw that she was slender and attractive. A girlfriend? A date? A pickup from a bar?

Together they walked to the back door of the house. They did not hold hands as they walked. They disappeared into the shadows. A moment later there came a light from a room in the back of the house. The window had half curtains. I could see a patterned floor, like linoleum. The kitchen, most likely. With tingling anticipation I waited and watched. Minutes passed. What were they doing?

And then came the moment that made everything worthwhile—my planning, my new identity, my mind-numbing work at the restaurant, my practice at the firing range. The moment that validated my plans of revenge.

A brilliant light came on in a window, throwing a bright splash of illumination in my direction across the back yard. This window was big. Plate glass, no doubt. The curtains, if there were any, were open. The window gave me a clear view into the living room of the house of Chris Mark.

I should have brought my gun, I thought bitterly. But the feeling passed. Careful, meticulous planning had gotten me this far. I needed to have patience.

With methodical detachment I studied the layout of the room. A black leather sofa faced a wide screen television. A coffee table, with three or four bottles standing on its glass top. An armchair, covered in gray fabric, placed with its back to the window.

For a few minutes I saw no people. Then Mark and his hookup came into the room and sat on the sofa. They each held a wine glass in their hands. Mark clicked the remote and the television flickered to life. I could not see what they were watching, only the play of light across the carpet.

Had I brought my rifle I could have easily drawn a bead on Mark's head and pulled the trigger. If the window glass deflected the bullet, it would not matter.

Before Mark—or any human being—had time to react to the shock of the suddenly shattered window, I'd squeeze off another shot. This one would not have to break the glass and would travel in a direct line to the target.

It would all happen soon enough. And then I would be free of the humiliation and shame of having been duped by this obnoxious man.

After a few minutes Mark put his arm around the girl. She kissed him. As he held her more tightly they kissed with increasing passion. His hand slid along her flank to her ass. She responded by twisting her hips to give him easier access.

After a few more minutes of intimate groping she broke free and picked up her glass of wine from the coffee table. Settling back into the sofa, he ran his hand through his hair. They talked before she put the glass back on the table. Then she stood up. She took his hand and he too stood up. After another long kiss, with their arms around each other's waists they walked out of the room.

In the darkness I waited.

No other lights in the house came on. I stared into the bright living room with its two empty glasses on the coffee table.

Suddenly I felt horribly and tragically alone. Damn my miserable life! And damn the anger that drove me blindly forward into the dark woods.

There was only one way to exorcise the demon in my gut. I would not be free until I had exacted my price from Chris Mark.

I was tempted to remain in my place in the dark as a voyeur. Heck, these two lovebirds rabbits might just come out to the living room sofa and give me a free show. But business was business. The longer I lingered, the greater the chance of discovery. With great reluctance I tore myself away from where I stood next to the tree. I had accomplished my goal for the night. I had proven to myself that my plan was feasible. It would work. All I had to do was to be patient and not get greedy.

At that moment I saw a set of headlights coming from over my left shoulder—from Swallow Lane. Amazed that anyone used this lonely road at night I instinctively crouched next to the tree. The lights came slowly down from the ridge, and as they passed I saw that it was a Gloucester police cruiser.

My blood froze and I dared not breathe. I watched intently as the cruiser slowly made its way along the potholed lane, its headlights bouncing with each impact. It stopped at the corner of Blackburn Road. After what seemed like an eternity its right turn signal began its rhythmic flash and the car slowly took the corner.

In a moment it had disappeared behind Mark's house and reemerged again before creeping up the road towards downtown.

Okay—I had passed another test. Clearly I was fated to be victorious!

I made my way back to my car. In the moonlight something caught my attention. An orange rectangle under the windshield wiper. Shit—a ticket. The bastard had given me a ticket! I took it and got in my car. Under the dome light I found the violation: parking the wrong way. I had pulled over to the left side of the road so that my car had been facing the oncoming lane.

People do that all the time on the back roads in Gloucester. The cop must have needed to make his quota.

This ticket created a problem. It meant that I had to wait at least a month before executing my plan. I did not want the cops to connect a ticketed car to a murder, even if I were going to be a thousand miles away by the time they figured it out.

Twenty bucks was the fine. I'd send a check to the court the next day. Problem solved.

As I drove my crummy used Ford down Swallow Lane and took the right onto Blackburn Road, I thought about the couple carelessly cavorting in the bedroom of the house, and how happiness can be fleeting. Soon enough, I would transform Chris Mark's pleasure into horror.

During the following month I went to the rifle range every weekend. I would have gone there every day, but I was thinking about the police investigation of the murder of Chris Mark, and I did not want to undue attract attention.

My marksmanship steadily improved, which presented me with a problem. I did not want to get the reputation of being a good shot. In fact, I wanted the opposite. I wanted the guys at the club to believe that I was an inept female who could barely hit the target. Validating their Neanderthal beliefs about women would give me cover.

On the day that I drilled ten shots into the two-inch-diameter black bull's-eye, I changed my strategy. Instead of aiming for the bull's-eye, I aimed for various parts of the target: the top of the far outer ring, or the left side of the inside ring. It was like a major league baseball pitcher would train: throw one low and outside, then burn one right down the middle. Then put one high and inside. It was all about control.

After my sessions Gus and the boys would examine my targets, which I made sure to show them. The hits appeared to be all over the place. They tried to be encouraging while making fun of me. "Well there, Darlene," they would say while exchanging witty glances, "Are you breathing slow? Squeezing the trigger slow? Compensating for the crosswind?" I think that one of them—Michael—sincerely wanted to help me improve. He offered to sit with me while I shot. I just shrugged my shoulders and thanked him, and tried to act coy. Maybe sometime, I said. He said okay, feel free to ask. It was funny because I saw his targets. In a competition I'd wipe the floor with him.

A week after my nighttime visit to the woods behind Chris Mark's house, I went back for one more reconnoiter. I was nervous about the cops and I wanted to see if the patrol was a regular occurrence or if the cop car had randomly targeted Swallow Lane.

When I drove by Mark's house it was dark. No lights, no car in the drive. Maybe he was out picking up another girl at a bar. I drove up Swallow Lane and parked in the wide area at the top of the hill. This time my car was facing Atlantic Road. I was legal.

Although the moon was nearly full, high clouds diffused the light. I picked my way through the underbrush and found my tree. Below me was the darkened house.

I stood and watched and listened. There were only the usual sounds of the city and the port: an occasional distant siren, the throbbing rhythm of a boat in the harbor, the whine of a jet airliner passing overhead on its approach to Logan Airport in Boston, twenty miles down the coast. Now and then a nocturnal seagull cried, and from a nearby pond came the steady croaking of frogs.

The clouds separated and the scene was bathed in moonlight. I could see every detail of Mark's house—the shingles on the roof and the muntins in the windows. Yet in the deep shade of the tree I was hidden, invisible.

A car approached on Blackburn Road. It turned into Mark's driveway. The Camaro. Another girlfriend, for sure! The Camaro pulled to the side of the house and the lights were extinguished. The car door opened. This time the passenger seat was empty. No companion. Mark got out of the car and reached into the passenger compartment. He removed a fat tube that was nearly as long as he was tall. It had not fit into the trunk of the car, I suppose, so he had laid it from the front seat across the center console to the back seat. He carried the tube into the house before returning to the car and recovering a large box. After closing the car door he carried the box inside the house.

The lights came on in the kitchen, and then in the living room. But this time I saw light only around the edges of the window. The living room curtains were closed.

For fifteen minutes I waited and watched. Nothing changed. The lights did not change. No sound came from the house.

There had been no cop car on Swallow Lane, either.

I returned to my car. After I started the engine I sat in the idling car for a moment, thinking about the immensity of my triumph. Soon this would all be a memory and I'd be living a thousand miles away. No one would mess with me again.

The night of the operation was cool, with a waning moon that hung behind drifting high clouds. At nine o'clock I packed my second Mossberg with its scope and sound suppressor into a long cardboard box that I had bought at the pack-and-ship store. With the ammunition in a camera bag, I nonchalantly left my apartment and went to my car. It's funny how you think everyone is staring at you as you walk down the sidewalk carrying a long box with a gun inside. Of course no one gives a crap. They're just going about their business. As I was carefully sliding the box into the back seat of my car a Gloucester cop drove by. My hands started to shake and I knew that he could tell exactly what I was doing. It was only a matter of a second before he'd turn on his lights and screech the cruiser to a halt, blocking my escape. But the cop did not turn on his lights and did not stop. Out of the corner of my eye—*do not stare*, I told myself—I watched as he slowly took the corner and disappeared behind a building.

Being careful to obey every traffic law, I drove to Blackburn road. As I passed Chris Mark's house my heart jumped into my throat: his black Camaro was parked in the driveway. I smiled to myself. Tonight was the night of sweet revenge.

I parked legally at the top of the hill on Swallow Lane. I felt comfortable now; it was my third visit here and I had the confidence of a veteran. After I stepped out of my car I stood and listened. The familiar woods were dark and quiet. In the distance a dog barked, and then others joined the chorus. It's always that way—it's never just one dog that barks; they all have to join in and annoy the neighbors for a few minutes until they all get bored and go back to whatever it is that dogs do.

Satisfied that I was alone, I took the rifle out of the box before closing the car door. From this moment my situation was serious: I was carrying a firearm at night in a residential neighborhood. The stakes could not have been higher.

It had rained earlier in the day, making the once brittle underbrush flexible. As I made my way to the tree I noted with satisfaction that my footsteps created no crackling of dry underbrush. Like a panther I moved silently and with stealth through the damp vegetation. The spiders had been busy, and using a thin stick I whisked away more than one web and its frantic, wriggling owner.

I arrived at my tree and stood for a moment against the dark trunk. Two hundred yards away, the kitchen light was on. Its glow cast a thin beam across the green grass of the small back yard. I could see no activity in the kitchen. The rest of the house was dark. The Camaro sat like a sleeping cat in the driveway.

I was confident that since the car was here, so was Chris Mark. I would wait for my opportunity. If for some reason the night passed without giving me what I came here for, I'd come back again. I was patient. I was willing to do it right. Chris Mark would not escape.

I needed to be ready to act at any time. Rather than sit on the damp earth I decided to stand and use the tree as a brace. After loading five rounds into the internal magazine I brought the gun to my shoulder and sighted through the scope. To get a sense of the trajectory I found the brightly lit kitchen window and drew a bead on a bowl on the table. I held the bowl rocky steady in the crosshairs.

This shot was going to be no problem.

Now I only had to wait.

I stood next to the tree. All around me I heard the tiny sounds of the woods at night: the lonely creak of the trees in the wind, the cries of night birds, the steady croak of frogs. Every now and then a jet, bound for Boston with its running lights blazing, would whine overhead. Across the still waters of the harbor a ship's horn echoed.

Above the dark lattice canopy of tree branches the gleaming quarter moon crept across the sky. My knees were growing stiff. Something with tiny legs crawled across the back of my neck and I swatted it away.

Suddenly, from the living room a flood of light streamed across the yard.

With every sense alerted I came to attention. The television was on, giving the scene a flickering quality. Visible just above the back of the gray chair facing away from the window was the top of a man's head. Had I missed something? Did Mark quickly turn on the lights and run to his favorite chair? No matter. I brought the gun to my shoulder and got the head in my crosshairs. I could see only the dark close-cropped hair. I could not be certain that it was Chris Mark. It might even have been a dummy.

I needed a better shot. I waited.

Over the next few agonizing seconds the head didn't move.

Then the person abruptly stood up and turned towards the window. He was talking on his cell phone.

There was absolutely no doubt: it was Chris Mark. I tried to keep him in my sights, but at that range it was impossible. As he talked he would take a step to the left and then a step to the right. My crosshairs were a millisecond behind him. Damn you, stand still! I tightened my finger on the trigger...and then relaxed. I didn't have the shot.

I was breathing too fast. Gotta slow down. Loosen my muscles. Focus on the target.

Chris Mark turned away from the window and walked out of the room.

Damn!

I realized that sweat was dripping into my eyes. I wiped my forehead with my sleeve. The night seemed oppressive. I heard a faint snap in the woods behind me. I whirled around. A woodland creature, no doubt. I was too nervous. Needed to get a grip. I looked back at the house.

The television was still on and the room was still empty. Okay. Relax. Take a deep breath. Pay no attention to the small sounds and rustles of the wind in the underbrush and through the leaves. I was utterly alone in the woods and my quarry was in the house. The living room lights were blazing. Chris Mark would come back. Maybe he went to get a drink or go to the bathroom. It wouldn't be long.

I checked the time. I had been standing by the tree for nearly an hour. C'mon, I told myself. Compared to what I wanted, it was a blink in time. I'd stand here for a week to nail my target.

A car came up Blackburn Road. It passed the house and kept going towards the end of Eastern Point.

I dared to lower my rifle and stretch my stiff arms.

There was motion in the living room. Chris Mark had re-entered. Now he was carrying a drink. He came to the window and stood facing in my direction. He seemed to be looking out the window into the darkness. He raised the highball glass to his lips.

I raised my gun to my shoulder.

In a moment I had his head in my sights. My heart beat faster and I struggled to breathe slowly. To my amazement he kept his position. Now was the time. All of my planning and training had led up to this moment. Slowly I squeezed the trigger.

Instead of a loud bang, the suppressor did its job and I heard only the click of the hammer and a soft thump, like someone punching a pillow. The silent recoil knocked me out of position. Quickly I sighted again through the scope. The window glass had shattered. I saw it shatter and I heard the tinkle of glass. This was not unexpected. I knew that the first bullet would be deflected by the impact with the glass.

I had to shoot again before my target had time to react.

But to my astonishment Chris Mark did not respond. He calmly brought the glass to his lips again as if nothing had happened. The window had nearly exploded—how could he not react?

No matter. I squeezed the trigger again. The rifle clicked and made its "thump" sound. I felt the recoil. My target's head was in the crosshairs. This time he seemed to waver, as if hit by a strong breeze. Then with his drink still in his hand he slowly turned towards the gray chair.

How could I have missed? How could he not respond?

Desperately I got him in my sights for the third time.

Against the back of my neck I felt the barrel of a gun.

"Drop your weapon," said a man's voice.

I froze.

A hand roughly grabbed my shoulder.

"Drop it or I'll drop you."

I was not going down without a fight. As I tried to turn around I felt an impact against the back of my legs and my feet left the ground. I fell heavily on my side. The rifle was torn from my grasp as a knee pinned me to the damp earth.

"Get off me, you motherfucker!" I shouted.

"Shut up," said the voice. "The game's over."

As he pinned me down he fastened my wrists behind my back. Then he hauled me upright and shoved me against the tree. In the darkness I could not make out his face.

"You're going back to prison," said the man.

At that moment the moon came from behind the clouds and pale light filled the dark woods. I was staring into the face of Chris Mark.

"How—?" I sputtered.

"I've been waiting for you, Angela," he said coolly. "The parking ticket. Big mistake. We traced your car. All the pieces fell into place. But I had to get you for attempted murder. I had to let you take a shot at me. So I made a little movie of myself. Got a rear projection screen. I knew you'd be out here so I set up the screen and ran the movie. It cost me a plate glass window, but it was worth it."

The rest is a blur. The cops came and took me to lockup. They put me on trial. My defense attorney was an idiot. For multiple offenses—too numerous to list here—I got twenty years.

Six months after I had shattered Chris Mark's living room window, I stepped off the bus at MCI-Framingham. I thought I'd never see this place again. I asked the intake guard if I could have my old number again. He laughed as he handed me my new red card with number 67430-317. Some of the ladies—the ones doing hard time— remembered me. We quickly fell into the old routines.

That's all for now. I've got a killer recipe for potato logs with melted cheese, and I have to get in line for the microwave.

The House on Cliff Lane

Chris Mark felt himself losing his edge. His hand had reached for the Jim Beam once too often. Over the course of the long evening there had always been one more easy swallow. When empty, the glass had been readily refilled from the bottle at his elbow.

The other four guys at the table were the same men with whom he played Texas Hold'em nearly every week. An affable bunch and only occasionally given to violence.

Mark looked at the cards in his hand and at the community cards. A lousy pair of sevens. Nothing to write home about and certainly nothing to put a buck on. The river card had given him no hope.

"What'll it be?" asked Bernie, the dealer.

"Fold," said Mark as he consigned his cards to the flat green grave of the table. He took a deep breath. The air flowing into his lungs gave him momentary clarity. But his brain was sluggish. His mouth was pasty. The last sip of whiskey had been bitter.

It was a too-familiar experience that regularly produced a lesson that Mark tried in vain to take to heart: *getting* drunk is always much more fun than *being* drunk. The journey is wonderful, the destination tiresome.

In his pocket his phone vibrated. Who could be ringing him at three o'clock in the morning? He took out the insistent phone. In his hand the caller ID glowed coldly: Chief Ray Frontiero. "Gentlemen, please excuse me," said Mark as he slid back his chair and rose to his feet. He walked with his phone into the tiny kitchen of Bernie's apartment. "Yes, chief," he said. "What's up? Okay. I'll be right down. No, it's no problem. Always glad to assist the Gloucester Police Department."

He went back into the living room and offered his apologies for cutting out early. After finding his way outside he breathed in the crisp and salty early dawn air that flowed in cool waves over the beach at the far end of the lane. He unlocked his Camaro, slid behind the driver's seat, and before putting the car in gear he punched up Gary Clark Jr. on the sound system. The searing neo blues agreeably reset his focus.

Ten minutes later, his brain having regained a semblance of clarity, Mark ducked under the yellow police tape and entered the alley behind the Red Lantern bar. Under the glare of portable lights he found the chief and his men standing around the body.

"Sorry to ruin your Friday night," said the chief wearily.

"I was only down a hundred bucks. You saved me from losing my shirt." How could Mark be upset with the late night call? He knew the chief's day had begun at seven that morning, when Mark was still blissfully asleep in bed.

"Suspicious death?" said Mark as he knelt next to the body.

"Anytime a thirty-year-old man drops dead in the street, it's suspicious," replied the medical examiner. "No obvious injuries. No defensive wounds. No blood on the clothing or on the pavement. Only this—" she rotated the right arm. "A needle mark. Fresh. And this—" she pointed to an object lying on the dirty asphalt a few feet from the body. "Hypodermic syringe. Looks clean, as if it hasn't been there long."

"Time of death?" asked Mark.

"Body's warm. No rigor. I'd say within the past four hours."

"The Red Lantern closes at one o'clock," said Mark. "The cleanup guys would be putting the trash out here in the alley until about one-thirty. Then they would lock up."

"He must have died here between one-thirty and a few minutes before three, when our patrolman spotted him," said the chief.

"Unless he died somewhere else and was dumped here," replied Mark. "Like you always say, we gotta keep our options open. Is there a security camera out here?"

Mark and the chief scanned the surrounding walls. "Don't see one," said the chief.

"We've got millions of goddamn cameras spying on us every hour of the day, and when you really want one, there isn't one," said Mark. "It figures, right?"

The corpse and the scene had been photographed and the area searched. Nothing had been found except the needle. The medical examiner bagged the body.

"You like working on Saturdays, right?" asked the chief as they walked to Rogers Street. In the soft glow of dawn, along the wharves and docks of the harbor the crews of the fishing and lobstering boats made ready. Under the supervision of the usual committees of strutting seagulls, the boats were loaded with ice and bait, and one by one the sturdy diesel engines rumbled to life.

"You know I'm trying to lead a peaceful and uneventful life," replied Mark with an ironic smile. "The problem is that peacefulness and uneventfulness constantly elude me. So, sure. Count me in. I'll come by your office at ten."

The morning came hard and bright. At ten o'clock Chris Mark presented himself at the office of the chief.

"We've got an identification," said Frontiero as he slid a file across the grey leather desktop. "The name is Carl Lewiston. He happens to be one of the owners of the Red Lantern. The medical examiner confirms he died from a heroin overdose."

"Was he a user?" asked Mark. "Known to the police?"

"That's got me puzzled," replied Frontiero. "We've got no records on him. No arrests. No connection to known dope dealers. If you asked me to name the heroin addicts in this city, I could print out a list. Not many of them manage to avoid interaction with the law. And look at this—" Frontiero pointed to a page of the file. "The medical examiner found just one needle mark on his arm. Either he habitually snorted the stuff or this was the first time he tried shooting it."

"Anything else in his system?" asked Mark.

"Yeah. His blood alcohol concentration level was point zero two."

"For a guy his size, that's one glass of wine," said Mark.

"His blood also showed traces of Rohypnol."

"Roofies," nodded Mark. "The odds that he would administer Rohypnol to himself are about zero. The dose of heroin was fatal, which means he had to have ingested the roofies and the wine before the heroin injection. Any prints on the syringe?"

"It was wiped clean but whoever did it missed one. We have a single partial. Looks like a thumb print. No match on the state police database."

"Did Lewiston have a car? Was it found?"

"Yes. It was parked on the street nearby. It was clean except that it looked like it had been to a state forest. Yellow pine needles were stuck under the wiper blades and along where the trunk lid meets the car body. We didn't find the car keys. They were not on the body."

"Sounds like murder to me," said Mark.

"The medical examiner wants to do a few more tests before signing off on accidental death, suicide, or homicide. To call it murder we need some evidence. Where do you want to start?"

"I'll pay a visit to Carl Lewiston's business partner," replied Mark.

The home of Skip O'Doule was a compact Gothic revival located at the end of a narrow street in Lanesville, the section of Gloucester that, because it's on the west side of the peninsula of Cape Ann, faces the setting sun over the placid Ipswich Bay.

Chris Mark rapped with his knuckles on the front door.

"Yeah, just a minute," came a groggy voice from inside. Presently the door swung open. Mark stood facing a heavyset man clad in a plaid bathrobe. His eyes were clearly pained by the invasive morning light.

"Skip O'Doule? My name's Chris Mark. I'm working with the Gloucester Police Department. May I have a few words with you?"

"Yeah, sure," replied O'Doule. "What's this all about?"

"May I come in?" Without waiting for an answer Mark stepped across the threshold. The home smelled of musty cigarettes.

"What's going on?" asked O'Doule. He scratched his armpit.

"Last night your business partner Carl Lewiston was found dead. His body was lying in the alley behind the Red Lantern."

"That's terrible," said O'Doule. "I saw him yesterday afternoon. At the bar. We did the inventory of the liquor. He was fine. What happened?"

"You didn't see him last night?"

"No. He left the bar around five. I stayed. I was there until closing."

"At one?"

"Yeah. The staff and I cleaned up. When we were finished I locked up and came here. I was tired. I went on Facebook for a while before going to sleep."

"You didn't see Carl?"

"No," said O'Doule. "You want some coffee? I've got the pot on in the kitchen."

"Thanks, but I'll pass," said Mark as he followed O'Doule through the living room with its enormous Bob's Discount Furniture Store reclining sofa set and its wide-screen TV bolted to the wall. Mark did not want O'Doule's coffee. He did not want to be indebted, in even the smallest way, to a possible suspect. His visit was strictly business.

The small kitchen looked as if it could have appeared in the pages of *House Beautiful* magazine in the nineteen thirties. The floor was uneven linoleum and the cupboards were old painted wood. Next to the refrigerator with its rounded corners was a gas range with heavy cast iron burner rings.

O'Doule poured steaming water into the French press. "It sucks about Carl," he said as he waited to plunge the coffee maker. "He was a good guy. Any idea what happened?"

"We're looking at a number of leads," replied Mark. "Did you ever know him to use drugs?"

"Carl? Are you kidding? No. His only vice was a good glass of wine. He had a nice collection in his apartment. He was always pestering me to upgrade our wine list, and I'd always say, 'Carl, we own the Red Lantern, not the goddamn Ritz. We sell beer and liquor to men and women who want to forget their troubles.' He'd laugh and say that of course I was right. He took the business seriously. We ran a clean operation. No minors and no fights. Never had a problem with the cops or the licensing board."

"Anything on his mind lately?" asked Mark. "Did he seem different in any way?"

"Only the problem with his father and the house," replied O'Doule.

"What kind of problem was that?"

After heaping several teaspoons of sugar into his coffee, O'Doule took the mug and sat at the Formica-topped kitchen table. Mark drew up a chair and sat opposite O'Doule.

"Carl was very close to his dad, Richard Lewiston," began O'Doule. "The dad had a rough life. He grew up in the family house on Cliff Lane. It's a big old rambling Victorian not far from here. Sits on a granite bluff overlooking the ocean. When Richard was a teenager he saw his older sister get shot in the house. Her boyfriend came to the door and bang! Put a bullet in her. Killed her. It was a fucked-up situation. Ten years later Richard inherited the house when his mother died. But Richard was never happy. I think it was the house. It was the scene of too much bad shit. Richard drank too much and barely made enough money to pay the property taxes. Then his wife—Carl's mother—left him. That was the last straw. Richard went over the deep end. He became violent. Couldn't function. So Carl and his younger brother Jeremy arranged for their dad to become a ward of the state. He was committed to a state facility. He made progress there. I went there a few times myself to visit him. He was trying to put the past behind him. But the bills started to pile up. The house was seized for back taxes. Carl was his father's legal guardian, but the court appointed a lawyer to be Richard's conservator. I didn't know what a conservator was, so I found out. Apparently a conservator is supposed to be responsible for the protected person's assets—things like his bank account or any property that he or she owns. There are certain things that conservators can do without getting court approval, like paying ordinary living expenses, paying debts and expenses, and managing the protected person's property and investments. One thing that requires prior court approval is the sale of a house or land belonging to the protected person."

"So Carl was his father's guardian, and was therefore responsible for everyday decisions, while the court appointed a conservator to oversee his finances?"

"Yeah," said O'Doule. "It was because of the taxes. The bills for the state care too. The state wanted to make sure it got paid back."

"And there's tension among the parties?"

"Carl told me that the conservator put the house up for sale. The house was in Richard's name, so there was nothing that Carl could do except try to buy it. Imagine having to buy the house that had been in your family for three generations! Carl was trying to raise enough cash for a down payment. That's all I know."

"Okay," said Mark. "By the way, the word around town is that you were pressuring Carl to sell his share of the bar to you. It sounds to me like he could have used the money."

"We disagreed on the business direction," shrugged O'Doule. "He had this idea that the bar could go upscale. Get a brick oven and serve fancy pizza. I told him over and over again that the Red Lantern had an image and a loyal clientele. It was too risky to change it. We were not going to try to cater to a bunch of hipsters. So yeah, on more than one occasion I offered to buy him out. It was nothing personal. Let him take the money and open a wine bar. I had no objection. But he would just laugh and say, 'C'mon, Skip, you're not getting rid of me that easily. We'll do it your way.' And we always did, which is why the Red Lantern always made a profit, even in January when there's not a tourist to be seen anywhere in town. He wouldn't sell out to me. Despite his ideas for an upscale place, I think that he loved the Red Lantern."

On the way back to downtown Gloucester, Chris Mark stopped at number 325 Cliff Lane. At the end of the curving gravel driveway stood a house that was once quite handsome, with Victorian turrets, tall windows, and finely carved trim. The view of Ipswich Bay from the driveway was impressive, and must have been even more spectacular, thought Mark, from the stately widow's walk perched high up on the slate roof. The house was built solid and had "good bones," as they say.

Now, after years of neglect, the balusters of the porch railing were gapped and the paint on the clapboards was peeling. But the new owner had already started work—the ground floor windows were freshly boarded up, and what had formerly been the lawn was now a field of mud criss-crossed by Caterpillar tread marks. Several big rocks and tree stumps had been bulldozed over to the edge of the property.

With a shudder Mark imagined the scene fifty years earlier: the boyfriend parking his car on that same gravel driveway, pounding on the heavy oak front door, pulling out his revolver, and putting a bullet into the head of Richard Lewiston's sister when she answered his knock.

Mark returned to his car, and as he pulled out of the driveway he noticed the "FOR SALE" sign with the added slat affixed to the top: "SOLD." The realtor was Bernard Oldman. While it was unfortunate that Carl Lewiston wasn't able to buy the house, it was good that the property would have a new owner. Give the old place a new lease on life.

Mark made a note to himself to find out who had bought the house.

That afternoon Chris Mark knocked on the office door of Brianna Collar, Esq. Like many law offices in small cities and towns, this one was located in a former private home, a grand turn-of-the-century residence on Middle Street in downtown Gloucester. In the old days, Middle Street was the street between Prospect, which runs along the crest of the hill above the harbor, and Main Street, which used to be the street closest to the water. But over the years the land between the wharves was filled in and a new street—Rogers Street—was created that serviced the docks. So now Middle Street wasn't in the middle of anything, but it still retained its share of magnificent old houses that housed condos, law firms, and the occasional bed and breakfast.

Mark pushed open the door with its oval panel of frosted glass. The receptionist smiled and waved him toward a second door. He dutifully opened the second door and entered a corner office with double-hung windows and a plaster medallion in the ceiling.

A well-dressed woman rose to greet him.

"Mr. Mark? Brianna Collar. Please sit down. How may I help you?"

"As I'm sure you know," said Mark as he pulled up the old leather-upholstered armchair that faced her big desk, "I'm assisting Chief Frontiero with an investigation."

"Ah yes." She resumed her seat and appraised Mark from behind big headlight eyeglasses. "Carl Lewiston. Very unfortunate. Today's paper said he was found in the alley behind his bar."

"Yes. An apparent heroin overdose. We're just trying to tie up some loose ends."

"Of course. Due diligence. Well, I'm not sure what I can add to the story. I didn't know him very well."

"But you know his father," said Mark.

"Yes. I'm the conservator for Richard Lewiston. I was appointed by the court."

"I happened to drive by the house on Cliff Lane today," said Mark. "It's a marvelous piece of property. I understand it was recently sold to a Ms. Diane Wheaton."

Collar nodded. "Unfortunately, selling the house was inevitable. Richard Lewiston will never be able to manage his own affairs again, and his estate owes the Commonwealth of Massachusetts for his care at a state facility. After careful consideration, it was determined that liquidation of this major asset was in the best interests of my client."

"According to RealtyTrac, the selling price was two and a half million," said Mark. "The realtor was Bernard Oldman. How did you come to choose him?"

"I don't recall. A recommendation from someone. You know how it is—you go online, you see a few names, you make a few phone calls. Someone says yeah, this guy is good, so you give him a call. Everything checks out and you say okay, let's see what this person can do."

"Did Carl Lewiston make an offer on the house?"

"I think he did. There were several offers. We took the best one." Collar's eyes narrowed. "Forgive me, Mr. Mark, but what does any of this have to do with the accidental drug overdose of a man who owns a bar on

Rogers Street? I mean, it couldn't it be any more obvious, could it? He comes from a troubled family. He has a drug habit. He makes a mistake. It's tragic but it happens. I feel sorry for the family. But that's the way it is for some people. Life hands them the short straw."

As Chris Mark walked back to his car he noticed that it was covered with what looked like yellow pine needles. He had parked it next to a big larch tree, which resembles an evergreen but is actually deciduous, and in the autumn they lose their needle-like leaves. After brushing off the pesky needles and getting into his car Mark took out his mobile phone.

"Chief? Mark here. You still like O'Doule for the murder? Yes, I agree he's the obvious suspect. If you want to bring him in, okay, but don't charge him yet. I've got a few more people to talk to. There are too many loose ends. I hate loose ends—one of 'em could come back and hang you. My next stop should be interesting. I'll call you later."

He eased the Camaro along Middle Street, through downtown, and along the coast towards Rockport. It was a beautiful autumn day and as he passed Good Harbor Beach he glanced wistfully at the wetsuited surfers poised on their boards, waiting for that one wave that was worth chasing.

For about a mile the road twisted and turned, following the rugged coast, until Mark saw the faux-antique sign that read GLEN HILL NURSING AND REHABILITATION CENTER. The facility was an all-purpose warehouse for the elderly and infirm who could not afford an upscale retirement village home or assisted living facility. For the lower-income geriatric set, this was the last stop before Calvary Cemetery.

The air inside smelled of disinfectant. The reception area was furnished with a vinyl-clad sofa and two big potted plants that, after a cursory glance, were revealed to be plastic. Behind a counter sat a woman in starchy white. She regarded Chris Mark with curiosity.

Mark glanced at her gold-colored Glen Hill nametag. "Hello, Grace—perhaps you can help me," he said in his friendliest tone.

"I'll do my best," she replied.

"I'd like to visit Richard Lewiston."

"Well, I don't know. You know that his son just passed away? I'm not sure that Mr. Lewiston's doctor would want him to have visitors. You're not a family member—?"

"No, I'm not. I'm a friend of Carl's. I just wanted to express my condolences to Mr. Lewiston and perhaps have a few words with him. I know he must be under a great deal of stress. To lose your child is a terrible thing."

"He doesn't get many visitors—Carl was the only one who came regularly, other than the woman from the court."

"Brianna Collar?"

"Yes," replied Grace. She leaned forward. "Richard adored his son. But Ms. Collar? Not so much. Whenever she visited him, after she left he'd be in a rotten mood. Morose. As if she brought him nothing but bad news. So now that Carl is gone, I don't know what's going to happen."

"His doctor must visit him too? I can't recall his name—doctor—?"

"Yellin. Franklin Yellin. Yes, of course he comes by. Once a week or so."

"So then—may I see Richard for a few minutes?"

"I suppose it would cheer him up. You'll find him in his room. Number twelve. On your left as you go down the hall."

As Mark made his way along the fluorescent corridor with its painfully cheery paintings of flowers bolted to the walls between the open doors, he glanced into the rooms and imagined himself a son or grandson visiting mom or grandma, and felt the inevitable hopelessness that comes with the knowledge that for the residents this dreary place was the end of the line.

At the threshold of door number twelve Mark knocked softly. "Mr. Lewiston?" he said to the man sitting in an upholstered chair looking out the window. The man turned—more quickly, thought Mark, than someone whose limbs were stiff with age. According to his file, Richard Lewiston was a relatively young seventy-two years old. He was not here because his body had broken down; it was his spirit.

"Yeah?" replied Lewiston. His brown eyes were sharp under furrowed brows.

"My name's Chris Mark." He advanced a few steps into the room. It was furnished with a single bed, dresser, and a small table with a wooden captain's chair. "I was hoping to have a few words with you. I'm assisting the Gloucester Police Department."

"Is it about Carl?"

"Yes." Mark drew up the captain's chair and sat. "I'm very sorry for your loss."

"Thank you. It was a damned shame. He was a fine boy. A fine boy."

"How long have you lived here, sir?" asked Mark.

"They put me in here—I don't know—maybe two years ago. I lose track of time."

"Did you see Carl very often? Did he come visit?"

"Oh sure," Lewiston nodded emphatically. "He'd come at least every week. He'd bring magazines and cookies. We'd sit and talk."

"Did you ever get any indication that he was using any kind of controlled substance?"

"Never!" Lewiston stabbed the air with his finger. "He once told me that he tried all the usual intoxicants when he was a kid, but he didn't go for them. They didn't appeal to him. What he liked was collecting wine. The good stuff. It was a hobby. No harm in that, is there?"

"No sir. No harm in that. I suppose the police told you how he died."

"Yeah, they told me. It told them it was a crock of shit. Somebody got it wrong. That medical examiner screwed up."

"Okay," said Mark. Richard Lewiston was becoming agitated. It was time to change the subject. "I drove by the house on Cliff Lane today. It's a nice piece of property. It was in your family a long time?"

"My parents bought the house. Back in nineteen-forty, when they were first married. They raised me and my sister there. Then Rebecca got shot there. I suppose you know that. Tore up my parents. They were never the same after. When my mother died I inherited the house. I tried my best with it but I had a hard time. I guess it just wasn't meant to be. The city took it and the court decided to sell it."

"That would be Brianna Collar—the conservator?"

"Yeah." Lewiston shrugged. "She calls the shots. She supervised the sale and made the deal with the people who bought the house."

"What was the sale price?"

"I don't remember exactly. Brianna told me that I could expect to receive two million. Just enough to pay my creditors. But there was something funny going on."

"Why do you say that?"

"One of the last times that Carl came to see me, he was excited because he was ready to put an offer on the house. He wanted the house to stay in the family. I guess he has better memories of it than I do. Anyway, he and his girlfriend had raised enough for a down payment, and he was going to get qualified for a mortgage. He thought he had a pretty good shot at getting the house. So did I. But it was Brianna Collar's decision. You'd think that someone representing me would be inclined to sell the house to the kid who grew up in it. But no. She chose someone else."

"Carl and his girlfriend got the money together? Do you know her name?"

"Lacie something. Sanborn. Lacie Sanborn. Lives across the bridge in Magnolia. She's no shrinking violet and she gave as good as she got, but they got along okay."

"What do you mean?" asked Mark. "Did they argue?"

"Oh, I dunno," shrugged Lewiston. "It's none of my business. But one day when they both came here to visit me I heard them arguing outside the door. I thought the nurse would come along and make them stop, but after a minute or two they came into the room and they seemed happy. I could tell there was some tension, but hey, what two people don't go at it once in a while? It don't mean nothing."

"Was it drinking? Another girlfriend or boyfriend?"

"All I could make out was Carl telling Lacie that they would discuss her boyfriend on the way home. That's all I heard before they came into the room."

At that moment Mark heard someone at the door. He turned to see a man in a white coat.

"Excuse me," said the man. "Who are you?"

"Name's Chris Mark. I was just visiting Richard for a few minutes."

"Well, visiting hours are over," said the man.

"And you are—?"

"I'm Doctor Franklin Yellin. Mr. Lewiston is under my care. I will thank you to excuse us now."

Mark turned to Lewiston, who gave a hapless shrug. "It's time to take my pills."

"Thanks for your time, Richard," said Mark. "It was a pleasure to see you. I'll come back sometime."

Lewiston nodded.

Dr. Yellin stood silently as Mark eased out of the room. Once he was in the corridor he heard the soft click of the closing door.

Chris Mark parked his car under the towering oak tree and walked to the broad porch of the house. Here in the village of Magnolia, a section of Gloucester located not on the peninsula of Cape Ann but on the mainland, the vibe was laid back, almost sleepy. Life moved at a slower pace here, unlike a century ago when the seaside village had been a popular resort getaway for the rich folks from Boston and New York. But the grand old wooden hotels had long since burned down, and whatever big money was left was discreetly hidden behind the walls of a handful of mansions tucked away down long driveways.

The handsome neocolonial house with a water view had become a duplex condo. Two front doors with two mailboxes. In the little name slot of one of the mailboxes was a paper slip that read "L. SANBORN." Mark pressed the corresponding doorbell. From within came a melodious chime. Footsteps. Then the door was opened by a trim woman with shoulder length straight brown hair.

"Good afternoon—Ms. Sanborn? Chris Mark. I phoned you a few minutes ago."

"Yes, of course," she replied in a clipped voice. "Call me Lacie. Come on in." She led him through the living room to the kitchen. The air smelled of pasta and sauce. "Do you want something to eat?" she said. "Friends have brought me a lot of food. On account of Carl passing away."

"No thanks," replied Mark. "I just wanted to talk to you about a few things."

"How can I help you?" she said. She leaned with her back against the counter. Since Lacie did not sit down, neither did Mark.

"I'm sorry for your loss. For how long did you know Carl Lewiston?"

"We met two years ago. At the Red Lantern. I was there with some girlfriends. He came over to talk to us and we hit it off. We started dating. Everything went well and about a year later we decided to get married."

"Is that why you wanted to help him buy the house?"

"Yes. I felt so sorry for him and the family. It's a beautiful old house. Well, it used to be. His father couldn't maintain it and it just kind of fell apart. But we were going to fix it up. Restore it. Carl wanted to get his father out of that nursing home and let him live there. The house is huge, so I didn't care—we could all live there with rooms to spare. And Richard is a sweet guy. He deserves better."

"I heard that you had been arguing with Carl. He thought you had a boyfriend."

Lacie rolled her eyes. "A silly thing. I happened to be downtown one day and I ran into Skip O'Doule. We were both hungry so we went into the Black Gull. We had coffee and fifteen minutes later we left. As we walked out the door we practically ran over Carl. He acted unconcerned about it and I went back to work. At his place later on that evening he ripped into me. We had a big fight. I didn't realize how jealous Carl could be. So I just played it cool and let him know that he had nothing to worry about."

"Did that affect your plans to buy the house?"

"The house quickly became a moot point," said Lacie bitterly. "The damned conservator gave it to another buyer. We were both shocked."

"Tell me about it."

"When the city seized the house and we learned that it was going to be sold, of course we were upset but we weren't surprised. We had seen it coming. Carl's money was tied up in the bar, and if he sold out and put his cash up for the house he'd have no income. So it took us a while to save up two hundred thousand dollars. Money doesn't grow on trees, right? I sold some stock I had inherited and we made our offer. Two and a half million dollars. The house was listed at two point eight million, which everyone knew was too high. The realtor—Bernard Oldman—told us we had a good shot. We assumed that because we were family, Brianna Collar would take our offer. So we waited. And we waited. Then suddenly it was announced that some bitch named Diane Wheaton was the buyer. And the price was two and a half million! Carl was furious. But what could he do? Nothing. His own father couldn't do anything. It was all up to the court."

"Why do you think that Brianna Collar awarded the sale to Diane Wheaton and not to you?'

"I have no idea. She was not required to give an explanation."

"With Carl dead, the only living relative of Richard Lewiston is his younger son Jeremy."

"You can forget about him," scoffed Lacie. "He moved to Hawaii. Grows pot for a living. Hasn't been back East in years. Said he just couldn't deal with it. I'm paying for Carl's funeral. I don't even want Jeremy involved."

"Seems like substance abuse runs in the family," said Mark. "The medical examiner said Carl died of a heroin overdose. Injected."

"That's crazy," said Lacie. She shook her head. "I never knew him to touch the stuff. He knew the family history was bad. He made a real effort to stay straight. He'd drink too much once in a while, but who doesn't? He took his wine collection seriously. He wanted to get out of the low-end bar business and go more upscale. More like a wine bar, like they have in Boston and New York. He thought the idea could work in Gloucester. People are becoming more sophisticated and there are more tourists. He thought the timing was right."

"So once you lost your chance for the house, Carl should have had a nice little nest egg saved up that he could use towards a new business. He could sell out to O'Doule and open his wine bar. Did he talk to you about that?"

"When we lost the house he was pissed. So yeah, I asked him. I thought maybe it was time to move on. Forget the house and look to the future. But Carl said to me that it wasn't over yet. He said that we should be patient, and that we had lost the battle but we were going to win the war. That's what he said. We were going to win the war."

"Where were you on Friday night?"

"Carl was at the bar until five. He told me that he got the car washed on the way home—the seagulls poop all over the cars that are parked downtown, and Carl hated having a dirty car. At six-thirty he and I went out to dinner at Fred's Clam Shack. I was in the mood for fried calamari. We left around eight. Carl told me that he had to meet someone about a business matter. I asked him who. He said don't worry—he didn't want me to get involved. Then he said that I should remember what he had said about winning the war. He said he'd call me later that night. I went home. He never called."

Chief Frontiero rubbed his forehead. "It's been a long day. I'm gonna go home and watch the Pats game. I don't care if the world ends." He closed the menu of the Harborside Restaurant, the venerable eatery on the waterfront that had been serving up comfort food since Frontiero was a kid working summers on a fishing boat. "I know what I want. The biggest boiled lobster they've got. How about you?"

"You do the surf, I'll do the turf," said Chris Mark. "Meat loaf. With mashed potatoes."

The waitress nodded, and once the question of side dishes had been settled she left them to their glasses of beer.

"Are you still not convinced that O'Doule is our guy for the Lewiston case?" asked Frontiero. "Jeremy Lewiston is the victim's only legal heir. From what I hear he doesn't give a crap about the Red Lantern and he'd sell out to O'Doule in a heartbeat."

"The house bothers me," said Mark. "According to Lacie Sanborn, she and Carl made an offer of two point five million. That's more than enough to pay the back taxes, pay Richard's long-term care bills to the state, and give Richard a bit of money too. Even though selling the house to Carl and Lacie was the rational choice, Brianna Collar accepted an identical offer from a stranger. Something is rancid about the way the sale was handled." Mark took out his mobile phone and began a search. "Brianna Collar told me that she didn't know the realtor, Bernard Oldman. She said that she found him online, just like anyone else would. I'm wondering if she's telling the truth. So I'm seeing if they show up anywhere together. And sure enough—look at this!" He turned the phone so that Frontiero could see it. "Two years ago the nonprofit organization Ocean Arts held a fund raising event. An auction and a dinner dance. Here's a photo of the auction committee. There are five people on the committee. Two of those five people are Brianna Collar and Bernard Oldman. They're even standing next to each other."

"So they knew each other," said Frontiero. "That doesn't make either one of them a murderer."

"Yeah, but it makes Brianna Collar a liar."

"Okay," said Frontiero as he wiped his buttery fingers on a paper napkin. "But what's the motive? Why should either of them care who buys the house? The price is the price. Two point five million from any buyer is two point five million. Unless maybe there's some connection between Collar, Oldman, and O'Doule. Maybe all three of them had some reason to give Carl Lewiston an early date with the grim reaper." He picked up a lobster claw, found that he had already picked it clean, and tossed it back on his plate. "Time is running out. We need to find the motive soon, or else the medical examiner is going to rule the death accidental and that will be the end of it."

Mark finished his beer. "What I see is a conspiracy. One that got out of control and ended up with a murder. My next stop is Carl Lewiston's apartment."

In the red glow of sunset the living room of Carl Lewiston's apartment looked as if the occupant had left only a few minutes earlier. A lightweight baseball jacket was tossed casually on the tan leather sofa. Next to it lay the remote control for the television. On the glass-topped coffee table was an empty bottle of wine. Chris Mark picked it up. A nice bottle of domestic Pinot Grigio, and definitely high end—not your usual supermarket swill. On the beige walls hung framed posters from California vineyards. An exercycle stood in the corner.

Mark moved into the kitchen. Pinned to the refrigerator with little magnets in the shapes of fruits were photos of Carl and Lacie in happier times—some at the beach and others eating dinner at a seaside restaurant. There was a photo of his father too. A pile of magazines filled a corner by the back door—mostly copies of *Wine Spectator* and *People.*

The bedroom was furnished with an unmade bed and a bureau with a mirror. More family photos were stuck on the mirror in the space between the glass and the wooden frame.

Placed against the window with a view of the harbor was a plain metal desk. On the green blotter was an open laptop. Next to the laptop was a stack of papers and file folders. On a small table next to the desk a printer stood with its "on" light illuminated.

After moving the black leather office chair aside Mark carefully picked through the stack of papers. The usual utility bills. Documents relating to the Red Lantern's operations. An unfinished novel.

Mark picked up a file folder on the front of which was handwritten "House—Copies." He opened it and riffed through the papers, which, as the folder title suggested, were photocopies of original documents. The offer to purchase was here. But there was more. Much more.

Mark punched a number on his phone. "Chief? We have what we need. Let me turn some screws on a certain individual. All I need is backup. Thanks."

"Mr. Mark, it's very late," said Bernard Oldman. His gaunt face peered through the narrow space created when he had opened the door—ever so slightly—to his house in the exclusive neighborhood of Eastern Point. "I cannot see what the urgency is."

"I understand, Mr. Oldman," replied Mark evenly. "But certain developments have come to light in the death of Carl Lewiston, and your cooperation will help the police make an arrest. May I come in?"

"I have no idea how I can help you, but if you must come in, I'll give you a few minutes. I have an important showing tomorrow morning and more work to do tonight." Reluctantly he opened the door wide and stepped back. Older than sixty, the realtor looked like tall matchstick topped by a shock of close-cropped white hair.

Stepping across the threshold, Mark entered the vestibule with its cool flagstone floor.

"Let's sit in the living room," said Oldman as he led the way through a set of pocket doors.

Mark waited for Oldman to sit on the sofa, after which he took a seat on a plain ladderback chair.

"I must advise you, Mr. Oldman, that at this moment a police detective is speaking with Brianna Collar. We expect her to be very cooperative."

"What are you saying?" fumed Oldman. "Cooperative how? For what?"

"Another detective is interviewing Diane Wheaton. She is also expected to be cooperative."

"I don't know what you're getting at," glowered Oldman.

"Carl Lewiston had the whole scheme figured out," said Mark. "Brianna Collar got herself appointed to be the conservator of Richard Lewiston. Normally this is a tedious, thankless job. You do it because the court asks you to do it. But Collar knew that Lewiston owned a very valuable home that was heading towards foreclosure. All she had to do was arrange the right sale to the right person under the right conditions and she could make herself a nice chunk of change. So the first phone call she made was to you. When I first interviewed her she told me that she didn't know you before she hired you. Of course that was a lie, wasn't it? You two go way back."

"Yes, I've known Brianna for many years," replied Oldman. "So what?"

"Once she had you on board to make sure the real estate deal was set up properly, the next step was to find the right buyer. Obviously that could not be Carl

Lewiston, for the simple reason that he and his girlfriend are honest people. They would never defraud Carl's father out of half a million dollars."

"You can't prove any of that!" spat Oldman.

"The offer from Diane Wheaton for two point five million was accepted," continued Mark. "The same offer from Carl Lewiston was rejected. Here's why. The sales agreement that you wrote between Wheaton and Collar included some very profitable clauses. Let's talk about the money, because that's what this is all about. For your commission you were paid a cool five percent. That's one hundred and twenty-five thousand dollars for very little work. But what about the other fifteen percent?"

"What are you talking about?" demanded Oldman.

"Richard Lewiston told me that Collar told him to expect two million dollars—just enough to pay his debts and keep him in a crummy rest home until they shipped him off to Calvary Cemetery. Carl Lewiston's research backed this up. To buy the house, Diane Wheaton paid two point five million. The difference is twenty percent, or five hundred thousand dollars. We know that five percent of the purchase price went into your pocket as your realtor's commission. In a legitimate deal that would leave Ms. Collar with nothing for her troubles. But you wrote an escrow agreement into the contract. The escrow agreement states that fifteen percent—three hundred and seventy-five thousand dollars—was to be placed in escrow to pay for property cleanup if necessary. Now there's a sweet deal! As you had arranged, a scant week after papers were passed, the proud new owner, Diane Wheaton, billed the estate three hundred and seventy-five thousand dollars! She claimed that lead had been found in the soil on the property. Of course, several previous inspections had found no trace of lead. It doesn't matter; all Wheaton had to do was make her phony claim. So the escrow account refunded Wheaton three hundred and seventy-five thousand dollars for her phantom lead removal, and she kicked it back to

Brianna Collar. Everyone went home happy except Richard and Carl Lewiston, who both got screwed."

"You've got a flimsy case that means nothing," sneered Oldman.

"You've got a point. Normally such a deal would be consigned to the cesspool of countless other slimy real estate ripoffs, and would be forgotten. But Carl Lewiston didn't forget. He was pissed and he kept digging. He discovered this shady deal and he threatened to expose the three of you. So Brianna Collar invited Lewiston to her office to negotiate. We know he parked in the driveway of Collar's office because on Cape Ann there is only one larch tree situated near a street or driveway. Every autumn, larch trees shed their distinctive yellow needles. We found them on Lewiston's car. At the meeting, Collar told Lewiston that if he backed off, she would have the sale nullified. She offered him a glass of wine. A vintage that he would appreciate. You were there too. The wine was spiked with Rohypnol. Once Lewiston was unconscious, you could take your time. You waited until one in the morning before injecting him with heroin. When you were sure he was dead you put him in his car and drove it to the alley, where you dumped him. You parked his car on the street and threw away the keys."

"This is completely outrageous," sputtered Oldman.

Mark leaned forward. "Here's what you need to know. A single fingerprint was found on the syringe. I know that it belongs to either you or Brianna Collar. Once we arrest both of you and take your prints, we'll know. By that time the district attorney will not be willing to cut any deals. You'll be sent to Cedar Junction and she'll go to MCI-Framingham. The only hope for you is if you start talking now."

"It's Brianna Collar's fingerprint!" shouted Oldman. "I gave Lewiston the roofies. She had the dope. It was her plan. She ran the deal from the beginning to the end. The bitch even promised me a cut of the lead removal fee, and then after the deal was made she told me that I wasn't getting another cent—I should be happy with my commission! When Carl Lewiston threatened to call the attorney general's office, Collar freaked out. She called me and told me that we had to get rid of the guy. She was planning on running for the state senate and she didn't need to have a scandal dog her. 'Either we win together or we lose together' is what she said. I'm not gonna let her pin this thing on me!"

Mark tapped his mobile phone. "Chief? We have our guy. Send the officers into the house. We're in the living room. You can go ahead and arrest Brianna Collar and Diane Wheaton too. Mr. Oldman will testify against them. Tomorrow morning I'll pay a visit to Richard Lewiston—he'll want to know that we've got the people who murdered his son."

Missed Deadline

The light dusting of seasonal pollen across the windshield told Chris Mark that the gray Toyota Corolla had not been moved recently. The doors were not locked. The key was in the ignition. No personal items—no purse, no phone—were found in the car.

Mark opened the back door on the driver's side. On the seat he found a college sweatshirt, a few plastic water bottles, and a baseball cap. No blood. No signs of a struggle.

The trunk was inspected. Nothing there but a dusty road emergency kit.

According to the registration in the glove box, the owner of the car was Abbie Danson.

The young reporter had been missing for nearly three days. On Wednesday at six o'clock Abbie had walked out the front door of the *Gloucester Tribune*. On Thursday morning she didn't show up for work. Phone calls to her number went to voicemail. That afternoon her boss, the editor of the *Tribune*, had filed the missing persons report. With her family living in another state, the editor had assumed there was no one else to notice her star reporter was gone.

"Now that we've found the car," said Mark as he replaced the registration in the glove box, "we need to find the girl."

After stripping off the latex gloves, Mark rubbed the back of his neck. Eight o'clock on a Saturday morning was too damned early to be doing anything except sleeping off a hangover. The band last night at the Anchor Club had played solid blues and the drinks had been light on the ice. Mark hadn't scored, but an occasional tumble into his own bed, alone, wouldn't kill him. And then at dawn his phone had rung. Chief

Ray Frontiero needed his help. Sure, chief. Just let me get showered and dressed and I'll be right down. Where's the car? On Wayland Street. Off the beaten path. Okay, see you there.

"The car isn't giving me much," said Mark. "Abbie could have driven it here and walked away. Or the perp may have driven it here and dumped it. I assume your guys have interviewed the neighbors?"

"Yeah," answered Frontiero. "A woman who lives two doors down remembers seeing the car here on Thursday morning. But no one saw who parked it."

"No credit card or phone activity since Abbie left work?" said Mark.

"Records indicate that the last time Abbie used her bank card was Wednesday evening at nine," replied Frontiero. "She bought gas at the Hess station on Rogers Street. The security camera caught her. She was alone."

"And then twelve hours later her car shows up here," said Mark. "Okay—I'm going to talk to her boss."

The offices of the *Gloucester Tribune* overlooked the sweeping curve of Stacy Boulevard, which fronted Gloucester's broad outer harbor and was home to the big bronze "Man at the Wheel" statue. Like many struggling regional rags in the age of the Internet, the *Tribune* was lucky to roll the presses every day and make payroll every two weeks. The paper survived on its comics section, high school sports, fish industry reporting, food articles, and an opinion page featuring a reliable supply of angry letters from local loudmouths on both ends of the political spectrum. While this living embodiment of nineteenth-century mechanical technology stubbornly defied the onslaught of the digital tsunami, no one at the paper was getting rich.

Chris Mark pushed open the glass door and presented himself to the receptionist ensconced behind her plain grey desk.

"You'd like to see Pauline Weston?" she asked. "Who may I say is calling?"

"Chris Mark. I'm assisting the police with an investigation."

"Oh—you must mean Abbie," said the receptionist. "I hope she's okay. I mean, I'm sure she's okay."

"I'm happy that you're sure, but why?" asked Mark.

"Oh, I don't know. I guess just because she's a smart girl. Knows how to take care of herself. Anyway, you can go right in. Pauline's expecting you."

Leaving the receptionist to her blinking phones, Mark knocked on the door marked "P. WESTON—EDITOR."

"Yeah, come in," said a gruff female voice.

As Mark pushed open the door the heavy scent of cigarettes hit him like an old sneaker slapping him across his face. On the broad desk, nestled among piles of papers and books and junk, sat a big ashtray full of butts. Mark marveled that in this day and age anyone still smoked at work.

"You're Chris Mark?" said Weston without looking up from her computer screen. "Have a seat. It's a damned shame about Abbie. Got us worried. I hope we didn't miss some sort of warning sign." She coughed. It was a gravelly resonant hack. In his mind's eye Mark could see the pink flesh of Weston's lungs coated with layers of deep black of tar and years of tobacco residues. There wasn't much oxygen getting into this woman's bloodstream.

"What sign could there have been?" asked Mark. "Does anyone have it in for her?"

"Just about every crooked politician or dope dealer from Boston to Maine," said Weston. "She's good at digging up dirt. I call her 'the gold miner.' Every afternoon at deadline I ask her, 'What nugget did you unearth today? Medicare fraud? State employees who double dip? Shenanigans on Beacon Hill? More crimes against the fishing industry perpetrated by the federal government?' She's always got a couple of good stories in development. She publishes only once or twice a week, but she's worth it."

"How about here at work? Get along with everyone?"

"Oh sure." Weston leaned forward. "All the guys have the hots for her. You know what I mean. But as far as I can tell there's nothing going on. At least not here in the office."

"The last time you saw her was Wednesday at six?"

"Yes." Another pause for a deep and watery hack. Then a good clear breath. "She didn't show up for the staff meeting on Thursday morning. I called her and got voicemail. Tried a few more times during the day. Finally I called the police."

"I need to see her computer," said Mark.

"Sure. I'll have Gary help you."

Weston made a call. A moment later a young man poked his head in the door. Mark followed him through the maze of desks in the newsroom to the last cubicle on the left.

Mark noticed that tacked to the grey fabric surface of the dividers in Abbie's little space were a handful of pleasant beach scenes. No personal photos.

"Does Abbie have a boyfriend?" asked Mark.

Gary shrugged. "Last year she was seeing a guy. They broke up a few months ago. She dates once in a while. No one special that I know of. Not for a lack of supply—every guy who meets her falls in love with her. She's one hot cookie."

"How about you?" asked Mark.

"I've got a boyfriend, thank you very much."

Gary sat in Abbie's chair. With a few taps on the keys the monitor sprang to life.

"Show me the stories she's working on now," said Mark.

Gary obligingly sorted the document folders by date.

"Okay," said Mark as he read the first file. "She's got notes on the new shopping center construction project. The flagship store is thirty feet higher than specified on the permit. The city may sue the developer, whose name is Larry Pickett. The project is getting bigger, and Abbie writes that Pickett is moving ahead without amending his agreements with city hall. Pickett figures that once something is built, it's impossible to tear it down."

Mark opened and studied the next folder. "Here's a story about how a community activist is trying to block a hotel development on the site of an abandoned factory. The property has been vacant for twenty years. It's prime real estate. Right now the parcel is an eyesore with zero value, but this activist—his name is Claude Fontaine—says that a hotel will destroy the character of the neighborhood and that it violates zoning restrictions. He claims the city council has no authority to create a zoning override so that the hotel can be built.

"Next we have some notes on a murder case from five years ago. A guy named Gary Oldston was convicted of shooting his boss after the guy fired him. Oldston has been set free on a legal technicality. A technician at the State Police crime lab has confessed to falsifying evidence, and convictions are being overturned all over the state.

"There's one more—an investigative piece on that secretive religious cult whose leader lives in the big castle on the coast. Abbie says that Stephen Hawks, the founder of the Church of the One Divine Kingdom, has subjected his followers to a pattern of mind control and virtual slavery. He makes them turn over all of their assets to the cult. There is a fear that he's preparing them for an apocalyptic mass suicide."

"Like Jim Jones did in Guyana with the Peoples Temple," said Gary. "Back in 1978 he convinced over nine hundred of his followers to poison themselves. It was one of the biggest mass suicides in history."

At that moment Mark peered at the monitor. "That's odd," he said. "See that tiny red light on the front of the computer? The internal camera is on."

"The one you use for video conference calls," added Gary. "Let's see... I'm not sure how it was activated. Perhaps Abbie had something set up."

The light blinked off.

"Hmmm," said Gary. "Oh, well. Must have been some peculiar computer thing."

"Okay," said Mark. "Thanks for your help. Make sure no one touches this computer. Right now we've got a missing persons case, but if that changes we'll need to bring the computer and all of Abbie's paper files down to the station."

"What'll you gentlemen have today?" said the waitress as Chief Frontiero perused the lunch menu at the Harborside Restaurant.

"I'm thinking about fish and chips," said the chief.

"I'll stick with a burger and fries," said Chris Mark. "Medium rare. Swiss on the burger. Coffee."

"What have we got so far?" said the chief after the waitress had left them alone at a table by the window overlooking the busy harbor.

"Abbie Danson, age twenty-seven, beautiful but tough reporter for the *Tribune*, not afraid to get in people's faces," said Mark. "I've got a binder full of people who would be happy to see her go away. And then there's the possibility of a jilted lover. That would be another binder full of men, including a few at the paper. We need to start somewhere—anywhere. Did you get the phone record?"

"Yeah," said Frontiero. "Right here." He took a paper from a folder and slid it across the table.

"She made and received a lot of calls," said Mark. "On our list is just about every suspect or their lawyer. She was talking to the guy who's developing the shopping center and the guy who's trying to block the hotel. Also the convicted murderer who's getting released, and a representative from the cult. The last conversation she had was at five minutes after nine. That would be just after she bought gas at the Hess station. The number she called was 978-555-3495. She spoke for a minute and a half. During the past two months she's had calls to and from this number almost every day. Let's see—" he tapped a lookup number on his phone. "The number is a landline. It belongs to a Timothy Berdon. And Timothy Berdon is—" he punched a search— "Thirty years old. Works at a high-end metal fabrication company in Gloucester called FormCo. He lives over in Lanesville. Has a degree in mechanical engineering. Tufts University. Not bad—one rung below Ivy League. Sounds like a boyfriend. I wonder why he hasn't called the cops to report Abbie missing. Let's pay him a visit and get his side of the story."

It was two in the afternoon when Chris Mark pulled his Camaro into the parking lot at FormCo. The company occupied a sleek unadorned two-level box of a building in Gloucester's bustling Blackburn Center, a village of tech and light manufacturing companies huddled on the high ground next to the highway leading into town. Mark pulled open the glass door and was greeted by a wall of chilled air that would have made a polar bear feel at home. The receptionist was redheaded and did not act like a stranger.

"Hi there," she beamed. "Welcome to FormCo. How may I help you?"

"I'm here to see Timothy Berdon. Name's Chris Mark."

"Yes," she smiled as she punched some buttons. "He'll be right out."

A moment later a tall, well-dressed man came through the swinging door that led to the offices next to the manufacturing floor. Without hesitation he extended his hand. His grip was confident.

"You wanted to see me about something?" he asked.

Mark steered Berdon away from the eager receptionist to a small seating area used by salespeople and job seekers. This afternoon there were neither, so they had the space to themselves.

"It's about Abbie Danson," said Mark. "Do you know her?"

"Sure I do," replied Berdon. His voice sounded ragged, and Mark could see the slight droop of fatigue in his eyes. "Nice girl. Works as a reporter for the *Tribune*."

"Would you call yourself her boyfriend?"

"No, not really. We're pretty casual."

"When was the last time you saw her?"

"I saw her on Sunday. We had dinner at the Lobsta House."

"How about phone calls?"

"The last time we spoke was on Wednesday night. About nine. I was leaving for Portland, Maine. Had to see a client early Thursday morning. It took me two days to get them sorted out. I got back last night after midnight. I haven't called or texted her yet today. Why? What's going on?"

"She's missing. She was last seen buying gas on Wednesday night. We found her car this morning. But we haven't found Abbie. Do you have any idea where she might be?"

Berdon's face turned ashen. "No, I don't," he stammered.

"What did you talk about during that last phone call?"

Berdon sat down in one of the vinyl-covered chairs. His slender fingers gripped the armrest as if he needed the support to stay upright. "Ummm—nothing much. She wished me luck in Portland. The client is one of the difficult ones. I told her I'd give her a call when I got back. She told me that she was free over the weekend, and we were going to try to get together."

"Did she say anything about where she was going on Wednesday night?"

"Yes. She said that she had to meet someone."

"Professional or personal?"

"For the paper. A story she was working on."

"She didn't say which story?"

"No. Just a story."

"Okay. Thanks."

Mark returned to his car. His next stop was Abbie's apartment on Overland Drive. Mark knew the building. The former elementary school, with its imposing brick exterior, tall windows, and a grand staircase up to the front door, had been converted to residential rental units. They don't build schools like that any more, except in very wealthy towns where the kids drive their own Audis and BMWs.

As Mark was pulling up to the curb in front of the apartments his phone rang. The tone said it was Frontiero. Mark answered.

Bad news. Gary Hiler, the young man from the *Tribune* who had showed Mark the computer used by Abbie Danson, had been found dead. Shot once in the back of the head as he sat in his car at a stop sign on the way out of the paper's parking lot. The police had detained a witness.

Mark drove to the scene, where Frontiero met him. The crime techs lifted the tarp covering the car. Hiler was still strapped in the driver's seat, slumped over the steering wheel. Blood and bits of skull and brains stained the dashboard.

The techs lowered the tarp over the grisly scene.

On a curb nearby the witness was sitting. Mark approached him.

"You saw what happened?" asked Mark.

"Yes," the guy nodded. He seemed dazed. "Gary was making a run to Dunkin' Donuts. My office faces the parking lot. I saw Gary get into his car. He drove to the stop sign at the end of the lot. I happened to notice a guy on a motor scooter pull up next to him. I thought maybe it was a friend and they were talking. Suddenly I saw something in the scooter guy's hand. There was a puff of smoke and Gary sort of lurched in his seat. The guy on the scooter jammed the object—a gun, I suppose—into his pocket and took off. I ran outside to Gary's car. I saw him sitting there. I could hear the scooter in the distance. I ran back to my car and raced out of the parking lot. I stopped to listen but I couldn't hear the scooter. I drove towards downtown but didn't see him. So I gave up and came back. By that time Kristen—our receptionist—had already called the police. When I dialed nine-one-one the officer said they were already on their way."

"How about the shooter? You said it was a guy. Are you sure it was a male? Do you remember anything about him or her?"

The witness shrugged. "Dark clothes and helmet. Could have been a woman, I suppose. He or she was wearing a sweatshirt that had a pocket. That's about it."

"How about the scooter?"

"It was dark too. Had small wheels covered by the fenders."

A uniformed officer approached Mark.

"Excuse me," said Mark as he turned to face the officer.

The cop pulled Mark aside. "Chief Frontiero asked me to tell you that a black scooter has been found abandoned on the road into Dogtown, in the woods," said the officer. "A hiker saw it lying on its side. The engine was still hot. The hiker called the police. We're taking the bike in for processing now."

"Gun?"

"No gun. But there's a slug buried in the dashboard of the victim's car."

Mark thought for a moment. Why Gary Hiler? Why now?

He took out his phone and punched a number. "Hello—Julio? I've got a job for you. Right away. Come down to the *Tribune*. Don't come in the main driveway entrance—you'll see that it's a crime scene. Go around back. Tell the cops you're here to see me. I'll be waiting in the reception area by the front door."

Mark went inside the building. The paper's employees, who had not yet been released by the police, were milling around wearing stunned expressions. No one was talking. Pauline Weston was in the lobby, standing with her arms folded. Tomorrow's paper was on hold.

"Ms. Weston," said Mark. "I'm going to need Abbie Dalton's cubicle. A man named Julio Rivera is meeting me here. No one else is to go near her space. Okay?"

Weston nodded. Mark walked through the deserted maze of desks. At the entrance to Abbie's cubicle he paused. The computer monitor was there, on the desk. The red light was lit. Mark took a post-it note and stuck it over the built-in camera lens.

As he expected, a moment later the red light went out.

"Hi Chris—you've got something for me?" said a familiar voice behind him.

Mark turned to see Julio. His bright brown eyes shone behind his horn-rimmed glasses. Julio always enjoyed a good piece of computer forensics.

"I need you to check out this computer," said Mark. "Tell me if it's infected."

"You got it, boss," said Julio. He took a seat in Abbie's chair and began to type commands.

After a few minutes Julio gave a low whistle.

"You've got something?" said Mark.

"Good thing you blocked the camera," replied Julio. He turned to face Mark. "This computer has a RAT."

"A remote access tool," said Mark.

"Yeah. It's a piece of software that allows an unauthorized operator to secretly control an infected computer as if he or she had physical access to that system. The operator directs the RAT through a network connection, which can be accessed through the Internet."

"The criminal can control everything in the victim's computer," said Mark. "They can use the on/off switch, log on and off the network, manage files, grab passwords, drop viruses and worms, and hijack the home page. They can also control the built-in camera."

"That's right," said Julio. "The remote operator can watch you as you work at the computer."

"And if you're a reporter, the interloper can access stories that you're working on," said Mark. "Any clue as to how this RAT program was introduced?"

"The most common way is through a Trojan horse—an attachment or external link that seems benign but is actually carrying the program. Typically you'll get an email that looks legitimate. You open the attachment and bingo! the spyware is downloaded. Your computer is toast. Or you'll download something off the Internet that looks okay, but it's really a virus. Same result: once it's in your computer, you're like a victim of a vampire. Your computer is one of the undead, doing its master's bidding. But rather than actually stealing from you, the remote operator usually uses your computer to send viruses to other computers. If the emails are tracked, the trail leads back to your computer. The crook gets away scot free."

"Is there anyway to know how long the RAT has been in place?" asked Mark.

"My guess is that it's been living inside this computer for at least two months. The operator has been very discreet. The goal was not to defraud Ms. Danson or steal from her, but to spy on her. If, for instance, they tried to hack into her bank account, she'd notice and alarm bells would go off."

"And some smart IT guy like you would detect the invader," said Mark.

"Exactly. Whoever planted the program didn't want anybody to find out about it. Ever."

"Here's the million-dollar question," said Mark. "Can you get the location of the invader from an IP address?"

"I'll try," said Julio as he worked the keyboard. "Geolocation involves deriving the city, ZIP code, or region from which a person is or has connected to the Internet by using their device's IP address or that of a wireless access point, such as those offered by coffee houses.

"Because a country name is required information when an IP range is allocated, and IP registrars supply that information for free, determining the host nation of an Internet user based on his or her IP address is relatively simple and accurate. But determining the physical location down to a city or ZIP code is more difficult and less accurate because there is no official source for the information, users sometimes share IP addresses, and Internet service providers often base IP addresses in a city where the company is basing operations. So it can be hit or miss. Ah—we have something here."

"What is it?" asked Mark.

"There's been an attempt to shield the source, but what I'm getting is that the origin of the malicious program is a computer located on Rocky Lane, over on the west side of town."

Mark quickly reviewed in his mind the stories that Abbie had been working on. He knew Rocky Lane. It was a very private road, not given to much traffic. The few residences on Rocky Lane enjoyed spectacular views across Ipswich Bay to the distant shores of the New Hampshire coast.

The most well known structure on Rocky Lane—and indeed, one of the most well known in the region of the North Shore—was Forsythe Castle.

In the nineteen-twenties Forsythe Castle had been constructed of solid Cape Ann granite in the style of the gothic manors of Europe. The owner, a wealthy American widow named Juliette Forsythe, had taken extensive tours of the Old Country. With a richly endowed checkbook she had bought fully intact interiors of bankrupt ancestral manors. After the rooms were disassembled, she had the pieces—including the furniture and artwork—carefully packed and shipped back to Gloucester. These interiors were meticulously fitted into the shell of the newly built château, so that upon entering by the wooden drawbridge the visitor was miraculously transported back eight hundred years to the age of chivalry.

After the death of Juliette Forsythe, the castle declined. It was expensive to maintain and the fortunes of her heirs couldn't keep pace. Finally in the nineteen-eighties the decrepit pile of stones was sold to the highest bidder, the Church of the One Divine Kingdom and its flamboyant leader, Stephen Hawks.

This was the man who was rumored to have subjected his many thousands of followers to a pattern of mind control and to lives of virtual slavery. It was even whispered that he was preparing his adherents for an apocalyptic mass suicide.

Whoever killed Gary Hiler had probably done something evil to Abbie Danson. Perhaps she had been murdered too. But her body had not yet been found.

Chris Mark assumed that because he and Gary had both been observed investigating Abbie's computer, he too was on the murderer's death list. The enemy was out there, watching. What was the best response?

The best defense was a strong offense. He needed to strike at the belly of the beast.

At ten o'clock the next morning Chris Mark wheeled his Camaro up to the big iron gates of Forsythe Castle. A small bronze plaque affixed to one of the stone pillars read "CHURCH OF THE ONE DIVINE KINGDOM—PRIVATE." Mark drove through the open gates and along the gravel drive. After negotiating a sharp curve to the right he rolled into a small parking area.

Before him loomed the castle. It was larger than he had expected, impressively detailed, and well maintained. The copper downspouts were gleaming and the shrubs were neatly trimmed. The gravel on the driveway appeared to have been raked.

There was big money at play here. What kind of people would want to commit suicide and leave all of this behind?

Mark crossed the faux moat and stood before the immense wooden door with its black iron bolts. Surely there had to be another entrance that was used by

Hawks and his cronies— something a bit more utilitarian. No matter—this was where the spokesperson for Hawks had told him to come. Mark pushed the little bronze buzzer. Presently a smaller door within the larger door opened.

"Yes?" said the mousy young man dressed in khakis and blue button-down shirt.

"Chris Mark for Minister Hawks."

"Of course. Please come in." The mousy man stepped aside and allowed Mark to enter the gloomy vestibule. "This way," he said.

The man led Mark up a curving flight of stone stairs. The handrail was of finely wrought black iron. Dim, dark oil paintings of pale people in renaissance garb lined the walls.

Mark and the man emerged into a vast great room over which soared a high vaulted ceiling. Around the perimeter of the room knights in gleaming medieval suits of armor stood guard. Hanging from the smooth stone walls were tapestries upon which more knights—these were on horseback—parried with coiled dragons blowing smoke from their nostrils. Here and there a unicorn pranced, unconcerned about the duels being fought in the woven landscape.

A long banquet table commanded the center of the room. It was attended by twenty heavy carved chairs and lit by a big chandelier made of antlers and lights that looked like candles.

At the end of the great hall soared a tall stained glass window, no doubt bought at a deep discount from an ancient private chapel in France whose owners had fallen on hard times after the carnage and upheaval of the First World War. On either side of the window hung two portraits, each in a carved gold frame. To the left was an older man with a halo behind his head. He looked vaguely Roman and was smiling. To the right was a middle-aged man with no halo. He was not smiling. He resembled a Hollywood movie star cast in the role of the dean of an exclusive private college.

"Quite an impressive room," said Mark as a conversation starter. His voice echoed in the vast space.

"Thank you," replied the mousy man.

"What do you use it for?" asked Mark.

"Special meetings."

Mark let the conversation wither. The man led him to a wide opening in the long wall of the room at the end by the stained glass window and the portraits. Mark now saw that above this opening was the balustrade of a balcony or gallery, from which you could observe the proceedings in the great room.

They entered the opening and ascended a set of stairs to the balcony, which was part of a long hallway that extended the length of the great room. The man led Mark past a marble bust of Julius Caesar and to a door. He knocked. A man's voice told them to enter. The mousy man pushed open the door and stood aside so that Mark could pass.

The room was an office. Behind a big ornate desk sat the middle-aged man who was depicted in one of the paintings. He was typing at a computer. On the burnished leather top of the desk there was nothing except a telephone and some books. Lining the walls of the office were bookshelves laden with leather-bound tomes. In the one space that was free of bookshelves hung a portrait of the haloed man that was similar to the one in the great room below. Floor lamps with silk shades and incandescent bulbs cast a warm glow. Heavy velvet drapes were drawn over the single tall window.

At that moment a side door opened. Silently into the room came a young woman wearing a plain skirt, blouse, and low heels. She gave Mark a quick uncertain glance before handing a paper to the man behind the desk. Without looking up he took the paper and began to read it. The woman tiptoed back through the door and closed it softly behind her.

The man set aside the paper. His sharp blue eyes met Mark's.

"Mr. Mark, how may I help you?" he said. His voice was as smooth as fine Cognac.

"You must be Minister Hawks." Mark hated the tedious and transparent mind games that powerful people enjoy playing, which often include not introducing themselves. You're supposed to know that their fame precedes them.

"Yes." Hawks made no movement. His gaze was steady.

"I'd like to ask you a few questions, if you don't mind."

"When you called you said it was something about a missing woman," said Hawks. "I'm happy to help but I have no idea how."

"Her name is Abbie Danson. She's a reporter for the *Tribune*. Does investigative stories. Crime and corruption—that sort of thing. She's pretty good at it too. Have you ever heard of her?"

"I suppose I've seen her name in the paper."

"She disappeared Wednesday night. Vanished. No phone calls, no charges on her credit card, no ATM withdrawals. We happen to know that at the time of her disappearance she was working on a story about the church."

Hawks smiled. "I cannot begin to tell you how many stories have been written about us. We've been under attack by the press for over fifty years, ever since our spiritual father, Hosiah Stewart, was commanded by God to found this church. Every week I see a new story—an exposé about the vast empire we're supposed to have, or a revelation about rooms full of treasure chests of diamonds and jewels. They're all rather ridiculous. I hope she wasn't wasting her time with such nonsense."

Mark shrugged. "Perhaps coincidentally, her computer had been hacked. Someone managed to implant a remote access tool. One of the things they did was control the camera on the monitor."

"I try to avoid computers whenever possible," said Hawks. "I'm forced to use this one for church communications. Otherwise I'd be happy if they had never been invented."

"Our technician traced the hacker to this address."

"That's absurd," replied Hawks coolly. "We're a church. Devoted to peace and goodwill. We don't hack into the computers of reporters or anyone else. Besides, I'm hardly an expert in this sort of thing, but isn't it true that tracing an IP address is an inexact science? In this neighborhood there are several houses. And next door to us is a state park where people park their campers. I'm sure that most of them have access to the Internet. Your hacker could be almost anyone."

"I'm just trying to do some legwork for the police department," said Mark. "With the shooting of the *Tribune* employee coming on the heels of the disappearance of Abbie Danson, the authorities are stretched pretty thin."

"Well, I'm sorry that you had to waste your time by coming here," replied Hawks.

"It hasn't been wasted. Just a few more questions. How many people live here?"

"Ten or fifteen. Church members come and go as they are assigned to ministries in other parts of the country and around the world. It is a great privilege to live here in Forsythe Castle. Additional members live in the surrounding area."

"The ones who live here—do you know where each of them was on Wednesday night?"

"Of course not," said Hawks. "I cannot possibly keep track of the daily comings and goings of everyone here."

"You've got a nice website," said Mark. "Very informative. On one page I read about how Hosiah Stewart was walking through the woods under a full moon and received a revelation. After writing down what had been revealed to him he began to preach. Despite opposition from the mainline religions his ministry grew. Fifteen years ago he died and you became the head of the church."

"Yes—?" said Hawks with impatience.

"Your webmaster and information technology guys—do they live here?

"Yes, of course. This is the communications center of the church."

"Mind if I have a word with them?"

"Yes, I do mind," Hawks said sharply. "This is a private facility. A church. You can't just come barging in here and pry into our business. I've been very generous with my time. Now if you'll excuse me I have work to do. Sister Juanita will show you out." He pressed a button under the edge of his desk. Almost instantly the side door opened and the woman whom Mark had seen earlier stepped in. After closing the side door behind her she went to the main door and opened it. With her hand on the doorknob she waited with her head lowered.

"Minister Hawks, thank you for your time," said Mark. He walked through the door and heard it close behind him. He waited for the woman to come around to lead him out. When she was abreast of him he spoke to her. "You name's Sister Juanita? That's a very pretty name."

"Thank you," she replied. She began to walk slowly along the hallway towards the stairs.

"Where's everybody else?" asked Mark. "Minister Hawks told me that ten or fifteen people live here. It's a pretty big place. What's everyone doing?"

"Working, mostly."

"And what's your job?"

"I help Minister Hawks in the office, keeping track of work hours and assignments."

"He runs a very tight ship," said Mark. "Very disciplined."

The girl seemed as though she were willing to talk. Mark walked as slowly as possible.

"Yes," said Juanita. "We all need to stay focused on the church. The life we have chosen is very demanding."

They came to the bust of Julius Caesar.

"It seems odd—if you don't mind my saying—that you've got a bust of a Roman emperor here," said Mark. "Wasn't he a pagan?"

"Our spiritual father admired many of the strong leaders from ancient times," replied Juanita. "Genghis Khan, Alexander the Great, Charlemagne—each of them transformed human civilization."

Mark paused to consider the sculpture. Juanita gave him an impatient look but allowed him the opportunity.

"Those were all ruthless men," said Mark. "They were not men of peace. They killed people."

"We are taught that harsh measures are sometimes necessary. You must meet evil with even greater force."

Mark looked into Juanita's dark eyes.

"So what happens when someone screws up around here? Must be hell to pay."

Juanita's eyes slid to the side. "Corrections are made."

"That sounds serious," said Mark.

"Whatever it takes."

"A big gloomy castle like this—there must be some sort of dungeon. Maybe in the basement?"

"I'm sorry," said Juanita abruptly. "I really think that you need to be going now." She turned to descend the stairs that led to the great room.

"I can't imagine that Minister Hawks personally does the enforcing," said Mark to Juanita's back. "He's above all of that sort of thing, isn't he? I'll bet he's got someone who keeps the troops in line and who weeds out the ones who are a threat. Am I right?"

Juanita stopped and turned on the stairs. "Please!" she hissed. "You don't know what you're saying. You must leave." She hurried to the bottom of the stairs and impatiently waited for Mark to descend the last few steps.

When Mark came close to her he said quietly, "On your wrists I see red marks. Abrasions from restraints. You've recently undergone this 'correction.' What did you do wrong?"

"That's church business."

Mark glanced around the vast great room. He heard the distant echo of a door closing. From another direction came the faint tapping of footsteps. He could see no one but he knew that this was not the place to talk.

"Okay," said Mark. He dutifully allowed Juanita to lead him across the expansive Persian carpet to the door that went downstairs. After descending the stairs they emerged into the lower level vestibule.

"Thank you for showing me out," said Mark. "But before I go, just one more thing." He reached into his jacket pocket and took out a photo of Abbie Danson. He held the photo so that Juanita could see it. "Have you seen this woman here?"

She glanced at the photo before quickly turning her eyes away. "No."

"Her name's Abbie. She's about your age. Nice girl. Works hard. Her mom and dad are worried about her. You can imagine how they must feel."

"When we enter the church we leave the past behind."

"She would not have come here willingly," said Mark.

"I wouldn't know."

As Juanita opened the door to the outside, sunlight streamed into the vestibule, sweeping away the gloom. Reflexively she squinted against the glare.

"It's a beautiful day," said Mark. "Why don't you take a walk with me? Tell me about yourself."

"It is forbidden."

"Are you afraid you'll be sent back to the dungeon?"

Saying nothing, Juanita stared at the ground.

Mark again showed her the photo of Abbie Danson. "This woman—are you sure she's not in the dungeon? Is she receiving correction?"

"No one is sent there who does not deserve it."

"How long is she supposed to stay there?"

"As long as it takes."

"You mean as long as Minister Hawks chooses?"

Juanita lifted her head. "It is not for me to question. Now please leave."

"Okay," said Mark. "Thanks for your help."

As he stepped onto the drawbridge that crossed the faux moat he glanced up at the high stone walls of the castle. In one of the tall windows on the second story the heavy velvet drapes gave a little shake as one of the panels fell back into place.

"You think that Abbie Danson is being held against her will in Forsythe Castle?" asked Chief Frontiero. With both elbows planted on his desk he rubbed his bald head with his hands.

Chris Mark looked into the gray eyes of the man who was responsible for keeping the citizens of Gloucester safe. This was not your ordinary case of robbery or even murder. It was something much more sinister.

"The cult member, Juanita, indicated that there was some sort of dungeon or cell in the castle where members were sent for punishment," said Mark. "She herself had marks on her wrists from restraints. She reacted when I showed her the photo of Abbie Danson."

"What about Gary Hiler?"

"I think that Abbie is of special interest to Stephen Hawks. Either as a challenge or as an object of his sexual sadism. Hiler was just a threat to be eliminated. Just as I may be."

"What do you want—a SWAT team to go into the castle?" asked Frontiero.

"No." Mark reached for a long cardboard tube that he had brought to Frontiero's office. After opening one end he gently shook the tube and a rolled-up document slid out. "If you'll excuse me," he said as he moved some of the clutter to one side of Frontiero's desk. He carefully unrolled the document, which was brittle with age.

"What is this—some sort of plan?" asked Frontiero.

"Exactly. In City Hall there's a storage area of old city documents. You've heard about it—they've been trying to raise money for a climate control system. They've got all kinds of stuff down there, including a set of the architect's plans for Forsythe Castle. Back in the nineteen-twenties the city must have demanded a copy to ensure that there weren't any flagrant zoning violations."

"In those days they could have built the damned Eiffel Tower there and the zoning guys wouldn't have cared," grunted Frontiero.

"It was a formality," said Mark. He pointed to a section of the yellowed sheet. "See this area? It's in the basement, but it's not directly accessible from areas used every day such as the kitchen pantries. It's set off by itself. You can see that it's got a notation: 'Pontefract.'"

"Pontefract? What's that?"

"In West Yorkshire, England, Pontefract Castle was renowned for its terrifying and bloody series of don-jons, or dungeons, hollowed out of the bedrock deep below the castle. Prisoners were trapped in the winding, pitch-black pits for weeks at a time, and scratched their names into the walls during their miserable imprisonment. You can see the prisoners' names, inscribed into the dungeon walls, when you visit the castle today.

"It's believed to be the site of the demise of King Richard II. And in Shakespeare's tragedy *Richard III*, Rivers is sent to his death in the dungeon of the castle, which was also known as Pomfret; and as he is led away he bitterly proclaims,

"'O Pomfret, Pomfret! O thou bloody prison,

Fatal and ominous to noble peers!

Within the guilty closure of thy walls
Richard the Second here was hack'd to death;
And, for more slander to thy dismal seat,
We give thee up our guiltless blood to drink.'"

Frontiero winced. "It sounds grim."

"On the plan," continued Mark, "you can see the notation that in order to construct the basement levels considerable blasting had to be done to clear away the bedrock granite. They created four cells in the deepest part of the castle. My guess is that Mrs. Forsythe used them as attractions during the many parties and social events she threw there."

"Give the guests a little thrill," said Frontiero. "Have them pose for gag photos while they're chained on the rack or manacled to the wall."

"Exactly. It would have been quite amusing to the rich folk. My guess is that when Minister Hawks bought the place, he put the dungeons to more practical use."

"What's your plan?" said Frontiero.

"A frontal assault would be much too dangerous," said Mark. "Any hostages would be killed before the team could penetrate to every area of the castle. And there may be a secret escape route. I need to go in alone. You can see on the architect's plan that there are a total of four entrances to the castle. One is the big front door that is accessed over the phony drawbridge. It faces west, towards Ipswich Bay. The second opens onto a terrace that faces north, also towards the ocean. It's a short walk from the garage. Both of those entrances are no good for me. On the southern side, the third door leads into the kitchen pantry—in the old days it was probably used for deliveries. The fourth door is on the back of the building, to the east. It leads to a set of stairs that descend directly into the basement boiler room. In the nineteen-twenties this door may have been used for coal deliveries."

"I thought you said the dungeons were in a separate area," said Frontiero.

"They are, but there's a narrow passageway that connects the dungeons with the rest of the basement. I intend to get into the dungeons and then get out with Abbie before the cult security people realize what's going on. The SWAT team backup needs to be well out of sight—perhaps waiting in a civilian camper in the state park."

"Okay," said Frontiero. "I hope for your sake that you're right."

The night was moonless. At one o'clock Chris Mark left the nondescript mobile home that was parked along the road in the state park adjacent to Forsythe Castle. Inside the vehicle waited six highly trained members of the state police SWAT team.

Mark picked his way through the woods separating the park from the castle. Between the tall maple trees the formidable silhouette of the manor loomed before him. Save for one light high up on the third floor, the windows of the castle were dark. At the edge of the grove he paused to listen. The only sounds were of busy crickets and, far away, the rhythmic sigh of ocean waves as they broke against the rocky shore.

After crossing the shadowed lawn he stood against the castle's stone wall. In his right hand he held a hardened steel crowbar. Instinctively he slid his left hand to his lower back. The Walther was there in its holster, loaded and ready.

Quietly Mark made his way along the wall of the castle to a projection that he knew from the plans was the first floor library. Around a corner and behind a clump of shrubs he found his target: the door that led to the basement boiler room. As he expected, the door was secured with a heavy padlock. Mark slipped the crowbar into the hasp and, once he could feel that he had leverage, firmly but slowly began to pull the crowbar in a downward direction.

He had to work carefully. It would be dangerous if the lock or the door gave way with a loud explosive sound.

With a faint creak the hasp gave a little. The old wood splintered. After waiting a moment to listen for sounds of human activity, Mark resumed the downward pressure. He could feel the crowbar move slightly as the hasp loosened. The screws holding the hasp to the door began to work their way out of the wood. Mark reversed the pressure before pulling down again.

With a crack the hasp broke away from the doorjamb and fell to the ground.

Mark paused to listen. The only sounds were the crickets and the ocean.

Slowly he pulled open the door. With a complaining creak the rusty hinges gave way and the door swung open. From the dark opening came a gush of dank air.

With the crowbar in his right hand, with his left hand Mark took his phone from his pocket. Its light illuminated the stone stairs that led to the basement. Brushing aside cobwebs, Mark descended the uneven steps. At the bottom of the stairs was another door, which Mark pushed open. He peered into the gloom and listened. Nothing. The weak light of the phone showed that Mark was in a small windowless room. Around the perimeter, cardboard boxes huddled against the damp walls. The air smelled of mold.

Cut into the wall to Mark's right was an open doorway. Mark went to it and showed his phone to the darkness. Just as the plans had indicated, this was the building's heating plant. The big oil-fired boiler was here. Overhead, its attendant inbound and outbound pipes formed a complex pattern. Visible in the shadows just beyond the boiler were the building's three gas-fired hot water heaters.

Mark turned his attention to the door directly in front of him. He went to it and as he slowly pulled on the old iron handle the stubborn hinges creaked. When the door was open just enough for a man to pass through Mark paused again, and again he listened.

Silence. From somewhere far above came a gentle vibration. Most likely a pipe. Then a faint skittering along the wall. Mark pointed his phone in the direction of the sound but saw only the dirty floor of a narrow passageway.

According to the plan, the dungeons were to the left. Slowly, carefully, Mark made his way along the rough corridor, ducking under the low-lying iron pipes that crossed overhead.

He came to a wooden door. After putting away his phone and laying the crowbar on the cement floor he removed his gun from its holster. In the darkness, after pausing to listen and hearing nothing but his own breathing, he gently but firmly grasped the handle, put his shoulder to the door, and pushed it open.

He was greeted by the dull yellow light cast by a single overhead bulb. This was another corridor, larger than the one he had just come through. The air was fresher and the floor not as dirty. This was a space that people used.

Along the corridor were four doors. Two of the doors were open. Two were closed.

With his Walther leading the way, Mark stepped through the first open door. The cell, hewn from granite, was furnished only with an iron cot topped by a thin mattress. Bolted to the walls were iron shackles. On the floor next to the bed was a tin pot. There was no window to the outside; the only light would enter through a small barred opening in the door.

Mark retreated to the corridor. The second cell was bolted from the outside. Mark gently slid back the bolt and pushed open the door.

The dim light showed an identical cell. Here, though, a figure was lying on the cot. The person was covered by a thin blanket. A heavy chain snaked from an iron ring on the wall to a shackle on the person's ankle.

The person stirred. Mark saw that it was a man. The man wearily raised his head.

"Who are you?" said the man.

"A friend," said Mark. "I'm going to get you out of here."

"Why?" said the man. "I've got another day remaining in my sentence, don't I? Did Minister Hawks say I could be released?"

Mark thought for a moment. He didn't have time to analyze why this man was here or why he was passively accepting his fate.

"Is there anybody else down here?" asked Mark.

"Yes—the woman. The noisy one."

"Noisy?"

"Yes—always screaming and yelling. Demanding to be let out. I guess she doesn't understand that complaining only gets you a longer sentence. At the rate she's going she'll be down here forever."

"Okay," said Mark. "Thanks. Keep quiet. I'll be back."

After closing and bolting the door, Mark went to the next cell, which was open. Like the others this cell was furnished only with an iron cot, and on the walls were the grim rings and shackles.

The door to the fourth cell was closed but not bolted. Mark gently pushed it open.

To his astonishment he did not find Abbie Danson.

This cell had been recently occupied. The blanket on the bed was rumpled. Mark placed his hand on it and felt a trace of warmth. And unlike the other cells, here there were signs that someone had occupied this place for more than a few hours: a bottle of water, a toothbrush, a towel, and a tray with a spoon and a plastic bowl.

Abbie Danson had been here only moments ago. She had either escaped or—for some reason—had been taken out.

Suddenly Mark heard the faint echo of a door. Distant footsteps. The sounds became louder— nearer. One person. Mark did not want to be discovered. Not yet. With his Walther cocked, he pressed himself up against the wall behind the open door. The footsteps came along the corridor. Closer. There was the flicker of a flashlight. Mark's muscles were coiled and ready to explode into action. The footsteps paused at the open door. A brilliant light swept the room. Then the footsteps went further down the passageway. In the darkness Mark heard the bolt slide and the door to the man's cell creak open. But there was no talking. The man shackled to the cot said nothing and nothing was said to him. After a moment the door was closed and the bolt slid shut. The footsteps and the flashlight passed by the cell where Mark was hiding. In a moment they were gone and all was again darkness and silence.

Abbie's absence was not a cause for alarm. She had been taken out.

Mark tapped his phone and scrolled through the plans to Forsythe Castle. The master bedroom—the one used by Mrs. Forsythe and which occupied the most commanding position with the best view of the ocean—was on the second floor, off the corridor that circled the great room.

Putting his phone in his pocket, in the gloom Mark followed the corridor along the same path taken by the visitor. It led to a set of stairs, at the top of which was a door that according to the plans led to the library. He gently pushed open the door. By now the moon had risen in the east and a pale light suffused the richly paneled room. Noiselessly he crossed the carpeted floor. At the door to the great room he paused to listen. Somewhere far away a toilet flushed and a door closed. Then all was silent.

Swiftly he crossed the great room to the broad staircase. Once at the top of the stairs, instead of going in the direction of Hawks's office he went the other way, which took him around the end of the great room to the side facing the woods. The corridor, softly lit by wall sconces of ornate crystal, was quiet. Mark went to the door of the master bedroom. It was closed.

He paused to listen. All was silence.

With his gun in his hand he grasped the handle of the door.

Now was the time.

With one fluid motion he turned the handle and burst through the door.

In the glow of moonlight Mark saw a big brass bed with luxurious pillows and a comforter. Sitting on the edge of the bed was a woman. She was naked. In her hand was a blade.

"Abbie—Abbie Danson!" whispered Mark.

The woman raised her head. Her face showed no expression.

Mark took a step forward. "Where's Hawks?"

Abbie rotated her body and weakly nodded in the direction of something next to her.

Mark approached the bed. In the shadows he could see the figure of a man. The sheets and comforter were soaked in blood. With his gun trained on the man, Mark carefully reached for the exposed foot. He gave it a shake. The flesh was warm but the man did not respond.

"I'm sorry," said Abbie. "I killed him. I didn't know what else to do. He was—" her voice trailed off.

"Put down the knife," said Mark.

Abbie dropped the dripping blade on the carpeted floor.

Mark took a robe that was draped across a chair and put it over Abbie's shoulders. After standing up and covering herself, Abbie sat on the bed again. Holstering his gun, Mark sat next to her.

"Killing a man is a nasty business," he said. "But I know why you had to do it. You had no choice."

For the first time she raised her eyes to meet his.

"Will I go to jail?"

"Not if I can help it," said Mark. He took out his phone and tapped a number. "Chief? I'm here with Abbie. Up in the master bedroom. Hawks is dead. Send in the SWAT team to secure the building. We'll wait here for you."

He turned to Abbie. "You did what you had to do. Now you're going home."

Love Eternal

At noon on a crisp September day Chris Mark had reluctantly abandoned the rollers off Long Beach for an appointment that had been arranged for him by a client. The morning had provided acceptable surfing on four-foot waves, which in fair weather are about as good as you're going to get on Cape Ann. After loading the dripping surfboard onto the rack of his old Jeep and stripping off his wetsuit, Mark had driven home, showered, and put on a sports jacket over a button-down shirt and black jeans.

The Jeep being reserved for local beach duty, at two o'clock Mark stepped out of his black Camaro at the appointed address. He paused for a moment to consider the grand old house upon which he was calling.

Built in the late nineteenth century by a prosperous quarry owner, at the time it had been a modern showpiece boasting a massive turret and big wrap-around porch. Providing counterpoint were a jumble of gables, bay windows, and dormers collected under a steeply pitched roof. Two—no, three—stone chimneys suggested a cozy hearth in every room.

There had been a time when its current owners, George and Glenda Aniston, had done very well for themselves. According to their daughter Rose, at whose behest Mark was making this visit, nearly sixty years earlier George Aniston had graduated from Boston University with a degree in English, and then, newly married to his college sweetheart Glenda, had settled down to a comfortable if wholly unremarkable life as a high school English teacher. A few years later Rose was born, and all was well; the only challenge facing the family was the narcotic effect of ordinariness that permeated the days of their lives.

But George had a secret ambition. In his off hours he wrote hard-boiled detective novels. He had no particular training in law enforcement, and there was nothing about him or his past that suggested an inclination towards the brand of fiction that made your hands sweaty and your pulse pound. Even though he entertained few thoughts that anyone else would ever read his creations, this was the genre in which he happily immersed himself.

His efforts would have remained nothing more than the personal hobby of a high school English teacher if something amazing had not happened. Of the many manuscripts that George had dutifully mailed to publishers, one had not been returned. By mere chance a junior editor had plucked it from the slush pile. The book—*The Faded Red Stain*, starring detective Wade Drake—had been accepted and then published. George had been pleased to see his little novel appear on the shelves of bookstores next to those of authors whom he admired, and he was equally pleased to give a reading or two before scattered audiences at local book clubs. He assumed that this brief fling with professional authorship would be the end of it, and that *The Faded Red Stain* would soon be consigned to the remainder bins.

But the feisty little book had caught on, and kept selling. The publisher inquired if George had additional titles featuring Wade Drake. Indeed the author had several, buried deep within his filing cabinet. He found them, dusted them off, and sent them to his publisher.

And thus the Wade Drake detective series was born. George wrote more of the books, and many of them were best sellers. Movie offers soon followed. Being a practical man who knew his strengths, George never once flew to Hollywood. He was content to make the deals that his agent recommended and cash the six-figure checks that the postman slipped into his mailbox at the end of his driveway.

George and Glenda's ordinary suburban house was soon swapped for the one at Oak Acres, where Chris Mark had arrived on this crisp autumn afternoon. The property had been bought with earnings from the Wade Drake books, after which additional income from movies had allowed George and Glenda to buy up surrounding acreage to create a sprawling estate with a magnificent view of the Atlantic Ocean from the front door and rugged unspoiled woods out the back door.

Today, many years after those flush times, the house showed the ravages of age. The faded paint offered scant protection to the cracked clapboards. The roof shingles were broken and tired from decades of pounding by sun and snow. Reaching towards the gables with clawlike branches, the ancient oak trees provided not comforting shelter but an ominous sense of foreboding.

As Mark's shoes crunched against the gravel and dead leaves on the driveway he thought that despite the dreariness of the scene there was no harm in spending an hour or two with a wealthy literary couple in their moldering retreat, asking them a few pro forma questions, and then sending a brief report along with his bill to the concerned daughter. It would be an easy way to make a few bucks.

After climbing the granite steps he crossed the creaking floorboards to the front door. At his feet he noticed an antique boot scraper, beside which were a pair of men's black galoshes. A black umbrella poked its curved handle from a tall glazed ceramic urn.

Mark pulled the old-fashioned doorbell and heard the chimes within. Footsteps, and then the door swung open. Not all the way, though. Just enough to establish contact.

The woman who stood before him was older in appearance than he had expected, perhaps because the photographs he had uncovered during his brief background research had been taken ten or twenty years earlier. Indeed, it had been a decade since the Anistons had retired from public view. They both had dropped off the various charity boards on which they had served and stopped accepting invitations on the cocktail circuit, and George had even withdrawn from writers' conventions and symposiums. This change had not gone unnoticed by those who knew them, but it had been accepted; after all, the world is full of authors who achieve best-selling status, immerse themselves in the white-hot glare of the public spotlight for a few years, and then retreat to a more comfortable anonymity.

"You must be Mr. Mark," the woman said without smiling. Her keen eyes, the steadiness of which contrasted to her general appearance of unsteady frailty, bore into him. Yes, she was old, but the superficial deterioration of skin and hair could not disguise the proud bones. Once she had been beautiful, and she had the good sense to let go of her beauty rather than attempt to preserve it by succumbing to the greedy ravages of plastic surgery.

She wore a simple but well-designed cotton housedress. Her jewelry consisted of a gold wedding band and pearl earrings. Her grey hair was cut above her shoulders. Over her forehead curled one stray strand, providing a solitary hint of unplanned dishevelment.

"Yes—Mrs. Aniston, I presume," replied Mark.

"Yes. How may I help you?" The door was not opened further.

Interesting, thought Mark. She's not inviting me in. Rose had told me that her parents were reclusive, and the fact that her mother had agreed to see me was no guarantee that she would go so far as to invite me into the house. This might be a very short visit indeed.

"Thank you for taking the time to have a few words with me," said Mark. Might as well start off on a note of gratitude.

"My daughter told me that you were coming," said Mrs. Aniston. "It's only to please her that we agreed to see you. But I can assure you that you're wasting your time. George and I are perfectly fine, and you can tell Rose not to worry."

It was not Mark's imagination that Mrs. Aniston shifted her weight onto her heels and the door began to swing shut.

"I don't think that Rose was trying to be intrusive," said Mark quickly. "In fact she told me that I would find you to be quite charming."

The door paused.

"Just because we value our privacy does not mean that we're dull people," she said with a wry smile.

"No, of course not. And as much as I'd enjoy talking with both you and your husband, I think I should be perfectly honest about why I'm here. Rose asked me to see her father. She's gotten the impression that his desire for solitude has gone too far. She told me that she hasn't spoken to him in over a year."

Mrs. Aniston put a hand on her hip. "Yes, yes, I know all about Rose's concerns. I'm not going to air the family laundry with someone who shows up on our front door. You can tell Rose—as I've told her over and over again—that her father is perfectly fine, and that he's just not a phone person. He likes social media. He's very active on Facebook. In fact, I have to tell him to not spend so much time on the darned computer!" She laughed and then gave Mark a conciliatory smile. "So please tell Rose that you've been here and that we are both perfectly happy."

What Mrs. Aniston said about Facebook was true. George Aniston maintained an active page and regularly posted both professional news about reprints of his books as well as personal tidbits about the gardens, which he tended with great care.

"I was hoping to ask George about his asters," said Mark. "I saw the post that he put up about them last week. They're from your garden? They look terrific."

"Thank you," replied Mrs. Aniston. "We both think it's important to cultivate native species. George first planted asters about ten years ago, and in the fall they really come into their own. I'll tell him that you saw the post. I'm sure he'll be delighted."

At that moment Mark heard from within the house an indistinct woman's voice. The tone was questioning. Mrs. Aniston turned. "Yes, Maria," she said to someone in the gloom behind her. "I'll have tea with cheese and crackers." She turned back to Mark. "Every afternoon I have a little pick-me-up." Her expression became indecisive. "Well—as long as you're here, why don't you come in? We rarely have visitors, but I don't think that George would mind."

For the first time since Mark had arrived, she backed away from the door, giving him space to enter.

"You have help here?" asked Mark as he stepped into the vestibule. Before him the grand staircase ascended to the gloom of the second floor. The air was suffocating and smelled of mold.

"Yes," replied Mrs. Aniston as she led the way through the dismal formal living room to a sunroom on the south side of the house. "Maria comes in three times a week for a few hours. She's a godsend."

Unlike the living room, which in its strict arrangement of furniture looked as if it were never occupied, the sunroom was a casual environment with books and newspapers stacked on the low table that fronted the cozy chintz sofa. There was a small TV set too, and on the walls hung framed posters of some of the movies that had been made from George's books. A window was open an inch or two, providing breathable air.

"Please," said Mrs. Aniston as she motioned to an easy chair. Mark sat down and Mrs. Aniston took a spot on the sofa. She cleared an area on the coffee table by putting aside a stack of magazines. "I apologize for the clutter. You must think we're terrible housekeepers. I must lay the blame on George. He never picks up after himself. Always leaves things lying here and there."

Maria brought in a tray with a pot of tea and a plate of cheese and crackers. After pouring two cups she asked Mrs. Aniston if that were all. Mrs. Aniston thanked her and Maria excused herself.

"Maria seems to be very efficient," said Mark. The teacup was old porcelain and hot to the touch. He let it rest on the saucer.

"Yes," replied Mrs. Aniston. "This house is very big for two people. There's simply no way we could do it all ourselves. And besides, I think that both George and I should use our time more productively than by cleaning bathrooms, don't you think?"

"Yes, I suppose so. Is George working on anything new? His Facebook entries don't reveal his current projects."

"And that's how he likes it," said Mrs. Aniston with a note of pride in her voice. "He never discusses his projects until they're ready. Even I have no idea what he's writing. His study is strictly off limits. No one goes in there."

"I've heard that authors often create a defined space for themselves," said Mark. "Sometimes it's a separate building, like a little hut. Where does George do his work? Has he got a bungalow somewhere on the property?"

"Oh no. It's upstairs. No doubt you noticed when you arrived that this house has a tower. That's one reason George fell in love with this place. The minute he saw it he told me that the tower would be a perfect place for his study. It's on the third floor. I thought it was a lovely idea. The space is big and sunny and utterly private. The day we first saw the house, George claimed the room for his own."

"His sanctuary," said Mark.

"Exactly!" replied Mrs. Aniston. "He's a very creative person. He really needs big blocks of time to get his work done. Soon after we moved into the house, together we set up the room. I found him a nice old antique desk and chair. He also wanted a chaise longue, in case he wanted to take a nap. We built bookshelves and hung pictures, and I made curtains. When it was ready he said, 'Thank you dear, now please give me the key.' That was it. The room was his alone. At first I'll admit that I was a bit jealous. 'You love your room in the tower more than you love me,' I would say to him. He would just laugh and kiss me. 'When I come out after a long day's work, the very first person I want to see is my beautiful bride,' he would reply. So what could I say? He needs his privacy, and I cannot complain. I love this house and our gardens, and I know how I got here. So I let him stay in there for hours. It makes him so very happy."

"You never go into his study?" said Mark.

Glenda lowered her eyes before raising them again. "I don't want to fib. Just between you and me, I have a spare key. I go in there once in a while, when George is out of the house. I only want to make sure that the room is clean and tidy. Of course I don't touch anything. If I did then he would know that I had been there. If I notice something like a dirty drinking glass, when I see him later that day I'll remind him to bring downstairs with him anything that needs to be washed. Sure enough, the next morning he'll bring down the dirty glass. So my little system works out just fine."

Mark ventured a sip of his tea, which by now had cooled sufficiently. He carefully replaced the cup on the delicate saucer.

"Mrs. Aniston, I—"

"Please call me Glenda," she offered.

"Certainly. Glenda, I'm sure that George would not object if you asked him to come out of his study for one moment, just to satisfy the concerns of his perhaps over-imaginative daughter. I'm sure that my intrusion into your private life is not what you want, and perhaps if your daughter were reassured then she'd be less interested in hiring people like me to knock on your door."

"You're some sort of private detective?" asked Glenda.

"More like a consultant. I do what I can to solve problems for people."

"How interesting. I'm sure you've read some of my husband's books?"

"Yes—the Wade Drake series. Very entertaining."

"But you're the real thing, so to speak."

"I suppose. But my life is not nearly as exciting as Wade Drake. I don't go around shooting people."

"Have you ever—you know—shot someone?" Glenda's eyes were sharp and focused.

"Not around here. I was in the military. So I had some experiences there. But let's get back to my question. I'd like you to call your husband and ask him if he'd mind just coming down and saying hello."

In response Glenda smiled and poured herself another cup of tea. "May I freshen your cup?" she asked.

"No thank you."

She set down the teapot.

"Of course you're quite right, Chris. May I call you Chris? I don't want to make assumptions. I'm sure my husband would be more than happy to say hello to you, particularly because you have admired his asters. But at the moment he's on one of his rambles."

"Rambles?"

"Yes. That's another reason why we bought this house. When we first moved here twenty years ago, the house occupied a relatively small lot. It was only three acres. But we learned that in the woods behind the house there were several undeveloped tracts of land. During the following years, one by one these properties came on the market. Five acres here, ten acres there. We snapped them up. We did this to not only prevent other houses from being built directly behind our own, but to establish a green area of undisturbed woods. At the moment our property totals over thirty acres. We hope to make it even larger. It's a very lovely area, with both deep woods and an old quarry. Scattered about are those big granite boulders that you find all over Cape Ann. They're called 'erratics' because fifteen thousand years ago the retreating glaciers randomly dropped them onto the surface."

"Thirty acres isn't so large," said Mark. "I'll bet I could find him. Doesn't he carry a phone?"

"He does carry a phone," replied Glenda. "A new one, in fact. I forget which version it is—I can never keep track. He's more in tune with technology than I am. But he keeps it turned off. He only agrees to carry it so that if he has an accident he can call for help. He's quite spry for a man who's eighty years old. And as for our thirty acres, our property abuts the big expanse of Dogtown. That's three thousand acres of wild woods and fields. He likes to hike through there. Sometimes he leaves in the morning with nothing but a sandwich and a bottle of water, and I don't see him until well into the evening."

"What time did he leave today?"

"You just missed him. He went out around one. I don't expect him back until after sunset. And then he wants his supper."

Mark glanced out the window at the vast expanse of dark woods. Somewhere out there George Aniston was tramping around with his dead cell phone. It would be impossible to sit here and wait for him. Staking out the house wouldn't work either, because George wasn't driving a car.

At that moment Glenda's phone rang. After a quick glance at the caller ID she said, "Please excuse me for one moment—I need to take this." She pressed the answer button. "Yes—you're from Kingston Electric? You can come out next Tuesday? Good. Yes, either Mr. Aniston or myself will be here. Yes, thank you."

She put the phone down. "When we bought this house we knew that sooner or later we'd have to replace the old knob and tube wiring. But you know how it is—the years go by and you just keep putting things off. But we really need to do it because we keep adding new appliances like computers, and everyone tells us that our wiring is dangerous. It could cause a fire. So we're finally asking some contractors to give us estimates."

"Yes, I understand," replied Mark.

"Chris, you've been very kind to visit," said Glenda. Her voice had an unexpected sweetness. "I want you to understand something. When I first married George, he was a very private person. Reserved, you might say. I liked that about him. Nothing ruffled him. What you saw was what you got. I had grown up with two parents who were, shall I say, volatile. Never a moment's peace in the house. When George and I were married and he was teaching, I thought we had it made. We had our little house in the suburbs and he had the summers off. I worked part-time at an antiques store. Life was very tranquil. And then George's writing career took off. Bang! Just like that. It seemed to happen overnight. Book signings and television and radio appearances. And groupies! Did you know that there are literary groupies? They have no shame. They'll come right to your door and ask to see your husband. As if you're the hired help! George had to travel and we both felt like we were living in a fishbowl. After we moved here things got a little better—we had more privacy—but the pace was exhausting. One day George sat me down and said, 'My dear, we need to get off the merry-go-round. We have enough money. I'm going to get out of the spotlight.' To tell you the truth, I was overjoyed. It meant that I got my husband back again. We could spend time together. And sure enough, the spotlight faded. Our life became very peaceful. The days did not fly by so quickly. Rose had grown up, gotten married, and had moved to Seattle. I regret not seeing her more often, but her husband is a difficult person. I won't burden you with all of that. The point is that George and I don't want anything to change. We're very happy. We could stay here forever."

The afternoon sun was now casting long shadows through the grasping trees. Mark set down his empty teacup and stood up.

"I want to thank you for your time, Glenda. It's been a pleasure to meet you and to see your lovely home. I'm sorry that I missed George. I would very much have liked to have met him too."

Glenda stood up. "I'll be sure to tell him."

At this moment of their parting, Chris Mark's feeling of disquiet intensified. Glenda Aniston was a frail woman, and while her husband at the age of eighty was apparently capable of tramping around in the woods for hours at a time, one slip and fall could spell disaster. Maria came to the house only three days a week, and their only child lived thousands of miles away. If anything were to happen to either George or Glenda, they might be trapped in this big decaying house until they were discovered by Maria, and by then it would certainly be too late. With the passing of every day, George and Glenda risked losing everything they had worked for.

Mark reached into his jacket pocket and pulled out a business card. He offered it to Glenda. "Please," he said. "Take my phone number. If you or George should need anything, please don't hesitate to call. I'm not far away."

Glenda accepted the card. "I'm sure we'll be fine," she said cheerfully. "But I'll keep your card just in case."

At that moment Maria came to the door of the sunroom. "If you don't need me for anything else, Mrs. Aniston, I'll be going now."

"That's fine, Maria," replied Glenda. "I'll see you on Thursday."

Chris Mark was happy to be walking out of the house at the same time as Maria. After the front door closed behind him he strolled around to the side of the house by the garage. Maria was opening the door to her car. He asked her for a moment of her time.

"How long have you worked for the Anistons?" asked Mark.

"About six months," she replied.

"What's your impression of Mr. Aniston?"

Maria shrugged. "I've never actually seen him. He's always working in his study. Once in a while he'll leave me a note in the kitchen. A little yellow post-it. He'll ask me to make him up a ham and cheese sandwich for one of his walks. I leave the sandwich in the refrigerator. They seem like a very nice couple. I have no complaints."

"You've never entered his study?"

"Oh, no. When I first came to work here, Mrs. Aniston told me clearly that it was off limits. Mr. Aniston needed his privacy."

"Okay. Thanks."

After dinner with friends at Lobsta House that evening, Mark returned to his house and turned the game on the television. He had sent his report to Rose Aniston saying that while he had not actually seen her father, Glenda was perfectly fine. Other than the general state of decay, nothing seemed amiss at the house. The Aniston case was almost too easy, but that's the nature of the business: one week you get a job that's almost like getting free money, and the next week you nearly get yourself killed for what seems like chump change. You take the good with the bad.

After setting his glass of Wild Turkey on the table next to the chair, Mark took out his phone. He opened Facebook and went to George Aniston's page. There was a posting from five o'clock that afternoon, which was about two hours after Mark had left the house. George described his walk through the woods and included a photo of the fall foliage in Dogtown. Some of his friends had commented favorably on the posting.

Such a sweet old couple, thought Mark. The familiar wave of bitterness came over him. His own parents would never know those golden years. He wished that he had more memories of them, and clearer ones; but they had both died when he was a small child, and in his mind they survived as little more than the flickering images of an old movie. It had happened so suddenly and with such brutality. One day he had been picked up at school by his aunt Rina, who told him that Mommy and Daddy had been taken to heaven. He soon learned the truth about the mad gunman who had burst into the restaurant and sprayed the place with bullets. A senseless and horrifying act for which no reason was ever learned.

Mark took a swallow of Wild Turkey. Banish these thoughts! They served no purpose. Everyone has their own path in life to follow. Aunt Rina had loved him and raised him as her own. Some kids don't even get that much.

Rose Aniston had thanked him for his service, and that was the end of it. Perhaps the circumstantial evidence of her father's well being was enough to satisfy her, and she had chosen to accept the painful reality that her father had moved into some later stage of his life in which contact with his only daughter was somehow less important than the small pleasures to be gained by working on his books and his garden. Some parents remain close to their adult children, while others grow to see their children as people who are not much different from strangers whom they encounter on the street. Rose had concluded, perhaps more out of expediency rather than knowledge of fact, that her father had simply forgotten his love for his daughter, and that she should be content with regular phone calls with her mother.

It was a cold night in November when Chris Mark's phone rang. He was at Fred's Clam Shack having a lobster roll and a beer. His mind was focused on a new and baffling case, and when he glanced at his phone he did not recognize the name on the caller ID. He had forgotten that he knew "G. Aniston."

Absent-mindedly and with no small feeling of annoyance he answered the phone call.

"Chris? Chris Mark?" The woman's voice had the edge of desperation. The tone was familiar. Mark searched his memory.

"Glenda! Is that you?" he said.

"Yes—please—you must come right away! The house is on fire and we must save George!"

"Where are you?" said Mark as he rose from his seat.

"I'm outside but I'm going back in," she said.

With his free hand Mark hurriedly slapped a twenty on the counter before heading to the door. "Glenda—are you still there? Yes? Good. I'm calling nine-one-one. Don't go inside the house. It's too dangerous. I'll be there in five minutes."

As Mark rushed to his car he called emergency services and reported the fire. Two people—both elderly—were living at the residence. He knew that he was closer to the house than the fire station was, and that he would almost certainly arrive before the first responders.

As he slid into the gravel driveway at Oak Acres he saw in the bright moonlight that from nearly every window of the house poured thick black smoke. There were no flames visible. While the fire had not yet grown out of control, Mark knew that it would not be long before the entire house was fully involved.

He did not see Glenda in the yard. Foolish woman! He had told her to stay outside. He hoped that she had not decided to go back into the burning house. If the smoky blaze became a conflagration before he could get both Glenda and George out safely, the chances of saving them were exceedingly slim.

Leaving his car parked on the lawn out of the path of the soon-to-be-arriving fire apparatus, Mark ran to the front door. It was open. From the upper half of the opening came dense acrid smoke. He dropped to a crouch and went inside. There in the vestibule he saw a huddled form.

"Glenda!" he shouted. "Where's George?"

She turned to him with wild eyes. "Upstairs! In his study! He must be trapped in there! You must get him out. Please!" Her tone was plaintive, beseeching. Her hands were shaking and her body quivering.

"Yes—I will," replied Mark with as much calm in his voice as he could muster. "First, *you* need to get out. Come on—come with me." He grasped her by the shoulders. Her frame felt thin and insubstantial— almost weightless. He gently but firmly steered her to the front door as she twisted around in an effort to look back towards the staircase. "Go!" insisted Mark as they crossed the threshold.

"Please!" she implored. "You've got to save George!"

"Yes, yes, I will," said Mark as he hustled her across the porch and down the steps and onto the safety of the gravel walkway.

In the distance he heard the wail of the sirens. There was no time to lose. He could not wait for the first responders. He had to go back into the house.

"Where did the fire start?" he asked.

"In the basement I think," replied Glenda. Shivering, she drew her thin housedress around her shoulders. "The wiring."

"Stay here!" he commanded. Meekly she nodded.

Mark turned and ran back through the front door. Keeping low, he made his way through the thickening pall to the base of the stairway that led to the second floor. Grasping the carved wood banister he vaulted up the stairs. Half-seeing and half-feeling his way, he quickly found the second-floor landing and then the stairs to the third floor. With smoke stinging his eyes, in a crouch he made his way up the narrow stairs to a landing. The heat was building and Mark knew that he had only moments left before the flames erupted from inside the walls.

There were three doors. Two of them were open. Ducking low, Mark entered the first room and found himself in a musty old bedroom with a four-poster bed. He dodged into the second door. A bathroom.

Mark pounded on the third door and called for George. He heard no sound other than the crackling of fire as it worked its way up inside the walls. Gingerly he reached for the antique metal doorknob. It was not hot. Good—there were no open flames on the other side. With greater force he grasped and turned the knob. The door was locked. Damn! Again he pounded and called. No answer. With his head bent low against the blinding smoke he stepped back and gave the door a solid kick with the heel of his shoe. With a sharp crack the wood splintered but the old door held. He kicked again and the door flew open.

Instinctively Mark crouched in a defensive position in case the door now being open created a draft that would cause the fire to explode. But there were only waves of bitter smoke.

"George!" Mark called as he entered the room. There was no answer. Yes, this must be the place—there was the desk with a computer, and piles of books and a file cabinet. A floor lamp burned with an eerie dirty glow.

Placed along the wall was an antique chaise longue. Lying on the chaise was a man. A blanket covered him to his chin. Perhaps he was sleeping, or unconscious. Through the dense smoke Mark could not tell if his eyes were open. No matter. There was no time to think.

Mark reached out his hand to the man's shoulder. He gave it a firm shake. "George! Wake up! We gotta get you out of here!" George didn't move. Through the swirling haze Mark could now see that his eyes were closed.

He must be unconscious. I'll have to carry him out. Without hesitation Mark grasped George by both of his shoulders and jerked him upright.

To Mark's shock he heard the sound of a snap. George seemed to be made of brittle plaster, not living flesh. And—penetrating through the acrid smell of smoke—into Mark's nostrils came the unmistakable odor of death.

Mark put his palm to the side of George's face. The skin was cold parchment. He ran his hand over the head. Great clumps of grey hair came off between his fingers. He felt an arm. It was a lifeless stick.

With wrenching revulsion swelling in his gut, Mark realized that the man he had been sent to rescue was nothing more than a desiccated corpse.

Damn you Glenda Aniston!

Better to leave the rotten body here. Let it be consumed by the fire.

There was movement at the door. A woman. "Please!" she shrieked. "You must save him!"

Mark whirled round. "Glenda! Are you insane? Get out of here! Get out now before you die!"

"I won't leave without George," she wailed. Before Mark could stop her she had thrown herself onto the body of her husband.

"He's dead!" said Mark. "Let him go!"

Suddenly through the black haze came an orange glow.

"Glenda!" said Mark as he roughly hauled her to her feet. "We need to get out of here now!"

"Not without George!" Great tears rolled down her cheeks. "He's everything to me. I'd rather die than leave him!" A wave of coughs wracked her frail body.

The heat was increasing. Mark wiped the sweat from his smokestained forehead and neck. To Glenda, this was not a rotting corpse but the person and memory of her dear husband.

"All right!" shouted Mark. "We're all getting out of here!"

Brusquely he hauled the corpse to an upright position and threw it over his shoulder.

Glenda turned and attempted to fuss with the blanket that covered her husband.

"Forget it!" shouted Mark. "I've got George! You go first! *Now!*"

Startled by Mark's vehemence, after releasing the blanket Glenda stumbled to the door. With his ghastly burden Mark followed close behind. The flames had not yet reached the staircase. Together they clumsily descended to the second floor. Mark felt his lungs seared by the hot fumes. With his eyes burning he followed Glenda down the stairs to the main floor. Every breath was an effort. In his dizzy mind he felt the floor rocking beneath his feet.

There—just ahead—was the front door! A timber crashed behind him in a shower of sparks. Where was Glenda? With his stomach churning in revulsion at the touch of the grotesque corpse on his shoulder, he twisted around to look for her. In the roaring smoke he saw nothing. The only place to go was towards the front door. Carrying the rancid body, Mark stumbled across the vestibule. As he came to the open door he saw figures coming through. Men in bulky uniforms, with helmets and masks. As his world dissolved into a black void, the gloved hands of these angels reached out to him.

Mark awoke to feel cold air on his face and intense heat on his head. He was lying on his back on a stretcher. He twisted his head to determine the source of the heat. Behind him the great house was engulfed in towering flames. The brilliant orange light was too intense and he turned away.

In the flickering haze someone bent over him.

"Where's Glenda?" asked Mark.

The person—a man—shook his head. "She didn't make it," he said. "Heart attack. She fell in the vestibule. By the time we got her out of the house it was too late."

She had joined George in death. Now it was all clear. It was Glenda who had preserved her husband's body long after he had died. Glenda had created the Facebook page and had written the notes. She couldn't bear to see him go, so she had kept his spirit—if not his body—alive.

As the oxygen mask was placed over his mouth, Chris Mark surrendered himself to the welcome embrace of darkness.

A Good Day to Bury Charlie

The punk had talked tough, but after a good beating he quickly caved in. He had begged for his life like a frightened kid. Heck, at age nineteen Charlie Kasko practically *was* a kid. He was in way over his head. Thought he was slick by playing both sides. But you can't be an FBI informer and a member of the Rock Hill Gang for very long. The kid should have known that. And his stupidity had been confirmed when he agreed to come to a meeting at the house on Willow Street. What a naïve fool! When Johnny "Pistol" Carrigan had suggested to the kid that he come to the house to "clear up a few things," Johnny half expected the kid to make up some excuse: he had to work or take care of his mother, or some crap like that. To Johnny's satisfaction the kid had readily agreed. Sure, Johnny, no problem, he had said. His eyes were big and full of trust, like a hound dog. What an asshole. No one crosses Johnny Carrigan and lives to tell about it.

Johnny and Junior had led Charlie to the basement. The rec room, they told him. For privacy. Didn't want anyone snooping into their business. Charlie had hesitated—a glimmer of apprehension had flitted through his overactive mind. But Johnny had clapped him on the back and reassured him that everything was cool. They were brothers.

Johnny believed that you can tell anything to a rat. It's okay to lie to someone who has broken the oath. Charlie had relaxed, said okay, no problem. We're brothers. And with a swagger in his step he had gone down into the basement.

At the point of a gun Charlie had allowed himself to be chained to a chair. He thought maybe he had done something wrong and Johnny was going to give him a beating. Nothing serious, just a slapping around for some stupid infraction. He didn't believe that Johnny, the guy who had brought him into the organization, would kill him.

When the chains were drawn tight around his chest he realized what was going on. Tried to stand and twist free. A whack with a two-by-four across the kneecaps had solved that problem. Then Charlie tried to bargain. Appealed to Johnny's sense of kinship. Hey Johnny, he said, I look up to you. Respect you. You're like a father to me. C'mon, let's talk about this.

Johnny didn't want talk. He wanted answers, and to get them he used the two-by-four. When Charlie's face started to look like a mangled tomato he broke down. Begged for his life. The rat became a singing bird. Confessed everything.

Yeah, he worked for the feds. They were going to bust him. Send him to federal prison. He had no choice. Said he'd do anything to make it up to Johnny.

It was hard for him to talk because of the busted teeth and the blood that kept filling his mouth. Pissed his pants, too. A mess on the floor to clean up, but that would come later. Bleach will do it.

This bird will never sing again, said Johnny as he twisted the clothesline around Charlie's neck. It took about five minutes for Charlie to have no pulse. The bastard took a long time to die! No matter. Dead is dead. He won't sing again.

Johnny had planned the operation with meticulous care. He wanted nothing left to chance. No possibility of Charlie escaping the snare. No possibility of discovery. That's the way Johnny was, and it was why he was both successful and feared. When Johnny pulled off a job it was always clean. No tracks, no evidence.

The house had been scouted and bought for cash. It had a small back yard. Maybe half an acre. There was a tall fence around the perimeter and lots of lilac bushes. You couldn't see into the yard from the street because the house blocked the view. The neighbors couldn't see into the yard either. It was secluded. Private.

The previous owner of the house had been a woman who was a gardener. She had planted all kinds of shrubs and flowers. Johnny didn't know anything about flowers but when he visited the house he liked to look at them. He was a brute who fancied he possessed a certain level of sophistication. It was summertime now and many of the flowers were in bloom. There were red flowers and blue ones.

Johnny also liked to watch the hummingbirds that patronized the flowers. He'd watch as they hovered at the flowers and probed them with their slender beaks. After a few seconds they'd zip away in a zigzag pattern, and then fly up to a tree to perch for a while.

They'd fight, too. Johnny liked that. If one hummingbird was at a flower and another approached, the first one would defend its territory. They'd tussle in midair until one gave up and flew away.

That's what life was like, thought Johnny. Always a battle for the flower.

As the warm corpse of Charlie Kasko lay on the basement floor wrapped in a sheet of plastic and secured with duct tape, Johnny sat for a moment at the little garden table on the back terrace of the house. He knew exactly which spot would be the best to bury the body. The grave had to be dug good and deep, and it had to be dug by hand. There was a maple tree in the far corner of the yard, but trees have roots, and roots can make digging with a shovel difficult. He and Junior couldn't use a backhoe. One would never fit through the narrow path that led from the street to the back yard, and anyway it would be too noisy, too conspicuous. Goddamn Charlie—not only did you have to be a rat, but now you needed a hole dug, which meant several hours of backbreaking work.

Johnny mopped his brow. The day was humid. He flexed his hands. Whacking Charlie with the two-by-four had made them stiff. No matter. There was work ahead.

Junior had wanted to take the body out in a boat and dump it at sea. Johnny nixed that idea. Bodies tended to float. You had to weigh down the body with chains and concrete blocks, and even then there was no guarantee that the bloated corpse wouldn't bob to the surface or get caught in a fishing net. And the Gloucester waterfront was busy twenty-four hours a day. There were security cameras too. Any fisherman seeing suspicious activity would get nosy and maybe even call the cops. Or worse, get that private detective Chris Mark involved. The guy was dangerous. He had a knack for putting people in jail. One of these days someone—maybe Johnny —was going to put a bullet in his head. Take him off the streets and out of the business of people who just wanted to make a living.

Then Junior suggested chopping up the body in the bathtub and leaving the parts in various dumpsters around town. Idiot! said Johnny. Someone would find an arm or a leg. That would trigger an investigation by the state police. Media attention. Headlines. And you can't always be sure you get rid of traces of blood on tools and from the plumbing. Hacking up Charlie was a stupid idea.

No, they were going to plant Charlie right here in the back yard. Good and deep. No evidence would leave the house. When they were done Junior would put on some gloves and drive Charlie's car across the bridge. Park it on a side street in Salem. Let the cops find it in a week or two. Even better, some neighborhood entrepreneur might steal it.

As he pondered the details of his foolproof plan Johnny took stock of his environment. Except for two noisy crows squawking on the overhead power lines on the street, the immediate neighborhood was quiet. From many blocks away came the faint hum of a lawn mower. In the harbor a ship blew its horn. These everyday sounds were not a problem. Johnny took pride in his ability to sense anything unusual, especially any peculiar noises from beyond the fence and the protective barrier of lilacs. His senses had never failed him. Maybe that's why he was still alive when so many of his competitors were either dead or in jail.

He watched the hummingbirds as they darted amongst the flowers. Over the past few weeks he had counted five. Johnny thought that there were two males and two females. And then there was the one extra hummingbird. Johnny couldn't figure out exactly what it was. It had the dull coloring of a female, but was a little bit bigger than the other two females. She never stayed at a flower very long. She would come into the yard, fly around, hover, and then zoom away.

She had been here earlier today, but he didn't see her now. She must be in some other garden.

Johnny noted with satisfaction that it was a good day to bury a body in the back yard. The late afternoon sky was overcast and the light was dim. Johnny craned his neck to look up through the branches of the trees at the dense blanket of clouds. The cops had drones now. Goddamn little helicopters and airplanes that could fly hundreds of feet overhead and watch you on a video feed. On a clear day they could be high enough to be invisible. But not today. They'd have to fly low, which meant you could see them or hear them.

No neighbors, no wiretaps, no cameras. Good.

Johnny went into the kitchen and told Junior to finish his beer. It was time to get to work. After retrieving two shovels from the basement Johnny showed Junior where they were going to dig. It was a spot around the corner from the kitchen door, out back by the property line. Out of the direct sight of the path that led to the street. And for extra insurance Johnny had bought a magnolia tree sapling from the garden supply store. Supported by its big round root ball of clay mud, the sapling sat on the scrubby lawn. If anyone happened to walk into the back yard—maybe some asshole from the gas company who had to read the meter—two guys digging a hole would make sense. They were planting a tree. Only this tree was going to have some extra fertilizer.

After pacing off six feet, Johnny used the tip of his shovel to turn up the sod at each end. He then paced off two feet for the width. He wanted a nice neat job.

Junior fetched the tarp from the basement. Johnny insisted they put a tarp on the lawn next to the hole. The top layer of sod and the dirt would go on the tarp so that when they were done they could easily refill the hole and replace the sod. The lawn wouldn't be ruined and the outline of the grave would quickly disappear as the pieces of sod knitted together.

After the sod had been set aside they started to dig. Johnny hated digging. It seemed like such a ridiculous activity, and dirt was always much heavier than you had imagined. But it had to be done.

After an hour they had gotten down only about three feet. Junior wanted to quit and dump the body in the hole. His back hurt and the hole was adequate.

It was much too shallow, insisted Johnny. We don't want a neighborhood dog digging up the corpse. And we need to make it deep enough to plant the magnolia tree on top of him.

Plant the tree? asked Junior.

Of course—what did you expect, that we would just leave the goddamn tree sitting in the middle of the yard? We gotta plant it. Right on top of Charlie.

They kept digging and dumping the dirt on the growing pile on the tarp. The hole was now deep enough so that Johnny had to stand in the hole in order to keep digging. It was a laborious process to heave the dirt out of the hole and on top of the pile. Johnny was grateful that during his life he had never had to earn a living as a gravedigger. He'd rather put a bullet into his head than dig up dirt every day.

Junior set down his shovel and announced that he needed to take a leak. Okay, said Johnny. We'll take a break for five minutes. He climbed out of the hole and brushed off his pants. Junior went into the house while Johnny sat at the little garden table on the terrace. He was tired. Getting too old for this shit. He wiped his brow with his sleeve.

The hummingbirds were out. The presence of people doesn't bother them. While you're in your back yard they just go about their business. They aren't scared the way most birds are. They're not bothered by the busy sparrows that congregate in the lilac bushes and on the lawn. Speed gives them confidence.

Johnny saw that there were two hummingbirds in the yard. One was poking around the red flowers by the back fence. The other was that oddball bird that was larger than the others. She zipped into the yard and hovered near some blue flowers. Then she inspected the magnolia tree. Finding nothing of interest, she flew over to the hole in the ground. Then she flew near to where Johnny was sitting and hovered for a moment before abruptly zipping away over the high fence in the direction of the neighbor's yard.

Johnny shrugged. If that hummingbird ever came near enough to him he'd snare it and kill it. But it was too fast and too clever to be caught. And who cared, anyway? Just a stupid bird.

The sound of an aircraft engine intruded into Johnny's thoughts. A small plane. There was an airport nearby and during the summer the little Cessnas and Beechcrafts would circle Gloucester. Sightseeing, looking at the boats and the beaches. Johnny peered up at the cloud cover. With the houses around to reflect sound it was hard for Johnny to tell from which direction the plane was coming. Then he saw it. Single engine, high wing. The plane made a lazy circuit around the harbor before motoring off to the south. It became a speck and the sky was quiet again.

Junior emerged from the house. Ready to get back to work. They took up their shovels and resumed their labors. They dug another foot deeper, and then another. Sweat trickled down the back of Johnny's neck. The handle of the shovel was slippery. His arms ached. God, what a thankless task.

As the sun was setting over the harbor Johnny told Junior that the hole was finished. It was well dug and professional. Six feet deep and with good straight sides.

The time had come to bury Charlie. This was the most dangerous part of the operation: bring the body outside, dump it in the hole, and cover it up. It would take about five minutes to get the body sufficiently covered with dirt so that the hole would no longer be a grave but would become a flowerbed with a magnolia tree in the center.

Those five minutes were critical. Johnny and Junior needed to act quickly.

Johnny had planned the operation very carefully. After they had buried the corpse and planted the tree, they'd go down to the basement and wash the floor with bleach. The floor was old concrete and stained with decades of paint and grease. The bleach wouldn't change that—after they were done, the cement surface would look like it hadn't been touched. Then they'd bust up the chair and burn it. Take the chains and drop them in the harbor. A few days in salt water would destroy the DNA.

An hour from now, Charlie Kasko would be just another missing person.

Johnny and Junior dragged the wrapped corpse across the basement floor and up the rough stone steps leading to the bulkhead door to the outside. When they were halfway up the stairs they paused. Wait here, said Johnny. He stepped around the body and grasped the old latch to the bulkhead door. From around the edges of the door burned the rectangle of bright daylight. He was about to shove open the door when he stopped. It would be safer if he went around through the basement and up into the kitchen, and then out the back door into the yard. Once he was in the back yard he could verify that no one had entered the property while they had been in the basement.

Johnny told Junior to wait with the body until he had opened the bulkhead door from the outside. Junior nodded.

Johnny went through the basement and out the back door. In the early twilight the yard was quiet. The hole was there, and the big pile of dirt on the tarp too. The magnolia tree waited in its root ball. A hummingbird zoomed to a blue flower, hovered, and zoomed away. Overhead a seagull gave a harsh cry. Johnny looked to the sky. No planes. A light wind rustled the trees. Johnny peered down the path that led to the street. The path was deserted. On the street, a car passed the house and was gone.

Johnny went to the basement bulkhead door and pulled it open. Junior squinted up at him. So did the gaping face of Charlie Kasko from inside its plastic cocoon.

Okay, let's move, said Johnny. He grabbed a handful of plastic and pulled. Junior picked up the feet. They hauled the body out of the bulkhead and slid it onto the brick pathway. Junior scrambled out of the bulkhead. Johnny bent down and grasped the plastic that was bunched by the body's shoulders. Junior hoisted the feet. They carried the corpse across the lawn, past the magnolia tree, to the edge of the hole, where they brusquely dropped it on the ground.

Let me get his watch, said Junior. He bent down to open the plastic wrapping.

Are you fucking crazy? said Johnny.

Junior protested that it was a Rolex. No sense in wasting it.

Fuck the watch. We're gonna bury it with him. Now let's get going.

At that moment Johnny saw the hummingbird. The big one. It had flown up the garden path from the street. It circled the yard. Its tiny wings were a blur. It darted around the magnolia tree and then ventured close to the hole. At a distance of ten feet from Johnny it hovered.

Goddamn little bugger! Johnny picked up his shovel and swung it at the intruder. The tiny bird instantly flew backwards a few feet, the way a boxer leans back to avoid a punch.

Junior laughed. Who cares about a stupid bird? You'll never catch him.

From the corner of his eye Johnny saw the intruders running into the yard from the garden path. Helmets, boots, flak jackets, automatic weapons. All black. Sharp commands to drop the shovel and get down on the ground. Johnny and Junior were encircled. Facing a dozen black muzzles of automatic weapons. There was no escape. No hope. With his hands over his head Johnny knelt on the soft grass and then lay flat on his stomach. Rough hands searched him as his arms were yanked behind his back and his wrists cuffed. A voice said that Johnny Carrigan and Robert Holmes, Jr. were under arrest for the murder of Charles Kasko. They had the right to remain silent. Johnny was hauled roughly to his feet.

One of the cops wasn't a cop. He was dressed in jeans and a baseball jacket. He approached Johnny, looked him in the face, and smiled.

Chris Mark, sneered Johnny. You think you got me. Good for you.

We know we have you, replied Mark. Courtesy of our little friend it's all on film. You and Junior brought Charlie to the house. Took him into the basement. And now his corpse is wrapped in plastic on your lawn.

Over Mark's shoulder flew a hummingbird. The same bird at which Johnny had swung his shovel. Mark held out his hand with the palm up. The bird hovered over his hand before gently setting down on it. The wings stopped moving and the bird lay inert. It was now that Johnny saw that the bird's eyes were nothing more than dull plastic. Embedded in its white feathered breast was the tiny lens of a camera.

The great Pistol Carrigan, said Chris Mark. The great Pistol Carrigan was laid low by a hummingbird!

The Quarry Murder

The steel cable of the tow truck groaned under the weight of the car.

"Hold it a second," shouted the tow driver to his partner. "We need to let the water drain out."

The tattooed kid working the levers halted the winch. As the silver Cadillac hung suspended over the dark pool of the old quarry, water gushed from its undercarriage.

With the car's front end exposed like a trophy fish on a line, Chris Mark could see the figure of a man still strapped into the driver's seat.

"Okay," said the tow driver. "Lift her slow."

The tattooed kid threw a lever and the winch shook to life. Hanging by the thick cable, the dripping car emerged from the water and slowly rose until its rear bumper cleared the edge of the quarry. The driver inched the big tow truck forward until the rear of the Cadillac was well clear of the edge. Resuming his place by the controls on the side of the tow truck, the tattooed kid worked the levers and carefully lowered the car to the ground.

As the tow driver was unhooking the car, Chris Mark and police chief Ray Frontiero approached the driver's side door. It was locked.

"Pop the window," instructed Frontiero to one of his officers.

Once the glass had been broken and the door opened, Mark could instantly see in the driver's arms and hands the stiffness of rigor mortis.

"The water's cold," said Mark. "Looks like he's been submerged for at least five hours. That would jibe with what the studio assistant said about hearing the car last night." He turned and looked back at the tracks in the grass. "The car came down the driveway, but instead of stopping at the house he barreled off the pavement, crossed a section of lawn, smashed through a split rail fence, crossed another short stretch of lawn, and hurtled over the edge into fifty feet of water. No evidence of braking. A straight shot into the quarry."

"He's not a young man," shrugged Frontiero. "You know how old folks are. Every month I read a report of a senior citizen hitting the gas by mistake and ramming their Buick through the front doors of a Wal-Mart."

"Yeah, but Gustav Fredericks is no ordinary geezer," said Mark as he watched the medical examiner pry the victim's hands from the steering wheel. "He's a renowned sculptor. He works with stone and bronze. He's not someone who has problems with motor coordination."

As they watched the medical examiner, Mark stifled a yawn. He was not being disrespectful. He was tired. Eight o'clock in the morning was too damned early, especially after a late night poker game at Bernie's. Mark had ended the night fifty dollars in the black and unable to walk a good straight line home. Once he found his way into his bed he had gratefully anticipated a solid night's sleep that would last until the sun was high in the sky. But as dawn broke Frontiero had called, and so here he was, in the sharp light of early morning seeing the body of one of the most successful artists in Gloucester being loaded into a body bag.

After the bag had been zipped shut and hoisted into the medical examiner's van, Mark took a moment to familiarize himself with the old quarry. Many such water-filled pits dot Cape Ann; in the nineteenth century they were a source of high quality granite blocks that were shipped from Rockport and Gloucester to building sites all over the world. But an industry-wide strike followed by too many men enlisting to fight in the First World War crippled the business, and the increased use of concrete and steel for building, and asphalt for paving, ensured that it would never recover. The abandoned quarries—some as wide as football fields and others no bigger than the footprint of a small house—quickly filled with water. It is said that at the bottom of some of them there still remain the rusting hulks of cranes and machines that were simply left behind by bankrupt operators.

This pit—identified as Smith's Quarry on old maps—was a quarter-mile in diameter. It was ringed by trees that were interrupted only by three houses that were built close to the edge: Gustav Fredericks's house and studio, a white Greek Revival on the property next door, and a brick colonial visible through the trees directly opposite the Fredericks place.

The death car having been lifted from the depths, the scene was restored to one of perfect idyllic tranquility.

"Where's Fredericks's studio assistant?" asked Mark.

"In the house," replied Frontiero. "He hasn't been to sleep yet. He's been awake since he called nine-one-one at two o'clock this morning."

They turned and walked toward the big house.

Gustav Fredericks, the immigrant from Norway, had done well for himself. From his early student days living in a rented room on the Lower East Side of New York to his comfortable late career at his home and studio on four acres in Gloucester, it had been a long journey marked by international success. Fifty years ago he couldn't give away his sculptures; now museums and collectors waited in line to pay six figures for one piece.

"I don't get it," said Frontiero as they walked past a ten-foot-high bronze dog, which from its spot on the lawn commanded the view of the old quarry. "It's just a gigantic mutt."

"It's all about making the commonplace monumental," answered Mark. "And Fredericks shrewdly realized that everyone loves dogs. If he made cats, they'd sell for half the price."

The house was a magnificent example of Arts and Crafts architecture. Mark and Frontiero stepped onto the flagstone veranda that embraced the first floor like a mother's protective hug. Under its sheltering eaves they lingered to watch the silver Cadillac being winched onto the flatbed truck.

"Nice car," said Mark. "I can't imagine it having a mechanical malfunction."

Frontiero shrugged. "Let's see what the state police mechanics say. Not to mention the medical examiner. Maybe the old guy's ticker gave out."

Mark pulled open the screen door and entered the kitchen. Sitting at the big wooden table was a young man about twenty-five years old. His spiky black hair made his skin appear to be as pale as parchment.

"Are you the studio assistant?" asked Mark. "Jerry Winston?"

"That's me."

Mark pulled up a chair. "You called the police last night. You want to tell me what happened?"

"Not much to tell," shrugged Winston. "It was like any other night. Gustav often went out for a late dinner at a local restaurant—usually Lobsta House. Then he'd go to a bar and see some friends or hear some music. He'd come back around two and then stay up working until three or four."

"Do you know whom he was with last night?" asked Mark.

"He told me he was meeting his wife," said Winston. "Her name is Amelia. They're separated, but recently they've been seeing each other. To be honest, I think she's been trying to get Gustav to come back to her, but I don't think he was particularly interested. Getting back together with Amelia would have meant giving up his other girlfriends."

"Where were you last night?" said Mark.

"I was in the studio," replied Winston wearily. "Working on a piece that's in its final design stages. At a few minutes before two I saw the lights of the car come down the driveway. But instead of stopping in front of the house the lights kept on going. It seemed strange so I went outside and saw nothing—no car. I ran into the house, got a flashlight, and returned to the driveway. I saw that the fence had been smashed. The tire tracks led straight to the quarry. I ran to the edge and looked down. Deep under the water I could see the faint glow of the lights of the car. It was horrifying. I hoped that maybe Gustav had gotten out. I waited by the water, just looking down at the lights. I called his name. He wasn't there. Then the lights of the car went out. I had left my phone next to the computer, so I ran back to the studio and called the cops. They came right away, but the divers couldn't go down to the car until it was daylight."

"I'd like you to show me where you were when you saw the car come down the driveway," said Mark.

Winston roused himself from his chair and slouched to the kitchen door. Mark followed him across a patch of lawn to a big wood-sided barn that was adjacent to the house. Winston pulled open a sliding door and they entered. Inside was a vast space full of big bronze castings of dogs in various poses. It looked like the kennel of the gods on Mount Olympus. Along one wall was a set of steel stairs. Winston led Mark up to the second level, which was a loft space that overlooked the main floor. Here there was a room that looked less like a sculptor's studio than a tech firm in Silicon Valley, with computers and small plastic models of dog sculptures.

"I was here, at my desk," said Winston. "As you can see, the window overlooks the front yard and the driveway. I can see anyone who drives in."

Mark scanned the room. "Is this where the sculptures are designed?"

"Yeah," nodded Winston. "It's all done by computer. We make a one-tenth-scale maquette of the sculpture. Then we photograph it with a 3D scanner. The scanner digitizes the object. The reverse engineering data is imported into a CAD/CAM program, and then sent to a prototype-sculpting machine. The sculpting machine makes a full sized version in polyurethane foam. The foam model is sent to the foundry, where they make the molds and do the casting. The cast bronze piece is brought back here for finishing."

"You must have a background in design," said Mark.

"I was a computer engineering major at Boston University," replied Winston. "But I've always loved art. So here I am."

At that moment Mark heard raised voices. He went to the railing. In the studio below, a distraught woman was talking to a cop.

Winston came and stood next to Mark. "That's the estranged wife," he whispered.

Mark descended the stairs and approached the woman and the cop. "Thanks, officer," he said before turning to the woman. "Are you Amelia Fredericks?"

"Yes," she replied with a long glance down her nose. "And you are—?"

"Chris Mark. I'm an investigator. May I ask you a few questions?"

"I'm the one who has questions," she snapped. "I heard there was a terrible accident. Is Gustav here?"

"No. I'm afraid he's deceased. His body had been taken to the medical examiner's."

Nearby was a plain ladderback chair to which Amelia retreated. After sitting for a moment she went into her alligator purse and extracted a tissue, with which she dabbed her eyes.

"I can't believe he's gone," she said. "Such a genius! The world will never see the likes of him again."

"You were with him last night?" asked Mark.

Amelia nodded. "We had dinner at Lobsta House. He was so sweet. He wanted me back. I know he did. That's why he never signed the divorce papers. In his heart he knew that I was the only one for him. I understood him—his moods and his inspirations. No one else could connect with Gustav the way I did."

"So you're still legally married to him?"

"A year ago I moved out of this house. I just couldn't take the lies and the cheating. Everyone assumed we were divorced, but it was never finalized. So yes, we're still married."

Mark's eye strayed to the glittering diamond on her ring finger. With her thumb she worried the platinum band.

"What happened after dinner?" asked Mark.

Amelia took a deep breath. "He came back to my place for a drink. He wanted to stay, but I was tired and I told him that I just wanted to go to sleep." She gave a shrug. "I suppose that idea did not please him, so he left."

"What time was that?"

"About eleven fifteen."

"Do you know where he was going?"

"Probably to a club. The Catboat is his favorite place."

Mark knew the Catboat. It was on Rogers Street down by the harbor, but it wasn't a local hangout. The prices were high and the atmosphere self-consciously trendy. While to call it pretentious would be unkind, the practical reality was that if you were a wealthy older gent looking for top shelf single women, the Catboat was the place to go.

Two and a half hours after leaving Amelia's, when Gustav Fredericks had plunged his car into the quarry, apparently he had been alone. Sometimes, it seemed, even the mighty Gustav struck out.

Mark's thoughts were interrupted by a quick movement by Amelia. She had stood up and was glaring at the loft.

"You!" she hissed.

Mark's eyes followed her sharp pointed finger to its target: Jerry Winston.

"If you had done your job Gustav would still be alive!" spat Amelia. "It was your responsibility to watch over him. You got paid to live here and to make sure that Gustav's vision was protected. Where were you last night? With one of your trashy girlfriends? How could you let this happen? You failed him!"

"I tried to *save* him!" shouted Winston. "If you hadn't made him so fucking miserable in his marriage, maybe he wouldn't have to go out every night. What did you ever do for him except to suck him dry? You're nothing but a vampire!"

"All right—enough!" said Mark. "Winston, go back to the office. Amelia, sit down. Nothing will be gained by making accusations. We're conducting a full investigation. If this was not an accident, we'll find out who's responsible."

"Can't you get her out of here?" called Winston from the balcony.

Mark turned on his heel and ascended the stairs. Quickly reaching the loft, without hesitation he took Winston by the arm.

"Listen to me," said Mark. "Be a good boy and sit down and shut up. The fact is that unless you can prove otherwise, Amelia Fredericks is the legal heir. Until we declare this house and studio to be a crime scene, she has a right to be here. As for you, you're an employee. Unfortunately Gustav Fredericks is out of business. Your employment has been terminated."

As Mark released his arm Winston slumped into his office chair. "Sorry," said Winston. "I'm just tired. It's been a long night. Every time she comes around here she brings nothing but misery. Gustav used to complain incessantly to me about her. Called her 'The Great Medusa.' Said that any man who looked at her would turn to stone."

"And yet he went to see her," said Mark.

"Yeah. Go figure. Maybe they had some sort of weird chemistry. But who cares? For the past ten years Gustav Fredericks has been nothing but a brand name. No one knows what goes on around here."

"What do you mean?" asked Mark.

From the studio below boomed a man's voice. "I insist on being allowed to exercise my rights!"

Mark peered over the balcony railing. Standing in the center of the studio was a burly man with a sheaf of papers in his hand. Between the man and a group of finished bronze dogs stood Chief Frontiero.

"You stay here," Mark instructed Winston before he hurried down the stairs.

"Listen, fella, you can't just walk in here and start taking things," Frontiero was saying as Mark approached them.

"I have a right," retorted the man. "Gustav Fredericks owes me a hundred thousand dollars."

"Who are you?" asked Mark.

"My name's Edward Hill. I own Northeast Foundry. We do all of Gustav Fredericks's casting. Listen, I'm sorry about the old guy, but business is business. The last five pieces we cast for him were never paid for. He was a longtime customer so I let him slide. I asked him over and over again. He kept putting me off. He said he had a big museum sale in the works that would take care of everything. That's why I'm here. Those five pieces are right over there. They each have my foundry mark. I'm ready to take them. I got bills to pay like everyone else."

"Are you insane?" interjected Amelia. "Those five works of art are worth a hundred thousand dollars *each*. Maybe if you go to court and get a judgment you'll be lucky to get one of them as payment. But five? You're crazy. Over my dead body."

"One corpse is enough for now," said Frontiero.

"Amelia, let us handle this," said Mark. He turned to Hill. "None of these works are leaving this studio. The estate will be inventoried. You'll have your chance to be heard. By the way, where were you last night between midnight and two o'clock?"

"I was at home," replied Hill. "Why?"

"Just getting everybody on the record," replied Mark. "Now I need you to leave. If the estate owes you money, get a lawyer. Middle Street is full of 'em. Just knock on any door and you'll find one."

With a sour look Hill took his papers and left.

"I never liked that man," said Amelia.

"Why not?" asked Mark.

"Many years ago Edward Hill got his start making industrial bronze castings—things like gears and crematorium urns. Gustav hired Hill to cast his early small dogs. They were no more than three or four feet high. They sold well enough, and Gustav started making them bigger and bigger. At first they were five feet high, and then ten feet, and then fifteen feet high. Edward Hill couldn't handle the bigger sizes that Gustav wanted. His foundry is second rate but he charges top dollar. In the past few years Gustav had to have several pieces recast because of flaws. Gustav told me last night that he was looking for someone new. 'He's not getting another nickel out of me' is what Gustav said."

"How about Winston—when did he come on board?"

"About five years ago. Gustav realized that by using traditional clay models there was no way to cast the big pieces that he wanted. It was inefficient. He hired Winston so that he could design the pieces on a computer. Using the computer's data, you can have a full sized maquette made out of polyurethane. Then you just ship the polyurethane maquette to the foundry, where they use it to make the mold. It's many times easier than the traditional method, where you've got a heavy steel armature or skeleton that you must cover in clay. For a big piece you need several tons of clay and steel."

"A work can be cast more than once," said Mark.

"Absolutely," said Amelia. "Multiple castings of bronze sculptures are made routinely. Take 'The Thinker' by Rodin. Many were cast during Rodin's life, and many more after his death. Posthumous castings of 'The Thinker' include the ones at the National Gallery in Washington, D.C. and the Vatican Museum in Rome. In an effort to limit these endless castings, in 1956 France passed a law that say the maximum number of examples that can be made from an artist's original and still be considered his work is twelve. Most other nations agree."

"How many castings of each piece did Gustav have made?"

"Never more than three or four. He didn't want to dilute his market."

Mark surveyed the jumbled studio, with its many models of dogs and unfinished full-sized castings. "Assuming there are no surprises in the will, all of this will be yours," he said. "You'll have the responsibility to manage the estate."

"I'll do a better job of it than the sycophants who hang around here," said Amelia forcefully. "I'm going to run things a bit differently." She leaned forward. "First to go will be Jerry Winston. He's a shady one."

"What do you mean?"

"Gustav put Winston in charge of the accounts. He told me that he wanted to be free to focus on his work. Gustav never liked handling money. He was an artistic genius. He was never very good at everyday things. I had to tell him where his car keys were! I offered to handle the money but Gustav would brush me off and tell me that it was something that I shouldn't have to worry about. But lately Gustav told me that he was worried. He saw statements come in the mail from banks that he never heard of."

"He thought Winston was stashing cash in secret accounts?"

"Maybe," shrugged Amelia. "I don't know. Gustav kept his world very compartmentalized. I was in the 'wife' compartment. Some things he told me, and some things he didn't. I was in the dark about many parts of his life."

Mark's phone rang. The state police crime lab manager told him that the Cadillac had arrived for examination.

"If you'll excuse me," he said to Amelia, "your husband's car is being looked at. They need me there."

"But the state trooper who examined the car told me that there didn't seem to be anything wrong with it," said Amelia.

"Mechanically, perhaps," replied Mark. "The people looking at it now are the Digital Evidence and Multimedia Section. They focus on the computers in the car."

"Computers?"

"Your husband's car has nearly a hundred computers that control various actions. They range from big ones that control the powertrain to smaller ones for the brakes, dashboard, power windows, electrically controlled mirrors, sunroof, running lights, windshield wipers—you name it, if it moves it's probably got a computer controlling it. Then you've got the event data recorder—what people call the black box. The lab has to check out all of them."

As Mark hurried to his car, which was parked on the gravel drive near the road, he saw a woman walking her dog—a white Westie. Mark and the woman made eye contact, which Mark instantly regretted. He did not want to engage a nosey neighbor, at least not now. Shifting his eyes to his Camaro, he hoped that his diffidence would discourage interaction.

"Excuse me!" came an insistent voice.

She could not be ignored. Mark turned his head. The woman was not ten feet away. In her hand she held the leather leash against which the dog strained in its desire to inspect the base of a rock.

"Twinkle! Behave yourself!" said the woman as she gave the leash a sharp tug. The dog dejectedly gave up on the rock and sniffed about in the grass for another scent that could prove equally as fascinating.

"What can I do for you?" said Mark as blandly as possible.

"I couldn't help but notice all the police cars. Is everything all right? Has there been an accident?"

"Yes, there has been an accident," replied Mark. "And you are—?"

"Eleanor Listwick. I live next door—just past that line of lilacs. The white colonial. My husband and I have been here for thirty-two years."

"I'm afraid that Mr. Fredericks died last night," said Mark as he made a show of looking at his watch. "He drove his car into the quarry."

Eleanor Listwick frowned. "Oh dear. How very sad." She moved closer. "Well, as much as I hate to wish ill upon anyone, I suppose it's high time that there was a change around here."

"What do you mean?"

"Ten years ago this was a quiet neighborhood. Then Mr. Fredericks bought the place and the neighborhood went downhill. Suddenly there were cars coming and going all night. He let kids come and swim in the quarry, which all the other trustees absolutely forbid. We asked him many times to keep the kids out but he just laughed in our faces. And then all of these horrible sculptures started appearing!" She waved a bony hand across the grounds. "Such hideous things they are. I serve on the board of the Gloucester Museum of Art, and Mr. Fredericks wanted to donate one of them to the collection. I persuaded the board to decline the offer. I mean really—would *you* call these things works of art that deserve to be in a museum?"

"The Museum of Modern Art in New York has one," replied Mark.

"They've got all kinds of junk at MOMA," retorted Eleanor Listwick. "Anyway, whether or not you think a big bronze dog is any good is beside the point because of one important fact: Gustav Fredericks was an arrogant prick. I wouldn't give him the satisfaction of being in our museum if he wanted to give us the *Mona Lisa*." She gave Mark a sharp look. "Amelia—is she safe?"

"Yes. She's inside the house now."

"I'm happy to hear that. She's a fine woman who frankly deserved better. I don't understand why she put up with his shenanigans for as long as she did. Everybody thinks that just because you're a hotshot artist you can drag your loved ones through the mud. As if success gives you a license to abuse people. Well, I hope that she can bring back some dignity to this neck of the woods."

"She's a friend of yours?" asked Mark. He was becoming increasingly interested in this nosey neighbor.

After bending down to pet Twinkle, Eleanor Listwick drew herself up to her full height. "Yes, we are. Amelia Fredericks is a sweet and decent woman. I chose not to judge her on the basis of her husband's behavior. Why do you ask?"

"Just getting a picture of the neighborhood," replied Mark. "You said you're a neighbor and that your house is the white colonial that you can see from this property—"

"Yes, that's us," replied Eleanor Listwick.

"I assume that you have a view across the water to the Fredericks house and the studio."

"Oh, yes," nodded Eleanor Listwick. "We can see every damned bronze dog on the lawn. Every bunch of kids who go swimming in the quarry. Every near-accident caused by Gustav Fredericks when he comes careening down the driveway at two in the morning, drunk. It's a miracle this didn't happen years ago."

"Did you see what happened last night?"

Eleanor Listwick's eyes slid to the side. "No. I didn't see anything. After *The Late Show* ended at twelve thirty, I went to bed."

"So last night you happened to miss Gustav Fredericks as he came careening down the driveway at two in the morning?"

"Yes. That's correct. I was asleep."

"Thank you, Mrs. Listwick. If you'll excuse me I really must be going."

As Chris Mark drove south to the state police crime lab he mulled over the events of the day. After weighing all the evidence, or lack thereof, his first impression was that Gustav Fredericks had died in a tragic accident. It seemed impossible that anyone could have been in the car with him when it went into the water; the doors were locked and the windows rolled up. Anyone exiting the car as it was sinking could not possibly have closed the car door because of the massive rush of water. On the grass at the quarry's edge there were no skid marks. Fredericks had driven straight into the water without even trying to stop. His body showed no wounds.

And the car had been in good condition. The brakes were fully operable.

Mark's phone rang. The call was from the medical examiner's office. Gustav Fredericks had a blood alcohol concentration of point zero six percent. In Massachusetts the legal limit is point zero eight percent. Fredericks was impaired but did not meet the legal definition of drunk. He had bruises on the sides of his hands consistent with hitting the door or window in an effort to escape the car. Otherwise he was uninjured. Cause of death was drowning. Manner of death—natural, accident, suicide, homicide, or undetermined— had not been established pending more tests.

Mark thanked the caller and hung up. Natural death had been ruled out. Suicide seemed preposterous. That left accident or homicide.

Mark felt the corrosive tide of resentment rise within him. Damned Frontiero! Couldn't he have handled this case on his own? Was Mark's skill so extraordinary that he had to be dragged out of bed every time a citizen of Gloucester met with an unusual or untimely demise? He was tempted to turn the Camaro around, drive home, and go back to sleep. He did not need this aggravation. Some old coot drives off his driveway and into a quarry and drowns. Sad but not earth shattering. Everyone's gotta go somehow.

But Chris Mark hated loose ends. Once a case had been opened it had to be closed. Every lead had to be chased down. It was a matter of personal integrity. And so he knew that regardless of his ambivalence he would dutifully put one foot in front of the other until he had arrived at his destination. And maybe then the good citizens of Gloucester would do him a favor by not getting themselves murdered and not dying under mysterious circumstances. If they gave him a break he might get in more quality time on his surfboard. There was a competition coming up soon in New Hampshire, and he didn't want to miss it. He could use the prize money.

The silver Cadillac sat in the state police garage. Like a giant lab rat, it was hooked up to a web of wires that led from the car to a set of diagnostic computers.

"Ah, Chris Mark," said Dawes, the lab technician. "It's been a while. Still making the surfing circuit?"

"Yeah, at least whenever people aren't getting themselves bumped off. Last week I was down in South Carolina. Folly Beach. Did pretty well at the Liquid Shredder Open. This morning I saw on Surfline that the tropical storm off Bermuda is producing six footers there. But hey, I gotta pay the mortgage. Tell me about this car."

Dawes consulted his notes. "The first thing we checked was the black box. It records fifteen vehicle data points. These include vehicle speed at five seconds before impact, brake status, throttle position, ignition cycle count, airbag deployment, and more. All the data points checked out as unremarkable. By all accounts, they show that the victim drove straight into the water and didn't even apply the brakes."

Mark felt his heart sink. "So why am I here?"

"Because there's something else," said Dawes. "I had to do some deep digging, but I've found evidence that your victim was murdered."

"Murdered? How? No one else was in the car."

"They didn't have to be. Several of the computers on board show evidence of being hacked."

"How could a hacker cause an accident?"

"By introducing a set of destructive codes or malware and selectively disrupting the computers that control the various systems in a vehicle. A hacker can take over the car's computer systems to turn the engine on and off, disable the brakes, change the cruise control settings, and control many of the electrical systems including the lights, climate control, locks, and even the sound system."

"How does a hacker gain access?" asked Mark.

"There are several different ways. Most modern vehicles have an on-board diagnostics port. This is an access point through which car mechanics get data on the vehicle's functions and make adjustments to various performance metrics such as the timing of the engine. A hacker can also get in through the car's mobile phone hardware, which is linked to the car's computer system. Malware can be installed that enables a thief to unlock the car remotely and to take over various other systems. Remote access can be gained using the car's Bluetooth system using a laptop or cell phone."

"And someone did this to Fredericks's car?"

"Yes. His Cadillac is equipped with OnStar, the network service that provides vehicle security, hands free calling, turn-by-turn navigation, and remote diagnostics systems. You've seen the ads on television where a stolen car is speeding down the highway, and control of the car is taken over by the cops. The stolen car slows down and comes to a stop. That's a good example of remote control achieved through an internet connection. The OnStar system is encrypted, but if you broke the code you'd gain access to the vehicle controls. My guess is that when the car was on the driveway and pointed in the direction of the quarry, at that moment the hacker disabled the brakes and commanded the car to accelerate. The victim was impaired by alcohol and did not—or could not—react quickly enough. Before he knew what was happening he was in the water. The hacker terminated the commands and the car reverted to its normal functionality. By that time it was too late. The Cadillac is a heavy car. It sank like a rock."

"So we're talking about someone interfering with the systems of the car for a period of less than five seconds," said Mark.

"Yes—just long enough to drive across the lawn and plunge into the water."

Mark was electrified. The death of Gustav Fredericks was not an accident. It was murder. The method was very sophisticated. No need to use a gun, which after all is not much more than brutish seventeenth-century technology. All the killer needed was a computer and knowledge of software programming.

Unfortunately, software programming was no longer the private domain of a few select geeks in Silicon Valley. Almost anyone with computer skills could go online and learn how to create and use malware for any purpose.

"The chicken teriyaki looks good," said Mark. "With a Sam Adams on draft."

"I'll have the steak tips," said Chief Frontiero. "I'm on duty so I'll stick with cranberry juice." He handed the menu to the waitress. He looked at Mark. "Your first time here at the Catboat?"

"For dinner, yeah. I've been to the bar a few times. They make a pretty good vodka martini. I thought we'd come here because this is the last place Gustav Fredericks was at before he was murdered."

"Or so says the on-again, off-again wife," said Frontiero. He consulted his phone. "Ah—just what I was waiting for. Well, it looks like we may have embarked on a wild goose chase. Unless he paid cash, which according to people who knew him he never did, Fredericks was not here last night. His bankcards show no activity here. What they do show is a charge to the Rock Point Motor Inn. It was made at eleven forty-five last night. One room. Obviously he didn't use it for the full time that he paid."

"Okay," said Mark. "He made a booty call. He met someone who couldn't stay overnight at his house—someone who had to go home by two o'clock. Let's get the security camera tapes from the motor inn and find out who our mysterious companion is."

"We may not have to do that," replied Frontiero. "His cell phone records just came in. At eleven twenty—exactly five minutes after the missus said he left her house—he placed a call to a local cell phone. The call lasted three minutes. Let's see—the cell phone belongs to Cynthia Jasper. Her address is fifteen Winding Way in Gloucester."

"I know the street," said Mark. "It's in Fredericks's neighborhood. It runs along the side of the quarry opposite Fredericks's property. It's a short road—only a few houses. I'll bet I know which house it is." He consulted Google maps. "Just as I thought. Fifteen Winding Way is the brick house that you can see from the Fredericks place. It's directly across the quarry. And the owners of the house are Cynthia and Robert Jasper."

"Gustav Fredericks leaves the wife at eleven fifteen," said Frontiero. "He calls Cynthia Jasper at eleven twenty. At eleven forty-five he checks into the Rock Point Motor Inn. At two o'clock he arrives home and drives into the quarry."

"I think I'll pay a visit to the Jasper residence," said Mark.

Nestled among a stand of oak trees, the fine old federal style house showed the patina of well cared-for age. Chris Mark pushed the glowing doorbell button and was rewarded by the soft shimmer of chimes from within. Presently the door swung open. In the late evening light stood a woman. A stylish forty years old, slender, with hazel eyes that spoke of deep sadness.

"Mrs. Jasper? Chris Mark. May I come in?"

"Yes, of course." She led Mark through the vestibule to the library, which opened onto a terrace at the rear of the house. Beyond the terrace lay the dark waters of the quarry.

"May I get you something to drink?" Cynthia went to a cabinet that opened to reveal a bar. Without waiting for Mark to answer she took a glass, scooped in some ice cubes, and reached for a bottle of Jack Daniels.

"I'll have whatever you're having," said Mark.

While Cynthia prepared a second glass Mark took stock of the room. Books lined the tall shelves, and in the corner by the fireplace stood a federal rolltop desk. Yet on the floor next to the desk, from its circular base rose a slender stainless steel sculpture that Mark recognized as being by a contemporary artist in New York.

The Jaspers had eclectic tastes.

"Here you are," said Cynthia. After handing Mark his drink she sat lightly in a leather-upholstered chair. With her legs crossed to reveal trim ankles and satin house slippers, she waited for Mark to begin.

"Thank you for seeing me at this late hour," began Mark.

"It's not so late. I've always been a night owl."

"I think that you know why I'm here."

"Yes," she nodded.

"If I may ask, where is your husband?"

"He's upstairs in his office. He works seven days a week. I think it's an escape. But whatever makes him happy."

"Does he know—?"

Her eyes narrowed. "He knows that I was out with my girlfriends last night at a club."

"You know that your story is going to be blown apart."

"Yes, I suppose it's time to face the music. To be honest, for several years Robert and I have not been happy. We lead very separate lives."

"And Gustav Fredericks was—?"

She gave a shrug. "Someone exciting. I know that he was separated from Amelia." She laughed, showing white teeth. "It's a regular soap opera around here, isn't it? Maybe I'll write a book someday. *Fifty Shades of Sneaking Around.*"

With a final swallow she drained her glass. "How's your drink?" she said.

"I'm good, thanks."

Cynthia got up and went to the bar. Mark did not think it was his imagination that as she walked he saw in her hips an extra sway. While she fussed with the ice tongs he watched her, as she knew he would.

With fresh ice cubes and a full glass of whiskey Cynthia returned to her seat.

"Where were you at the time of the accident?" asked Mark.

"What time was that?"

"Two o'clock."

"I was driving home. I had to stop for gas at a twenty-four-hour station by the harbor. I arrived here about two fifteen. Robert was not happy. We argued and then I went to bed."

At that moment Mark heard the sound of footsteps. Cynthia subtly changed her posture so that she was sitting more upright, with her back straight against the chair.

A man entered the room. Fiftyish, stocky, graying hair. He looked first at Cynthia and then at Mark. "I saw the car outside," he said abruptly. "A black Camaro."

"Yes—it's mine." Mark rose from his seat. "Chris Mark. I'm investigating the death of Gustav Fredericks."

"Oh yes—terrible tragedy," said the man. "I'm Robert Jasper. I can see that you've met my wife. Do you have any questions for me?"

"Yes, if you don't mind. Where were you last night at two o'clock?"

"In my office upstairs. Waiting for my wife to come home from her evening out. With her girlfriends. What happened to Fredericks? I saw the car being pulled out of the water this morning."

"We thought it was an accident," said Mark. "But there's evidence that the car may have been tampered with."

"Do you mean like the brake lines were cut?" asked Cynthia.

"Something more sophisticated. The vehicle's computer may have been hacked."

"So he was *murdered*?" said Cynthia. She took a swallow of her whiskey.

"Possibly," said Mark.

"Well, that's certainly shocking," said Robert Jasper. "In this day and age, no one is safe. Now if you'll excuse me, I have a business videoconference with a client in California. Mr. Mark, if you have any more questions for me please give me a call." He turned and left the room.

"That's Robert," said Cynthia. "Man of few words."

"Mrs. Jasper, why don't we go outside on the terrace? We can speak more freely there."

"Suits me fine. I could use the air."

She rose and, with drink in hand, pushed open the French doors that led to the terrace.

The night was starry and crisp. From across the dark water the lights on the Fredericks property gleamed.

"From here you have a direct view of the house and the driveway," remarked Mark.

"Yes," said Cynthia. She shuddered. "It gives me the creeps to—you know—see where it happened. What an awful way to die."

"Who would want to kill him?"

Cynthia grew pensive. "Many people were not happy with him. Gustav was not happy either. He told me that he felt as if his creativity was gone. He was making lots of money, but the sculptures were all designed by his assistant on a computer. His work had become big business. It was no longer art. He told me that he missed the old days when he worked with his hands in clay and plaster. The problems with Amelia brought him down. He knew that a divorce would be terribly expensive. And the neighbors were not kind to him. They're all a bunch of old fossils."

"When you were with him at the Rock Point Motor Inn, how was his mood?"

"He called me at eleven twenty. I was at the Anchor Club with some friends. He told me that he wanted to see me. He sounded a bit drunk. I said okay, and after I got to the inn I waited in my car while he rented the room. I didn't want the clerk to see me. Gustav had brought a bottle of wine. We were in the room until one thirty, when I said that I had to go home. He was very sweet and made sure that I got to my car. Then I left."

"Okay. Thanks. By the way, what do you and your husband do for a living?"

"Me?" She laughed and her teeth shone in the glimmering light. "I'm a trust fund baby. Dad was president of a company that made the first industrial optic fibers. He was killed in a plane crash, but in his will he had established a trust for me. I just watch the portfolio go up and down with the stock market. You win a million, you lose a million. As for Robert, he's involved in an internet startup. Selling real estate advice. Not getting rich yet. Sometimes I think that he only puts up with me because of my money."

The rising moon threw splashes of light over the dark treetops. Across the water the lights of the Fredericks house burned brightly. And then another set of lights came on: the Listwick house. Mark saw a figure—Eleanor Listwick, perhaps— walk from the house to the water's edge. She stood in the gloom for a moment before turning and walking back into the warm glow.

"Do you know Eleanor Listwick?" asked Mark.

"I see her now and then," said Cynthia. "The quarry is owned in trust by the abutters. Every six months we have a meeting. She's the queen of the Hate Gustav club. She spends most of the meetings ranting about the sculptures and the kids swimming. What a bitch. For some reason, though, she and Amelia are tight. They really seem to like each other. Go figure."

The moon had climbed into the sky. Having decided to take the rest of the night off, Chris Mark was driving south to Beverly, where a band that he wanted to see was playing in a bar. As the highway rolled by he tried to rid his mind of the deadly soap opera into which he had been plunged. The primary characters—the studio assistant, the estranged wife, the irate neighbor, the owner of the foundry, and perhaps even the husband of the girlfriend—all had good reason to wish ill upon Gustav Fredericks. But who had the technical expertise to pull off a sophisticated hacking job?

As the speedometer reached eighty-five the highway led him into a bend to the right. Too fast, thought Mark. I don't need to get pulled over by the state police. He eased off the accelerator. Instead of feeling the speed slacken, he felt no change. The car maintained its velocity. Odd, thought Mark—I never use the cruise control. To disengage the cruise control—if for some reason it had become activated—he tapped the brake. On the softly glowing dashboard the brake light indicator light flashed but the car did not respond. The speedometer crept up to ninety. Mark passed a pickup truck in the right-hand lane as if it were standing still. Now he was on a long straightaway. His headlights cut a sharp path through darkness punctuated only by the taillights of cars upon which he was rapidly closing.

Mark downshifted from fifth gear to fourth. The engine screamed as the tachometer jumped to five thousand RPM. He held his foot on the brake pedal.

No response. The speedometer read ninety-five. To downshift again would destroy his engine.

A truck ahead was drifting from the right lane into the left. Idiot! muttered Mark. Carefully he steered the hurtling Camaro to the edge of the left lane, as close to the center guardrail as he dared. The truck was now straddling two lanes, leaving the white line in its wake like a boat.

They'd impact within seconds.

The truck continued its infuriatingly slow drift to the left. Mark realized that he was not going to make it on the left side. He was going to smash into either the truck or the guardrail.

As gently as possible—do not oversteer!—he edged the Camaro to the right. Hugging the pavement, the roaring car slid into the right lane before edging into the roughly paved breakdown lane.

As Mark struggled to control the car he flew past the truck on his left.

On the highway ahead shone a pair of taillights. Two cars, side by side. No chance of getting around them.

Mark pushed in the clutch and popped the transmission into neutral. The engine screamed to six thousand RPM as the car gradually slowed. Mark punched the kill switch on the engine. It did nothing. The powerful V-8 howled and vibrated the car as if it were a toy. He was now off the highway on the grass, rolling to a stop.

Mark reached in his pocket and pulled out the electronic key fob. He punched the car alarm button. Instantly the headlights flashed and a siren wail filled his ears.

The engine went from redlining to zero.

Mark punched the alarm button again. The wailing stopped and the headlights burned steady.

He was enveloped in silence.

The truck that Mark had passed came up from behind him and rumbled into the darkness ahead.

Mark sat in his car. Only now did he become aware of his heart pounding in his chest, his shirt bathed in sweat, his hands shaking.

He sat quietly as his body and his emotions eased back from their adrenaline-fueled hyper-awareness.

After a few minutes a car pulled up behind him and stopped. In the glare of its headlights Mark couldn't determine what kind of car it was. Had the killer come to finish the job? Mark's hand went to his holster behind his lower back.

Suddenly the Camaro was enveloped in the brilliant flashing lights of the police cruiser.

Mark powered down the window. A state patrolman wearing the familiar flat-brimmed hat approached his door.

"Sir, do you require assistance?"

"Yes. My name's Chris Mark. I work with Chief Frontiero in Gloucester. I need to get this vehicle flatbedded to the state police lab. The Digital Evidence and Multimedia Section. I have reason to believe that an attempt was made on my life."

"What's the report on your car?" asked Chief Frontiero. The late morning sun slanted through his office window.

"Whoever hacked Fredericks's car tried to do the same thing to me," replied Mark. "But this scheme was different. A piece of malware was inserted into the coding of my car's main computer that controls the drive train. When the speed hit seventy miles an hour—which would be the first time after the hacking that I would take the car onto the highway—the accelerator would clamp down and the brakes would become inoperable. The car would continue to accelerate until it hit something."

"But you survived."

"The criminal did not take into account the fact that my Camaro has a six-speed manual transmission. Once I got over the initial shock and had safely passed the truck, I popped the car into neutral. After I had coasted to a stop I used the car alarm system to override the CPU and shut the vehicle down. But it was a very close call. If it had happened at rush hour the results could have been disastrous."

"Any clue as to who planted the code?"

"Nope. It was engineered to erase itself after its one-time activation."

With a sigh Frontiero leaned back in his chair.

Despite Mark's occasional resentment towards being asked to risk his own life and limb to solve murders in Gloucester, he had great affection for the chief. Frontiero was decidedly old school. This business of computer hacking had him flummoxed. The chief liked crooks who killed people the old-fashioned way, with guns and knives. He liked seeing physical evidence—fingerprints and gunpowder residues and telltale marks. What had been done to Fredericks, and had almost been done to Mark, was both devious and cowardly. No evidence. No trail to follow.

Then the chief brightened. With his rough fingers he shuffled through a pile of papers. "I've got something for you. It ain't much, but who knows." He produced a report and slid it across the desk to Mark. "At five minutes after two on the morning of the murder, Officer John Linquata pulled a guy over for speeding. The location was a half-mile from the Fredericks place. Officer Linquata had observed a car leaving the residence of Eleanor Listwick. He followed the car and determined it was speeding. Pulled him over and gave the guy a ticket for doing forty in a twenty-five-mile-an-hour zone. The guy was cooperative and Linquata let him go on his way."

Mark scanned the report. "The driver's name is Scott Wonston. Aged twenty-eight. Home address in Gloucester. Who is Scott Wonston?"

"Something tells me you're going to find out," replied Frontiero.

At five o'clock that afternoon Chris Mark opened the door to the conference room of the Gloucester Police headquarters.

"Ah—Mrs. Fredericks and Mrs. Listwick," said Mark. "Thank you for coming down to the station. I hope we haven't inconvenienced you."

"As a matter of fact you have," said Eleanor Listwick. "At eight o'clock I'm supposed to be on a plane to Chicago. I hope this won't take long."

"I could use some coffee," said Amelia Fredericks sharply. "With cream and sugar."

"If you don't mind police station coffee, I'm sure one of the officers would be happy to oblige." Mark pulled up a chair and sat opposite the two women. "To be honest, Mrs. Listwick, I do not think that you'll be making your flight."

"And why not?" she spat.

"Because of the confession of Scott Wonston."

"And who is Scott Wonston?" said Eleanor Listwick.

"He's a software engineer. He's the guy who hacked into both Gustav Fredericks's car and my car. He'll be facing a long list of charges."

"And how does this involve me?" said Eleanor Listwick.

"In order to signal Fredericks's car at just the right moment—when he was coming down the driveway—Wonston needed to see the car. It would have been too dangerous for him to be on the Fredericks property, especially with Jerry Winston sitting at his window that overlooked the driveway. He had to be somewhere else. At two o'clock on the morning of the murder, Scott Wonston was sitting on your terrace with his laptop. The terrace provided him with a perfect view of the Fredericks house and property. He watched as Gustav Fredericks's Cadillac crashed through the fence and plunged into the water."

"But I had nothing to do with any of it!" protested Eleanor Listwick.

Mark shrugged. "The district attorney doesn't care. Wonston has made a full confession. Both you and he will be going to prison."

"There's no proof that I knew anything!" said Eleanor Listwick.

"He was on your terrace at two in the morning. You're saying that you didn't know?"

"Yes. I was in bed, asleep. He must have snuck onto the property."

"There's more," said Mark. "Aside from the statement by Scott Wonston, we have a record of two deposits into his account. Each deposit was ten thousand dollars cash. These are convenient amounts because according to the Bank Secrecy Act you have to report deposits exceeding ten thousand dollars."

"I didn't pay him anything!" said Eleanor Listwick.

"Sorry, Mrs. Listwick," said Mark. "All the evidence points to you and you alone. Conspiracy to commit first degree murder." He turned to Amelia Fredericks. "Mrs. Fredericks, it appears as though you are free to go."

"What?" shouted Eleanor Listwick as she rose to her feet. "Amelia, tell him!"

"Tell him what?" she replied coldly.

"Tell him the truth! That you came to me and said that you couldn't live with Gustav's abuse a moment longer. You begged me to let that man sit on my terrace that night. You said that no one would ever know."

"Eleanor, shut up," hissed Amelia Fredericks.

"Mrs. Listwick, don't try to pin this on Mrs. Fredericks," said Mark. "I don't believe for one moment that she has the guts or the imagination to plan something like this. You're clearly in a league that's far beyond hers."

"I'll prove it," said Eleanor Listwick. "The fact is, Mr. Mark, my husband and I are nearly bankrupt. We lost everything in a bad investment. We're putting the house up for sale and moving to an apartment. I haven't got twenty thousand dollars. I've barely got twenty dollars. If Scott Wonston were paid that kind of money, he sure as hell didn't get it from me."

Mark turned to Amelia Fredericks. "You are a cold bitch, aren't you?"

Now Amelia Fredericks stood. "Screw you, Mr. Mark. You have no idea what it was like to live with that man. The great Gustav Fredericks! What a fraud. Jerry Winston designed and built the sculptures. I could go to any art college and hire someone just like Winston. Make more silly giant dogs and slap the Fredericks name on them. I stood to make millions from his estate. I planned the accident. For the pleasure of getting rid of Gustav, ten grand was chump change. If I weren't surrounded by pathetic weaklings we'd all be walking out of here. Eleanor, you're nothing more than a whiny mouse. And Scott Wonston is a fool. I told him to keep cool and to especially not get stopped by a cop! What an idiot! And you, Mr. Mark—thanks to Wonston's incompetence you're still alive. Ten thousand dollars wasted."

Mark went to the door. "Officers, come in. Put the cuffs on Amelia Fredericks and Eleanor Listwick."

The Body on the Rocks

There are many different ways human beings scream.

At the amusement park you hear the shrill cries of rollercoaster riders who, with arms held high not in surrender to the enemy but as expressions of death-defying hubris, giddily anticipate the breakneck plunge down the first big hill. In movie theaters you hear the excited shrieks of patrons who have paid to be scared half to death by the maniac on the screen. There are the squeals of delight from children who tear open Christmas presents to find that Santa has brought that coveted toy. And there are angry howls of sports fans who somehow expect that the nearsighted referee who is far out in the middle of the playing field, surrounded by thousands of the screamers' fellows, will somehow hear and be affected by each one's individual complaint.

Of the many varieties of excited utterances made by people, the scream of genuine terror is singular and unmistakable. It penetrates to the core and demands a response.

On that raw morning while walking on the desolate stretch of rocky coastline, the last thing that Chris Mark expected was an interruption to his solitude. Nursing a hangover, he only wanted to take a stroll and clear his mind. Of course, the shore was not totally deserted; it rarely is, and even in cold weather you will see people here and there, walking their dogs or just enjoying the briny air. But the rocky wasteland is expansive, and at low tide you can easily chart a course that will allow you to avoid interaction with any of your fellow walkers.

And so Chris Mark trudged along, just out of reach of the spray of the waves as they crashed against the boulders, with his hands in his pockets, not thinking of anything in particular except how the bracing air and the rhythmic murmur of the surf was making him feel like he hadn't made a huge mistake at the club last night. When Jack Daniels is your drinking buddy, it's easy to know when to stop. It's much harder to put down the glass and walk away.

The instant Mark heard the scream he knew something was very wrong. At the edge of a narrow chasm a woman was backing away from something. Her dog strained at its leash. Mark took his hands from his pockets, broke into a run. The woman saw him and pointed. The dog pulled excitedly, trying to get close to whatever was down there.

Mark approached the crevice and looked down. On the rocks ten feet below him a man lay on his back. He was clad in jeans and a sweatshirt. While the body was in bad shape—bloated and discolored—the waxy face still had its nose and ears, and the two bluish hands were at the ends of the arms.

The limbs and small bits had not yet been devoured by predators.

"I'm sorry that I screamed like that," stuttered the woman. "I just looked down and there he was. What do you suppose happened?"

Mark shrugged. "The ocean can take you any which way." On his mobile he punched nine-one-one. He heard the well-rehearsed voice say, "Gloucester Police, this is Officer Campbell. What is your emergency?"

"Tony, it's Chris Mark. We've got a body washed up on the rocks. White male in his forties. Been in the water awhile. Tell Chief Frontiero that I'm a quarter-mile south of Brace Cove. Okay. Thanks."

The cool afternoon light filtered through the half-drawn blinds of Ray Frontiero's downtown office.

"I know you're trying to avoid entanglements," said Frontiero. "I appreciate your assistance with this case."

"No problem," replied Mark. "Did the medical examiner provide an identification of the body?"

"Yes," replied Frontiero. "His wallet was still in his jeans. Name's Howard Galvin."

"The captain of the *Ace of Hearts*," said Mark.

"Captain and owner," agreed the chief. "Seventy-foot longline swordfisher. Sank off the coast last month in that big nor'easter. Galvin survived. He was plucked from the water by the Coast Guard chopper. One other crewman was lost." He picked up a computer printout. "The sea was not responsible for Mr. Galvin's demise. Cause of death was strangulation with a heavy rope. Finished off with a single bullet to the head."

"Somebody was not happy to see him back on dry land," said Mark. "When was he killed?'

"He marinated in the water for four days. That would put his death sometime on Thursday."

"Given the currents around Cape Ann, his body could have been dumped almost anywhere south of Gloucester Harbor," said Mark. "Or out at sea, with the waves bringing him in."

At that moment there was a disturbance at the front desk of the police station—officers shouting and a woman's insistent voice. The door to Frontiero's office flew open and a woman entered as if riding a whirlwind. With her hands on her hips she glared at Frontiero.

"You're the chief?" she demanded.

"Yes, I'm Ray Frontiero. And you are—?"

"Karen Hopper. Howie Galvin's next of kin."

"His wife?" asked Mark.

"Not yet," she spat. "We were engaged. But he has no other family. No parents, no brothers or sisters. I'm all he's got. I'm here to find out who killed him."

"You were informed—?" asked Frontiero.

"I got friends on the force," said Hopper. She looked at Chris Mark. "Who's he?"

"Mr. Mark is assisting with the investigation," said Frontiero. "I'm very sorry, Ms. Hopper, but we have no new information. But perhaps you can help us. Why don't you sit down?"

Reluctantly, Hopper slid onto the empty chair next to Mark's, facing the chief's desk.

"When did you last see Mr. Galvin?" asked Mark.

"Thursday night," said Hopper. "We had dinner at the East Main Bistro. Just the two of us. Romantic. He was very sweet. Then as we were leaving—it was around nine—he said that he was real sorry but he had to go talk to someone. He said it wouldn't take long. He dropped me off at the house. As I was getting out of the car he gave me a kiss and said that it was just some business, and that he'd be home in an hour. He seemed totally normal. Then he drove away. That's the last time I saw him."

"Any idea about who would want to kill your fiancée?" Frontiero asked Hopper.

"No," she replied. "He got along with everyone. He was a sweet guy. We never had a fight."

"What about after the *Ace of Hearts* went down?" asked Mark. "He lost a crewman and was nearly lost himself. That's a pretty traumatic event for anyone."

"Yeah, it was," nodded Hopper. She took a deep breath. Her face tightened. "After the boat sank he was shook up pretty bad. When we'd go out in public he was on edge, as if he was worried about something or someone. His phone would ring and he'd excuse himself and leave me alone while he talked to the person. Then he'd come back, and if I asked him what was wrong he'd say, 'Nothin', baby, just business. Don't worry about it.' But I did worry about it. We were supposed to be planning our wedding. Not a big affair—just our friends. But you still have to plan. Find the church and arrange for the reception. But during the past few weeks he kept putting me off. He'd tell me that he was real busy and that in a few weeks he'd be able to take up where we left off."

"Did you ever overhear any of the phone conversations?" asked Mark.

"Only once. We were at his house, watching a movie on cable. His phone rang. He glanced at the caller ID and went into the kitchen. In Howie's house there's a bathroom next to the kitchen. You get to it by a short hallway. So I got up and walked in the direction of the bathroom. I feel terrible about doing this, but I wanted to know what was going on. I wanted to know if it was another woman. In the hallway I stopped to listen. Howie wasn't saying anything. I guess he was listening to the person on the phone. Then I heard him say, 'Okay, Arnie. I'll take care of it. I understand. Yes. It will happen.' Then Howie walked near the doorway to the hallway where I was standing, and I thought he'd see me so I pretended to be walking to the bathroom. I went into the bathroom and closed the door. After a minute or so I flushed the toilet and ran the water. When I came out Howie was already sitting on the sofa in the living room. When I sat next to him I asked him if everything was all right, and he said that it was. He quickly changed the subject."

"That was the name—Arnie?" asked Mark. "Did he ever mention this name at any other time?"

"No, just that once."

"Okay," said the chief. "Ms. Hopper, thank you very much for stopping by. We'll let you know if we need to talk to you again. I'd appreciate it if you didn't leave town."

After Karen Hopper had left the office, the chief turned to Mark. "How many guys do we know who are named Arnie?"

"Not many," said Mark, "and none that jump to the foreground as people who might threaten Howie Galvin. I want to know more about the sinking of the *Ace of Hearts*. I'll see you in a while."

"Yeah, that was a rough night," said Harbormaster Rich Jackson. Leaning back in his office chair, he nodded his head in the direction of the harbor and the many boats riding at anchor or tied up at the wharves. "During the nor'easter we got beat up pretty bad, even here in the inner harbor. A couple of boats broke their moorings and we lost some of the big stone blocks off the breakwater. But the most serious tragedy was the loss of the *Ace of Hearts*. A real shame. She went down just east of Stellwagen Bank in ninety meters—about three hundred feet—of water. Greg Lewis was a good seaman. I know his parents. They were devastated. No matter how much you understand the risk, when it happens to your family it's unbearable."

"Howard Galvin was pulled off the boat," said Mark.

"The Coast Guard managed to get a chopper in the air. The chopper crew saw two men on the forward deck of the boat. They were both wearing immersion suits. A wave came along and swept one of them overboard. The chopper lowered the basket and managed to pull up the other one. That was Galvin. Lewis's body was never recovered."

"How long had the boat been at sea?"

"She left port on Monday the fifteenth. The storm was on the following Thursday the twenty-fifth. That would be ten days."

"Isn't that a short cruise for a longline swordfisher?"

Jackson shrugged. "Anywhere from ten days to a month is normal. Before she left Gloucester the *Ace of Hearts* took on eight thousand gallons of fuel, thirty tons of ice, and seven thousand pounds of bait—mackerel and squid. All of her gear was in order."

"And yet there were only two men on board," said Mark. "Longline fishing is an all-hands-on-deck business. There's no way two men could handle it. You need at least five or six good hands."

"It was my understanding that Galvin was going to pick up more crew in Provincetown."

"But he didn't," said Mark. "He was out for ten days with one other guy. How could they have caught any fish? My guess is that they were picking up something else." He thought for a moment. "The *Ace of Hearts* must have had a regular crew. Five or six guys who would normally have shipped out with Galvin but for some reason weren't hired. Are any of them around?"

Jackson shuffled through some lists on his desk. "You might try Johnny 'Sparks' Johnson. He was a regular hand on the *Ace of Hearts*. He's in town. Last I heard he had a room at the Lookout Bar on Rogers Street."

Chris Mark sidled up to the horseshoe-shaped bar and caught the eye of Shirley, the formidable woman who had been the proprietress of this harborside watering hole since most of her patrons had been in grade school.

"What can I get you?" she asked.

"I'm looking for Sparks Johnson," replied Mark. "I heard he bunked upstairs. Is he in?"

"Most likely," shrugged Shirley. "He's not shipping out until next week. Go upstairs and give his door a knock. Number six."

Mark ascended the narrow stairs to the second floor. He knocked on door number six.

"Yeah?" came a languid reply.

"Johnny Johnson? I want to ask you a few questions."

The door was opened by a rail-thin kid in his twenties. Flannel shirt, black hair, tattoos.

"Yeah?"

"My name's Chris Mark. May I come in?"

"You a cop?"

"No. Just helping the chief with an investigation. I want to talk to you about Howie Galvin."

"Okay." Johnson stepped to the side to allow Mark to enter the nondescript, functional room furnished with two twin beds, TV, refrigerator, and microwave. A window provided a view of Rogers Street, beyond which was Manny's Marine with its big gas tanks, and then the harbor.

"Smoke?" asked Johnson.

"No thanks," replied Mark.

"Shirley's gonna kill me for smoking in the room," said Johnson. "But I don't feel like standing out there on the sidewalk. So what's up with Howie? Is he in trouble?"

"Howie Galvin's dead. Murdered. His body washed up on the rocks near Brace Cove. When was the last time you saw him?"

"Wow," said Johnson. "I don't like seeing anyone get hurt, but I'm not surprised. He was a cheap bastard. A lot of people didn't like him. When did I last see him? Maybe two weeks ago. Here at the Lookout. I was sitting at the bar and he was playing pool with some guys. I knew them—they were fishermen. Regular guys."

"What do you know about the sinking of the *Ace of Hearts*?"

Johnson took a nervous drag on his cigarette. "Nothing."

"Weren't you a regular crew member on his boat?"

"Yeah. So what?"

"So what? On the last trip he didn't hire you. He didn't hire *anybody* except Greg Lewis. He loaded up the boat with fuel and ice and bait and sailed around for ten days. On the return trip he was caught in the nor'easter off Provincetown. Maybe the boat got hit by a couple of rogue waves. The Coast Guard rescued Galvin. Lewis was lost at sea and the boat went down. You knew that Galvin was going out, didn't you?"

"Uh huh."

"What did he tell you?"

Johnson dropped his cigarette into a drinking glass. At the bottom of the glass was a small pile of soggy butts steeping in an inch of brown water. He stood up and paced the room. "He told me just to be cool. He was taking the *Ace of Hearts* out with another crew from Provincetown. No big deal. He'd use me the next time."

"But there was no crew from Provincetown. There's no evidence he even stopped in Provincetown."

"That's all I know. I swear."

"Okay," said Mark. "Do you know his girlfriend, Karen Hopper?"

"Yeah," answered Johnson. "She's a piece of work."

"What do you mean?"

"Just between you and me, I don't know why Howie put up with her. She nice and everything, but she has a big gambling problem. She likes to fly to Vegas on the weekends. Stays at a fancy hotel and plays the slots. Howie told her she was crazy but she does it anyway. Howie told me that on one trip she lost five thousand dollars. On an office assistant's salary it adds up. One night Howie and some of the guys were having beers at Fred's Clam Shack. He was not in a good mood. Sour. We asked him what the problem was. 'You don't want to know,' he said. We told him to either stop being a pain in the ass or tell us what was going on. So he said that Karen was fifty thousand dollars in the hole. She was going to lose her house. So Howie got a loan to bail her out. We asked him, How'd you get a loan for fifty grand to cover your girlfriend's gambling debts? He said that he went to see a guy named Smiley."

"I know Smiley," said Mark. "Loan shark. Operates out of Salem. Did some time in state prison for racketeering and extortion."

"Yeah," nodded Johnson. "That's the guy. We told Howie he was nuts. No woman was worth that. Smiley would break his legs if he couldn't pay on time."

"But Galvin didn't get just broken legs. He got killed. Seems like an unproductive move for a loan shark."

"Yeah—that's what I thought." Johnson lit another Marlboro and stared out the window.

Chris Mark wheeled his Camaro across the high bridge that spanned the Danvers River before taking the long swooping curve into Salem. He followed Bridge Street into the center of town, with its witch museum and occult shops jostling for space with venerable nineteenth-century houses that had been built by wealthy ship owners and their captains. Presently he found what he was looking for: the Clipper Tavern Restaurant. From the outside it looked like one of those insular places that makes no attempt to attract new customers. There was no menu posted by the door, no cheery awning to beckon you inside. The small windows were expressionless.

Inside was chilly and dark. As Mark's eyes adjusted from the glare outside to the gloom inside he appraised the bar with its few solitary patrons watching sports on the suspended TV screen. On the main floor a row of tables in the center was bracketed by parallel rows of booths along the wall. Just as Frontiero had told him, sitting in a booth near the back of the room was a man. On the table before him was a coffee cup. He did not appear to be eating. He was on his phone.

Mark approached the booth. The man noticed him and gave a slight scowl. With a smile Mark slid into the booth.

"Lemme call you back," muttered Smiley into the phone. He clicked it shut and his black eyes drilled into Mark. "Who the fuck are you?"

"My name's Chris Mark. Ray Frontiero told me where to find you."

"Yeah, well you tell Ray that this is Salem, not Gloucester, so maybe you should go back across the bridge. I ain't bothering nobody in his town." He leaned forward. "Unless you need a loan. You need a loan?"

"I want to talk to you about Howie Galvin."

"What about him?" Smiley's voice grew icy.

"Galvin's dead. Murdered."

"You gotta be kiddin' me," said Smiley. He thought for a moment. "You think I had something to do with it? I run a clean business. People come to me who can't go anywhere else. They can't get a bank loan. They can't get a payday loan. They can't even get a title loan on their fucking car. I'm the lender of last resort. *They* come to *me*. I don't force anybody to borrow money."

"Yeah, it's a real friendly business," said Mark.

"Banks have nice polite ways of getting their money back," said Smiley. "They send their lawyers after you.

Repossess your car. Foreclose on your house. Get the sheriff to throw you out on the street. It's all very respectable. My loans are private. If you screw me, I got no nice polite way of gettin' my money back. I'm a sole proprietor. No one's looking out for Smiley but Smiley. Sometimes customers need to be persuaded to honor their agreements."

"What about Howie Galvin?"

"He paid most of it back. The day before he headed out on the *Ace of Hearts*, he came to see me. Sat right where you're sitting now. I was ready for a sob story, right? I figured I'd have to persuade him to pay up. Then he pulled out a paper bag. I'll be damned if he hasn't got fifty thousand dollars in cash. I said, where's the juice? I want another five thousand dollars in interest. He said he'd have it for me in ten days, when he got back. I said, ten days? Make it six thousand. He used some choice words and I told him to go fuck himself if he didn't like it. I'm not doing this for my health. The longer you take to pay, the bigger the nut. It's simple economics."

"Did he say where he got fifty grand?"

"He didn't say and I didn't ask," glared Smiley. "Maybe he took it from his grandma. I don't care. It's none of my business."

"All right. He borrowed fifty grand and paid back the fifty but not the interest. Thanks. You've been very helpful. Let me buy you lunch." Mark took a new hundred-dollar bill out of his wallet and slid it across the table. Smiley followed it with his eyes. He did not reach for it.

"Just one more question," continued Mark. "You know a guy named Arnie?"

"What if I do?" Smiley's mouth turned down at the corners.

"We heard that Galvin had a conversation with someone named Arnie. Sounded like some sort of deal."

"There's only one guy named Arnie around here who matters," said Smiley.

"You mean the Duke?" asked Mark incredulously. "Arnie 'The Duke' Masserat, the boss of the Tremont Corner gang in Boston?"

"Hey," Smiley turned his palms up. "Look in the goddamn phone book. There are a million guys named Arnie. It could be any one of them. I ain't sayin' nothing. But if you want to know who might have an interest in Howie Galvin and his boat, the field becomes very narrow."

"Okay. Thanks. Have a nice day."

With a glass of Jim Beam at his elbow, from his usual table on the back deck of the Tiller Restaurant Chris Mark contemplated the pleasure boats tied up to the buoys and docks of Rocky Neck. In the glow of the half moon the masts of the sailboats pierced the sky like exclamation points. A solitary man in a skiff rowed slowly into the still waters of Smith's Cove, and with a gentle "chunk" his boat met the wooden piling of one of the docks. After unloading his fishing gear he tied up the boat and made his way to shore and the golden light of the back porch of a house.

"What can I get you tonight?" The voice of the waitress broke his reverie.

"A half-dozen oysters to start. Then a boiled lobster. Thanks." He handed her the menu.

The case of Howie Galvin was tough. The captain had an unhealthy devotion to his fiancée, Karen Hopper. She had racked up gambling debts that Galvin felt obliged to pay. Love will make you do crazy things, including risking your health by borrowing fifty thousand dollars from a loan shark. But Galvin had repaid the loan—mostly, at least—and he had expressed confidence that he could pay the balance after the last trip in the *Ace of Hearts*. But where did he get the fifty thousand to pay off the debt? And why did he hire only one crewmember when the *Ace of Hearts* had been supplied for a month-long trip to hunt swordfish? And why had an experienced captain like Howie Galvin been caught in a nor'easter that he could have sailed around?

As Mark swished the ice in his whiskey, from the corner of his eye he saw two women enter the back deck of the restaurant. The hostess showed them to a table by the window. After they were seated one of the women glanced in his direction. Hurriedly she stood up, and after giving a reassuring smile to her companion she made her way to Mark's table.

"Ms. Hopper," Mark said as he stood up.

"Mr. Mark—I'm so glad that I found you." She seemed agitated. "May I sit for a moment?"

"Certainly. Can I get you a drink?"

"Just a glass of white wine. Thanks."

"If you're wondering about the investigation, we're really just starting, and if you need information—"

"No, no," Hopper interrupted. "Well, not exactly." She lowered her voice. "Earlier this evening I received a phone call."

"From who?" asked Mark.

"Greg Lewis."

"The crewman on board the *Ace of Hearts*? He was swept overboard and presumed lost at sea."

"He survived," said Hopper. "He was wearing an immersion suit. After five hours in the water he was picked up by a lobsterman out of Provincetown. Greg made the guy swear that he wouldn't tell anyone. The lobsterman brought Greg to Provincetown and he checked into a motel. He stayed there for a week until his credit card was maxed out. Then he bought a bus ticket to Boston and borrowed some cash from friends. Another friend brought his car to him. Now he's staying at a cheap motel in Lynn. He's afraid to go home. That's why he called me. He wanted to talk to Howie. When I told him Howie had been murdered he freaked out. He said that he would be next. 'You don't know these people,' he said. I tried to get him to tell me where he was and he refused. I asked him how I could get in touch with him. He said that I had his number. Then he hung up."

"Do you have your phone with you?" asked Mark.

"Yes."

"Okay, then call him. Tell him that someone is here who can help him."

Hopper nodded. She took out her phone and punched the number.

"Hello—Greg?" she said. "Yes. It's me, Karen. Listen, don't hang up. I'm with a guy who wants to help you. No, he's not a cop. But sooner or later you'll have to tell someone what happened. You can't hide forever. The guy who's with me? His name is Chris Mark. Yes. You can trust him. Okay. Here he is."

She handed Mark her phone. After introducing himself, for a moment Mark listened. "Yeah," he said. "I'm a vet. Marines. Second Recon Battalion, Charlie Company. Now I just try to stay out of trouble. I'm helping the Gloucester police with the investigation into the death of Howard Galvin. I don't want to have to do the same thing for yours. Let's meet somewhere and talk it over. A public place. Okay, the IHOP on Route One in Danvers. Sure, I know where it is. Open twenty-four hours. I'm driving a black Camaro. Eleven o'clock? Sounds good. I'll be there."

After giving Lewis his mobile number, Mark handed the phone back to Hopper.

"By the way," said Mark, "Not that it's any of my business, but a certain hobby of yours has come up in the investigation. You know what I'm talking about?"

The waitress brought Hopper's white wine. She took a quick and unceremonious swallow.

"Yeah, I guess. I like to go to Vegas."

"You like to *lose money* in Vegas. Not that it matters, except that Howard Galvin borrowed fifty thousand dollars to pay off your gambling debts."

"Yeah. He was a sweetheart."

"Do you know where he got the loan?" asked Mark.

"I dunno," she shrugged. "I never asked."

"Does the name 'Smiley' ring a bell?"

"No."

"Okay. To be honest, what's more interesting to me is that Howie suddenly found fifty thousand to pay back the loan. How did that happen?"

"I don't know," said Hopper. She took another gulp of her wine.

"At the police chief's office you mentioned that you overheard Howie talking to a guy named Arnie. Do you have any idea who that might be?"

"I have no clue. There are lots of guys named Arnie, aren't there? My own brother works for a guy named Arnie. They do blacktopping and seal driveways and stuff like that. So who knows?"

"What's your brother's name?"

"Stephen Hopper. He's three years younger than me. The baby of the family. Our dad died when I was a kid. My other brother and sister both live in Phoenix, near mom, who's in a nursing home. Stephen lives just outside of Boston, in Somerville. Working-class town."

"When was the last time you spoke with your brother?"

"At Christmastime. A phone call. Even though he lives only an hour away from here, I don't talk to him very often. He's always been difficult to get along with. He did time in juvie for stealing a car. Stupid kid stuff. He always wanted to hang out with the tough kids. All of his buddies call him 'Crackers' because of his temper. I guess it runs in the family, huh?"

"Did you ever mention your relationship with Howie Galvin to him?"

"To Stephen?" Hopper snorted. "Not on your life. I keep my personal life to myself. The last thing I want is my little brother interrogating me about whom I'm dating. I was going to tell everyone in the family once we had set a date for the wedding. Until then, the less he knows the better." Hopper drained her glass. "I gotta go," she said as she stood up. "My girlfriend will wonder what happened to me."

"Thanks for coming forward," said Mark.

At that moment the waitress arrived with Mark's oysters. Hopper hurried back to her table and Mark settled into his dinner while he thought about the strange phone call with Greg Lewis and their appointment later that evening.

The IHOP parking lot was not crowded. Chris Mark assumed that Greg Lewis was sitting in his own car, carefully watching who went into the restaurant. Mark went to the glass front door and pulled it open. He was greeted by the chilly odor of sugar and corn syrup and fryolators. The hostess allowed him to sit in a booth in a far corner of the restaurant. While keeping an eye on the door Mark glanced at the menu with its endless varieties of dough and sugar and bacon. Chocolate chip pancakes. Red velvet pancakes. Cinn-a-Stack French toast. Bananas & cream Belgian waffle. Just the thought of them made him feel ill. He ordered a black coffee and an appetizer sampler of Mozzarella sticks, onion rings, and chicken strips. At least it would look as if he were eating something.

At five minutes after eleven a man entered the restaurant. Late twenties, brown hair over his ears, muscular build. Black t-shirt and jeans. His eyes scanned the room. They locked onto Mark then surveyed the room again. Satisfied, he approached the booth. Mark kept both hands visible on the tabletop.

"Greg Lewis?" said Mark.

"That's me." He sat across from Mark in the booth.

"Chris Mark. Thanks for coming out tonight. Are you hungry?"

"Yeah. Maybe I'll get some pancakes." His voice was surprisingly soft. Almost a whisper.

"You've had a rough time," Mark volunteered after the waitress had left them alone.

"You got that right," said Lewis. "Fuckin' nightmare from beginning to end."

"Tell me about it," said Mark.

Lewis took a deep breath. "I've been crewing for Howie Galvin for three years. Doing longline swordfishing. We'd do trips of two weeks, a month. Made decent money and no one got seriously hurt. We were lucky, I guess. The *Ace of Hearts* was a good boat. Never any problems. Howie was very tough and a lot of the guys badmouthed him but he always managed to get the fish and bring the boat home. Everyone always got paid. What more can you ask for? It's not summer camp out there. Either you love it or you hate it. There's no in-between.

"Before the last trip, Howie called me. He said that he had a special job. It was a chance to make some big money. We all knew that he had debts. His girlfriend had gambled away all their money. But the guys kept their noses out of it. It wasn't any of our business. So I listened to what Howie had to say. He wanted only me to go with him—nobody else. We were going to load up the *Ace of Hearts* as if we were heading out fishing. Fuel, ice, bait—the whole works. Howie spread the word that we were picking up four more guys in Provincetown. He told me that all we had to do was rendezvous with a freighter at a spot a hundred miles west of the islands of Madeira. Pick up some cargo and bring it back to the States. We'd be met by a private boat off the coast of Massachusetts and transfer the cargo. That was it."

"What was your cut?" asked Mark.

"Howie gave me two thousand up front and he promised another three thousand after the trip. Not bad for ten days' work."

"Did you know who the client was?"

"Howie never told me. He said the less I knew the better. But when we were stocking up the boat I overheard him on the phone. It seemed like he was careful not to say any names, but he used the name 'Arnie' once. That's when I knew this was serious business. The only guy I knew by that name who could be responsible for something like this was the Duke. A seriously evil guy. When I realized who we were working for I nearly backed out. I went to Howie and asked him point blank if we were working for the Duke. He said 'yes' but it was strictly business. Nothing could go wrong. Ten days to Madeira and back. Simple. So I thought, okay, I'll do it. I could use five grand."

Mark and Lewis sat in silence as the waitress delivered Lewis's plate of Harvest Grain 'N Nut pancakes.

"So you motored out of Gloucester," said Mark when she had left.

"Yeah. It was a Monday afternoon. We didn't stop at Provincetown. We kept a course due east. On Saturday we reached our rendezvous point near Madeira. Sure enough, we saw a freighter. Two-hundred footer. Panamanian flag. Name was the *Apollo Star*. Fortunately the sea was calm and we drew alongside. The forward crane was used to hoist sixty bales, each wrapped in grey plastic, and drop them onto our deck. Howie and I carried them down into the fish hold. I figured each bale weighed fifty pounds. I asked Howie what they were. He just smiled and made a sort of sniffing motion with his nostrils."

"Cocaine," said Mark.

"Yep," said Lewis.

"Sixty times fifty gives you three thousand pounds,' said Mark. "That would be a street value north of twenty million dollars."

"Yeah. Now I knew why Howie was doing the job. He was probably going to make six figures on the deal. It would have changed his life."

"Then what happened?"

"The transfer took about an hour. Then we turned around and headed for home. We were supposed to rendezvous with a big private cabin cruiser outside of Boston Harbor. On the way home everything was fine. Calm seas, no problems. On Wednesday night—the twenty-fourth—we started getting reports of a storm. But we were only two hundred and fifty miles offshore. We figured that in twenty-four hours we'd hit our rendezvous point, right on schedule. There was no way we were going to alter our course. We were too close, and in this business there are no excuses. By dawn on Thursday we were running ten-foot seas. This was not a big problem for us, but we were worried about making the transfer to the smaller boat. As the day went on the seas got worse. I started to get seriously worried. Then we took a big rogue wave over the stern. It came out of nowhere. The engine room was swamped. I went down to try to get the engine restarted. Meanwhile we're drifting and getting hammered by the waves. Water was flooding in from every direction. The windscreen of the wheelhouse was smashed. We knew we were screwed. Howie sent out a distress signal. The storm abated and the Coast Guard was able to send out a chopper. Howie and I were on the forward deck with the chopper hovering over our heads. I thought that we were going to escape with our lives. I could see the basket coming down. Suddenly I was lifted off my feet and I found myself underwater. I struggled to the surface. Another wave picked me up and tossed me further away from the boat. Then I lost sight of the boat. The storm intensified. I suppose the chopper had to get out of the area. I didn't know if they had rescued Howie, or if he had ended up in the soup like me.

"After a few hours the weather cleared. I didn't see the *Ace of Hearts*. I didn't see Howie. I saw only the empty sea. There I was in my immersion suit in the middle of nowhere. Once or twice I heard the sound of an aircraft, but it was too far away. Towards evening a boat came along. A fishing boat. Thirty-footer. Three guys on board. They picked me up. The captain went for the radio and I begged him not to call it in. I asked him what the nearest port was. He said Provincetown. I asked him to take me there, drop me off, and forget he ever saw me. I think he understood, because he agreed. Three hours later I was in P-Town. The immersion suit had kept me dry, and I still had my credit card. I checked into a cheap motel. I wanted to bide my time and see what was going to develop. I knew that the Duke would not be happy that his shipment was lost. It would be better if he thought I was lost at sea."

"So you were working for the Duke," said Mark. "And you lost his cargo worth twenty million dollars. I can see why he'd be upset. You're right to lay low. Let everyone think you're at the bottom of Massachusetts Bay along with the boat. One more question—the name 'Crackers' mean anything to you?

Lewis blanched. "Yeah. He works for the Duke. He's one of his enforcers. A really dangerous guy."

"Does Crackers by any chance own a boat?"

"I think so. A twenty-foot cruiser. Keeps it at a marina in Beverly."

Chief Ray Frontiero drummed his thick fingers on the desktop. His eyes were narrow and his lips tight.

"Are you tryin' to tell me that Stephen Hopper killed his own sister's boyfriend?"

"What I've pieced together," said Chris Mark, "is that Howard Galvin was hired by Arnie Masserat, head of the Tremont Corner gang in Boston. Masserat's cover is that he's the owner of Beacon Bay Construction. They do occasional roadwork for private and corporate clients. But it's a front. The real business is gambling, narcotics, and gun running. The feds have been on the Duke's ass for years but so far haven't gotten enough for an indictment. Masserat hired Galvin to meet a freighter off the coast of Madeira and transport a ton of cocaine across the Atlantic to Boston. There the *Ace of Hearts* was going to be met by a smaller boat that would take the cargo to shore, probably to a private marina. The Duke paid Galvin fifty thousand up front, with probably another fifty thousand promised after delivery. Galvin took the fifty grand and handed it over to Smiley. Everything was working out fine until the *Ace of Hearts* encountered a fierce nor'easter and the boat went down. Masserat lost twenty million. He ordered Galvin to be killed. Crackers may have been the one who did the job. He had no idea that Galvin was his own sister's boyfriend."

"Or maybe he did know and just didn't care," said the chief. "How did the Duke connect with Galvin?"

"My guess that it was through Smiley. Masserat told his buddy Smiley to keep an eye out for a candidate, and when Galvin, the owner of an oceangoing fishing vessel, came to him for a loan, Smiley knew he was a good prospect for a job."

"How are we going to make a case against Stephen Hopper?" asked Frontiero.

"We're going to set our rat trap with some irresistible bait," replied Mark.

Just before ten o'clock the following night, the Jodrey State Fish Pier, the eight-acre concrete platform jutting into the center of Gloucester's inner harbor, was deserted. The fish processing and freezer facilities were quiet and the semi trailers were parked in rows.

At the end of the pier Chris Mark waited in his car. A few parking places away federal agents huddled in a dry cleaning van. Chief Frontiero and three SWAT team members waited in an unmarked SUV. The cameras and recording devices were rolling.

At ten o'clock the car came slowly cruising down the length of the pier. Mark flashed his lights once before stepping out of his Camaro so that Crackers could get a good look at him. Crackers parked his big rectangular Lincoln Continental a few parking places away and opened the door. After scanning the pier he got out.

"You Chuck Owens?" asked Crackers.

"That's me," replied Mark.

"You want to talk to me?" Under the orange sodium vapor streetlight the big man's eyes were narrow and hard.

"Yeah," replied Mark. "I run a salvage company. A team of divers. We specialize in sensitive cargo."

"What kind of cargo you talkin' about?"

"Cargo that might be in the hold of a fishing boat in three hundred feet of water off Provincetown. Cargo that's particularly valuable and requires special handling."

"Why should I talk to you?" said Crackers.

"Because there are very few salvage operators who have the skills and the discretion to successfully execute this type of operation. Notice that I said 'very few.' We're not the only ones. The feds have plenty of divers who could do it. No problem. But I'm sure that's not who you want going down there. And I'm sure you'll agree that time is of the essence."

"What do you want?"

"Ten percent of the value of the cargo. I estimate that what's in the hold of the *Ace of Hearts* is worth twenty million. So that would give me two million. One million up front. One million on delivery."

"I'll get back to you," said Crackers. He turned to leave.

Mark sensed his opening. "Not good enough. Time is not on your side."

Crackers turned to face Mark.

"The cargo of the *Ace of Hearts* is up for bid," said Mark. "The auction has already started. The clock is ticking. If Arnie Masserat thinks that he can play games with me, he's wrong."

"How the fuck do you know about Mr. Masserat?" glared Crackers.

"I know what I know," said Mark. "The point is this: Are you just his errand boy, or can you make a decision?" He waited for Crackers to either pull a gun or take a swing at him. But the big man only scowled. It was a positive sign.

"I took care of Howie Galvin, and I'll take care of you too," he spat.

"Yeah—the boat ride," said Mark. "Galvin was stupid to get on your boat. But you screwed up too. You should have put weights on his body. The damn thing floated up like a cork. Now the cops have it. Very sloppy work."

"The Duke wanted him to be found," sneered Crackers. "To send a message. Don't screw around with us. He told me to dump him within sight of land. Make sure the tide would carry him in."

At that moment the side door to the dry cleaning van slid open and two armed federal agents emerged. "Stephen Hopper! Get down on the ground! Now!"

The chief's SWAT team closed in from the other direction.

"Hey, Crackers," said Mark as Hopper was being cuffed. "You want to know something? Howard Galvin was your sister's boyfriend! They were going to get married. Your putting a bullet in his head should make for a real friendly family gathering next Christmas. Of course you won't be there. Maybe Karen will visit you in federal prison. You can tell her all about how you killed the man she wanted to marry."

The Breath of Death

"Are you ready to go to the beach?"

How could Chris Mark resist such a melodious and seductive voice? He would have been no less willing to accompany her if she had said, "Are you ready to go to the laundromat?"

"Yeah—just let me grab the car keys," he replied.

Rochelle Nickerson was her name. Tall and slender, with legs like a gazelle, eyes like two sapphire pools, and a voice out of a dream. He had met her a few weeks earlier at a party. They had quickly hit it off. One of the reasons they got along so well was that they were both open about the fact that neither was looking for a serious relationship.

The afternoon was a tradeoff. Normally Chris Mark would never choose to lie for hours on a towel in the blazing sun. Not that the beach was an unpleasant place, but for Mark the burning sand was something that you crossed in order to get to the waves. Surfers are interested in action, not relaxation. Enduring a few hours of roasting his epidermis on a beach was a small price to pay for the favors that he knew Rochelle would later bestow upon him between the cool sheets.

After Mark parked his Jeep along the road overlooking Niles Beach, they descended the short concrete ramp. The tide was out, creating a broad swath of sweltering sand and plenty of room among the umbrellas and the families lined up in their lawn chairs with their well-stocked coolers at the ready. The hard blue water of Gloucester Harbor was dotted with recreational sailboats and the working vessels of fishermen.

"Over there," said Rochelle, pointing to a cluster of sheltering rocks by the stone seawall. A generous section of real estate in front of the rocks was yet unpopulated, waiting to be claimed. After picking their way among the earlier settlers, Mark and Rochelle spread out their towels. Mark rubbed suntan lotion on Rochelle's toned back and shoulders before they settled down with an afternoon's supply of books and magazines.

Not more than a few minutes later, Rochelle suddenly sat upright. "Oh, shit," she muttered.

"What?" asked Mark.

"I thought they were up in Bar Harbor."

"You thought who was in Bar Harbor?"

"Gwendolyn Goodman."

"Who?"

"A woman I used to be in business with. She's here with her husband."

Mark set aside his book. "Where are they?"

"Over on the ramp." Rochelle indicated the direction with a nod of her head.

Mark shielded his eyes. A man and a woman were inching their way down the concrete incline. The woman wore a flowered bathing suit that strained to contain her ample curves. A self-consciously huge wide-brimmed hat shaded a hatchet face. Her round Jackie-O sunglasses made her look like a startled owl. She was assisting a man who was dressed incongruously in a pair of long pants and a loose shirt. The man was stooped and was walking with great difficulty. They were making very slow progress.

"You were in business with her?" asked Mark.

"Yes. We owned an art gallery in Rockport. She ripped me off—pocketed commissions and made deals behind my back. Took me a year and a fortune in legal fees to get rid of her. Then I closed the gallery. I was sick of the whole business. But we both still live in Gloucester, so I see her now and then. She's with her husband Rupert. He's got a disease called Friedreich's ataxia. It destroys the nervous system. Late onset—it showed itself when he was in his twenties. It's now very advanced. He can barely function."

"That sounds terrible," said Mark

"He's a sweet guy. Deserves better than to be married to that witch. It's too bad, but the disease has really taken its toll. He rarely goes out."

"What does Rupert do for work?" asked Mark as he watched Gwendolyn slowly guide her husband down the ramp to the beach.

"He's a sculptor. Was, anyway. When Gwen met him he was exhibiting works made from old pieces of driftwood. He'd find these hunks of wood on the beach or washed up on the rocks, and put them together. Sometimes he'd add an old lobster trap or buoy. I always thought that his work was a bit touristy."

"He made money selling his art?"

"No. He never needed to work. He's got some property. He inherited a house here in Gloucester and another one in Bar Harbor. A fat trust fund too. It all came from his father's toilet paper business."

"Toilet paper?"

"I'm being facetious—they made all kinds of paper products. But the biggest brand was the bathroom variety. Don't laugh. Think about it. No matter what the state of the economy—even if people are standing in bread lines—they keep buying toilet paper. God, what a genius the father must have been to get himself into that business."

Supported by his wife, Rupert hobbled onto the beach.

Rochelle pulled her hat low over her eyes and seemed to shrink into her towel as if to become invisible.

Instead of turning in their direction, Gwendolyn and Rupert shuffled to the other side of the wide crescent of sand.

"Where are they now?" whispered Rochelle from under her hat.

"He's lying down," replied Mark. To see better, he lifted himself on one elbow while placing a protective hand on Rochelle's shoulder. Her oiled skin was hot to the touch. "She's walking towards the water," he said. "She's looking around. Now she's wading into the water. Still wearing the big white hat and her Jackie-O sunglasses."

"She'll parade around out there, making sure everyone sees her," replied Rochelle as she suddenly sat upright. "I'm sorry, Chris, but we need to go."

"Sure—okay," he replied.

Hurriedly they gathered their things. With her head tipped low under her hat, Rochelle led the way back across the sand to the ramp. Mark kept an eye on the duo. Rupert was lying on a towel, reading a book. Gwendolyn stood knee-deep in the gentle wavelets, pretending to be Venus on the half shell.

After the interruption and forced relocation, the day had not been wasted. Mark and Rochelle crossed over East Gloucester to Good Harbor Beach and lingered there until sunset, when hunger drove them to decamp. After dinner at The Visa restaurant—famous for its wine bar and hot popovers—they had retired to Mark's house. To his bedroom, to be more exact. At eleven o'clock Rochelle had reluctantly dressed and gone home, explaining, between parting kisses, that she needed to be up early for work.

Sitting at his desk the next morning reviewing a pile of boring tax documents, Mark was pleasantly surprised when the caller ID on his buzzing phone showed the name "R. Nickerson."

"Hey Rochelle, what's up?"

"Chris—something strange has happened." Rochelle's voice had an uncharacteristic edge of urgency.

"What's going on?"

"An hour ago I got a call from a friend of mine who lives next door to Gwendolyn and Rupert. There was an ambulance at the house. Julie saw the EMTs carry out a body. The person was dead. In a bag. Then Gwendolyn came out, following the body to the ambulance. Julie knows the cop who was there. She went over and asked the cop what happened. He said it was a suicide. Rupert had gone into the garage and started the car. He died of carbon monoxide poisoning. The cop said that the medical examiner told him it was an open and shut case."

"Too bad," said Mark. "I guess the poor guy got to the end of his rope. Decided to end it."

"I don't think so," said Rochelle.

"Don't think what?"

"I don't think that he killed himself. *She* killed him."

"She?"

"The bitch. Gwendolyn. She murdered him for his money. I'm sure of it."

"Hmm," said Mark. "Do you want me to look into it?" As soon the words passed his lips, he regretted saying them.

"Oh, could you?"

"It's not really something that I want to get involved in—" he backpedaled.

"Please—I really think that something's very wrong." The conviction in Rochelle's voice bent Mark's heart.

"Yeah—sure," he heard himself say. "Okay. I'll see what I can do."

Oh well. Having nothing else on his agenda for the day—that is, having no clients—Mark picked up his phone and dialed chief of police Ray Frontiero. The chief was his usual gruff but friendly self, and his comments were straightforward. At ten o'clock that morning the part-time nurse had arrived at the home of Rupert and Gwendolyn Goodman. Not seeing her patient in the home, she went looking for him and eventually entered the attached garage. She discovered the deceased, Rupert Goodman, inside the couple's car. The engine was running. After shutting off the car and opening the garage doors for fresh air, the nurse called for an ambulance. Goodman was pronounced dead at the scene. According to the preliminary assessment by the medical examiner, cause of death was carbon monoxide poisoning. Manner of death was suicide.

End of story, said Frontiero.

Mark thanked the chief and hung up after saying that the next time they saw each other he'd buy the chief lunch.

As Mark drummed his fingertips on the desktop he pondered the ironclad rule of the private detective:

Do not perform pro bono work for a hot woman, even if she's already having sex with you.

Mark called Rochelle.

"Hey," he said when she picked up. "I want you to know that I talked to the police chief. He says that there's no doubt about it: Rupert Goodman committed suicide. The medical examiner has made her ruling. I'm sorry, but I've got nothing to go on. I have no way of collecting evidence. I think that the best thing to do is to step away from the situation."

After a stunned silence Rochelle spoke. "You don't understand. She *had* to do it. I *know* she did. Before they got married—when Gwendolyn and I were still in business together—one day she came into the gallery acting as if she were the Queen of Sheba. She bragged to me that she had hooked a rich one. A gold mine, she said. Rupert knew he had a terrible disease but the symptoms were manageable. Gwendolyn told me that she was going to 'love him to death.' She told me about the houses and the trust fund. She was showing off. Letting me know that she had scored big, and that she was going to be set up for life."

"I understand," said Mark. "But let's try to step back from your personal feelings about your former business partner and think about the unfortunate Rupert. There's just nothing there to suggest murder."

"There *must* be," Rochelle insisted. "Listen—I want you to look in the house. Check it out."

"That's called breaking and entering. No can do."

"You can get in. When I was still friends with Gwendolyn, I went there a few times. There's a basement door that should be easy to open. Please. Something is very wrong in that house."

A fool and his freedom are soon parted, thought Mark.

Still, the risk was low. Get in, look around, get out. If one of Frontiero's men in blue showed up, the chief would give Mark a lecture about minding his own damn business and staying out of police work.

"When am I supposed to do this?" he asked.

"This evening. Gwendolyn told Julie that while Rupert's body was at the funeral home, she needed to plan the service for the scattering of his ashes. She'll be over at Wingaersheek Beach at sunset. Said she wanted to 'feel the energy of the place.' Whatever. I'll keep a lookout near the beach. If she happens to come home early, I'll call you."

"All right. Sunset tonight is at eight-thirty. You'll know when she's left the house?"

"Yes. I'll be watching."

At eight o'clock that night Mark drove his Camaro to the corner of Dalton Lane. At the base of the wooded hill he pulled to the side of the road. Being a careful man who verified everything a client told him—even if the client were a beautiful woman—he had confirmed that the home of Rupert and Gwendolyn Goodman was at 357 Dalton Lane, and a quick drive-by earlier in the evening had revealed a modest but sturdy stone house with a slate roof and casement windows.

He took out his phone and punched Rochelle's number. After she confirmed that Gwendolyn had left the house and had driven to Wingaersheek Beach, Mark put the car into gear and eased up the hill before parking on the street near the driveway.

He circled the house. In the warm twilight the only lights that were burning were on the front porch and in a window around the back, next to the wooden door to the basement. Mark stood next to the wooden door and waited. If someone—a neighbor, perhaps—had called the cops, it was better that they came now, before Mark had entered the house.

The neighborhood was quiet. In the distance a dog barked. Something moved on Dalton Lane—a young girl laboriously pedaling a bicycle. She passed the house without looking to the side. Mark shrugged. It was now or never. After easily picking the cheap padlock, he pulled open the creaking door. Before him a set of stone steps descended into darkness. Entering the musty gloom, he followed the description given to him by Rochelle and quickly found the stairs leading up to the kitchen. At the top of the stairs he pushed open the door.

The kitchen smelled of burnt garlic. There was a table, four chairs, dishes in the sink—the usual stuff. Mark listened. No sound. He went to the door to the attached garage and opened it. The garage, which was built for two cars, was empty. Interesting: either Gwendolyn had already gotten rid of the death car, which seemed unlikely to have been accomplished so quickly, or she had driven it to Wingaersheek.

Which seemed mighty cold.

Anyway, the car was gone. But there was something interesting here in the garage: two big tanks that supplied compressed gas. Mark went to them and read the labels. Medical grade oxygen. He lifted them. They were empty. Probably going back to the supplier to be refilled.

Were these for Rupert?

After returning to the kitchen, Mark went into the living room. Nothing special here: a worn leather sofa, two easy chairs, a tall brass floor lamp, a TV set, and bookcases with books. The titles on the spines spoke of art and travel. In the corner stood a pale shaft of driftwood as tall as he was. It had been shaped and sanded before being attached to its sturdy metal base.

Down a short hallway, the tiled bathroom featured a big bathtub with lots of bright chrome handles for easy accessibility by an invalid. The medicine cabinet lived up to its name by being well stocked with prescription bottles. Two-thirds of them bore Rupert's name and the rest were for Gwendolyn. Blood pressure, muscle relaxers, sleep aids. The modern American couple, prescribed pills for every occasion.

Entering the spacious master bedroom, Mark involuntarily grimaced at the sour smell of an invalid. It was the scent of a hospice, of urine, body odor, and disinfectant that reminded him of visiting his great-grandmother in the nursing home when he was a kid. It aroused feelings of guilt and pity.

Shaking himself free of his memories, Mark saw that the bedroom was entirely typical of one that had been furnished in ordinary style only to be adapted for use by invalid: a four-poster bed with an institutional scissor lamp bolted to the wall, additional railings bolted to the paneled walls, a dressing table with a cushioned stool. A wheelchair, folded, sat by the window.

Before Mark left the bedroom he paused to listen for sounds in the house. All was quiet. But then—was that a shadow crossing the window? Mark padded quietly to the glass and looked out. He could see a section of the front yard and the street beyond. No people, no cars.

It must have been a bird.

Leaving the bedroom, Mark closed the door behind him, crossed the hall, and entered what was once a guest bedroom. The compact room was made to seem even smaller by the incongruous presence of a hyperbaric chamber.

The device was basically a man-sized transparent cylinder supported by a sturdy wheeled base, like a see-through casket on display at a funeral home. The concept of a hyperbaric chamber is that the patient enters the chamber and lies comfortably on the bed. When the door is shut, oxygen—either pure or in some proportion to regular air—is pumped into the chamber at two to three times normal atmospheric pressure.

Under these conditions, the patient's lungs can gather much more oxygen than would be possible breathing pure oxygen at normal air pressure. Hyperbaric oxygen therapy is a well-established treatment for decompression sickness, a common hazard of scuba diving. Other legitimate medical conditions treated with hyperbaric oxygen therapy include serious infections and wounds that won't heal as a result of diabetes or radiation injury.

Like many other therapies, both legitimate and experimental, hyperbaric therapy had once been proposed by some practitioners as a treatment for Friedreich's ataxia. Clearly, Rupert Goodman was giving it a try.

On the side of the rolling base was a hinged panel. Mark pulled it open and peered inside. Cradled on its supporting rack was an oxygen tank similar to the ones he had seen in the garage. The pressure gauge indicated it was about half full.

After closing the panel door, Mark left the guest bedroom and went into the hallway. He scanned the hallway ceilings until he found the concealed ladder that provided access to the attic. He pulled down the steel ring and when the unit was halfway down he unfolded the two sections of the hinged ladder. When extended, the ladder's feet rested neatly on the floor.

Cautiously Mark ascended the stairs. When his head reached the level of the floor of the attic he twisted in place. Behind him, to the right, to the left, and in front, he saw a dusty space that contained only a few old boxes and a chrome clothing rack upon which hung one solitary ladies' coat. The space—and its fine coating of dust—did not appear to have been disturbed during the past few years.

After descending to the main floor Mark returned the folding ladder to its position in the ceiling.

Off the hallway between the master bedroom and the living room was a small home office. Aside from more pieces of driftwood affixed to metal bases, there was a desk, computer, printer, stacks of papers—all the usual household stuff. The papers on the desk yielded utility and healthcare bills. Mark noted that Rupert's illness cost him and Gwendolyn thousands of dollars each month in medical bills, medications, and home health care. The visiting nurse was supplied by North Shore Home Health Associates. Her name was Rosita Clemens and she cost them five hundred dollars a week. That was twenty-six thousand a year. It had to be a substantial trust fund to throw off that kind of cash—maybe five million or more. If you were deeply alienated from your spouse, that kind of money might be a motive for murder.

Here was the bill for the oxygen tanks. Sixty dollars a pop, delivered by Allied Gas Products to your home or medical center, with the empties picked up by the same. Rupert was going through a tank a week.

Phone bills, heating oil bills, car insurance bills. Nothing unusual.

In a corner of the room was a narrow closet door. It was the kind of closet that an architect would create to utilize an odd leftover space in the room layout, like the gap created by a chimney or stairwell. Mark pulled open the louvered door. There was a rod with clothes hanging on it— men's lightweight jackets and raincoats. On the shelf above were rain hats and old cardboard boxes.

On the floor were men's shoes and boots.

And there was something else.

A tank of gas.

This one was smaller than the oxygen tanks. It resembled a squat lobster pot with a valve set sticking out of the top. Using a tissue from the box on the desk to prevent his fingers from leaving prints, Mark rotated the tank so that he could read the label. Its contents were ninety-four percent pure carbon monoxide with six percent common atmospheric gases. The gauge indicated it was about half full.

If carbon monoxide had been used in the hyperbaric chamber, then Rupert Goodman had been murdered.

According to the label, the tank had been manufactured by TopFlite Gas, a big national company. But only major accounts such as hospital chains would buy gas directly from the factory; there had to be a local distributor. Mark looked for a sticker. He found only an oval residue of adhesive. Someone had scraped off the distributor's label.

Mark returned the tank to its place before sliding shut the doors. After extinguishing the lights he walked to the basement stairs and paused to listen. No sound. Stealthily he descended the stairs and made his way to the outside door. Carefully and slowly he pushed it open. The cool night air brushed his face. It was dark now, and a canopy of clouds obscured the moon. Mark stepped onto the lawn before turning and gently closing the door behind him. He replaced the padlock in its rickety hasp.

As he turned to walk back to his car, he was suddenly engulfed in the blinding glare of spotlights.

"Chris Mark, show me your hands," came a hard voice from the darkness behind the lights.

"Jimmy—is that you?" said Mark, squinting to see.

"Yeah, it's me," replied Officer James Carlson. "But this is no social call. We've got to bring you in. C'mon, don't make me take you down. Lemme see both your hands. You carrying a weapon?"

"No—of course not!" replied Mark as he showed his palms to the brightness.

From out of the shadows came a Gloucester police officer. Mark didn't recognize her. Without a word she expertly handcuffed Mark's hands behind his back.

"He's clean," said the cop after a thorough frisk.

The cop led Mark to one of the cruisers parked on the side of the road. Officer Carlson opened the back door.

"Jimmy, what's going on?" asked Mark as the first cop placed her hand on Mark's head to guide him into the back seat.

Carlson shrugged. "We got a call about an intruder in the house. We've got no choice but to respond. Now if it happens that you had some legitimate business in there while the owner was gone, then no harm, no foul. That's not my job to determine. So be a good boy and get in the car so we can take you in."

Mark remembered the fleeting shadow across the window. Had there been someone outside?

After a ten-minute ride downtown—Mark was grateful that Jimmy didn't use his lights or siren—he was hustled into the police station, but to his surprise not immediately booked or placed under arrest. As he stood by the desk with Jimmy at his side, Chief Frontiero came out of his office.

"Okay, boys, I'll take him," said Frontiero. After the cuffs were unlocked and his hands were freed, Frontiero ushered him into his office and closed the door.

"Sit down," ordered the chief.

Mark complied.

After taking his seat in his armchair behind his desk Frontiero regarded Mark with sharp eyes.

"Just what the hell were you doing in that woman's house?" he said. "You'd better have a good excuse."

"I was acting on a tip that Rupert Goodman was murdered."

"Oh yeah? Who gave you this tip?"

"I'd rather not say."

"You're a goddamn pain in the ass," said the chief.

"Sorry."

"Did you find anything?"

"As a matter of fact I did." Mark described the hyperbaric chamber and the tank of carbon monoxide gas.

"So you think that someone switched the oxygen tank for carbon monoxide," said Frontiero with a frown. "Goodman gets in the hyperbaric chamber and inhales carbon monoxide. The gas is odorless and colorless, so he never knew he's being poisoned. He's dead within five minutes. Then the perpetrator opens the chamber and carries Goodman's body to the car in the garage. He or she straps Goodman in the car, starts the engine, and leaves. The medical examiner determines that the cause and manner of death are suicide by carbon monoxide poisoning."

"Exactly."

"You got any suspects?"

"Goodman has been ill for a long time and his list of friends and associates is very short. There's his wife, Gwendolyn. Her former business partner, Rochelle Nickerson. Gwendolyn's uncle, Quentin Parris. She has no other living relatives. The home health aide, Rosita Clemens. On some of the papers I saw the names of a financial manager and an art dealer. Lots of doctors. I'm sure there are other people I'm not yet familiar with."

"I heard that you and the ex-business partner were getting cozy."

"Nice to know that my social life is of such great interest," said Mark. "You asked for suspects. The list is the list. And now I have a question for you. Who dialed nine-one-one to report a burglar at the Goodman house?"

"Don't know yet." The chief tapped his computer. The sound of a click was followed by a voice.

"Gloucester Police Department, what's your emergency?"

"I want to report someone breaking into a house at three fifty-seven Dalton Lane." The caller's voice was that of a middle-aged male. Cool, not agitated. "He's in the house right now."

"You saw this person break into the house?" asked the operator.

"Yes. He went into the basement door in the back of the house. He broke the lock."

"Can you describe him?"

"White male. About thirty. Short hair. His name is Chris Mark."

"You know this man?"

"I know who he is."

"Okay..." There were sounds of paper shuffling. "Sir, may I have your name?"

"Harold Simmons. I'm just passing by. Listen—I gotta go. But get someone down here right away."

"Sir, please do not interact with the person in the house. Officers are on their way."

"Yeah—no problem. Thanks."

Frontiero tapped his computer, ending the tape.

"You know anybody named Harold Simmons?" he asked Mark.

"No. Never heard the name," replied Mark. "And I'll bet that the call was made from a throwaway cellphone."

"As a matter of fact it was."

"Someone wanted you to bust me."

Frontiero leaned back in his chair with his hands folded across his belly. "Okay, let's assume that it was not a concerned citizen. Let's say it was some nefarious person. Why make the call?"

"Maybe I was interrupting something. After all, I found evidence of murder. The tank of carbon monoxide. The murderer needed to get rid of it."

"The wife?"

Mark shrugged. "Maybe. Maybe not. As far as I know, she was nowhere near the house."

"And she's not a man," added Frontiero.

"C'mon, Chief," said Mark with a smile. "You know that anyone could go to Radio Shack and buy a voice changer. A simple gizmo that drops your voice an octave. Over a crummy cellphone you'd never know the difference."

"So I'm not as young as you are," replied Frontiero with a tone of irritation that was supposed to sound genuine. "Not as tuned into technology. Yeah. I agree. The voice could be a false indicator."

There was a moment of silence.

"Okay, so what are you going to do with me?" asked Mark.

"Like I said, you're a pain in the ass," said the chief. "Not to mention an irritation to my highly qualified detectives. But the fact is that you've got a knack for putting scumbags behind bars. You've made yourself useful to the good citizens of Gloucester. Made the streets safer. Get it? So I'd rather not have you locked up. I'm gonna cut you loose. Just stay out of trouble."

"Thanks, Chief. What if the weeping widow files a complaint about the break-in?"

"Let me handle that. Go on. Get out of here."

"I'm buying you lunch tomorrow. At the Anchor Club. They're running a special on steamed lobster."

"Yeah. Okay. See you at one."

As Mark left the station under the sour eyes of the arresting officers he pondered the fact that he was starting from square one. He had a victim—the terminally ill Rupert Goodman. His suicide had been staged. Someone had substituted carbon monoxide for oxygen in his hyperbaric chamber. Then the murderer had stashed the CO tank in the closet, presumably to retrieve it later and dispose of it. Of course in any Crime 101 class the unhappy and narcissistic wife would be the number one suspect. But her guilt had to be proven. The investigation had to be thorough.

The person to start with would be the visiting nurse. She had discovered the body.

The next morning Mark drove to the home of Rosita Clemens, a tidy Cape at the end of a quiet street near Our Lady of Good Voyage Church in downtown Gloucester. It was a block where the houses stood shoulder to shoulder and every neighbor could see what the family next door was watching on their wide-screen television.

After parking his Camaro on the street Mark stepped up onto the porch and rapped on the aluminum door. It was opened by a compact woman who regarded him coolly. After explaining that he simply wanted to discuss the tragic demise of Mr. Goodman, and that he was not there to try to pin anything on her, she consented to his coming inside.

Seated on one end of the stiff sofa with Rosita at the other end as far away as she could get from him, Mark asked the nurse to describe Goodman's hyperbaric chamber treatments.

She said that it was not something that was medically indicated. It simply made him feel better.

"A placebo effect?" said Mark.

"Yes, I would say so," replied Rosita. "He did it every morning at nine o'clock. He entered the chamber, which was then pressurized with fifty percent oxygen at two atmospheres. He'd stay there for half an hour. Then he'd release the pressure, open the top, and climb out."

"He did this unassisted?"

"When he first started the treatments two months ago I insisted that I be present. But soon they became routine, and after a while he said that he didn't need anyone to help him. There were a few days when he felt particularly ill and either Mrs. Goodman or I had to help him get in and out of the chamber. But on most days he managed by himself."

"Tell me what happened yesterday morning," said Mark.

"Just what I told the police. I arrived at the house at ten. I expected that Mrs. Goodman would not be home. She goes to the gym every Monday and Thursday from nine to eleven. I called for Mr. Goodman. He didn't answer. I looked for him, and after searching the house I went to the garage. When I opened the door the terrible smell of car exhaust hit me. The car was running. Mr. Goodman was in the driver's seat. I rushed to him and he was unresponsive. I turned off the ignition, and because we needed fresh air I opened the garage door. Then I pulled him from the car and administered CPR. It was no good. I called the EMTs but I knew he was dead."

"When you were looking for him in the house, did you check the hyperbaric chamber?"

"Of course. When he was in there he couldn't hear anything, so that was the first place I looked."

"Was the lid open? Did it look as if it had been used?"

Rosita shrugged. "The lid was open. It looked the way it always did."

"Tell me about Mrs. Goodman. Did they get along?"

"Oh yes. They were devoted to each other. She would do anything for him. It was not easy. He required constant care. He really should have been in a long-term care facility, but she insisted that he stay at home. She said that she would never allow him to be 'warehoused,' as she put it. She helped him to bathe, helped him to dress, she took him out driving in the car—so many things she did for him."

"Did they ever argue?" asked Mark.

"No more than any other couple, I suppose. One day last week when I came to the house at my usual time I walked in without saying anything. It was not intentional; my mind was just preoccupied. I heard angry voices coming from the living room. I stopped because I wasn't sure what to do. I heard Mrs. Goodman say, 'But we can't afford that!' He said not to worry, it would be okay. Then she said that it would not be okay and that Mr. Goodman needed to take it back. That's what she said— 'You need to take it back!' I was feeling increasingly awkward, so I went to the kitchen door, opened it, slammed it shut, and called out in a cheerful voice. They stopped arguing and a moment later Mrs. Goodman came into the kitchen. She greeted me like she always did, as if nothing were wrong. A while later I saw Mr. Goodman in his office. He had wheeled himself to his desk and was writing something on the computer. That was all."

"Okay," said Mark. "Thanks. You've been very helpful."

As Mark pulled away from the house he reached for the dashboard button to activate the phone. After hesitating a moment he punched a number. Into the cabin of the Camaro came the sound of a dial tone, eleven beeps, and a phone ringing.

"Mars Risk Management," said a woman. The voice was without expression.

"Kevin Lone, please."

"Who may I say is calling?"

"Chris Mark."

"Please hold."

There was a long moment of nondescript instrumental music.

"Hey Markie! How've you been?"

Mark could not help but smile.

"Good, Kevin. How about you? Staying out of trouble? How's Washington?"

"Can't complain. The Nationals are doing okay—looks like they're headed for a second place finish. Too bad—it would have been nice to face the Red Sox in the World Series."

"Dream on."

"Yeah, dream on. What's up? Are you in town?"

"Nah. I'm home in Gloucester. Working on a case. I need your help."

"What, has a kid lost her puppy?"

"C'mon, gimme a break! No, a guy got himself murdered. A staged suicide in his own home. I need some computer forensics that are out of my league. The kind of stuff that MRM can do in its sleep."

"What can we do for you?"

"I need to know if my guy bought anything expensive recently. Someone overheard him and his wife arguing. She told him to return whatever it was he bought. It's a long shot. I'm looking for a motive."

"You got an IP address?"

"No. Just the guy's name and a physical address. He would have used the computer in the house."

"Why don't you just get into the house and have a look?" asked Lone.

"I played that card already. The Gloucester cops caught me inside. Someone tipped them off."

"All right. Anything for a fellow Marine. Listen, I gotta leave town tomorrow. Be gone for a few weeks. I'm going to hand you over to Lamonte in IT. He'll take care of you."

Chris Mark knew well enough not to ask Lone where he was going. As an undercover agent, Lone handled the most dangerous international cases. From the moment he walked out of the Mars Building in Washington until he re-entered the building through the multiple layers of security, no one other than his handlers would know where he was. If he happened to turn up dead or went missing, it would be as if he never existed.

"Thanks buddy," said Mark. "Come up to Gloucester anytime. We'll have a few beers and a couple of lobsters. Okay? Stay safe."

"You got it," said Lone.

As Mark pulled into his driveway he checked his email. Sure enough there was a message from Lone with instructions for contacting Lamonte through the secure servers at MRM. After typing in the information about Rupert Goodman, Mark hit the send button.

Mark didn't dwell on the past. A few years ago when Lone had applied for a job at MRM, Mark would have applied too, but he knew that having just one good eye would have made that an exercise in futility. MRM only considered candidates who were in the top one percent of physical fitness, and there was no leeway given to vets who had left a part of their anatomy on the streets of Baghdad—even if one such vet could kick Kevin Lone's ass any day of the week.

Being thus disqualified from chasing bad guys across the globe, Mark was grateful to get scumbags off the streets in his small corner of the world.

And now to do some online sleuthing of his own.

It did not take him long to find Quentin Parris, the uncle of Gwendolyn Goodman. Age fifty-seven. Occupation, cable television district manager. His territory included Gloucester and Cape Ann. Home address 768 Cambina Street, Rockport. About five miles from the house of Gwendolyn and Rupert. Not the nicest neighborhood—no water views and no wooded areas nearby. The photo showed a typical middle-aged guy with a white shirt, narrow tie, and big grin, like a salesman.

Mark picked up the phone.

Late that afternoon Mark walked into the Seaport Landing restaurant on the harbor. It was early for dinner, but what the interview subject wanted, the interview subject got. Mark quickly spotted Quentin Parris sitting at the bar.

As they shook hands Mark thanked him for agreeing to meet with him.

"Hey Rocky!" Parris called to the bartender. "A glass of Chablis for my friend. And a dozen oysters too." He turned to Mark. "You like oysters? Sure you do," he said, not waiting for an answer. "You know the cocktail sauce here? It's made by Bobo Dominick. The famous chef in New Orleans. Personal friend of mine. Met him when I played tight end at Tulane. Great guy! I spent many a night hanging out at his restaurant. Buying drinks for the whores. Ha ha! You've been to Bobo's, haven't you? No? Are you kidding? Everyone's been to Bobo's. You don't know what you're missing. When you get down there, tell 'em Quentin sent you. Okay?"

Mark suspected that if he ever entered that restaurant and dared to mention Quentin's name, they would throw him out on his ass.

"Mr. Parris that's all very interesting," said Mark as he reluctantly accepted the glass of Chablis. "I was hoping that you could help me with the death of Rupert Goodman. Your niece's husband."

Parris shot him a sideways glance. "Are you a cop?"

"No. I'm an investigator."

Now came a sly smile. "Oh I get it. Like that old-time detective from the nineteen-forties—what was his name? Ellery something."

"Ellery Queen? No—"

"That's it! Say, you know it was mighty peculiar how the books were supposed to be written *by* Ellery Queen, and at the same time they were *about* Ellery Queen! I never could figure that out."

"The books were ghostwritten by two cousins from Brooklyn—"

"So, you're like Ellery Queen, huh?"

"No. Not at all. I wasn't even born when—"

"You must get plenty of chicks, because of you being a detective and all. I'll bet they line up at your door. Right?"

"Chicks? No, not really. Mr. Parris—"

"Call me Quentin."

"Okay. Quentin. Tell me, how do you feel about Rupert Goodman committing suicide?"

Another sideways glance. "Too bad." A shrug. "He and I never connected. I always thought Gwennie could do better. She could have been a fashion model, y'know? I could have set her up with a top photographer. But she had her own ideas."

"Did they have any money problems?" asked Mark.

Quentin shook his head carefully. "No. Not that I know of. I think he had some money. I don't know much about his occupation other than his making those driftwood sculptures."

"Fights?"

A shrug. "No more than anybody else, I suppose. Gwennie doesn't exactly share with her old uncle every detail of her private life. I figure that if she wants me to know something, she'll tell me. I don't go prying and I don't make demands."

"There's evidence to suggest that Rupert was murdered, and the death staged to look like a suicide."

Quentin set his empty wine glass on the bar. "Well, if it was murder, I hope you catch the bastard who did it. Is there anything else you need from me? I've got an appointment."

"No. Thanks for taking the time to speak with me."

Mark watched him leave before resuming his seat at the bar.

"Hey buddy, here's the bill," said the bartender.

"Thanks, Rocky," said Mark. "I'll take care of it."

"By the way," said the bartender, "my name's not Rocky. It's Jim. I don't know what that guy was talking about."

"I thought he was a friend of yours."

"Never saw him before in my life."

With a wry smile Mark pulled out his phone to check his messages. There was one from Lamonte at MRM in Washington.

> Chris: Aside from medical bills and other routine household expenses, our inquiry into your subject has yielded one positive result. On the fifth of this month on his home computer the subject drafted a letter to the Hathern Foundation in New York. In the letter (copy attached) the subject states that pursuant to their discussions he is pleased to pledge five million dollars to the foundation to assist in their search for a cure for Friedreich's ataxia. The bequest is to be paid upon his death.
>
> However, the letter was not signed. It appears that at the time of the subject's death the bequest had not been formally presented to the foundation. The foundation itself has a very questionable background. There's no record of actual medical research. We're still looking into that.
>
> I also did some research on the wife. Aside from the legal dispute over the art gallery, she's clean. Nothing on her. Her father died when she was a kid, and her mother died five years ago of cancer. Her only relative is her uncle. He's a lifelong gambler. He loses big at casinos in Connecticut and occasionally Atlantic City. Doesn't spend much money anywhere else.
>
> I hope this information is helpful to you in your investigation.
>
> — Lamonte LaPierre.

That evening Chris Mark leaned into the window of the patrol car parked on Dalton Lane.

"Well, Jimmy," he said, "this may be your chance to make an arrest at this house that will stick."

"I don't know why we're wasting our time up here," replied officer Carlson. "You got no evidence. If you did, we'd have probable cause for an arrest."

"Don't worry. Sit tight. Give me fifteen minutes."

Mark went up the hill to the Goodman house and rang the bell. Gwendolyn answered the door.

"Mr. Mark, I think that this is an intrusion," she said. Her small eyes, narrowly set in her head, gave her the appearance of a trendy rodent.

"I want to thank you for taking the time to see me," replied Mark as he crossed the threshold. "I know this is a difficult time for you." He followed her into the living room. As Mark had hoped, Quentin Parris had already arrived. He was seated on the sofa with a glass of white wine in his hand. He gave Mark a cold nod.

Mark and Gwendolyn each took a chair, with a low coffee table between them. She did not offer refreshments.

"Mrs. Goodman, I'm going to be very blunt," Mark began. "You and I both know that your husband was murdered."

"Are you serious?" she stammered. "What makes you think so?"

"While he was in his hyperbaric chamber, he was poisoned with carbon monoxide. When he was dead his body was carried to the car and his suicide was staged."

"That's unbelievable," she insisted.

"C'mon, Mrs. Goodman," said Mark. "Let's not play games. The Gloucester police know all about the tank of carbon monoxide gas that I found in the closet. They know all about your husband's letter to the Hathern Foundation, in which he made a pledge of five million dollars. His bequest would have left you with a pittance. Barely enough to pay the taxes on this house, much less live the life to which you are accustomed. Not a very nice payback for your years of selfless devotion, would it be?" Mark shifted his gaze to

Quentin. "Even worse, Mister Parris, your expensive gambling habit would end. Your niece has been funneling her husband's cash to you, which you piss away at the tables and slot machines. You'd be at the mercy of your many creditors. Are there loan sharks among them?"

From Gwendolyn and Quentin came only shocked silence.

"Mrs. Goodman," continued Mark, "you needed to get rid of your husband before he finalized his bequest. The police are ready to arrest you for murder. I'm sure it will be a sensational trial. After a quick conviction you'll spend the rest of your life in prison."

"No!" she shouted. "All I ever did was try to make people happy. I tried to make Rupert happy." She turned to her uncle. "I tried to make *you* happy!"

"Hey, what you did was your choice," said Quentin.

"Yes, it seems cut and dried," continued Mark. "Mrs. Goodman, you were afraid of losing your husband's trust fund. He had not long to live. When he decided to will the bulk of his estate to medical research, you had no other choice but to kill him."

"But I talked to Rupert!" she protested. "I checked up on the Hathern Foundation. I discovered that the state attorney general's office was investigating them for fraud. The foundation has never funded any real research. Rupert was too trusting. He desperately wanted a cure. He was willing to give everything to anyone who was doing legitimate research. Who could blame him? But when I asked him to reconsider his bequest to the Hathern Foundation, he did. He told me that he wouldn't send the letter to the foundation."

"In fact, that's true," said Mark. "Rupert never signed the letter. Just out of curiosity, Mrs. Goodman, when your husband first announced his bequest of five million dollars to the foundation, did you tell your uncle?"

"Yes, I did," replied Gwendolyn. "I told him that after Rupert's death, circumstances would change for both of us. I'd have to watch my budget. I could not keep paying my uncle's gambling debts. It would be time for him to stop and get control of his life."

"And did you tell him about your husband's change of heart? That he had reconsidered and had decided to forgo the bequest?"

"Why, no," said Gwendolyn quietly. "I hadn't seen uncle Quentin in a few days. I was too busy. I was going to call him."

Mark turned to her uncle. "Well, Quentin, it seems to me that you killed Rupert Goodman for no reason."

"You're insane!" said Quentin. "It must have been someone from the foundation! After all, they were the ones who stood to lose five million dollars. Go after them. Leave me alone."

Gwendolyn sat quietly before speaking in a steady, controlled voice.

"Uncle Quentin, it was just last week that you asked me for a key to the house. You said that with Rupert being in such a fragile state it was a good idea if you could get into the house anytime. You could help him with his treatments. It would give me more freedom. So I gave you a key. And you know Rosita's schedule. You knew that I would be gone and that she wouldn't arrive until ten o'clock!"

Glowering, Quentin said nothing.

"You came back to this house to retrieve the tank of carbon monoxide gas," said Mark to Quentin. "When you saw me inside the house, you dialed nine-one-one. After the police took me away, you came in and recovered it. What did you do—throw it in the ocean?"

Jumping to his feet, Quentin hurled his wine glass to the floor. "Gwendolyn, that idiot husband of yours was going to give away a fortune!" He began to back towards the door. "I always thought you were a fool to marry him. I did you a favor by getting rid of him. His fortune was being wasted on endless treatments for a disease that was going to kill him anyway. If he had lived another ten years, he would have either given millions to that ridiculous foundation or he would have spent it on his quack doctors. Then where would you be? Living on the streets? And you, Mark—you're not a cop! You can't touch me! I'm going to walk out of here—and to hell with both of you!"

As Quentin opened the door Mark picked up his phone and punched a number. "Jimmy? He's coming out the front door now. He just confessed. I've got it on my phone. Yep. My pleasure."

It was the next day. Mark and Rochelle sat together on the rocks overlooking the ocean.

"When I called you and told you my suspicions about Gwendolyn," said Rochelle, "I was shooting from the hip. It was personal. I had no idea if she killed her husband. My only motivation was to make life miserable for her. I used you. I'm sorry."

"You wouldn't be the first," replied Mark. "And your instincts were correct. Rupert was murdered—just not by Gwendolyn. But if you hadn't convinced me to enter the house, Quentin Parris would have gotten away with it."

Rochelle gave a little nod. "I suppose I feel a bit less guilty now. Still, it seems so sordid. I don't feel good about any of it."

Mark shifted his position on the gray granite. As the ocean waves crashed against the rocks the salty spray misted high into the air. But the sun was shining and the onshore breeze, even down here by the cool water, was warm. It was the end of summer. The tourists were thinning out and the geese flew overhead in tight V-formations.

"So what do you want to do?" asked Mark. "About us?"

She turned and smiled. "It's been decided for me. You remember that job in New York that I applied for? This morning I got an email. They want me. I start next week."

"Well that's great!" said Mark. "Congratulations!"

"Yeah," she gave a happy lift of her shoulders. "Now I've got to find a place to live. I'm going to crash with a girlfriend. She's in Brooklyn. But I can't stay with her forever. I've got to find a roommate." She turned to Mark. "Got any girlfriends in New York who have an extra bedroom?"

"Can't say for sure, but I'll ask around."

In the moment of silence that followed, his gaze wandered to a lobsterman working the swelling sea. The lobsterman pulled up a trap and dumped it into his boat. Mark squinted into the glare. On the gently rolling craft the fisherman took a lobster out of the trap. After examining it, he threw it overboard. Probably undersized.

"Have *you* ever thought about New York?" said Rochelle.

Mark turned and looked into her cool blue eyes. Her gaze was inviting but not pleading. Behind her eyes Mark could sense the spark of sexual heat. The feeling was dangerous.

"Only as place to visit," he abruptly replied.

Feeling the subtle contraction of the space she occupied, he immediately regretted his glib answer.

"I've dropped anchor here," he offered. "This is where I am today. I can't say what'll happen in the future."

She nodded.

"The reason I came to Gloucester," he continued, "was because when I was a kid our family spent summers here and the place felt like home. There's something about this little island that's in sync with my life—the rugged rocks, the rhythm of the waves, the ebb and flow of the fishing boats as they head out of the harbor before dawn and return at sunset. After my discharge from the Corps I needed a place to land, and this was the best fit. Here you can drive from the eastern shore to the western shore in fifteen minutes. Gloucester's got a little bit of everything, including people who need my help. I can be useful here. I may not stay here forever, but right now I feel like the chaos of what happened overseas needs to settle and fade. I need to get my life back into alignment."

"I understand," said Rochelle. "Me, I've been here long enough. Time to pull up anchor and sail somewhere new. Somewhere with more possibilities." She smiled. "No offense. I get bored easily. Sometimes I think that I'm just shallow. Can't commit to one place." Her eyes softened. "But I won't forget you. If I don't see you in New York, maybe I'll make a return visit sometime."

"Sure," said Mark. "You do that."

Behind her smile Mark knew that neither one of them was going to carry a torch for the other. Once there was distance between them, their spans of attention would drift to new partners and new possibilities.

They sat together in silence, listening to the plaintive cries of the gulls, feeling the newly formed and delicate intertwining of their lives slowly unravel.

About the Author

Thomas Hauck is a writer living in Gloucester, Massachusetts. His first novel, *Pistonhead,* tells the gritty story of a guitar player in a rock band who faces a life crisis. *Lucas Manson,* his second novel, is a literary horror thriller that pits agent Mark Dylan against a charismatic evangelist who is the leader of a bloodthirsty hominid species.

His third novel, *Avita Doesn't Love You* (Whiskey Creek Press, October 2014), is an international thriller that traces the moral and physical challenges faced by agent Kevin Lone as he battles an implacable global enemy.

Thomas's short stories have been published in *The Armchair Aesthete, The Bitter Oleander, Over My Dead Body!,* and *The MacGuffin.* His collection of short stories and poems, *Public Image: Stories and Poems*, was published in 2009.

Thomas is the editor of *Renaissance Magazine*, America's leading national magazine devoted to contemporary renaissance faires and culture.

A former member of the Boston powerpop band The Atlantics, he's a rock musician who has released two solo CDs available through CDBaby and iTunes. His most recent CD, *Valentine to the Future*, was released in April 2014 under the name Telamor.

Thomas earned his B.A. in History of Art at Tufts University, graduating *magna cum laude*. He earned his M.B.A. at Endicott College in 2004.

Thomas lives with his wife Kim Smith, a published garden book author, photographer, and documentary filmmaker. Thomas and Kim have two children.